ON LEAVING PARADISE

Other books
by Frank Hercules

WHERE THE HUMMINGBIRD FLIES
I WANT A BLACK DOLL
AMERICAN SOCIETY AND BLACK REVOLUTION

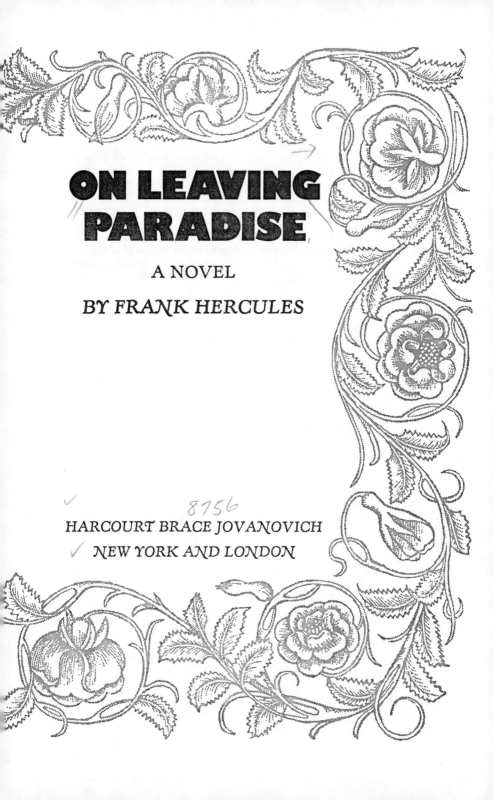

ON LEAVING PARADISE

A NOVEL

BY FRANK HERCULES

HARCOURT BRACE JOVANOVICH
NEW YORK AND LONDON

Set in CRT Gael

Library of Congress Cataloging in Publication Data

Hercules, Frank.
On leaving paradise.
I. Title.
PZ4.H538On [PS3558.E655]   813'.5'4   79-3354
ISBN 0-15-169921-6

First edition
B C D E

TO THE MEMORY OF MY AUNT,
CHARLOTTE ALEXANDRA DOTTIN,
OF
SAN FERNANDO, TRINIDAD,
WHO
REVERED LIFE AND BELIEVED IN LAUGHTER,
AND OF MY SON, JOHN,
SO LOVED AND SO LAMENTED

ON LEAVING PARADISE

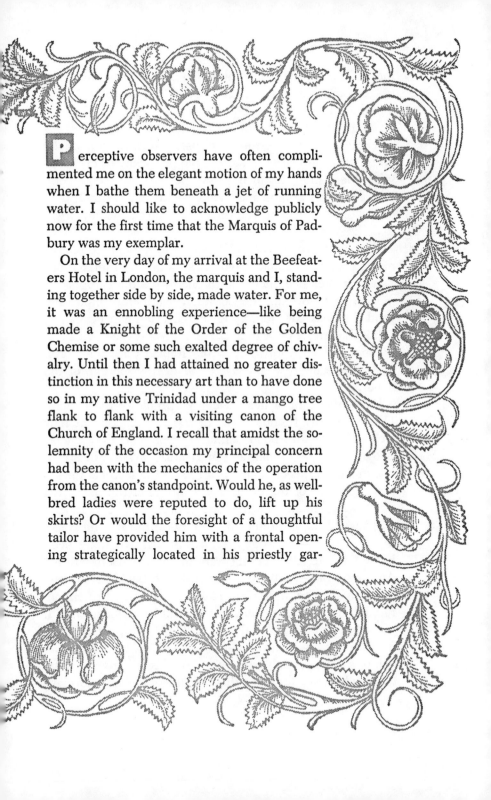

Perceptive observers have often complimented me on the elegant motion of my hands when I bathe them beneath a jet of running water. I should like to acknowledge publicly now for the first time that the Marquis of Padbury was my exemplar.

On the very day of my arrival at the Beefeaters Hotel in London, the marquis and I, standing together side by side, made water. For me, it was an ennobling experience—like being made a Knight of the Order of the Golden Chemise or some such exalted degree of chivalry. Until then I had attained no greater distinction in this necessary art than to have done so in my native Trinidad under a mango tree flank to flank with a visiting canon of the Church of England. I recall that amidst the solemnity of the occasion my principal concern had been with the mechanics of the operation from the canon's standpoint. Would he, as well-bred ladies were reputed to do, lift up his skirts? Or would the foresight of a thoughtful tailor have provided him with a frontal opening strategically located in his priestly garment? The churchman fumbled with the lower portion of his vestment and at length succeeded in springing his privy member. Having released it from confinement, he was obliged to wait several minutes before the recalcitrant organ could be prevailed upon to pass water. A sympathetic horse, grazing nearby, observed the predicament of the divine. Flourishing its own privy member in a confident, schoolmasterly fashion and then urinating forthwith, it both instructed and encouraged the clergyman's unwilling organ to do likewise.

Now here at one ocean-wide leap was I, Johnny de Paria, making water in London (you hear w'at Ah'm tellin' you? You hear me? In London) with one of the most important men in Great Britain, the Commonwealth and Empire Beyond the Seas. Me, Johnny de Paria. From San Fernando, Trinidad, British West Indies. Yes, me. Me-e-e-e—SELF. As Father Maginot, the priest at the Roman Catholic church in San Fernando, would say, I was deeply sensible of the honor.

I like that kind of talk. "Deeply sensible of the honor." That's the way thunder rolls in the rainy season at four o'clock in the afternoon behind Tamana and El Tucuche, two of the highest mountains in Trinidad. When I hear anyone making a speech, I always listen for the sound of the sea and the sense of the earth in the words of the speaker. I don't write much—maybe one short letter a year. But whenever I do, I am not satisfied unless the writing is like my breathing—easy, deep, effortless. Just as I don't even know I'm breathing, I don't want to know that I'm writing. Anyway, I'm not talking about that. I'm talking about the Mister-Man. The Marquis of Padbury. And me. In London. Me, Johnny de Paria, from San Fernando, Trinidad, B.W.I. "Last train from SANFER—NANDO-O-O-O . . . ! Last train from SANFER—NANDO-O-O-O-O . . . !" Man, that was a hell of a calypso. Calypso father, boy. Professor von Buffus told me he knew for a fact that because of this calypso, elev-

4

en thousand three hundred and sixty-four young girls lost their virginity in San Fernando alone—not counting Port-of-Spain—during the carnival season that year. The professor is a German. People say he is the greatest scholar, the most learned man in the world. He says so, too. So it must be true.

Herr Professor Dr. Dr. Dr. Dr. Wolfgang von Buffus zu Damnitz not only knows more than everyone else, but he is also the most impoverished man on this planet. These twin attainments are inseparable. Monumental learning goes hand in hand with abysmal penury. So I'm told. The professor is a man whose astral scholarship is untainted by anything so coarsely material as cash in hand. I speak of "cash in hand" because this learned man has always looked to the indefinite future to redeem the needs of the uncompromising present. He was one of the earliest pre-Keynesian pioneers in the economics of deficit financing. This is understandable, since his absorption in scholarship obliges him to carry on a somewhat Gregorian existence, several months behind the Julian calendar. Among his universal accomplishments, Professor von Buffus is also the world's leading authority on urinometrics, or the art of divination by measuring the parabolic arch of water passed in the act of urinating. I have picked up a thing or two along these lines from the professor and I can pretty much tell what a man's future is likely to be simply by observing the curve of the arch and the angle of descent of his water. The professor once told me that he had written a book on this subject. He said the title of the book was *The Relationship between Asymptotes and Hyperbolas Considered as a Factor in the Mathematical Theory of Probability*. He told me I needn't trouble to try to find the book, for there was only one copy and he had presented that to the Pope, who kept it in the Vatican under lock and key. The book was purely mathematical, he said, and so advanced that only two people in the world besides himself were able to understand it. One was a Hindu mystic three hundred and seventy-nine years old who lived in a deep crevasse in the Himalayas and the other was a Chinese sage who lived in a canyon in the Gobi desert, where he had just celebrated his four hundred and twenty-second birthday. According to the professor, this sage had spent the past two hundred and fifty-seven years annotating the Analects of Confucius.

Applying the principles I had been taught by the professor, I noted at once the high parabolic arch of the marquis's water. It was only a trifle lower than mine, though to be sure I was considerably younger than he. When in addition I had calculated the angle of its descent, it became plain to me that, eminent as he already was, there were even greater things in store for the marquis. Less than a week later, I chanced to pick up a copy of a London newspaper. There I read that the marquis had just been appointed His Britannic Majesty's Ambassador and Plenipotentiary to the Hedgehog and Iguana Islands of the Far Pacific. The newspaper also noted the marquis's authorship of a book entitled *Diplomacy and the Moral Imperative of Duplicity*. As His Lordship's views appeared to be identical with those of the newspaper, it had no difficulty in describing him as "a diplomat of extraordinary competence."

The marquis and I, having urinated, washed our hands at adjacent basins with equal care. I recall the manner in which the great nobleman revolved his hands, each serving in turn as an axis for the other, so as to distribute the soap's lather impartially. While he did so, a faint smile hovered on the threshold of his face, as if reluctant to suggest, by its intrusion, a capacity for anything so common as laughter in so uncommon a man. I noted his air of imperial abstraction. All Africa, I thought, India, the Dominion of Canada, Australia, New Zealand, the Pitcairn Islands, Tonga, Trinidad and Tobago, Tortuga, Tortola, etc., etc., all turned on the majestic spindle of his remote, proconsular concern. It was pure accident that I was handsomer than he, and my dinner jacket of a more impeccable cut. It was not necessarily to my credit that aesthetic considerations led me to prefer the bronze of my hands to the pallor of his own. What mattered was the consciousness of mission that informed each revolution of his thoughtful, viceregal hands. We were of about the same height, but while I was slender, slim-hipped, and broad-shouldered, he tended toward a diffident hint of Britannic port. Nothing obese: merely authoritative.

I glanced at him in the looking glass set above a row of marble wash basins and I began insensibly to mimic the movement of his hands. Watching him in the mirror, I noticed that he was turning off one of his water taps. I therefore did the same. But owing to the treacherous manner in which looking glasses refract images in reverse, when he turned off his hot-water tap, I turned off my cold water. He held his wrists beneath the flow of water, moving them slowly from side to side. I did the same. The water from my tap, which at first was warm, became warmer. I assumed the existence of a similar state of affairs with the marquis. He seemed unruffled. So, I thought, should I. But my wrists were being scalded and steam was rising from the basin. There was no question about it: unless His Lordship made quick work of his hand-washing, I should have need of first aid in a hurry. But he appeared to be sunk in untroubled meditation, while I was suffering third-degree burns. This imperial phlegm was altogether too much for me. In considerable agony, I uttered a short, colloquial word commonly employed as a synonym for fecal matter. I then withdrew my hands from the boiling water. The marquis turned to me and spoke with detached, impersonal gravity. "You really must learn to make rudimentary distinctions," he said. "That was hot water." There was no censure in his voice, only the aloof kindliness of a Builder of Empire. He was aware that a colonial could not reasonably be expected to make such subtle distinctions at once. I should have to be taught. Otherwise the West Indies could never be granted its freedom. Nor India itself. Africa (including Keenyah).

7

Nor the Maldives or the Seychelles, not to speak of Mauritius, Malaysia, Zanzibar, and the Spice Islands.

I thanked His Lordship and hurried away in search of a doctor.

That was a very important lesson, for which I have never ceased to be grateful to the Marquis of Padbury. He need have said nothing. Indeed, were he a lower-class person, he would have either been silent at my discomfiture or indulged himself in sadistic amusement. (Professor von Buffus always spoke of the latter reaction as *schadenfreude*. This was, he told me, an essentially untranslatable German expression.) But the marquis chose to instruct me, a mere colonial youth, in the very art in which the English, traditionally, have surpassed the rest of the world—the art of making useful, pragmatic distinctions. I have never since mistaken hot water for cold, thanks to that great man. Because few people can have had so illuminating a lesson from so distinguished a personage, I have chosen to set it down here. It cannot fail to be helpful.

What the marquis appreciated as I, a benighted colonial, did not, was that the *peine forte et dure*, a form of Judicial Trial by Ordeal to which earlier generations of Englishmen were subjected, had long since been abolished. But because we in the colonies always lagged a century or two behind developments in the metropolitan country, I was unaware of the abolition some five hundred years earlier of this mode of assessing guilt or innocence. I discovered this when I began to study English legal history. Meanwhile there were other fundamental lessons to be learned. After the curious fashion of improbable coincidences, I had a similar encounter only a few days later with another illustrious Englishman, the Right Honorable Sir Peter Coxlady, whose name is associated with some of the less glittering achievements of British imperial policy in the twentieth century. Finding myself at an adjoining stall in the same watering place with Sir Peter, I inspected the trajectory of his water. He was my

8

senior by several decades; even so, the arch of his flow was disproportionately lower than my own. I knew then that he would someday be accused of having been soft on Hitler. I did not have the opportunity of testing the elevation of Mr. Chamberlain's water. It would, I think, have been of the same level, give or take a fraction of a millimeter, as Sir Peter's. Since Sir Peter and I were in a manner of speaking both handling at the same moment the same matter, separately but equally, I ventured to address certain remarks to him on his mismanagement of the crisis over the phosphates-rich Sultanate of Jumbala several years before. I was able to tax Sir Peter on this point because Professor von Buffus had been principal adviser to the sultan in that unhappy affair. At least that's what the professor told me. A man, even one so outstanding as Sir Peter, with his privy member at large in his hand is not in a position to summon hostile emotion to his aid. He may squirm, writhe, or bristle, but for those crucial minutes he is in the power of his kidneys, a notoriously despotic pair of organs. The fifteenth- and sixteenth-century custom by which French monarchs were required to hold morning levées in their bedchambers while yielding to the importunities of nature should be reinstituted. Franco-American relations during the reign of General de Gaulle would have been a good deal better had Charles le Grand been constitutionally obliged to conform with this practice. The late President Eisenhower's press conferences, for example, were among the most tranquil of public events in the history of the American republic. The general's syntax made unmistakably plain what he was really doing while apparently discussing grave issues of domestic and international import. The republic suffered no harm and neither did the rest of the world, even if the general sometimes fell between two stools.

When I presumed to disclose to Sir Peter my disapproval of the forcible overthrow of the Sultan of Jumbala by the crew of a British gunboat expressly dispatched for that purpose at Sir Peter's instigation, I knew my ground. I was not astonished at his silence. For the moment there was nothing he could say. His hands were full. As usually happens, however, speech was restored to him with the cessation of his water. Like the great statesman that he was, he returned his privy member to the sanctuary of his breeches with the same meticulous care that he was accustomed to bestow upon his replies to questions directed to him by querulous members of the House of Commons. Then he turned to me. Although we had broken from the starting gate together, I, in all the copiousness of my youth, was only just arriving at the end of my water. As he was a gentleman he waited until I, too, had returned my member to its trousered niche—but not, of course, before I had brandished it, Excalibur-like, with all the famous panache that characterizes a Trinidadian. (No well-bred Trinidadian ever replaces his member, after making water, without observing this rite. The lesser breed from the smaller islands—Barbados, St. Lucia, Grenada, St. Vincent, Bequia, Cariacou, as well as British Guiana on the South American mainland—are typically in precipitate haste, after passing water, to return their member to confinement without ceremony. It is as if they had something to be ashamed of. Not so Trinidadians. Nor, to do them justice, Jamaicans. A Trinidadian—or a Jamaican—wishing to give himself as it were a medical checkup, simply brings his member out of hiding and swings it vigorously to and fro. If it makes a whistling sound, he is in good health. Otherwise he consults a physician.) Only when he had made certain that in no conceivable way was he taking me at a disadvantage did Sir Peter Coxlady respond. "It is not necessary to be offensive," he said, "in order to be noticed." There was just the slightest hint of magisterial reproof in his tone. More pronounced, however, was its courteous intimation of a desire to be helpful. Most reassuring of all, so as to spare me the least semblance of a desire on his part to be wounding, he did not look at me as he spoke. He seemed instead to address himself to some distant corner of the pungent, dimly lit *pissoir*. Then he washed his hands. As he did so, the resemblance to the Marquis of Padbury was dramatic indeed.

It is from the Right Honorable Sir Peter Coxlady that I acquired the modest reticence that so many excellent judges of character have found praiseworthy in me. Yet I have never felt that I deserved to be complimented on this score. It is the duty of a colonial to emulate his superiors. This is what Dr. von Buffus has told me. It must be true, because he is the greatest scholar, the most learned man in the world. Even if it's also true that he looks like a damn ole po'-me-one without a red cent to his behind. How the hell can anyone know as much as the professor and still be so damn poor? I tell you the truth, man: I don't understand this. I just don't.

I was still residing at my home in Trinidad when I saw the professor for the first time. I said to myself: "Jee-sus Chris'! But what the hell is this?" I couldn't believe my eyes. The man looked just like a little, old, white manicou. (A manicou resembles a rat, only it's bigger than a big rat. But the meat, man, the meat sweet too-much. Sweet like sweet 'self. O God, boy!) So when this old white manicou knocked at my door, at first I didn't even look up. I thought it was one of the servants. It was late afternoon. In a few minutes I would go out on the veranda, lie down in my hammock, play my guitar, sing calypsos, and drink rum punch. I had forgotten that this mister-man was coming to see me. My aunt Jocasta had told me to expect him. "He's going to be your teacher," she said. But to teach me what? I didn't want to learn anything except how to pick the right cock in a close fight. Now here was he, this mister-man, bowing and clicking his heels together with the sound that the tail of a horsewhip snake makes when it is whipping a pregnant woman.

Before he could say anything, I told the professor: "I know

why you come to see me. But I don't want you to teach me anything. I know enough."

"Ah!" He looked up at the ceiling. "Know-ledge—what is know-ledge?" But he wasn't asking me. He was talking to the ceiling. "Does one *know* anything? Is it really possible to know?" And he was sighing all the time he was talking. "Epistemology—"

His overemphasis of the second syllable blurred his enunciation. Why, I thought, was this sonofabitch talking about piss? And who was pissing? To come into my room, just like this, talking about piss, somebody pissing— Now if there's one thing I don't like, it's people bothering me. Irritation threatened to render me discourteous. He looked weary. That didn't surprise me. He was an old man. The young are never weary; the old are never anything else. I do not wish to be old. My nose itches with disesteem at the thought of decrepitude.

"I have no desire to teach you anything." He was studying me as if I were a bird in a tree and he was trying to find a way to put salt on my tail.

But I only looked at him and I thought to myself: "Go 'way, ole man."

I couldn't tell him so, for he was a guest in my room and Aunt Jocasta was always impressing on me morning, noon, and night that "A guest in your house must be regarded as rain in a season of drought." Well, this was the dry season, anyhow. So I said, offering him a drink: "Come, man, leh we fire one." And I began to move toward the veranda. But he raised his hand and, with no more than that gesture, stopped me dead in my tracks. Our eyes clashed. His won.

I gave in because he was a guest in my room. By winning I would have insulted him, displayed bad manners. And my mother was forever admonishing me that "Manners makyth man."

The pupils of the professor's eyes were black-black: black

as the seeds of that fruit of paradise, the soursop. This was one of the first things you noticed about him—those black-black eyes. And a huge head, round like a ripe calabash but twice as big. Otherwise he looked just like a manicou at five o'clock in the morning, tired after hunting for food and dodging its enemies all night long, and trying now to get back to its hole before sunrise. But you don't feel sorry for a manicou, and I didn't feel sorry for the professor. Besides, you couldn't feel sorry for anyone whose eyes glowed like his—dream-bright, star-proud, fierce and solitary as bon-fires burning on far-distant hills.

The daylight dimmed in the room. More insistently than ever I heard the inarticulate call of my guitar and felt the lure of the hammock on the veranda. The professor, howev-er, having successfully detained me, was speaking.

"I will not be long." The seat of his discolored twill trou-sers rustled against the cane-bottomed armchair, and rus-tled again as he shifted his body to cross his legs. I thought of turning on a light, but darkness might be more appropriate to whatever mysterious knowledge he was about to impart to me. "I don't think you have a taste for scholarship." His voice was an unresolved conflict between a squeak and a rasp. "Books have no compelling attraction for you. The learning you need will come to you in other ways. But there is one book—"

The room now was in total darkness. But I was aware of fugitive lizards on the walls, scurrying about in search of food under cover of night. They were always here at this time or whenever else they had a chance of being unob-served. Other little creatures of the dusk were either som-nolent on the ceiling or, as I knew from frequent observa-tion, streaking across the walls supercharged with alarm or propelled by hunting lust. An occasional hiss or rustle, inde-cipherable unless familiarity with the tropics provided the key, announced still other presences. A bird's enthralled cry to the enshrouding night, an owl's antiphony, the staccato plaints of choirs of cicadas, a dog's challenge to an intruder delivered in throat-constricted accents of fear and rage. Yet the deep interior silence of the night remained inviolable. A perfume of jasmines drifted into the room, voluptuous and indolent on the air. The odor of frangipani blossoms masked the smell of fish frying and meat broiling, bread baking, rice boiling, and fruit greening into ripeness, into mellowness, into rottenness. These massed pungencies concealed but also confirmed the miasma of ebb tide across the mud flats, the stench of mangrove swamps, the effluvia of latrines, and the malodorous reek of thousands upon thousands of un-washed human bodies. A muezzin's cry from a distant mina-ret arched in a long parabola of plangent entreaty across the town, imploring the faithful to pray. The bells of the Roman Catholic church took plaintive leave of the departing day. Within the shuttered house of the de Parias, servants, resur-rected by eventide, began to stir, gliding barefoot to and fro across the tessellated floors.

"You want me to make a light?" I asked the professor.

The silence in the room was as soft as a bat's wings brush-ing against midnight. The professor's voice, for all its creak-ing, rasping, unlubricated quality, was as soft as he replied: "In a minute. I want to finish what I'm saying to you." The darkness deepened his authority, inflecting his tone with oracular portent.

I waited. His breathing was clearly audible: systole, diasto-le; then, dactyl, spondee—one long, one short. I listened, as in a trance, to my own breathing, too.

"The book—"

My breath voyaged in serene progression, slow as a sailing ship in an idle breeze. I felt easy and content, only half-lis-tening to the professor. I was in fact engaged in an absorb-ing calculation. What was the exact ratio of lime juice to rum—this was the question I had posed myself—that would produce a perfect rum punch? Given six parts of rum, two

14

parts of lime juice would produce—what result? Or three—
But this—three, three parts of lime juice—would lead to
precipitate conflict between the lime juice and the rum. For
rum, being by nature what it is, would inevitably war
against any attempt by lime juice at domination. Three
parts of lime juice would be a *casus belli*, a naked provoca-
tion. Yet when all was said and done, the achievement of a
great rum punch was a matter of art, not chemistry. A great
rum punch could not be calculated. Too many variables
would enter into the equation. One's own mood was a factor
that at all times had to be taken into account. An overasser-
tive sense of oneself would be communicated to the lime
juice, which, itself aggressive by disposition, would seize the
opportunity to be unduly familiar with the rum. The latter
would respond with violent distaste, since it is by nature
hostile to foreign intrusion. Like a great nation-state, rum is
hospitable only when its constitutional sovereignty is respected. Then a transforming welcome rewards the devo-
tee. Men momentarily become gods. They sit in judgment
on human destiny. Or they become inspired prophets, uttering cryptic revelations in Delphic tongues. To crown all,
they ascend to Paradise, charioteering on clouds of liquid
ecstasy, swifter than light, more gossamer than sunbeams.
Men—and women, too—have been known to renounce every earthly tie and to repudiate the most sacred obligations
in order to consecrate their lives in single-minded zealotry
to the worship of Rum, a most jealous god, whose first com-
mandment, following Jehovah, is: "Thou shalt have no other
gods but Me." Me. Rum.

Some have seen in the élitism of rum evidence, so to
speak, of racist tendencies deriving from its fanatical insistence on elemental purity: the *limpieza de sangre*, so to
speak, of the Spanish Inquisition. I do not share that view. I
believe that rum, like man himself, is entitled to exist on its
own terms in accordance with the fundamental laws of its
nature. I am unable to see why rum should be expected to

behave like whiskey, a subversive drink of the Scottish Highlands inclined by its Jacobite character to lofty pretensions and lost causes. Whiskey is at its best in the society of demagogues, upstarts, and lawyers. But where sacrificial youths, vestal virgins, conquistadors, and kings are gathered together, rum finds itself among equals. Yet always (and this is its very signet) *primus inter pares.* So lime juice must be infiltrated into rum with the most delicate circumspection. And this is why sugar—a gravid, brown sugar, pregnant with conciliation—is indispensable as a mediator. Nothing else will do. Parvenus and other types of *arrivistes* have been known to attempt to use surrogates for brown sugar. I heard Father Maginot speak one evening on Aunt Jocasta's veranda of honey culled from Benedictine swarms as a substitute. Straightaway I knew that, whatever his good works and priestly zeal, he was destined for a protracted stay in Purgatory. Indeed, even before that time came, he would be damn lucky to escape excommunication at the hands of some fastidious, purist bishop. The sonofabitch. (Sorry, Father. My indignation just got the better of me.)

The ideal rum punch is a grail that men pursue in the all-consuming spirit of an unremitting quest for perfection. I, myself, have discovered, as I believe, a hitherto secret formula. Two and one-half parts of lime juice (the limes not a sunbeam less or more than precisely ripe, and their juices then expressed without bruising the tender pulp; otherwise, in its exquisite sensitivity, the rum will recoil and perfection remain elusive); say, six and seven-sixteenths parts of rum, a spoonful of brown sugar—mountain-high or hillock-low, according to taste . . .

"The book I want you to read—" The rust-hinged croak of the professor's voice recalled me to awareness of the unlighted room. By some trick of intangible transference, it emphasized anew the creature actualities—the musty odor of the learned man's clothing (probably, I thought, an unwashed shirt perhaps several days overdue for laundering). I surmised that the professor, except for a lapse caused by scholarly inattention, would have had a bath that morning. But if so, then I really could not account for the brazen reek of his armpits as he elevated his arms and folded them across his chest. I was reminded of Saint Anthony, who, according to Father Maginot, thought bathing sinful. Even the beasts of the desert gave him a wide berth, and only an angel could be persuaded to come within miles of him. So did that holy cleric stink. At any rate—

"This is the book—" I sensed rather than saw one of his hands disengage itself and grope beneath his jacket. "Put on the light."

I stretched out my hand. He blinked as the light swept aside the darkness. From the waistband of his trousers he extracted a book and, fondling it as if he were parting from a beloved child, handed it to me. "Yes," he said. "Homer." I was scrutinizing the title. *The Odyssey*. He gave me an intent, unwavering look. "Read it." His eyes were pronouncing their verdict in the trial they had held of me. "Every day."

I opened the book at random, puzzled and curious.

"In fact," he told me, as I began to turn the pages, "we'll read it together." Then, musing, he said, speaking more to himself than to me, "Ulysses sometimes occurs in the form of a Joe Caldeira—"

"Joe who?" I thought. "Who the hell is—?"

Herr Professor Dr. von Buffus zu Damnitz had come to Trinidad as a private tutor to the adolescent son of a former English governor of the island. It had been His Excellency's intention to have the boy prepared for entrance to a German university. There he would spend a year or two in philosophical studies before continuing his formal education in England. So he had engaged the services of the learned scholar, who was then, as it happened, at leisure in London

17

after making an extremely hurried departure from a teaching post at a finishing school for girls in Switzerland.

On arriving in Trinidad and becoming acquainted with his pupil, Dr. von Buffus lost no time in deciding that whatever distinctions the future might hold in store for the boy, it was unlikely that philosophical studies would be the path to their attainment. More than to anything else, the youth was devoted to cockfighting. This pastime was illegal, but it was carried on openly with the connivance of the police. Young Nigel, aged seventeen, discovered in the professor less a tutor and guide in the arcane mazes of Kantian Categories than a companion at the weekly rendezvous with other cock fanciers and devotees of this ancient sport. German verbs fared ill alongside the flurry and whir of fighting birds trained to gouge one another's eyes out and slit one another's throats with steel-shod claws. There was scarcely a Sunday when the professor did not find himself the winner, on balance, of the wagers he had made on the outcome of the contests in which his pupil's cocks were engaged. In those circumstances, it seemed disproportionate to spend overmuch time on the baroque splendors of the German language, for which, after all, he earned less each month than he made each week by betting on the gallant cocks. To do Dr. von Buffus justice, he had attempted to carry out his trust and to instruct the boy along the lines that His Excellency had indicated. Even now he did from time to time try to ingratiate the grammatical structure of the German language into the youth's interest. There were moments, as when for example he grew rapturous over the glories of German syntax, that he felt certain he had at last succeeded in claiming his pupil's attention. Almost at once, however, his sense of triumph would be rendered illusory by the boy's irrelevant inquiries, such as: "Wey de arse yo' t'ink, Prof, me red cock go' cut de Venezuelan t'roat in one roun'?" His forefinger traveled in a straight line of sanguinary anticipation across his own throat. In pure pedagogic desperation, the professor even resorted to reciting poems by Heine, reading from Schiller and Goethe, and to be sure he did not neglect the more or less contemporary, declaiming from von Hofmannsthal and Stefan George. Its only effect on the boy was his decision to give the name "Hynie" to a cock about to fight its maiden battle. The cock was killed in the very first flurry. So heavily, for sentimental reasons, had the professor wagered on the bird that it took him more than three weeks of careful betting before he could fully recoup his losses. German studies sank still lower in his pupil's esteem.

One of the aspects of the young man's personality that fascinated the professor was the Trinidadian dialect that he habitually employed in contrast to his father's extremely correct, upper-class British speech. In his capacity as the boy's tutor, Dr. von Buffus occasionally dined at His Excellency's table. At such times he was always struck anew by the boy's deliberately cultivated Trinidadian persona in contradistinction to the Anglicism of speech and manners that otherwise prevailed within the cultural stronghold of the governing Anglo-Saxon community. Why His Excellency should have thought that his son, constituted as he obviously was, would find German philosophy congenial was beyond the professor. In rueful introspection, Dr. von Buffus could only remind himself that the English were a very peculiar people.

His Excellency sometimes inquired about his son's progress. The professor would then attempt to reveal something of his pupil's recalcitrance to learning in general and to German studies in particular. His Excellency would brush him aside, however, with a brusque though cordial show of incredulity that anything so carefully considered as his plan for his son's future could possibly go awry. He would afterward dismiss Dr. von Buffus with an offhand remark about the weather or the caprices of the local legislature. Disconsolate, the professor would return to his pupil. "Say after me," he would tell the boy:

> *"Mein Vater ist ein Dummkopf,*
> *Meine Mutter ist eine Kuh.*
> *Ich bin ein Sportsmann—*
> *So eins und zwei macht vier."*

But to no avail. "Yo' t'ink me red cock go' cut de black cock arse? Ah bet—" The professor was sure to lay his bet, too.

Mistakes occur, of course, no matter how well regulated the circumstances. The police raid on that Sunday afternoon's cockfight was a mistake. There could be no question about it. For the inspector of police himself was among those arrested; and that was a clumsy error indeed. So was the arrest of the governor's own son along with his tutor, the distinguished German scholar, Dr. von Buffus zu Damnitz, and a score of others not quite so highly placed, perhaps, but in no instance nonentities. Except in the case of Joe Caldeira, the bartender at the Black Cat Bar in San Fernando, the very cream of the local sporting crop had been harvested in that ill-judged raid.

Dr. von Buffus's efforts to explain the misadventure went coldly unheeded. After making some unfortunate references to Kaiser Wilhelm and the First World War, His Excellency gave the professor a month's notice of termination of his services. Neither, in the circumstances, was His Excellency prepared to pay the professor's passage back to Europe. His Excellency's wife was a good deal more vehement. Normally, she was an unobtrusive lady with the appearance of an overgrown lobster that had been plunged into boiling water and then discarded as unfit for human consumption. Now, without warning, she became garrulous and offensive. She informed the professor that insofar as she was concerned, he should be repatriated to his native country—in the unlikely event that it would be so misguided as to readmit him. Certainly, England should be spared his presence. Her country, she said, had no need of Teutonic law-breakers posing as respectable scholars. She accused Dr. von Buffus of initiating her blameless son into the crime of cock-fighting instead of instructing him in the elements of the German language as he had been employed to do. Drawing on her knowledge of social and political history, she asserted that the Hanoverians had introduced the wretched sport of cockfighting into England. Strictly as a matter of historical accuracy, Dr. von Buffus pointed out that cockfighting in England had preceded the Magna Carta of King John by several centuries, having already been widespread in the time of Hengist and Horsa. Her Ladyship remained unimpressed by this display of scholarly precision on the part of the learned doctor and with distinct acerbity spoke instead of Bismarck's manipulation of the events that led to the Franco-Prussian War of 1870. That incident, together with Professor von Buffus's betrayal of his trust, as she conceived it, was conclusive evidence of national turpitude.

His Excellency's attempts to remonstrate with his son were not markedly successful. For the latter, with a casual offhandedness at least equal to his father's, summarily invited him in the broadest Trinidadian dialect to "kiss me arse, man." His Excellency declined the invitation. He also cut off his son's allowance. His object was to make all such invitations to him from his son as costly to the latter as possible. Not only must the boy be taught better manners, but what was a good deal more important—better English. Damn the beggar. He sounded like a bloody native.

Unable to leave the island for want of passage money, and unable to earn his livelihood by teaching the German language to Trinidadians, the professor fell headlong into scholarly seediness and chronic insolvency.

It was at this low point in his fortunes that he met the First Lady of San Fernando, my aunt, Jocasta Maria Esmeralda Victoria de Paria.

Aunt Jocasta was my mother's sister, though she always

21

treated my mother as she would have done a child of her own had she ever given birth to one. She had never married because of her conviction that only spineless women surrendered their personal independence to mere males. Aunt Jocasta was a large lady of commodious means. From the level of her imposing height and the relative scale of her financial standing, she dominated much of the life of her community. She possessed a consuming sense of "family" and of the importance of being a de Paria. The distinction of belonging to Aunt Jocasta's clan invested every member with the privilege of appearing, uninvited, at her table on any festive occasion, public or private. This was in addition to the inherent right of all members to be present at family celebrations and other tribal events. Aunt Jocasta's extended family system made possible the care and feeding of scores of impecunious relatives and the formal education of a considerably smaller number. Academic excellence was not regarded as a mark of significant achievement from the family's standpoint. Other attainments were more highly valued. The ability to sit a horse masterfully; to recognize at sight any of the innumerable specimens of the island's flora and fauna and to be aware of their potential for help or harm; to consume titanic quantities of rum without displaying offensive symptoms of excess; to wench lustily, to eat omnivorously, and to view the world at large after the fashion of a beneficent monarch contemplating his domain: accomplishments such as these were more lavishly esteemed within the family.

The admission of the learned scholar, Herr Professor Dr. Dr. Dr. Dr. von Buffus zu Damnitz, to this bloodbound circle of primeval materialists provoked wide local speculation. It was, however, carefully muted. For no one would have thought lightly of incurring Aunt Jocasta's displeasure by indulging in unseemly gossip about her private arrangements. Moreover, she had once been to England. This sovereign fact, and the authority of her hereditary position—as she envisioned it—gave her the unchallengeable liberty to dictate standards of personal conduct to those she deemed "the better people" in the community. Her benefactions were not confined to her kinfolk, but extended even to those imprudent enough not to have been born de Parias.

Aunt Jocasta possessed the bearing of a female conquistador. She was feudal in her social outlook and in the condescension of her benevolent regard. Her mouth was linear-lipped, her nose authoritarian, her jaw cast in granite against all heretics recusant to the motto of the de Parias: "*Écrasez les clochards.*" The family name had been handed down—somewhat irregularly—from an ancestor of noble lineage who had forfeited his life in circumstances of the utmost gallantry. Surprised in bed with a lady by her jealous and ill-tempered husband, he bravely maintained his horizontal position of protection above the lady, concealing her body with his own and his head with a pillow. Evidently preferring to have found them in a vertical rather than a horizontal position, the discourteous husband impaled them both on the point of his sword, exclaiming as he did so: "*Écrasez les clochards!*" Whence the family motto of the de Parias.

Her voluminous bosom billowing outward and her far-flung backside in full sail rearward, Aunt Jocasta gave the appearance, when in motion, of a great Spanish galleon beating slowly up a leeward passage, borne by winds of sovereign majesty. Aunt Jocasta's bottom was, in fact, the subject of much comment among the townspeople. There were no doubt bigger backsides than Aunt Jocasta's in the British Commonwealth and Empire Beyond the Seas. Within the memory of the oldest living inhabitant of the islands of Trinidad and Tobago, there once was, some seventy-five years earlier, a celebrated backside incontestably as large as hers. It was generally conceded, however, that never in all the history of the islands had there been, in proportion to its gigantic mass, a more dignified, a more commanding, a more transfixing eminence. So what might otherwise have been a low source of popular derision became a high symbol of insular pride. Aunt Jocasta's bottom was one of the accredited sights of the islands. Much piquancy was lent to this circumstance by the fact that there also resided in the town of San Fernando a maiden lady whose name was Lucinda Bottom, and whose rearward endowment, despite her declaratory surname, was negligible. "De two o' dem should 'change bam-bam" ("bam-bam" being a lewd Trinidadian colloquialism for backside). This observation, delivered in discreet whispers, was about as far as anyone dared to go. Except in a singular incident when a suicidal admirer succumbed to a compulsion whose consequences, while painful for him, provided the townspeople with a dramatic reminder of the capacity for feudal vengeance still retained by a de Paria.

Aunt Jocasta was accustomed to go walking of an afternoon in a parklike area called Mon Repos Savannah. On this particular occasion, she had stopped in the course of her stroll to admire a tumult of wildflowers in the shade of a sapodilla tree. She bent over to get a closer look. At that moment she felt a hand on her behind. She didn't scream; she didn't scold; she didn't faint; she didn't fuss. No. She simply turned and, by that measured, deliberate act of turning, removed her tectonic plate of a posterior from the clutch of her too-ardent aficionado. Then she gave him a look that cut him right in half. But she said not a word to him. She walked back to the entrance to the Savannah, where her buggy awaited her.

"Drive through the Savannah," she told her groom.

"Yes, Miss Jo."

As they neared the exit, she saw the fellow who had insulted her. The buggy came abreast of him. "Stop," she said to her groom.

The buggy came to a halt.

"Horsewhip that man." She indicated the ill-mannered molester.

The groom dismounted, whip in hand. When she thought that the man had had enough, she signaled to her groom. Then she threw the man some coins. She was always generous.

Aunt Jocasta never explained to her groom why she wanted the man horsewhipped. That would have been beneath her dignity. A relationship, intolerable to Aunt Jocasta, would have been initiated between herself and her servant, in which the latter would have appeared her champion. In dealing with the matter as she did, she maintained her proper distance from her servant while conscripting him to assert the sanctity of her person. Lastly, I noted her good manners in throwing the offending fellow some coins to salve his bruises.

The incident was entirely unexpected to Aunt Jocasta. She was taken by surprise. It is not every afternoon of a lady's life that a strange man caresses her "bam-bam" in a public park. A lesser person would have made quite a to-do about it. But not Aunt Jocasta.

I came to hear of this only because the two sons of Aunt Jocasta's groom were my bosom companions. They were Chinese and we were inseparable. Ah Sam and Ah See. Those were their names. They had heard their father relating the incident to their mother. He, in turn, had overheard Aunt Jocasta relating it to my mother.

The matter did not end there.

Ah Sam, Ah See, and I lay in wait for the horsewhipped man. He then endured a Second Purgatory. We ambushed him in a crossfire of stones from which he barely escaped with his life.

Actually, I was closer to Ah Sam than I was to Ah See. Ah Sam and I were of the same age. Ah See was two years younger. Each day, from the rising to the setting of the sun, Ah Sam and I were together. He was squat, round-headed, and bowlegged. His distaste for books was profound. Tree and water, earth and sky, wind and starshine, bird and beast, everything that lived and everything that didn't (or seemed not to), the discovered no less than the undiscovered world: all these things were the staple and center of Ah Sam's existence. We would summon each other at daybreak, whistling a bar of an old tune: "I hear you calling me-e-e-e-e!" Depending on the time of year, we would begin the day by raiding someone's mango tree, running two or three miles for exercise, playing cricket or soccer, going down to the beach for a swim, or teasing girls on their way to school.

We lived off the land. We had no time for set meals. When we were hungry we ate what was at hand—fruit for the most part, which we usually took from whatever tree was available without regard to legal ownership. Technically, as I afterward discovered, we were committing an offense known to the law as praedial larceny. None of us, however, had any leaning toward the law at this stage and were largely unaware of its numerous prohibitions. We simply did as we pleased. Within, of course, reasonable limits. We did not maim anyone, commit murder, or anything so beastly. But as I look back on it, we were a three-man gang that effectively terrorized the neighborhood in which we operated.

I did not wholly share Ah Sam's distaste for books, but I was unreservedly with him in his contempt for school. A brief acquaintance with all the artificial nonsense of formal schooling had aroused in me an implacable hostility. The outdoors had more to teach, and an intelligent youth more to learn from the rain it dispensed and the sun it bestowed, than in all the schoolrooms in the world. Aunt Jocasta took much the same view as I, insisting only that I consult with tutors whom she periodically engaged for this purpose. I had, in fact, a somewhat indistinct regard for books. I was willing to bestow upon them a grudging admiration, provided they kept their distance from me. Some doubtless were useful, and many no doubt were not. But I had carefully refrained from exploring my assumptions at first hand, and so they remained, as I well knew, mere uninstructed opinions. For the moment, more interesting matters claimed my attention. Invariably at some point during the day, I would retire into a tree for an hour or two and meditate. On such occasions, Ah Sam would go foraging for supplies or execute some other commission. In any case, he would shield me against interruption. "He's thinking," he would admonish would-be intruders. "Don't bother him." When I came down from the tree, if something had occurred to me that I judged to be of interest or value to Ah Sam, I'd tell him about it and answer any questions he had. In this way, although he did not go to school or read any books, or even meditate as I did, he became quite well educated. His powers of observation were extraordinary; his memory capacious, retentive, and accurate in the highest degree; his judgment keen and penetrating. He is, beyond all comparison, the most intelligent person I have ever known. I do not claim that he is Professor von Buffus's equal as a scholar. Yet to be a scholar and to be intelligent are not one and the same thing. It is possible to be a scholar and at the same time a damn fool. Scholarship has very little to do with intelligence. Ah Sam was not an academic person. Neither, of course, would I describe him as an intellectual. For at the time I speak of, he wrote his name only with the greatest difficulty. Whenever he was obliged to do so, the arduousness of the task was emphasized by his pendant tongue, which, escaping from its glottal constraints, hung down elongated and salivary well toward the base of his chin. Thus suspended, it went about its business of assisting him to form each letter of his name in a slow and laborious calligraphy.

Like me, Ah Sam retained his virginity until a relatively advanced age. We had heard that sexual intercourse depleted a man's strength. Weakness was repugnant to us. Our manners toward girls were usually correct but distant. The biblical story of Samson and Delilah had made a strong impression on us. I discussed the matter with Aunt Jocasta, who said that Samson was strong but that he lacked common sense.

Aunt Jocasta really was my mother's half-sister, since she was of a different mother, my grandfather's first wife. Twenty years older than my mother, she was almost as much in the relation of aunt to my mother as she was to me. Indeed, she had reared my mother as if the latter were her daughter. Her father's second wife had been, in her view, of unsuitable antecedents. Not only had Aunt Jocasta refused to have anything to do with her, but she had excluded her from any part in my mother's upbringing. She had inherited a comfortable fortune from her own mother, which made her financially independent. Upon her father's death, her share of his estate brought her substantial wealth in addition. To say that Aunt Jocasta was a formidable lady would scarcely do justice to her mountainous dignity. Her fundamental beliefs, as I recall them, were not excessively complicated. She worshiped the late Queen Victoria, was suspicious of the Virgin Mary, and censorious of the Almighty on the ground that His dispositions of human affairs would be so much the wiser were He to resort more often to her, Jocasta de Paria, for counsel and guidance.

Aside from her ample means and immense self-assurance, she had made the crowning pilgrimage to England. She had stayed there for seven days, three hours, and fifty-six minutes before returning to Trinidad. As a result, her social position, which had always been paramount, became unchallengeable. Her exordium to each assertion of her personal opinion, her invariable preface implying a weight of authority too powerful to be contested by any ordinary mortal, was: "When I was in London ..." Every dissentient point of view collapsed in the face of this reiterated fact. No matter what the subject under discussion, the project under way, the end to be achieved, opposition dissolved at the mere incantation of the formula: "When I was in London . . ." Her father himself, a man of strong character, was so overawed by his daughter's attainment of a visit to England that he never mentioned her without appending: "She's been to England." Neither did any of the townspeople ever forget this stupendous achievement of Aunt Jocasta's; nor were they permitted to do so. As well as this, she stood above six feet in height and weighed three hundred pounds. The only lady in recent times who has seemed to me to be worthy of comparison with Aunt Jocasta from almost every known point of view was the late Queen Salote of the Tonga Islands. I cannot speak of Queen Victoria, although, as I have said, Aunt Jocasta thought very highly of her. Because so much of Aunt Jocasta's embonpoint was arrayed at her rear, envious and ill-disposed persons made this the subject of covert gibes and coarse witticisms. Yet I had seen quite a number of substantial gentlemen appraise it with evident admiration and had even overheard some of them exclaiming among themselves: "O God, man, what a backside!" The most fervent of them was a dwarflike Chinese, Mr. Ching Po Lee, a prosperous merchant, of whom it is said that he had lost five mistresses and won seven at the gaming tables. As further proof of the esteem in which Aunt Jocasta's behind was held by persons of taste and discrimination, I myself once overheard Mr. Ching Po Lee confide to one of his cronies that he would like nothing so much as to "climb that big bam-bam." The worthiness of his ambition was confirmed by the general agreement that it would be a feat equal to the ascent of Mount Everest. To witness Aunt Jocasta's progress along the middle aisle of Saint Paul's Anglican church in San Fernando any Sunday morning at ten o'clock to her pew, first row front and center, was an object lesson in the art of transporting the human backside with supernal assurance and celestial dignity.

There was Mr. Deschamps, the town druggist, a gnome-

like man with a massive head, who was the only resident besides Aunt Jocasta (I mean, born resident and not, as Dr.
O'Flaherty and some others, come from abroad) who had
actually made the journey to Europe. And Mr. Deschamps
had not, even so, achieved the supreme distinction of a visit
to England. He had got only as far as France, which ever
after subordinated him in social status to Aunt Jocasta. No
matter the multitudinous repetition with which he referred
to "the time when I was in Paris." (He had arrived at the
Gare Saint-Lazare at nine-thirty-one in the morning and,
without once quitting the precincts of the railroad station,
had left at ten-twenty-three for Le Havre to take the boat,
the S.S. *Flandre* of the Compagnie Transatlantique Géné-
rale, for the return voyage to Trinidad.) No matter that he
had in impressive and undeniable fact spent a grand total of
fifty-two minutes in Paris. No matter that he had "crossed
the water" and brought back a lavish French accent, which
he never afterward discarded, to prove it. No matter the
steamship labels on his luggage, which possessed the status
of religious relics in his home. No matter. He remained distinctly below Aunt Jocasta in the social hierarchy of the
town. It availed him nothing that, having spent less than
one hour in France, he now had great difficulty understanding English though he could not speak a word of French—
except for the phrases *n'est-ce pas* and *comme il faut* and
the words *non* and *oui*. But his elaborate French accent
more than made up for these minor deficiencies. With the
most touching consideration for his clientele, he now employed an interpreter in his shop. All in vain. For she was
able to say, as he could not, "When I was in England...";
able to produce, as he could not, a parasol purchased at
Swan and Edgar's in Piccadilly Circus at the point where
Regent Street began "its radial progress into Nash's sculptured crescent." She had read this description in a guide-
book, memorized it, and never forgotten it. These words
were like an evocation of witchcraft in their effect upon her

listeners. Unfailingly, an awed silence descended upon any company in which she uttered them. By comparison, Mr. Deschamps had not even so much as a gaudy little miniature of a Paris scene—not even of the Eiffel Tower—to show for his visit; and even if he were able to produce such an artifact, it would have been unequal in its potency as a status-generating symbol to Aunt Jocasta's parasol, "purchased"—no less; not merely bought, but "purchased"—from—let the commercial superscription in all its gravid imperiousness sink in—"from Swan"—pause. Build the appropriate suspense. Don't be in a hurry. Let them wait as for a royal visitation. Take your time. They will appreciate it better and never afterward forget it—"and"—hold it. H-o-l-d it. Now—now— Let it go: "Ed—g-a-r's." Silence. Except for a single stertorous sound. The awed breathing of shut-in, untraveled yokels.

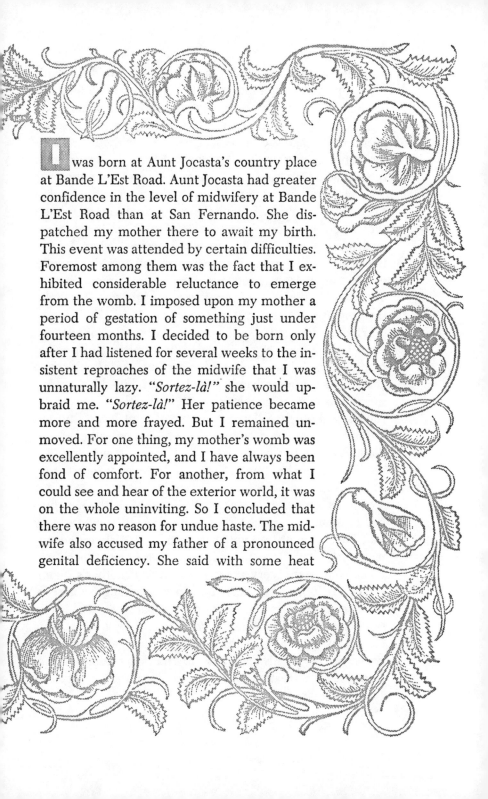

I was born at Aunt Jocasta's country place at Bande L'Est Road. Aunt Jocasta had greater confidence in the level of midwifery at Bande L'Est Road than at San Fernando. She dispatched my mother there to await my birth. This event was attended by certain difficulties. Foremost among them was the fact that I exhibited considerable reluctance to emerge from the womb. I imposed upon my mother a period of gestation of something just under fourteen months. I decided to be born only after I had listened for several weeks to the insistent reproaches of the midwife that I was unnaturally lazy. "*Sortez-là!*" she would upbraid me. "*Sortez-là!*" Her patience became more and more frayed. But I remained unmoved. For one thing, my mother's womb was excellently appointed, and I have always been fond of comfort. For another, from what I could see and hear of the exterior world, it was on the whole uninviting. So I concluded that there was no reason for undue haste. The midwife also accused my father of a pronounced genital deficiency. She said with some heat (speaking in the local patois) that he had tried to do a man's job with a boy's equipment. So I was ashamed to face the world. She and my father nearly came to blows. Aunt Jocasta had to separate them, ordering my father to leave the premises (he had, in any case, turned up without her consent) and making no secret of the fact that she agreed with the midwife. Aunt Jocasta did not approve of my father.

Much in my subsequent life up to the present has tended to confirm the midwife's opinion as to my laziness, though there are times when I am capable of cataclysmic exertions. Such occasions are only possible, however, when I have been sufficiently aroused over a protracted period. I am otherwise the most relaxed and easygoing of men. A true Trinidadian. Which is to say, I live and let live. This is the sovereign principle of my existence.

When I was a few months old, my father died of chagrin. Aunt Jocasta had always regarded him as a sort of praying mantis who, in the proper course of nature, should have ceased to exist immediately after he had fulfilled his species' specific destiny by copulating with my mother. He was not robust, and when, following my birth, Aunt Jocasta turned the full force of her disapproval upon him, he withered and died. After a not quite seemly period of mourning, my mother terminated her widowhood. If my aunt Jocasta's attitude to my mother's first marriage had been chilly, to her second its temperature was arctic. Worst of all, the new husband's name was, rather improbably, Pooch. The possibility that Pooch might be hyphenated with de Paria into a surname gave Aunt Jocasta cold, quotidian shivers. Pooch was unsuitable from every point of view. My mother's *mésalliance* can only have been due to a headlong impulse of some overmastering aberration. According to the family physician, it was a case of self-destructive neurasthenia caused by grief at the death of my father (and—he whispered the rest of his diagnosis—my mother's resentment at Aunt Jocasta's treatment of him). So, from merely displeasing Aunt Jocasta by her marriage to my father, my mother, by marrying Pooch, a virtual pariah, had engaged in an act of vengeful self-mutilation in order to punish, outrage, and horrify my aunt.

Whatever the accuracy of Dr. O'Flaherty's diagnosis, I had never consciously known my father. I did have some fetal awareness of him and, in particular, had eavesdropped on heated exchanges between him and the midwife. Of the two, I then thought the midwife much the stronger character. It was clear to me, reposing at my ease in the amniotic fluid of my mother's womb, that insofar as I might have been responsible for choosing a father, I had not been wisely discerning. Besides which, I had been put off by his habit of engaging in sexual acts of superfetation with my mother during her pregnancy, ignoring my presence in her womb and obliging me to be a voyeur. He seemed to think that I was drowning in the fetal pond and he was throwing me a rope, which, however, was too short to reach me.

At six months of age, my nurse found me in my cradle one day covered from head to foot with big red ants. In Trinidad, red ants can be so big that just a few of them could have pulled the damn cradle out of the room. And there was I with a million of them having a big fête on top of me, crawling and dancing all over me—playin' mas', yes—so many of them that you could hardly see me at all. I tell you, man, I was in a hell of a fix. Every one of those red ants could bite like a dog. I was in some crab-hole.

The nursemaid screamed, and my mother came in to find out what was going on. Then she also screamed. Aunt Jocasta came. She took one look at the situation I was in and she said: "Send for the priest. The baby must receive extreme unction. But never mind," she told my mother. "You can always have another child—with another husband."

At the same time, since Aunt Jocasta simply wasn't the sort of woman who just stood about and did nothing in an emergency, she ordered the nursemaid to pull herself together and go and fetch a candle and a box of matches. The woman returned with the candle and Aunt Jocasta lit it. Then she stood over my cradle, holding the lighted candle in front of her, and she prayed. Nobody knows to this day how it happened, but all of a sudden those big red ants ("batchak"—the worst kind) started to leave the fête they were making on me. Aunt Jocasta just stood there with her candle and prayed. By the time the priest arrived to give me the last rites of the Church, there wasn't a single "batchak" on me. No one knew where they had gone to, but I was completely unharmed. Not a mark, not a scratch, not a bite. "Such," said the priest, "is the power of prayer."

Another time I and my cousins, about two dozen of us, were all staying at Aunt Jocasta's place at Bande L'Est Road one August. I was then six or seven years old. Although the house was large enough, with room to spare in ordinary circumstances, there were just not sufficient bedrooms for the considerable horde of children. So a number of us were put to sleep on mattresses on the floor here and there about the house. In those days there were no electric lights. Pitch-oil lamps gave the necessary illumination.

Sometime during the night, Aunt Jocasta decided to make a round of the house to see how the children were faring. To enable her to make her way in the darkness she carried a portable lamp. When she reached my pallet and shone the light on me, something caught her attention. Peering closer, she saw a large snake stretched full length on the wooden partition directly above my head, just a foot or so away. I was sound asleep.

Aunt Jocasta made a quick decision. She went in search of the night watchman. Returning with him, she held the lamp while he slowly pulled the mattress and me with it away from the wall. The maneuver had to be carefully performed so as neither to awaken me nor disturb the snake. A venomous snake at large in a house full of sleeping children is a matter of some delicacy. With a single blow of his cutlass the night watchman severed the snake's head.

I slept through this incident, just as I had done when as an infant I was overrun and occupied by the army of big red ants. This is why I believe, above everything else, in sleep. God is sleep, man.

It was years later that I learned from Aunt Jocasta of the danger I had been in. And then I was not told directly about it, but overheard her relating the incident to someone else.

In addition to all this, the family physician, a fat Irishman with Edwardian mustaches and a Regency belly, had given it as his firm medical opinion after my birth that I would in no case survive to be more than six months old owing to a defective heart. The whole course of my life was determined by this pronouncement. For from that day on I was treated as an invalid, regarded as fragile, and labeled "Handle with care." If I sneezed, it was taken as a sign of my imminent dissolution. If I had a cold, it was looked upon as the prelude to pneumonia. If I whimpered in the night, it was a major crisis. If I showed a loss of appetite, I was thought to be going into a fatal decline. And whenever the doctor was sent for, which was nearly every day, the priest was also summoned. Indeed, the ministrations of the latter were deemed more valuable to me, since hope had been abandoned for my body but the Christian faith demanded belief in the survival of my soul. The needs of my body were to receive attention, but only to a minor degree as compared with the lavish preparations devoted to the prospect of my life in the hereafter. I was a delicate child. I was not to be spoken to in a loud voice. Only dulcet whispers were to be directed toward me. As a consequence, to this day my nervous system is easily jarred by noise and I can be seduced with discomfiting ease by ladies whose voices are pitched below the normal level of audibility. I am a creature of acute sonar sensibilities. For this, my childhood invalidism is wholly responsible. To some extent it also explains why I found Dorothea as irresistible as I did. Whenever she spoke, I heard the wind, half-asleep at midday in the coconut palms at Moruga (on the Atlantic coast of Trinidad), murmuring softly in my ear. Dorothea's voice made me homesick, yet at the same time was ambrosial medicine for this melancholy ailment.

Because, too, of my enfeebled condition, I was nursed at the breast until I was well past my fourteenth birthday. I had a succession of wet nurses, all East Indians, whose services were terminated only when my advancing years gave them—and me—undue pleasure in the performance of their duties. They were thought by my mother to be carrying out their function with excessive ardor. I myself was aware of the marked degree of affection they brought to their task. I could hardly have failed to be, for the warmth of their caresses as I sucked at their breasts left me in no doubt of their zeal. I grew exceedingly fond of my nurses and showed temper when my mother insisted that it was time I was weaned. I was going on fifteen years of age, and, as a result of the breast-feeding I was enjoying, I had grown into every appearance of being a sturdy lad. Since Ah Sam, Ah See, and others of my contemporaries had been weaned from the breast before they were a year old, I was the object of much envy on their part as they watched me feeding daily from the lactating breasts of luscious East Indian ladies. To this day I cannot see an East Indian lady without expecting her to offer me her breast. I have had to impose a stern discipline upon myself in this matter. It has not been easy for me to arrive at the point at which I no longer regard the entire female population of India (and their Caribbean cousins) as my copious and ever-flowing, ever-feeding wet nurse. Some adventures have also befallen me with male East Indians whom I discovered to be lacking in sympathetic understanding of my early conditioning. They exhibited impatience with me because of the continuance into adulthood of the dietary demands of my childhood. So they misjudged my infantlike behavior toward their womenfolk. My predilection for sitting in the laps of their ladies mystified them, and they found in my tendency to nuzzle at the breasts of these Indian ladies a constant source of exasperation. I did my best to reassure them. But when I realized that their presence invariably led to misunderstanding, I was obliged to arrange for their exclusion. But this was in later years. At the time I am speaking of, I was still an infant going on fifteen years, and still unweaned.

It was Aunt Jocasta who succeeded in effecting my ablactation. I regret to say (and it is the only criticism I have ever made of Aunt Jocasta) that it was by means of a trick. As I discovered years afterward, she instructed the last of my wet nurses to place the juice of the aloe—a bitter, astringent liquid—on her breasts. When I took the breast and put it in my mouth, I was repelled. After this had occurred several times, I was forced to choose in all the agony of my frustration between starving to death and finding some other source of nutriment. So I took what Aunt Jocasta offered me: milk drawn from a large, upstanding goat and contained in a prosaic water glass.

Now, at length, I can understand why Aunt Jocasta was driven to such extreme measures. For it is not difficult for me to recall the passionate intensity with which I was nourised by my wet nurses. Instead of being *puer intactus* as I was at the age of twenty-one, a young male virgin in unviolated standing, I would have certainly been seduced in the very bud and flower of my pubescence had I remained much longer unweaned. This prospect was clear to my mother, but she was perplexed in the face of it. Not so Aunt Jocasta; she knew the remedy and applied it.

The home of the de Parias (Aunt Jocasta, my mother, and me) stood on the main street that ran through the town of San Fernando. It was an eighteenth-century house that had come into the family's possession in somewhat left-handed circumstances. The claim to ownership was based upon a transaction of which there was no documentary evidence except a marriage certificate that was, some thought unkindly, an invention. But the family had now been in possession for more than one hundred years and it was increasingly unlikely that our precarious title would be put to a legal test. The house boasted a historical connection with a West Indian planter whose abundant wealth had been derived from sugar and slaves, and whose country house in England was one of a select group of national synonyms for execrable taste and vulgar ostentation. But the de Paria home was simple enough. Its living quarters comprised eighteen rooms on two floors, surmounted by a watershed roof of weather-beaten red slate. All the rooms on the upper floor opened onto a circular veranda. Beneath the lower floor was a basement formerly used as slaves' quarters. Leg irons and shackles, eroded by rust, remained attached to the rough, dank, concrete walls.

The veranda that encircled the house was broad and spacious. It was screened by a network of finely meshed blinds against the incursion of marauding insects. The sun rose on one side of the veranda and set on the other. With the rising of the sun the occupants of the house migrated to the opposite side of the veranda; with its going down we returned to the first side. The life of the household flowed with metronomic regularity between these two sides of the house. But after dinner we gathered in wicker chairs for coffee, liqueurs, and conversation on the front portion of the veranda, facing the street. The rear was left to the servants.

Dr. von Buffus's credentials as the former tutor of the son of the English governor were what, above all, had initially recommended him to Aunt Jocasta. She visualized him in a similar relationship to me, her favorite nephew. It soon became evident, however, that the learned man was, if anything, receiving more instruction from me, by way of tutorial classes in the art of playing the guitar and concocting rum punches, than he was giving in the rudiments of the German language and other academic disciplines. To be sure, under his tutelage, such as it was, I had taken to reading Homer. But under mine, he had taken to singing calypsos in a stormy Wagnerian manner when adrift of a late afternoon in heavy squalls of rum punch. Whereas I, at Aunt Jocasta's express command, never touched a drop before sundown, the professor was prone to decant his first drink directly after breakfast. Yet Aunt Jocasta felt that Dr. von Buffus's scholarship was bound to manifest itself before, during, and after drinks, and that I, insensibly as it were, would acquire in time a modest learning to adorn my status as a gentleman. It turned out to be a race between education and corruption. Aunt Jocasta saw that it would be a near thing, but she was willing to take the chance. If the worst should come to the worst, I would be in no poorer shape than the governor's son. And, as it happened, the professor also proved to be more immediately useful in other matters.

One such matter had to do with my stepfather, whom Aunt Jocasta had expelled from the family. Expelled? This is not quite accurate. For though he was married to my mother, Aunt Jocasta had never accepted him. So he really was never a member of the family. Anyway, she had been at some pains to reject him in full view of the townsfolk. Shortly after the marriage, she arranged to pension him off. She had disliked him from the moment she first set eyes on him. Divorce was not possible as a legal solution to the problem since the laws of the island did not provide for it. In any case, as a practical matter it would have been unthinkable. The religious mores of the island community were explicit and binding on the point. "Those whom God hath joined together, let no one put asunder." So my parents lived in the twilight zone of an indeterminate relationship, neither married *de facto* nor divorced *de jure*. Many people at that time existed in a similar situation in the small community of Trinidad. No one seemed unduly incommoded. All made their

41

public peace with the regnant norms and their own kind of accommodation in private. This was especially true of the women. They did not defy the inconvenient custom, but simply circumvented it, whatever it chanced to be. As for my mother, her marriages were the sole acts of defiance, the solitary instances of disobedience, that she had ever been guilty of in her entire relationship with her sister, Aunt Jocasta. She had then resumed at once her ingrained habit of acquiescence to her sister's will. It was as if by marrying in the teeth of her sister's disapproval, she had consummated the essential expression of her personal independence and would ever after be content to submit, to please, to humor, and to defer.

Dr. von Buffus had been acting as my tutor and adviser for a year or so, and by then was more or less regarded as a member of Aunt Jocasta's household, when the latter dispatched him on a family matter of some consequence. He was to call on my stepfather, Mr. Pooch, whom she had pensioned off, and inform him that his request for an increase in his monthly allowance had been denied. In the past, such rejections had usually engendered troublesome scenes. My stepfather was inclined to think that his *de jure* status as the husband of a de Paria should be more generously reflected in the standard of living provided him by Aunt Jocasta. Dissatisfaction on this score was apt to inspire him to street-corner denunciations of the miserliness of the de Parias, in which disclosures of family secrets (fabrications for the most part) were a prominent and distasteful feature. Most distressing of all from Aunt Jocasta's point of view was his repeated allegation at such times of a longstanding liaison between the Roman Catholic priest, Father Maginot, and herself. As proof of this charge, he asserted that my mother was in fact not Aunt Jocasta's sister, but rather her daughter by the Roman Catholic divine. (Some color was lent to this assertion by the fact that Aunt Jocasta was about twenty years older than my mother.) Not content with declaiming these inventions at street corners, he was also in the habit of stationing himself in front of the Roman Catholic parish house and there, liberally refreshing himself from a bottle of rum, cry out against Father Maginot as a licentious seducer of profligate women. Nor did his catalogue of the priest's incelibate conduct end there. He went on to allege against the Reverend Father carnal relations with livestock—cows, sheep, horses, mules, goats, jackasses, and farmyard fowls. All of which gave great scandal to the parishioners but, curiously, only amusement to Father Maginot.

"Imagine, Miss Jocasta." With a hairy forefinger he would swirl the ice around in his rum swizzle as he sat with her on our veranda. "Imagine—me—with a cow!" Their eyes would dance together in a secret minuet of remembered delight, and in a silent toast to memory they would refill their glasses from the crystal goblet standing on a silver tray perched on the three-legged rattan table between them. To be sure, no one took the displaced husband's fulminations at all seriously. The general attitude toward him was that he was insane. And whenever Father Maginot preached on the theme of Christ dying by crucifixion between a pair of malefactors and in his final agony saying to one of them, "This day shalt thou be with me in Paradise," this citation from the New Testament was generally taken to imply a charitable reference to the priest's public tormentor. Thus was the noble compassion of the Reverend Father illuminated.

Of late, however, my stepfather had begun to hint in his public denunciations that my mother was now sharing with Aunt Jocasta the sexual attentions of the Reverend Father. Here Aunt Jocasta drew the line. As soon as she learned of this new development, she summoned Dr. von Buffus. Insane polemic was one thing, insidious poison quite another.

The mission the professor undertook at Aunt Jocasta's request was one of exacting delicacy. He was to silence the slanderous husband without incurring the risk of recurrent and escalating financial demands.

43

The professor laid his plans with infinite care. He took as his model the local practice of ensnaring birds by placing adhesive substances where they were accustomed to perch.

He ran his quarry to earth at the Black Cat Bar on High Street. With the assistance of the bartender, Joe Caldeira, a Portuguese from Madeira, he quickly reduced my stepfather to a state of exuberant drunkenness. In furtherance of his plans, he had recruited a young lady of lavish charms and a most generous disposition to bring the proceedings to their preconcerted climax. The professor reported that my stepfather had exhibited vast delight on being introduced to her.

"Look here, man," he said to von Buffus, "let me tell you something, eh? You and I are friends, man, friends for life." He was agreeably stroking the young lady's behind. "Don't let anybody tell you different, you hear?" His sense of appreciation demanded some explicit gesture toward the professor himself. So, "You go first," he invited von Buffus, grandly propelling the young lady in his direction. But the learned scholar declined the honor. This only deepened the gratitude of his drinking companion. "Lissen, nuh, man," he told the professor. "I'se a coolie-creole." He bared his teeth in an explanatory grin. "My father was a coolie and my mother was a nigger." He disclosed several more teeth. "So I am a Dooglah—" His mouth transformed itself into a whitewashed dental picket fence. "Coolie-creole." And feeling now on terms of unreserved intimacy with Dr. von Buffus, he gave him a look of rapturous approval. "You are a hell of a man, yes." His eyes were candescent with admiration. "I hear you can speak forty languages." The odor of rum and the scent of ill-digested onions were in pungent conflict on his breath.

The professor did not find it in his heart to disenchant his admirer. "O, just a few." But the very diffidence of his reply hinted at a modest concealment of prodigious attainments.

"Give me another rum," my stepfather told the bartender. "Have one, too, Professor. And you"—with an air of easy, confident proprietorship, he smiled at the young lady—"you don't know my name—" He was smiling down at her, his dark, aquiline face aglow, one hand fondling a glass of liquor and the other straying, briefly, from her behind in order to smooth the thick, rippling hair away from his narrow, convex brow. "I'm going to tell you," he said, as if about to confer a supreme honor upon her, "I name Sultan Pooch. I does carry my mother name." He felt himself enveloped in a transfiguring mist of alcoholic happiness. "What's your name again?" The young lady had not previously told him what it was, but she did not point this out. She was always polite to her clients. It was good for business. So she smiled at him. "Carmela," she said.

"Carmela—" He repeated her name as if it were a cabalistic word whose sound could elicit a magic key to the central mystery of the universe. "Carmela—" His free hand resumed its ardent pilgrimage up and down her backside, and he gazed at her with the reverent delight of a black man who has been permitted to look upon the face of God and has seen for himself that, sure enough, the Almighty is black just like him. To such a man it would not occur to remark with all due respect to the Almighty: "Well, my Friend, since You black like me, why the hell You kicking my arse so?" In his quasi-religious ecstasy, Pooch was seized by a desire to perform a sacrament. "Leh we fire one," he said to Carmela.

Overhearing this, Joe Caldeira, attentive as always to his customers, poured some rum for Carmela and refilled the two men's glasses.

Dr. von Buffus pondered the dark, amber fluid, trying—if one might judge from his intent study—to penetrate its opaque interior. Pooch brought his glass up toward his nose and inclined his head in obeisance to the fragrance of the liquor. Meanwhile his other hand reposed at ease on the shelving portion of Carmela's behind at the point where it

45

began its ballooning descent from the base of the spine. His hand would shortly resume its impassioned wanderings up and down, around and across the woman's backside, but for this brief, sacramental moment it simply lay there in pleasant surcease from its amorous explorations. He shifted his head toward Carmela, lowered it in a ritual of simulated tenderness, and now with gentle ardor he exhaled on the nape of her neck, smiling as he did so with a knowing, self-satisfied assurance. His lips made contact with Carmela's neck just below the hairline, his tongue forked out, and he licked the spot, slobbering, sucking, and salivating. At the same time his hand recommenced its travels about her backside. Then he raised his glass, first to Carmela and next to Dr. von Buffus. "Chin-chin!" he exclaimed.

"Chin-chin!" they each in turn repeated after him.

He clinked glasses with Carmela and then with the professor. "Chin-chin!" Ecstasy quickened his breathing. He hurried the glass to his lips and, tossing his head backward like a galloping steed defiant of the wind, he drank at one impetuous gulp a mouthful of scalding rum.

His hand abruptly abandoned Carmela's backside, the pupils of his eyes lost their focus and bolted distractedly from corner to corner. When at last he recovered his breath and regained his speech, he yelped in mingled anguish and gratification: "Mama!" Then without warning he burst into a calypso: "Come an' leh we go, Carmela/Come an' leh we go—"

As an a cappella performance it fell distinctly short of virtuosity, but what it lacked in technical accomplishment it more than made up in enthusiasm. "Play mas'!"—the cry of revelers at carnival—he exhorted Carmela and the professor. The latter was unable to comply, except to the extent of a restrained Hanoverian jig, but Carmela joined him in a rhythmic shuffle, the typical dance of the participants in carnival. They moved their feet in unison with a dragging, syncopated gait up and down the length of the bar, their arms flung upward and their backsides oscillating. Meanwhile Carmela's high, caterwauling soprano reinforced Pooch's bull-bellowing baritone.

When they had had enough, Pooch proposed another drink. "Leh we fire anudder one." He was swaying slightly and his eyes were glazed, but he was otherwise in excellent fettle. "Pro—fess-sorrrr!" He laughed and slapped Dr. von Buffus in a comradely fashion on the shoulder. "What's the matter, man? You don' play mas'?" Without awaiting a reply, he began to sing again. As before, Carmela accompanied him, and they repeated their carnival shuffle the length of the bar and back.

Joe Caldeira and the professor furtively traded signals. The former then nodded to Carmela, who sang out to my stepfather in her high-pitched calypso voice. "Come an' leh we go—!" She thrust her arm through his, and, their feet shuffling in rhythm, their backsides vibrating in unison, she led him out of the Black Cat Bar. Up the High Street they went, executing their carnival steps, her voice shrill above the clamor of the traffic, Pooch augmenting it with the grating dissonance of his untuneful clamor. "Come an' leh we go—!" they sang together. "Come an' leh we go—!"

They attracted little attention, as it was the privilege of the islanders to "play mas' " at will provided it was not organized on a public scale outside of the period officially designated for the annual celebration of carnival. Otherwise, if people felt they had some private occasion to "play mas'," that was their business. So Carmela and Pooch made their way up High Street, gradually becoming objects of general curiosity as they shuffled and sang, "playin' mas'," on their way to the residence of the de Parias, as some astute observers had already guessed. An increasing throng of inquisitive spectators trailed after the two revelers, some shouting encouragement and others joining in the refrain, "Come an' leh we go—!" A few also shuffled and shook their backsides like terriers drying themselves after immersion in water. Joe Caldeira was conspicuous among these. He had temporarily left the Black Cat Bar in charge of his assistant so as to be present at the impending dénouement.

As they approached the house, Pooch, perhaps because he felt challenged by the sight of it, sang more boisterously. Taking her cue from him, Carmela grew shriller. They came to the wrought-iron gate, on which a bell was suspended from the ceremonial apex. The profuse tendrils of a climbing plant rendered the gate as much an espalier as an entrance.

When Pooch and Carmela reached the gate, Pooch turned to the onlookers. "Play mas'!" he cried, flinging his arms above his head, cocking his bottom, and beginning to shuffle. No throng of Trinidadians could be unresponsive to such an appeal. Numerous backsides commenced to swing from side to side, a sensuous, collective pendulum, synchronized to the rhythm of shuffling feet orchestrated by a chorus of jubilant voices singing "Come an' leh we go—!"

Dr. von Buffus stood across the street from the house observing these developments with the air of a man whose hour was at hand.

In a single, insolent movement, Pooch thrust his behind outward and upward, then abruptly retracted it. With one upraised hand he signaled to the crowd in the manner of a conductor at a rehearsal of an orchestra. "Ab-bre-vi-a-SHUN!" he exclaimed. "Make a bar!"

The singing and dancing ceased. My stepfather's arms dropped to his sides and he began to speak. "Jus' now," he told his listeners, "Ah was playin' mas', but now Ah go' cut she arse." He gestured at the house and the mob rewarded him with their raucous approval.

"This woman—Jocasta de Paria—you hearin' me?" He shouted up at the mullioned windows. "Jocasta de Paria—you lissenin' to me? Jocasta de Paria—you makin' s'amie with my wife!"

Thus alleging a homosexual relationship between my aunt and my mother, he turned to the laughing, jeering crowd in

48

full and exhilarating confidence of their support. The derisive tumult spurred him on. He swiveled to face the house again. "Ah'm tellin' you, Jocasta de Paria—woman, you'se a damn bitch!"

Wholly inspired now, and certain of popular favor, he asserted: "You an' de French priest—Big-belly Maginot," he elucidated for the benefit of the crowd—"de two o' you is like husban' an' wife. He does give you 'holy communion' mornin', noon, an' night!"

This was the vilest sacrilege, to say the least. By now the crowd had increased to a considerable size, filling up the narrow street so that traffic either came to a standstill or threaded its way hesitantly through the cluster of spectators. It was just like carnival.

Pooch's last sally, charging a sexual relationship between Aunt Jocasta and Father Maginot, had pleased the crowd. To demonstrate her own delight, Carmela stood on tiptoe and kissed him. Laughing and fondling him intimately, she volunteered to the crowd: "He goin' upstairs to see she. Go on, man!" she encouraged Pooch.

Until that moment, the idea of calling on Aunt Jocasta had not occurred to him. But now that it had been mentioned, its appeal was irresistible. What he would never dare to contemplate when sober was alluring to him when drunk.

"Ah go' gi'e you somet'ing good." Carmela dangled Paradise before him. But the delectable prospect did not entirely obscure from his vision the possibility of hell.

"You hear, boy, w'at she tell you," Joe Caldeira supplied in ribald support. "Tonight she go' gi'e you sugar-cake!"

"Go on, man!" Carmela insisted. She kissed him again. Perhaps by accident her hand brushed against his penis, and perhaps by accident lingered there. "Show dem"—she indicated the crowd—"show dem you got balls. Don' 'fraid, man. Ah got somet'ing nice for you. Nice, nice, nice." She caressed him with candid intimacy, to the delight of the onlookers.

Yet now for the first time the enormity of the undertaking penetrated his drunkenness. He seemed to hesitate. Sensing this, some among the crowd shouted at him, "W'at's de matter, man? Yo' frighten'?" Other queries followed in a similar vein, preludes to imprecation. Indeed, a voice from the crowd accused him of being deficient in "bam-bam." (This term was popularly associated with courage, the "bam-bam," or backside, being regarded in the local folk value system as the seat of virtue.)

My stepfather stood momentarily irresolute on the cobbled street. He had to choose between the certainty of a near-lynching, if not worse, at the hands of a frustrated mob and the certainty of an inhospitable welcome by an infuriated Jocasta de Paria. He prepared to take a chance on the latter. Shaking off his indecision, he walked with a theatrical show of insouciance up to the gate. "Jocasta de Paria!" he called out at the top of his voice, placing his face against the bars. "Big-belly Maginot sanga-wanga-in' [that is, he's having sexual intercourse] with you and my wife." He pushed the gate open. The bell clanged harshly, giving off a sullen, fretful sound. The violence of the bell's tone startled but did not deter him. With that expectant mob at his rear, he really had no choice but to go forward. Turning back was unthinkable. So, teetering slightly, he angled his body through the gate, which now stood ajar. Then, with the crowd in the street baying at his rear, he began a slow progress up the wide stone stairs. His unconcern was dissembled, yet the crowd was impressed. Caldeira voiced their admiration. "He got bam-bam, boy, plenty bam-bam!"

As Pooch reached the door after crossing the veranda, Carmela's voice shrilled above the clamor: "Knock on de damn do', man! Knock on de do'!' Don' 'fraid, boy!"

Pooch knocked on the door. It was a wide French door that opened onto a vestibule between itself and an inner door that led into a drawing room.

There was no response, so Pooch knocked again, hammering with his clenched fist in a brusque, demanding fashion. The crowd meanwhile was shouting encouragement to him and engaging in unseemly speculations as to just what intimate details of her toilette might be preventing Jocasta from opening the door at once. A thesis that presently gained wide acceptance, and was circulated vociferously among the crowd, was that she was "makin' s'amie wid she sister." An alternative thesis, hardly less popular, was also canvassed, to the effect that Jocasta was "sanga-wanga-in' wid de French priest." By thus accusing Aunt Jocasta of having sexual intercourse with either Father Maginot or her sister, the crowd gave proof of their acceptance of the plausibility of Pooch's allegations. "Don' be 'fraid, boy," they reassured him. "She boun' to hear you." To which Carmela added her own keening injunction: "Wake up de damn bitch, man! Wake up de damn ole bitch!"

"Yes! Wake she up, de damn ole soucouyant!" Joe Caldeira added. (A "soucouyant" is, in Trinidadian folklore, a witch who at nightfall assumes the form and function of a vampire.)

The door suddenly opened inward to disclose Aunt Jocasta standing there, indeed, face to face with Pooch. At the sight of her, unassailable in her dignity, formidable in her embonpoint, incandescent in her rage, the crowd became silent. Pooch quailed. One voice only was heard from the crowd. It was Carmela's. "Douse him, Miss Jocasta! You got him. Yes, you got him now. Douse him with the piss! Douse the sonofabitch, Miss Jocasta!"

Three servants stood with Aunt Jocasta, each carrying a commodious chamber pot of a design once fashionable at the court of Louis Quinze. Students of the social history of France will recall that period as a time when chamber pots were fashioned on exceedingly generous lines in view of the fact that the French were unwilling to dispose of human waste before it had attained an odoriferous ripeness indoors. The unusual size of these pots was also intended to accommodate with reposeful ease the ample and aristocratic bottoms of feudal France *avant le déluge.* In addition to their size, these chamber pots were exceedingly ornate, as befitted the tastes of the nobility in the royal afterglow of the vermilion reign of the Sun King. A peasant lady could easily have immersed herself in such a vessel to enjoy, on her wedding day, the only bath she would have during her lifetime. Napoleon had a number of these chamber pots installed at Malmaison for the use of Josephine Beauharnais. The hips of the beautiful Martiniquaise were slim as a sugar cane, and her ladies-in-waiting were constantly obliged to fish her out after she had fallen in while sitting on the pot, her body jackknifed and her legs at right angles to each other, while she expressed her indignation with the aid of the choicest creole expletives of her native island. If *merde* seemed to have a certain primacy among them, it is perhaps because there was distinct objective justification for it.

At the sight of Aunt Jocasta's servants armed with chamber pots, an expectant hush fell over the crowd. Pooch stood transfixed, Aunt Jocasta dominating him from her superior height while she contemplated the mob in the street below with a mixture of outrage at their presence and satisfaction at what they were about to witness.

The silence was broken by Carmela, who called out again: "Douse 'im wid de piss, Miss Jocasta! Douse 'im wid de piss!" As though that were the awaited signal, the servants, acting in well-rehearsed concert, simultaneously emptied the contents of the chamber pots over my stepfather.

A malodorous stench enveloped the crowd. Pooch reeled backward and started down the stairs, where, missing his footing, he tumbled dripping wet and reeking high to the bottom. Aunt Jocasta withdrew across the veranda into the drawing room and the great French doors closed behind her.

A huge roar rocketed upward from the crowd. "Aie-y'aie-y'aie!" Their exultation soared above the stench. "The sonofabitch stink, oui!" "O God, man! Dat coolie-creole stink like shit-self! Aie-y'aie-y'aie!"

Dr. von Buffus, aided by Joe Caldeira, was barely able to rescue Pooch from the derisive violence of the crowd. They themselves, the members of the crowd, had no cause of grievance against the evil-smelling figure of sodden abjection slinking along the gutters, trying to make good his escape. But in the outcome of the personal combat he had ventured upon he had been vanquished. Yet that alone would not have sufficed to whet the mob's fury against him. It was the utter contempt of the manner of his defeat that provoked from them a corresponding contempt for him. "Kill de stinkin' sonofabitch!" they shouted in the wake of his flight, hurling stones at him, spitting, and assaulting him with the filth and rotting garbage strewn about at random. Were it not for Dr. von Buffus and Joe Caldeira, who covered his retreat, the mob would have made short work of him. In this way did the great scholar atone for his role in the conspiracy to defend Aunt Jocasta's honor.

Carmela did not go unrewarded. She acquired a wardrobe of pure Shantung silk dresses that was the envy of the town. Never thereafter did she want for anything. Aunt Jocasta saw to that. And the professor told me later on that Aunt Jocasta was grateful to Joe Caldeira, too.

At that time, however, I did not know Caldeira. I used to pass the Black Cat Bar on my way up and down High Street. But what the hell would I have been going in there for?

Joe Caldeira was happy in Trinidad. He probably would have remained there forever had it not been for the intrusion into his affairs of an incident as malign as it was unexpected.

Everything had been going so well. He was making a good living at the Black Cat Bar. His clandestine relationship with his employer's wife gave him the dual satisfaction of cuckolding his boss and at the same time increasing his earnings in the indirect form of the generous subsidies he received from his grateful mistress. Nothing could have been more agreeable, except perhaps, as sometimes it seemed to him in moments of high ambition, a monopoly of the very lucrative business of pimping in Madeira. Meanwhile the boss's wife was paying him a "salary" even larger than the one he was earning from the boss himself. He had taken to wearing a silk shirt and a gold wristwatch, and he had had an incisor tooth capped with gold purely as a sign of his prosperity; there was nothing whatever the matter with the tooth. On the whole, though, he lived modestly, was diligent in his work, and never stole a penny from his employer. He really had no need to do so, since he could not have stolen as much—undetected—as the boss's wife was giving him from week to week. He was her lover, and she liked to think of herself—indeed, she often referred to herself in the secrecy of their assignations—as his "little parakeet." (Parakeets are birds inclined to prattle.)

It cannot be said that the "parakeet's" husband was in any sense complaisant in the affair. He knew nothing about it. Perhaps he should have known long before he did, but he was himself engrossed in an affair with his own "outside woman." This lady was a sister of Mr. Balgobin Maraj, an East Indian merchant doing business in San Fernando.

In the welter of intimate cross-relationships typical of small island communities, the "parakeet" was a cousin, twice removed, of Aunt Jocasta.

Family connections in these cloistral, insular circumstances tend to be more of a palimpsest than a mosaic. For they are not really constructed in precise and variegated geometrical forms according to a set familial design. They occur instead on many layers superimposed one upon the other after the fashion of successive writings and interlineations inscribed on old parchment. On any given layer they would be capable of an astonishing complexity, testimony itself to the myriad permutations of human contact across the centuries of interbreeding.

Thus Joe Caldeira, a bartender by occupation, a "sweetman" in his leisure, dwelt happily in his secluded little corner of Eden. And so he might have done ever after had not envy, treachery, and indiscretion forged a flaming sword to drive him out of the Garden.

His assistant at the Black Cat Bar was a fellow expatriate from Madeira. He was a shriveled little runt of a chap whom Caldeira had rescued from the clutches of a black Amazon who had seen in her victim a heaven-sent opportunity to avenge the enslavement of her ancestors. She had kept him in chains, worked him incessantly to maintain her in a state of petit-bourgeois comfort, and beaten him with frequent regularity as a matter of historical principle. "He white; I black; I beat he arse."

When Caldeira discovered him and saw the plight he was in, he negotiated his emancipation. He bought him his freedom from the Amazon, paying (in the view of the lady herself) the excessive sum of forty dollars for him, which was twice as much as she had thought of demanding for his release. In addition, he had thrown in two bottles of rum and three pounds of saltfish as lagniappe. He afterward got the newly freed slave a job at the Black Cat Bar washing glasses and cleaning up the place. Between times he taught him the art of dispensing drinks. But gratitude is a fickle emotion. As a man of Caldeira's experience should have known. He may have been led astray, however, by the fact that he and the subject of his compassion were compatriots. Few sentiments are so misleading as those prompted in people by their common derivation from the same territory: the same town, the same island, the same village, the same country. No sooner does this notion make its appearance than prudence vanishes. Caldeira proved to be no exception to this rule. Worse yet, he was so misguided in his naiveté as to expect gratitude. So he grew careless with his assistant—the position to which he had now promoted him.

One day he handed the latter a key to his room and asked that he go there and fetch him, Caldeira, a clean shirt. He had an appointment with the "parakeet" that evening, but he was busy at the bar and could not spare the time to go himself and fetch it. There was a further complication. He had taken to supplementing the "parakeet's" affections with those of a Chinese woman, a laundress in less affluent circumstances than the "parakeet" but whose sexual allure he found a good deal more compelling. He was in the habit of explaining this to himself—and, latterly, to his compatriot from Madeira—as the result of the contrast between his own weedlike, wild-grass hairiness and the Chinese lady's relative lack of body hair. In the beginning, he had frankly been seduced by the prospect of discovering for himself if, as he had so often heard, the vaginal arrangements of Chinese ladies were horizontal rather than vertical. When he had seen with his own eyes that rumor lied, he also discovered that in some curious, metaphysical way sexual intercourse with a virtually hairless lady was considerably more stimulating and enjoyable to him than with other ladies whose pleasure gardens were lush with heavy overgrowths of rank and luxuriant hair. Such a lady, for example, was the "parakeet." When in bed with her, he often felt like a hunter making his way through a trackless forest. Or so he confided to his compatriot. "Jeez Chris', man! Me hairy so, and she hairy so—we jus' like two monkey!" At such moments his compatriot would reward him with prolonged fits of convulsive laughter. "But wid me Chinee, she don' have to look fer me, an' I don' have to look fer she. Ah does find she at Stroke One." His compatriot would come near to swooning with insuppressible glee.

So with the long hours he was putting in at the Black Cat Bar and the allurements of the ineffable Chinese lady, he was growing neglectful of his hirsute though generous benefactress, the "parakeet." He was also spending substantial amounts of his subsidies from the "parakeet" on the Chinese lady. "But w'at de hell, boy," he would rationalize this development to his compatriot, "Peter does pay for Paul." His compatriot readily endorsed this point of view. He also added to the fund of worldly wisdom a local proverb that he cited with marked approval: "T'ief from t'ief mek God larf."

His compatriot had been gone for some time when Caldeira suddenly remembered that he had an assignation with the Chinese lady, as well, that evening. He had been careless, or, under the pressure of his work at the Black Cat Bar, forgetful. In any case, he was, he told himself, "in a hell of a fix." The only good thing, he realized, groping for reassurance, was that he had been lucky enough to make the two

58

appointments at different places although at the same hour. The "parakeet" was to meet him at the Colonial Hotel, while the Chinese lady was to await him at his room, to which he had given her a key. This was a trifle reckless of him, as the "parakeet" also had a key to the room.

He served a customer a rum swizzle when the latter had requested a plain rum and lime. He served another a Caroni rum when a Forest Park had been ordered. Something was troubling him. It wasn't the fact that he had bungled his trysts. He could straighten that out easily enough. As soon as he closed the shop for the night, he would "bu'st dirt" (that is, go quickly) to his room, where the Chinese lady would be awaiting him. He would give her a stroke or two—just to keep her quiet—and then he would run to the Colonial Hotel, where the "parakeet" awaited him. He would give her in turn a stroke or two—to keep her quiet—collect his subsidy from her, explain that he had some business to transact for the boss, make another assignation with her for the following evening at the same time and place, and then return to the Chinese lady for the rest of the night. It could all be managed with comparative ease, for his room on Chacon Street was within comfortable walking distance of the Colonial Hotel on lower High Street near the waterfront. A smile, pleased and lubricious, floated buoyant as cork, bobbing up and down on the sweat-slicked surface of his face. He served vermouth to a customer who had asked for gin, corrected his mistake, and then once more and quite unaccountably experienced an uneasy foreboding. He was disquieted by a haunting sense of something amiss, something gone wrong, he did not know what. In his nervous fret, he accidentally dropped a bottle of Carypton, which shattered on the concrete floor. When he stooped to gather up the shards, he suddenly remembered. The appointment with the "parakeet" was also to be kept at his room this evening. They had decided on this because her husband, the boss, would be at the Colonial Hotel tonight. O God, man! De-

59

spite the sultry atmosphere of the bar, an icy chill numbed him from head to foot. "Jee-zuz Chris'l!" he repeated over and over to himself. Subconsciously, he made the sign of the cross. And in some inexplicable way, connecting his compatriot with his profound unease, he wondered what the hell was keeping that sonofabitch so long.

As to that: when, on entering Caldeira's room, his compatriot and assistant (whose name was Layal, though it was spelled "Leal" so as to confuse people) pulled open a drawer, he quickly shut it again. He never knew why. He just stood there, momentarily abstracted, hesitant, and, it seemed, unwilling to proceed any further. This was strange enough, for all he had been asked to do was fetch a shirt for Caldeira. Then, with a sudden burst of resolve, he again opened the drawer. It was, he thought, the drawer he had been directed to, but he saw that instead of shirts it contained a miscellany of odds and ends—papers, trinkets, and the like. It was the wrong drawer. Clearly. So he tried the adjoining one. There indeed were shirts. Nice shirts. Elegant. Silk. Cotton—so fine you could almost see through the material. He shook his head. A smile uncoiled across his face. He selected a shirt more or less at random, then shut the drawer. Now he returned to the first drawer and reopened it. He lingered over it, looking down at the contents. An antique corkscrew caught his fancy. He picked it up, put it down again, took up a tortoise-shell comb, put it down again, took up a pair of sunglasses, put them down again. He was like a hound picking up a scent. The alchemy of inquisitiveness had transformed the innocent-seeming objects, in all their haphazard diversity, into clues leading to a quarry, concealed and fugitive, to be run down, to be cornered. His instinct quivered, fibrillate, in the nostrils of his hunting-beagle's nose. Breathing hard and pawing with stubby, splayed fingers, he rummaged in the drawer, jettisoning keepsakes, discarding personal trivia, digging deep into the disorder of unsorted papers, the private moraine of Caldeira's memories. All at once his curiosity was rewarded by an instinctual certainty of a discovery. He knew, he just knew, that he would find something. Sliding his hand beneath a mound of miscellany in a corner of the drawer, he explored it with his fingers. When he withdrew his hand, it was clutching an unsealed envelope. He slipped the envelope inside the shirt he was wearing and closed the drawer. As he began to extract the contents of the envelope, the inaudible bay of a triumphant hound glittered in his eyes.

He started at an unexpected sound. Cowering and panic-stricken, his eyes stampeded in his head, searching for a hiding place for him. But a key had turned in the lock and the door was opening. There was no chance of escape.

A Chinese lady stood there, outlined in the doorway, and for a few scurrying seconds divested of speech. So was he. She, however, regained the use of her tongue before he did. "Wey de arse you doin' here in Joe room?"

He was at a loss for a reply. Overawed by the scowling, voluptuous Chinese apparition in the doorway, he stammered out: "Joe send me."

She eyed him with plain disapproval. "Sen' you? Sen' you fer w'at?" She entered the room, closed the door behind her, and began to advance upon him. "W'y de arse 'e keah come 'eself?"

Still recovering from the shock of her unexpected appearance, he fumbled for an answer. "'E busy," he said.

With ceremonial care she placed on the unmade bed a package she had brought with her.

"'Is clothes," she announced, less to him than to the universe. "Ah wash an' iron dem." She swiveled around and glared at him. Intimidated, he shuffled from one foot to the other. "Don' 'fraid," she reassured him. A smile of Oriental splendor, radiant as the rising sun, overspread her face.

He construed this change in her humor as direct encouragement to him. "Buh yo' nice, yes." He essayed this thanks-offering to her in the hope of richer rewards. And he accompanied it with a well-oiled grin.

She was not ill-pleased. Moreover, to her emphatic delight, she now saw that he was open-toothed, that there was a space between his two front teeth—a sure sign of a passionate sexual nature. "'E's a hot man," she told herself. And to him she said: "Yo' nice yo'self." She considered him with heightened approval, having also remarked in him the possession of a large, elongated charm pendulous and pestling in his faded, skin-tight khaki trousers—a charm that had riveted his former Amazon owner to him as firmly as the iron shackles by which she had bound him to her service. Her breath caught in her throat. "Me blood take you." This was a local colloquialism expressive of liking and incipient affection, an explicit indication of the existence of a basis for closer personal intercourse.

He noted with satisfaction the impression he had made on her. When he smiled at her, the gap between his two front teeth, betokening uncommon sexual ardor, was again disclosed. "Me blood does take you, too." His voice was soft, yet confident with the certainty of conquest. "Ah does gi'e on you, man." This meant that he found her sexually irresistible, that such was his eagerness—indeed, readiness—to make love to her that he was already in ardent fancy ejaculating his semen on her. His loins surged and he felt his penis cresting. With inward exultation he sang silently to himself a popular calypso:

> "Ah warnt a boat to go to China . . .
> Ah warnt a big, fat Chinee mama . . ."

She saw the drawer that in his alarm he had left open when she came into the room, but her gaze, fascinated, was intent on exploring his genital area, traveling thence upward to the opening between his two front teeth and back to his penis, shuttling to and fro between those two points in a lustful journey that left her moist, captive, and breathless. "Come," she said, "doux-doux..." She crooked an index finger and, slowly retreating backward to the bed, beckoned him to her. "Come, dahlin'." Her magnificent teeth, saliva-pearled, glowed between her parted lips. Her eyes, bright-burning agate and bow-shaped, compelled him. The retroussé nipples of her untrammeled breasts and, in her backward progress, the sway of her pneumatic hips, galvanized him. He commenced to move toward her like a sleep-walker on a high wire. "Come, sugarplum ... doux-doux ... dahlin'," she enticed him. The back of her knees made contact with the side of the bed, onto which she sank, her legs forking, her breasts heaving, her hands hitching up her skirt.

He stood over her, his divided teeth uncurtained by his lips, his penis straining for release, and his fingers fumbling impatiently to undo the buttoned front of his trousers.

And now, once again, a key grated in the door lock.

To do her justice, the "parakeet" behaved with admirable composure in the face of the situation she encountered. "W'at de hell is dis?" she exclaimed, amiably enough, heaven knows. "All-yo' sanga-wanga-in' in Joe room?" Although her tone was inflected with the ascending lilt of an astounded query, it carried all the unequivocal impact of a flat statement of clearly observed fact.

Quickly closing her legs and, as a preliminary to mounting a counterattack, pulling down her skirt, the Chinese lady sat up in bed and with a brusque jab of her foot thrust aside Caldeira's compatriot, who had teetered so perilously on the brink of betraying his emancipator. "Mind yo' damn business," she said to the "parakeet." Then, pursuing the matter, "Wey de arse yo' warnt?"

The "parakeet" was less angered than amused by the aggressiveness of the Chinese lady. Her knowledge of world history was not commodious, but it was sufficient to acquaint her with the bellicose, warlord traditions of the Chi-

63

nese people. She ignored the rough menace of the Chinese
lady's tone and replied quite simply: "But lissen, nuh"—this
Trinidadian locution, "nuh," is a corruption of the French
non, and is used in the local parlance to achieve colloquial
emphasis—"dis is my room, yes." And, in response to the
arching surprise in the upward twitch of the Chinese lady's
eyebrows, she climaxed her claim to tenancy. "Ah does pay
de rent."

The Chinese lady's astonishment expressed itself first in a
derisive sneer of disbelief, and then in a skeptical inquiry intended to reinforce that sneer and also to convey the speaker's outrage at such a barefaced lie. "Yo' does do w'at?"

"Pay de rent."

Enlightenment descended in swift flight upon the Chinese lady. A number of things that until then had mystified
her, but to which she had closed her eyes and sealed off her
ears, now began to assert in her sudden comprehension, lu-
cid contours of prior incident, and unmistakable clarity of
internal detail. "Well, well, well!" she pondered inwardly.
"But look at my Judas cross, nuh—" This interior contemplation of her betrayal still did not absolve her of the obligation
to engage in personal combat as a matter of principle. So she
was about to launch a fusillade of expletives at the "parakeet" when she caught sight of the object of her frustrated
attempt at seduction trying to slink through the door. She
turned on him instead. "Wey yo' goin', yo' shit-tail sonofabitch, yo'?" For a woman who only a few minutes before
had been wooing him with dulcet blandishments, there was
now a painful absence of tenderness in her voice. He himself gave no sign of his feelings at this abrupt change in her
attitude and he promptly obeyed her command to "haul yo'
arse back in here." She demanded to know his name, who
exactly he was, and how it had come about that she had
found him here, in this room, where instead she had expected to meet her "Po'tagee sweetman, Joe Caldeira." And
"Wey de hell yo' was puttin' in yo' pocket w'en Ah come in

here? Yo' stannin' up dey lookin' like a squingy-arse white manicou—lemme see wey yo' got in yo' pocket." Suiting deed to word, she seized hold of him and in a moment had relieved him of the envelope he had taken from his compatriot's drawer. "Wey de hell is all o' dis?" she demanded, examining the contents of the envelope. In a minute or two she looked at the "parakeet" and broke into mocking laughter. "So Joe's yo' sweetman, too! Eh-eh! Yo' ever see t'ing so?" She read from one of the letters she had withdrawn from the envelope, then paraphrased it: "So yo' like de way 'e does move?" she observed to the "parakeet." Her sloe-black eyes were incandescent with malice. "I's a fonny t'ing, but me—Ah'm always tellin' 'im: 'Joe, don' move so much, man.'"

The "parakeet" did not need to be told that her letters to Joe Caldeira had been discovered. Her crow-black face turned ashen. Those letters must be recovered at any cost. So she got down to business at once. "How much you want for them?" The ridge of her jaw jutted out.

The Chinese lady shuffled the letters with leisurely, scornful deliberation, then arranged them in a neat pile and handed them over to the "parakeet." "Dat damn Po'tagee make a blarsted fool o' both o' we. Take yo' letters, girl." She turned on Caldeira's compatriot, Layal, a man who couldn't even spell his own name. "As to you—" She moved close to him and, lightning-quick, brought her knee up to his groin.

He doubled over, howling with pain.

"Out wid you!" She spat at him. "You is a damn' ma commère' man. You come in here wid yo' open teet' an' yo' big to-tee"—the latter was a reference in the local vernacular to his penis—"macco-in' people business." (In the Trinidadian dialect, to "macco" is officiously to poke one's nose into someone else's affairs.) "Out!" And she kicked him in the backside, jackknifed over as he was, clutching his groin, out of the room. She consoled the "parakeet": "Man stink too much, yes—all o' dem." Unhurried, unruffled, she moved toward the door. She paused before closing it behind her and said to the "parakeet": "Ef Ah was you, girl, w'en Ah done wid Joe Caldeira, a monkey in de zoo would have to lend 'im balls." She threw the key that Caldeira had given her onto the bed.

Perhaps the "parakeet" should not have prattled about what had taken place. Perhaps the others—the Chinese lady and Joe Caldeira's compatriot—also tattled. At any rate, the "parakeet" did talk to her best friend, to whom she disclosed the incident, being careful to omit no detail, however unsavory or unflattering to herself. Though sworn to secrecy, her best friend confided what she had learned to her own best friend, whom she also swore to secrecy and who, exacting the same pledge from her own best friend, passed on the secret. The repetition of this process created a chain of "best friends" privy to the secret, which in no time at all came to the ears of the "parakeet's" husband, Antonio Caetano.

Now, Caetano was not an especially jealous man. In any event, he was himself attached, not very discreetly, to an Indian lady. As a husband, however, he had his pride. When the news of his cuckolding reached him, he reacted as most men would in such circumstances. He felt that his manhood had been affronted. Yet he would have been content to ignore the whole business if only an insistent curiosity as to the identity of his betrayer—as the phrase goes—had not got the better of him. Even so, when he discovered that it was his trusted bartender, he was merely reproachful. "But eh-eh," he said to Caldeira, "how you could do me a t'ing like dat, man?"

"O Gawd, Chiefie"—Caldeira regarded his boss with genuine affection—"it wasn' nutt'n. Ah jes' t'ought you wasn' lookin'."

The boss laughed in unaffected good humor. "Come, leh we fire one." He poured himself some rum and handed the bottle to Caldeira.

66

They drank together, Caldeira meanwhile assuring his employer of eternal servitude. "Ah'll do anyt'ing fer you, Chiefie. Anyt'ing. So help me Gawd."

"O, don' bodder, man. W'at de hell. Ah know you's me frien'. Come, leh we fire anudder one." And they drank again. Again. And again. Until it was morning and nearly time to reopen the bar. For most of the night they had commiserated with each other, the boss advising Caldeira as to the best way of getting on with Mrs. Caetano (the "parakeet"), who, he said, was a very nice woman but inclined to be "strict" in her ways. Caldeira had agreed, adding a complaint of his own that Mrs. Caetano wanted him to spend too much time away from the business. With him, however, he assured the boss, business always came first.

The boss expressed his pleasure at Caldeira's devotion to his work, promised to raise his salary, and then began a recital of his own difficulties with his Indian mistress. "The woman," he confided to Caldeira, "want to see me mornin', noon, and night. She don' gimme no peace, man. Sometimes Ah does say to meself: 'W'y de hell yo' don' go an' get yo'self a nice li'l gal from de country, man, who you don' even have to buy shoes for?' " Impressed by the pristine charm of his own inspiration, he exclaimed in endorsement of the prospect: "O Gawd, man!" In this vein, then, did they settle the delicate matter of honor between them. They had fallen asleep in the bar in drunken camaraderie, and when they awoke it was past time to open the place to the public. They made a quick toilet and began the day's business.

The boss collected the previous day's receipts from the cash register and went off to deposit them at the bank. As he was going down High Street, an acquaintance of his, but still a man he barely knew, made him the sign of the horns. He turned around and went slowly back to the bar.

Caldeira killed his employer in self-defense. The witnesses all testified to the sudden, unprovoked attack by Caetano, in repelling which Caldeira used only such force as was necessary. The coroner's report noted the cause of death as a fracture of the skull resulting from a fall sustained in the course of a struggle. The witnesses were positive that Caldeira never struck his employer, that he only defended himself by warding off the latter's blows.

During the trial, the "parakeet's" loyalty to Caldeira was irreproachable. She was not called upon to testify. Though it had been made clear that the immediate occasion of the conflict between the two men was a dispute over a woman, it had not been thought necessary to identify her in open court.

The "parakeet" busied herself on Caldeira's behalf. She obtained for him the services of one of the leading lawyers in the island. She personally defrayed all of her lover's legal expenses. It was of course by now common knowledge that she was the woman in the case. Numerous attempts were made by the ill-intentioned to impress this fact upon her by a malicious assortment of hints and innuendoes. But the "parakeet" endured all with dignity. An aloof serenity and a firm self-restraint never deserted her while the trial lasted.

When the jury brought in a verdict of acquittal and the judge discharged Caldeira, the "parakeet" underwent an astonishing transformation. From the loyal and dedicated mistress of the former defendant, she became overnight his vociferous and implacable enemy. She dismissed him from his employment at the Black Cat Bar and remorselessly hounded him off the island. Her motives were inexplicable, most of all to Caldeira, to whom this startling metamorphosis appeared to be the work of some vengeful spirit from beyond the grave. There were two prosaic reasons, however, for the "parakeet's" change of heart. One was her infatuation with the lawyer whom she had engaged to defend Caldeira; the other was the role of Mr. Balgobin Maraj operating through his grieving sister, the erstwhile mistress of the dead Caetano, in persuading the "parakeet" that she was too important a woman to be mixed up with a "dirty, no-count Po'ta-gee" like Caldeira.

Caldeira was unaware that he had been displaced in the "parakeet's" affections by the lawyer who had successfully defended him. Had he known this, he would undoubtedly have taken it as a compliment that his supplanter should be a gentleman of such eminence. Indeed, it was probable that he would have disclosed the fact with swelling pride to the world at large. To be bracketed, even as a displaced lover, with a barrister-at-law would have been a tremendous fillip to his self-esteem, as well as to his social standing.

He discovered the machinations of Mr. Balgobin Maraj when at a final interview with his former mistress he urged her to give him some clue as to the reason for the surprising change in her feelings toward him. Anxious to preserve the secrecy of her new liaison with the barrister-at-law, she threw Balgobin Maraj to the wolves. Mr. Maraj had convinced her, she told Caldeira, that God would punish her if she continued to associate with her husband's murderer. Mr. Maraj also felt that Caldeira should be forced to leave the island at once. Here, then, was some money. Take it. She did not wish to see him again. Go.

Now, in a town as small as San Fernando, where people knew one another from the first generation to the last, where nothing remained secret for any longer than it took to whisper it to the very next person encountered on the street, Aunt Jocasta was bound to hear of how Balgobin Maraj had exercised a malefic influence on the fortunes of the Portuguese bartender at the Black Cat Bar. Joe Caldeira had always been exceedingly accommodating to her. He used to take the trouble to advise her in advance of new shipments of liquor or of a brand or vintage that might be of particular interest to her. She had a special fondness for Stade's (Barbados) rum, and Caldeira saw to it that she was kept well supplied with the best of this sagacious liquor.

There was also the service he had rendered her when it became necessary to chastise my stepfather for his intolerable behavior. This last piece of assistance was of great value to Aunt Jocasta, and she never forgot it. Naturally, she did not frequent the Black Cat Bar. In fact, she had never set foot in the place. Her business with the bartender had been conducted through intermediaries such as servants and other designated parties like Professor von Buffus. There really was little she could do by way of direct intervention in the current affair. Her sympathies were with Caldeira, and she expressed them in a practical way. She sent him a substantial sum of money with a message of Godspeed. And when she next saw Balgobin Maraj on the street, she snubbed his effusive cordiality by coldly ignoring his greeting. She could do no less, she thought, for a man like Caldeira who had been so helpful to her and so considerate of her taste for good rum.

As the intermediary whom Aunt Jocasta had chosen to employ on her mission of aid to Caldeira, Dr. von Buffus felt himself obliged to make as certain as he could that the utmost discretion should prevail in the circumstances. He was in the habit of making occasional forays to the Black Cat Bar. Caldeira had done him several kindnesses in the past, never pressing him for payment of overdue bar bills and even procuring him at times the favors of women who had caught his fancy. So there was from Dr. von Buffus's point of view an element of private gratitude which he was happy to acknowledge and eager to redress. He carried out his mission with diplomatic verve and adroitness. He also derived a high degree of satisfaction from the fact that he was able to reinforce in Caldeira's mind what the latter had already been told by the "parakeet" about the part Balgobin Maraj had played in bringing about the severance of Caldeira's relationship with her. What the professor did not tell Caldeira was that he himself was now paying fervent court to the "parakeet." From his highly varied experiences in many countries of the world, the great scholar was convinced that Paradise on earth and in the afterlife was to be found only in the arms of a black woman.

The "parakeet" seemed to him to promise lush fulfillment of his scholarly fantasies. She combined the statuesque proportions of a Nigerian "mammy"—a female trader in the open-air markets of Lagos—with Hottentot charms that did not rival Aunt Jocasta's, since they were not of the same amplitude. But so far as the professor was concerned, that deficiency was more than compensated by her blackness, to which he ascribed an arcane mystery that antedated the universe itself. For he believed that it was darkness such as hers that had given birth to light, form to the formless, matter to the void, and, in the course of an infinity of eons, had created eternal life out of eternal death.

In a way, the professor—"Hydrological Cabalist, Specialist in Urinometry," as his visiting card proclaimed him—reminded me of a dilapidated character who wandered about the town, a vagrant named Philo. This old and bearded outcast went barefooted and clothed—it would be more nearly true to say unclothed—in rags. He carried a small, dirty bundle containing, one supposed, all his worldly possessions. He also carried a pail that was never uncovered—at least, no one had ever seen what was in it. Most transfixing about him were his eyes, which burned like frenzied blue flames, fanatical with resentment of unknown and immemorial wrongs. He suffered quite visibly from a grotesque enlargement of the testicles, a condition I have since learned is known to the medical profession as "hydrocele." The townspeople called it "babbamcoo." The older folk among us said that nothing so infuriated those afflicted with this condition as the smell of burning feathers. Having heard this, I decided to put the matter to the test.

Philo lived in a hut sequestered in a meadow at the edge

of the town. Judging that he would still be asleep as the sun came up, I found my way to his hut early one morning. I peered inside. He was asleep. I applied a lighted match to a bucketful of feathers I had brought with me. He awoke. Tottering to the entrance of the hut, he shouted terrible curses at me. I stood there in a paralysis of uncertainty. He stooped, seized hold of the pail he customarily carried with him, uncovered it, and threw its contents at me. I saw a dreadful form uncoil and elongate itself in the air. As I leaped away and started running, I head the thud of its body as it struck the ground a few feet behind me. When I had covered several yards, I stopped running and looked back. Philo had come out of his hut, and, as I was standing there, he recovered possession of the snake he had hurled at me. Cradling the abhorrent creature in his arms, he continued to shout curses at me. In cultivated accents belying, astonishingly, the decrepitude of his appearance and the squalor of his surroundings, he said: "I shall put the snake on you. It will follow you all the days of your life." I laughed and trotted away lightheartedly. A day or two later, a note was found at Aunt Jocasta's gate. It was addressed to my mother. It was written in an elegant, cursive hand reminiscent of the elaborate penmanship of more leisurely times, and it read: "The snake will find him." It was unsigned. Enclosed with it was a charred remnant of a feather.

I only found out about this when, later on, the professor told me about it. Neither Aunt Jocasta nor my mother mentioned it to me.

At any rate, there I was in Trinidad, my home—Iëre, sweet Iëre, the Land of the Hummingbird—where I was as happy as a kingfish with all the damn sharks asleep and not a fisherman in sight. I was, as we say, "at me."

Father Maginot had come to call and he was now about to leave. "I have a mass at six o'clock," he told Aunt Jocasta and my mother.

"Just wait a minute," the former told him. "Johnny," she called to me, "go and cut some flowers for Father Maginot"—she patted me on the head—"like a nice boy." And she gave me that special smile, which, next to soursop ice cream, was what I liked best in the whole world (except rum punch. But I don't have to say this, for everybody, even my little dog, Fidèle, knows it).

I went from rosebush to rosebush snipping blooms to make a bouquet for Father Maginot. I had gathered an armful, just about enough, but there was one rose, an uncommonly lovely blossom, that I simply had to have. It would make the bouquet just perfect. So I reached out with the scissors.

Something immemorial—horrendous, implacable—reared up right in front of me. Its flat, triangular head swayed from side to side, its unblinking eyes cold, hypnotic, and evil. Je-e-e-sus Chris'! I am face to face with Brother Death himself. You hear what I'm telling you? Brother Death, otherwise known as the Mapepire Zanana, Mister Bushmaster himself, the Most High Lord of All.

I leap backward a shade of a shade of a shade faster than the Lord of All can strike. Merciful Father, Almighty, I thank You for Your help in my hour of need. I have not prayed since my confirmation, when the English bishop put his old, fever-bleached, malarial-yellow hand on my head and intoned in a pious, sacramental voice: "Defend, O Lord, this Thy child with Thy heavenly grace, that he may continue Thine forever until he come to Thy everlasting kingdom." I have not prayed since that time. But I pray now.

I am still clutching the flowers when I go indoors. But instead of presenting them to Father Maginot, I hold out toward him the garden shears.

"What is the matter, Johnny?" Aunt Jocasta is taken aback by my lapse; my mother is amused. She twists her lace handkerchief, corkscrewing it with one hand around the little finger of the other hand in an effort to repress her laughter. But my aunt is not amused. She looks at me intently. "What happened, Johnny?"

I recite, stuttering with uncharacteristic intensity, the tale of my unscheduled rendezvous with the Lord of All.

Straightaway, five strong and cunning men are rounded up and dispatched to seek, find, and do battle (*à l'outrance*, as Father Maginot said) with Brother Death. I choose myself Number Six. But the Lord Most High has vanished, leaving a trail of fear, unease, and horror in the wake of his dread apparition.

In the first darkness of the early evening of the following day, terror screams long and loud to the distant and complicit stars, then wails low and shuddering into mortuary silence. One of the five strong and cunning men is found dead beside the rosebush where I myself had had my unsought meeting with the Most High Lord of All. The hollow of the dead man's throat bears two parallel punctures, two inches apart, commemorating the spot where Brother Death located the portals of his entrance.

On the second, third, fourth, and fifth days at different places in the garden but at the same hour and in the same way, Brother Death, the Lord Mapepire Zanana, Emperor of the Silent Kingdom of the Bush, gave audience to the second, third, fourth, and fifth of the five strong and cunning men who came unbidden into his presence. Exactly as before, terror screamed long and loud to the distant and complicit stars, then wailed low and shuddering into mortuary silence.

On the sixth day, I, John Sebastian Alexander Caesar Octavian de Paria, did not attend when summoned to audience at nightfall by the Most High Lord of All. So he waited on me, as Aunt Jocasta had foreseen he would, in the hammock on the veranda, where it was my custom to recline at the end of the day and sing calypsos to the accompaniment of a beguiling cascade of rum punch. Aunt Jocasta became aware of his presence when, as she was sitting with my mother in another section of the veranda partaking of refreshments before dinner, the hair on her head suddenly stood straight up and guardian angels in the icy guise of freezing chills danced up and down her spine. At the same time, my protective deity caused Aunt Jocasta's hands to become clammy with sweat, and for a moment she sat immobilized by apprehension and rigid with foreboding.

Then she got up and sent for a watchman. "Get your gun," she told him. Presently, with infinite caution she led him to the front veranda.

The Most High Lord of All measured ten iridescent feet from head to tail. Five shots were required to return him to the Kingdom of the Dead. As became His Sovereign Majesty, he did not go unescorted. For after the fourth shot, the watchman, supposing him lifeless, incautiously approached within range. Whereupon the Master of the Bush, the Lord Mapepire Zanana, struck again: once, twice. And again, exactly as before, terror screamed long and loud to the distant and complicit stars, then wailed low and shuddering into mortuary silence. I, John Sebastian Alexander Caesar Octavian de Paria, fired the fifth shot.

So this is how I came to leave Trinidad. For Aunt Jocasta said that she would be uneasy as long as I remained there. Since the female consort of the departed Lord Most High would implacably seek and ineluctably find me. For the instinct of vengeance would lead the inconsolable mate to me no matter where I might be, unless immensities of seas and ocean vasts had obliterated all my traces.

Because of all this damn *bouleversé* business—everything so upside-down, my stepfather get douse wid piss, the Mapepire snake want to kill me (what the hell I ever do that damn snake, I don' know), and Aunt Jocasta feeling that she better get me quick out of that tatou-hole (that is a place where Mapepire Zanana like to sleep)—I wake up and find myself on the way to England. Me, Johnny de Paria, leaving Trinidad, leaving Paradise, leaving my guitar, my calypso, my rum punch, my hammock, my dog, my cane fields, my frangipani and immortelle trees, my poui blossoms, four o'clock flowers and sweet-scented ladies of the night, leaving my carnival, my Corpus Christi, my Christmas—every damn thing. O God, man! Is true: life funny, yes. You know how you born, Peter, but you never know how you goin' to die. J-e-e-e-s-u-s Chris'! The last thing Ah Sam said to me, the very last thing: "Lissen, boy, remember w'at Ah'm tellin' you. T'ree t'ing: (1) Don' tek trick to make luck. (2) Play hot but keep cool. (3) W'at sweet in goat' mout' is bitter in 'is arse." In other words: (1)

Honesty is always the best policy. (2) Whatever the outward appearances, never lose your head. (3) Be prudent at all times.

Reflections such as these dipped and wheeled in disconsolate circles about my thoughts as the German steamship *Frederick of Prussia* made its way out of the Gulf of Paria through the Dragon's Mouth and into the Caribbean Sea. It was a morning of intemperate sunshine. But I was already homesick. I leaned against the ship's rail keeping a melancholy watch as increasing distance first diminished, then blurred, and at length blotted out Trinidad from my sight.

My old life ended in an agony of seasickness. I had dined with uninhibited zest that first night out and drunk large drafts of German beer. But for the first time in my life, I and my stomach were at odds. On the way to my cabin after dinner, I realized that somewhere inside of me a full-fledged revolution was under way and that I should have to expel the contending factions as soon as possible. Going at high speed along the corridor toward my cabin, I saw an open door and plunged in. An extremely large lady with a continental shelf of a bosom barred my way, shouting at me in an unintelligible language (it was certainly not English), her massive arms bracketing her body at belligerent angles. In some extrasensory fashion I gathered she was informing me that this was the ladies' room. But I was in no position at that moment to adhere to so fine a distinction. Nor was a clarifying exchange possible between us. I lunged for the nearest wash basin. She cut me off. I lunged to the other side of her. Again she cut me off. I could do nothing more for her. All the insurgent cuisine of her native Deutschland stormed up from my stomach, prompted by an unsporting roll of the ship. I had no choice in the matter. I disgorged my vast dinner squarely upon her bosom. She shrieked. I retched and puked once, twice, thrice more upon her, holding her at arms' length for support, before the return roll of the ship disengaged my hold, removed me from the room, and dispatched me teetering down the corridor to my cabin. I had just time to bolt the door behind me and collapse onto my bed after nearly tripping over a brass-bound box protruding slightly from beneath it. There was a great pounding on the cabin door, accompanied by more of the same unintelligible language uttered in an angry and unnecessarily loud voice. I was unable to do anything but ignore it and yearn for oblivion. Dr. von Buffus subsequently informed me of the lady's resolve to get her hands on me. *"Bloss einmal,"* she told him. *"Bloss einmal."* (The professor, great scholar as he was and master of a hundred languages, translated this for me as meaning, in English, "Just once . . . just once . . ." The deep yearning implicit in the lady's voice was scrupulously reproduced by the learned professor.)

So I had to spend some of the rest of the voyage playing hide-and-seek with this woman. Me, Johnny de Paria, hiding from a big, fat woman. Still, I was finding out: that's how life is, boy. But what the hell, when you have to puke, you have to puke. That's all. When, at Dr. von Buffus's suggestion, the cabin steward (a mister-man about my own age, who looked like a scarlet ibis without wings) brought me some beef tea a day or two—or perhaps three or four or five days—later (I had lost all count of time), he stumbled over the box, then stooped and pushed it farther back beneath the bed. *"Himmel!"* he exclaimed as he straightened up. He mimed the exertion involved in handling an object of such considerable and unexpected weight. At the time, feeling as I did, I was incapable of speculation concerning the box, or anything else, for that matter. Afterward I never gave it a thought.

I spent several days in my cabin, sick as an old jackass with the colic. The professor came in often to see me. Once he brought the ship's doctor along with him. Between the two of them, judging by the way they smelled, they must have drunk the ship's whole store of liquor. I got sick all over again. Another time the professor brought two Indian ladies with him. That was the turning point in my seasickness. At the sight of the two ladies, I sat bolt upright in my bunk for the first time in days. They were exactly the medicine I needed. I knew that they could cure me. Reverting to my unweaned state, I would suckle myself at their breasts back to health. I mentioned the matter to the professor. He was not at all encouraging and merely said that he would see what he could do. But he did not refer to the matter again. Neither did I.

A day or two later I was able to leave my cabin, and in another day or so, after spending hours on deck in the semitropical sunshine, I was as frisky as a young goat who had just cuckolded his father, the damn ole piss-tail ram.

It was also while I was lying stretched out at my ease in a deck chair that an Indian gentleman tried to engage me in conversation. I pretended that I was too sick to talk. That did not deter him. He embarked upon a monologue lasting several minutes, beginning with his name, the nature of his business, his address and telephone numbers, his wife's name and his daughter's, a remarkably careless disclosure that his wife and he were no longer "makin' sanga-wanga," and that as a result he was now at liberty to pay more attention to his mistress, who, unlike his wife, was not a "cold drink of water." His wife thought he was a "capon" but, contrary to her belief, he was a "very hot man." He was also quite well off; he was making money in his business—Balgobin Maraj's Emporium: Dry Goods and Hardware. Had I never heard of it? Where was I from? My face looked familiar. But I couldn't be the boy he was thinking of—a boy wid a ole big-arse tan'-tan' (meaning, in Trinidadian patois, aunt), because that boy was a "stuck-up creole who, people say, douse his own father—his own farder, yo' hear w'at Ah'm tellin' you? His own farder—wid stale piss." Did I ever hear t'ing so? But people bad, yes! Especially the young ones an' dem, man. Bad too-much, too-much. He had a daughter whom he'd like to marry some nice young fella. "Yo' face look as if Ah know you," he repeated. He considered me with the calculating eye of a marriage broker from Madras. ". . . Some nice young fella, an' settle down an' mek baby." A young fella—he was studying me with predatory intentness—who married his daughter would get some nice money to start, become a partner in his business, and of course the couple would live in the same house with him and his wife. But if they wanted their own house, he would give them one. He owned several in San Fernando. One at Marabella, another on La Pique Hill, one at Royal Road, another on Upper Hillside . . . But it would have to be a nice young fella. Not like some of them scamps—he scowled—vagabonds who married your daughter an' de nex' t'ing, w'en you hear de shout, dey cuttin' she arse w'at's matter, an' she comin' home to you cryin', she husban' treatin' she so bad. . . . But a nice young fella . . . Yo' face look so familiar. . . ."

I pretended to be asleep. Out of the corner of my eye, I saw him wave to a black man who had just come on deck. He got up, muttering to himself: "I wonder if they find his luggage—if they find the box?" Lurching slightly with the roll of the ship, he proceeded across the deck toward the black man, whom he greeted and, after pausing to light a cigarette, engaged in conversation. The black man stood with his back against the ship's rail, peering up at the sun with an aggrieved air, as if disenchanted by the discovery of yet another blemish on its face.

When I related the incident to Dr. von Buffus, he said to me: "Ach, so. *Ja*. Those two. The black one and the Indian. Dr. Schwanz and Kapitän Gebumst." Mordant relish skewed up his face. "You were right to"—he clasped his hands together, brought them up to one side of his face, and slowly inclined his head against them—*schlafen* . . . sleep." He glanced at me with a distant expression of academic solicitude. "You feel better, yes?" And without awaiting a reply, "Then we have dinner tonight." He tottered off, carefully accommodating his gait to the heel and pitch of the ship.

I dressed for dinner with care, putting on my second-best suit of cream gabardine made for me by an Indian tailor in San Fernando. When he learned that I was about to leave for England, and that the suit would clothe me as I walked around London, he put a sign on his window that read: MAKING SUIT FOR ENGLAND. He refused to allow his assistant to aid him in the slightest detail. For nights on end he stayed in the shop until the early hours of the morning, a bright and naked electric bulb illuminating the sign for the benefit of the passers-by. He devoted many hours to his masterpiece, slanting the pockets at a stylish angle, adorning the buttonholes with intricate filigrees of colored thread, making delicate little appliqués around the buttonholes of the jacket and vest, as well as the trousers fly (since in that manly era, unisex contrivances like metal zippers on a man's fly were unheard of and, in any case, would have been thought to place his precious parts at the hazard of being pinched or even mutilated). He widened the bottoms of the trousers with such modish elegance that they looked like hooped crinoline skirts, permitting only fragmentary and intriguing glimpses of the two-toned Hollywood shoes that went with the ensemble. When he had completed the suit to his satisfaction—my own was not consulted—he then created the silken shirt that I was to wear with it. Last of all he chose the tie, a watered-silk cravat flowered in all the prismatic colors of a tropical rainbow. He was unable to find a pair of socks to match the tie, so he was obliged to leave this final detail to my judgment, only enjoining me, however I chose, to be worthy of him. I did my best.

My entrance into the dining salon did not go unnoticed or without audible remark. I arrived after the other passengers had been seated. As I made my way to the table reserved for Dr. von Buffus, I could hear the murmurs of admiration that arose on all sides. An ill-disposed onlooker might have misinterpreted them as comments of a derisory nature. He might even have construed the laughter that accompanied my passage across the room as being impolite. He might also have concluded that the steward who showed me to the professor's table was sardonic when he informed me that the captain's fancy-dress ball was scheduled for the following evening rather than that night. But I myself, having fully recovered from seasickness, was in the most cheerful of spirits, my appetite for food restored and sharpened by the hours I had spent on deck in the salt air. In addition, I was overflowing with gratitude for the genius of my tailor. I thought of sending him a wireless message acclaiming him the greatest practitioner of his art in the British Commonwealth and Empire Beyond the Seas.

The only discordant note was sounded, though faintly, by the Indian merchant whom Dr. von Buffus had referred to as "Kapitän Gebumst." "Boy," he said to me, clutching his knife and fork in the wrong hands, "buh w'ey de arse wrong wid you? You dress-up like a damn daddantique." (The allusion here was, in this vulgar fellow's Trinidadian dialect, to a garishly overdressed figure teetering precariously on high, wooden stilts.) But I ignored the remark. What the hell would a coolie-man like him know about clothes? I turned to acknowledge the compliments of the African whose name, as I had gathered from the professor, was "Dr. Schwanz." "*Magnifique,*" he was saying to me. "*Quelle inspiration!*" I was unacquainted with the language he had spoken, but it was easy for me to understand that he was expressing his pleasure at the way I looked. I have since learned that Africans are universally regarded as great judges of style. This is true, I have been told, even of those who lunch on Roman Catholic nuns and dine on Church of England missionaries. (For breakfast, according to that famous man of learning, Dr. von Buffus, they prefer deviled bones.)

Intent as I was on making up for lost time, I ordered a lavish dinner from the extensive menu. Meanwhile Kapitän

Gebumst, the Indian gentleman otherwise known as Balgobin Maraj, was experiencing considerable difficulty with his knife and fork, which were at irreconcilable odds with each other. He presently discarded them altogether and resorted instead to the use of a single, all-purpose spoon. After another frustrating bout with the spoon, he also cast it aside. "The fingers is better," he said, plunging them into the dish before him. It was natural, he emphasized, and more sanitary. The African, Dr. Schwanz, agreed with only a minor reservation. No civilized person, he asserted, ever ate except with the fingers of *one* hand. He drove his point home by holding up his right hand and making pronate motions with it.

The African in particular interested me. He had been on a visit to Trinidad from the Ivory Coast and was returning home by way of London. "Dr. Schwanz," I began, addressing him directly.

He seemed puzzled. "My name," he objected, "is not how you call me—'Dr. Pants'? Is that how you say? 'Pants'?" He gave me a quizzical look. "I am engineer. Civil engineer."

"But I thought—" I silently queried Professor von Buffus, who broke in at once, clearing up the matter.

"*Ja.* Is so but not so." Great learning cobwebbed the corners of his eyes and deposited massive pouches of erudition beneath them. "*Ja und nein.* My esteemed colleagues, Herr Doktor Schwanz and Herr Kapitän Gebumst—" There was, it occurred to me as he was speaking, an odd suggestion of a certain variance between the gleam in his eyes and the words on his lips. "They are here, yet they are not here. *Ach,* so." He contemplated me with the air of a despairing scholar in hopeless quest of a mustard seed of intelligence in a pupil of mountainous stupidity. "You understand? *Ja?*"

The Indian merchant—Kapitän Gebumst—came to the rescue. "But I tol' you today, jus' today—" A large, white table napkin depended from the collar of his shirt and partially concealed the dinner-inflated expanse of his stomach.

"This morning, in fac'. I tol' you—Ah'm dead sure I tol' you—" His eyes both deplored my mental backwardness and pitied my generally deprived condition. "My name is Balgobin Maraj. High Street, San Fernando. Balgobin Maraj. The Emporium: Dry Goods and Hardware. I am married. I have a wife and one daughter. My telephone number is—"

The African interrupted him, being anxious not to miss the chance of announcing his own name, which he now did. "Marcellin Gros-Caucaud. But"—there was a degree of asperity in his tone—"you—" His eyes conveyed his sense of having been offended. They had hardened into narrow discs of mahogany-colored stone. "You call me 'Dr. Pants.' Is that how you say? But I am not doctor. *Mais, non.* I'm civil engineer." He pushed his plate a few inches away from him. "Pants? *Pourquoi* 'Pants'? *Je ressemble à—*" He plucked at his trousers, looking down and frowning over the ridgelike crease that ran along their immaculate length of starched white duck. "Pants—?"

Dr. von Buffus cleared his throat with scholarly authority. The table was silent. Attracting the African's attention, the professor touched his own forefinger to his head, and then in an obvious gesture of explication for the benefit of the African, he glanced at me.

Monsieur Marcellin Gros-Caucaud nodded. He understood. Perfectly. Compassion flickered in his eyes, which were deeply entombed in his head and guttered in their graveyard sockets. With infinite gentleness he inquired of me: "Have you ever had a woman?"

For some reason or other, the question troubled me. I balanced my fork with the most precise equilibration my left hand could command. With my right, I held my knife at half-staff, as if in mourning for my inability to respond with masculine forthrightness to so candid though indelicate a query. I was, as I well and—let me at least be frank with myself—even painfully knew, in a state of sorely tried though technically unviolated innocence. I had not long since at-

85

tained my majority (as the old-fashioned phrase went) and I was still, invincibly, a virgin. In the hot, aphrodisiac climate of my native Trinidad and Tobago, one ambitious young lady after another had tried in vain to disencumber me of my maidenhead. Ingenious traps without number were set for me. At one stage, so massive was the siege that my aunt Jocasta held a conference with Father Maginot and the family locksmith as to the advisability of fitting me with a contrivance known as a "chastity belt." The conference foundered on the problem of how the periodic rioting of my privy member might best be contained. Father Maginot suggested a design in the form of a fig leaf made of stout canvas and bearing the Christian symbol of the cross. Aunt Jocasta thought this an admirable solution, but preferred a more elastic material such as rubber, lined with silk. My mother, belatedly consulted, considered that a penis-shaped glove of fine linen, edged with lace, would do. She dwelt at much length on the necessity of lace and insisted upon it with a vehemence so uncharacteristic of her, twisting her handkerchief around her little finger and displaying such impassioned intensity, that Aunt Jocasta summoned a maid and bade her fetch my mother some sal volatile. For his part, the locksmith held out for iron. "A boy young like dat," he said, "will buss [that is, burst] steel." He shook his head in vigorous assertion of his superior technical acquaintance with the problems of metallurgical stress. And at Father Maginot he directed a look that called quite candidly into question the credentials of the former to discuss with competence so incelibate a matter. In the end, the fortress was left undefended except by the moat of my own disinclination, filled with rum punch, and with my guitar, my calypsos, and my hammock keeping watch on the walls of my beleaguered penis. I also knew, well in advance, that no sooner had I arrived in England than a youthful horde of female imperialists would lay siege to me in a determined and savage attempt to devirginate me in the sacred name of their

86

civilizing mission. Most young men of my standing from Trinidad and Tobago (and the large majority of us hailing from that distant suburb of the British Commonwealth and Empire Beyond the Seas are accommodating as well as handsome) have been obliged to undergo this tribal rite of initiation into the metropolitan society. It is, in fact, a form of circumcision by attrition. I differ from the rest only because I am, extraordinarily, *puer intactus*. How have I so improbably conserved my maidenhead despite tons of spices, oceans of rum, a score of carnivals, and the persistent endeavors of the most beautiful and enterprising maidens, demi-maidens, ex-maidens, and matrons in all the known world? This was a question of much concern to Professor von Buffus. He invented many hypotheses to account for the unique circumstance. None of them, however, or any combination of them, was wholly adequate. Von Buffus's scholarship, vast as it was, had never before contemplated, let alone investigated, so rare a phenomenon as a male Trinidadian virgin of mature years. His puzzlement led him to theorize that I was given, by some malfunction of my genetic structure, less to defloration than to something he called *défleurage*, which, he clarified for me, was an oral method developed by Frenchmen for extracting scent from—his mouth took on the appearance of a suction cup—flowers. Whenever he explained this Gallic art to me, his mouth would execute a highly suggestive transformation. Sometimes it would assume the shape of an inverted isosceles triangle and at other times that of a bivalve mollusk, such as a clam, agape and gradually, barely perceptibly, opening up in a state of dehiscence.

All of this passed through my mind like a lightning bolt as I responded to the African. "No," I told him. I had a feeling—I can't explain why—but I had a feeling that in amplifying my reply to him as I was about to do, I would be defending not only the inviolacy of my private parts (to which Aunt Jocasta usually referred as "the pencil," while my mother, who was more of a stickler than Aunt Jocasta for strict propriety in such matters, spoke of it as "your person"). I would also be justifying the training I had received from my aunt and my mother and vindicating the soundness of the precepts they had striven to instill in me. I felt I owed it to them to do so, to show myself to all the world, and in particular to this inquisitive African, as the burnished product of their patient handiwork. Besides which, anyone who put such a question to someone else laid himself open to the suspicion of being deficient in good breeding. And I did not care for commonness in any form. J-e-e-e-s-u-s Chris', boy! You could say w'at the hell you please about Johnny de Paria, but the one thing you could never say about me is that I am common. You say that about me, an' no matter who you are—you could be King George or the Prince of Wales—I will call you a damn liar an' kick you in yo' arse. No matter w'at kind o' mister-man you t'ink you is, boy, I will kick—

I looked straight at the African, this Dr. Schwanz—this Monsieur Marcellin Gros-Caucaud. I captured his eye and imprisoned it in a stern and unforgiving glare. Then I declared, addressing myself of course to him but also to the entire ship's company there gathered together in the dining salon: "Sir, I would have you know that I am a virgin." My voice rang high above the din of general conversation, the scurrying to and fro of waiters, and the clatter of tableware. A respectful, attentive, and admiring stillness ensued. And indeed the whole room, I felt, would have broken into applause except that an old, carrot-faced Englishman swiveled in his chair toward me and, screwing his monocle into place and adjusting it with deliberate precision, exclaimed in an elegant, drawling, pukka-sahib tone: "I say! By Jove! Eh, w-h-a-a-t?" And his wife, sitting across from him, her face red and long as a radish that a starving horse has declined for supper, said in a voice shrill and neighing with approval of my manly defense of my impregnable virtue: "How extr'o'r'dinry!"

Needless to say, I was pleased. So, bearing in mind my mother's constant injunction to me that "Manners makyth man," I arose from my seat and bowed in the direction of the English couple. At the renewed sight of my ensemble, my crinolined trousers and crenellated jacket, they both slumped backward in their chairs, closed their eyes, and folded their hands across their chests in an attitude of prayer. I regarded this as the ultimate compliment, for the English usually do not pray unless a favorite dog is about to be wormed by a veterinary surgeon.

I resumed my seat, conscious that the eyes of the whole room were upon me, a situation that I did not find at all displeasing.

Perhaps because of his discomfiture, the African presently got into an altercation with a waiter who had, he alleged, delayed overlong in refilling his wineglass. He called the man a "fascist" and when Dr. von Buffus remonstrated with him, he assailed the great scholar as a "white colonialist" and spoke angrily of a South-West African tribe known as the Herreros and of what had befallen them at the hands of Dr. von Buffus and his compatriots. Becoming more and more heated, what with the wine and his indignation mutually reinforcing each other, he openly pointed, with a lamentable absence of good manners ("It is rude to point," my aunt Jocasta was always saying), at the carrot-faced Englishman, whom he asserted to be a spy. "They're all spies—every one of them. And he"—with another deplorable lapse of manners he pointed again at the Englishman—"for all you know, is the director of British Intelligence himself." By now he had worked himself up into a dreadful temper, so that he was almost shouting (yet another breach of good manners. "In polite conversation, never raise your voice," was one of my mother's constant admonitions to me). "Just a damn spy! Spy! Spy! Spy!" And, nearly speechless and inarticulate now with sheer rage, "Lice! Lice! Vermin! Filth!"

The amazing thing was that he spoke in excellent English during the whole of this denunciation, although he had previously expressed himself in this language in a most halting and imperfect manner. I could only attribute the improvement in his command of English to the inspiration of his theme. But, as the professor when discussing language has occasionally said to me, "Swear in English, make love in French, and reason in German." However that may be, I did not like the African's show of temper and the display of bad manners it entailed. I was thinking that I myself should call him to order when he suddenly returned to me, charging that the only possible reason I could be a virgin was that I did not possess that appendage which he called a "foo-foo-tay" and which, as I have already revealed, my aunt Jocasta liked to refer to as "the pencil."

Now, I have a rule that I do not discuss my penis with anyone. My penis is mine. It is a personal matter. It is private. I decided to ignore the vulgar intrusion. In another few weeks, I thought, he'd be running naked about the African bush looking for my great-grandfather in order to sell him into slavery to the Portuguese, the English, or the Arabs—so to hell with him. In any case, by this time I had become intrigued by the spectacle of a number of the diners who were dancing between courses to the music of a jazz band in a small, circular area in the center of the dining salon. I was seized by an urge to join them. Yet I had never acquired the art of ballroom dancing and did not know how I would fare if I should attempt it without previous experience. But it seemed to me unlikely that a Trinidadian would be unable to master within a few seconds the extremely limited and stylized choreography of the fox trot, waltz, or one- or two-step, so I had no qualms about getting out on the floor. I lacked only a partner. I looked around the room. The situation was unpromising. There seemed to be no extra ladies

90

available. But, as by providential coincidence, the Englishman withdrew from his table, leaving his lady unattended. I saw my opportunity. I rose from my seat and went over to her. Bowing with formal ceremony, as I had seen gentlemen do at seasonal balls at home, I asked her to partner me.

Her response was not unenthusiastic. Though it was, I must admit, a trifle guarded. "O, I say!" she noted, rather than welcomed, my invitation. She was scrutinizing me with a sort of connoisseuse's interest, the way I had seen visitors to Aunt Jocasta's examine a piece of wood carving in the native Trinidadian style among her collection of West Indian statuary. "D'yew think we can manage it?" It may have been the result of her English taste for the exotic, or simply the lure of my flowered silk cravat, that magnetized her. Whatever it was, she threw aside her hesitancy and, like a resolute horsewoman at the challenge of a seven-barred gate, decided to take the jump. Her arm in mine, we mazed and skirted past the intervening tables to the dance floor.

Now, to begin with, I had never held a lady in my arms for the purpose of dancing or for any purpose at all, and I did not intend to start this evening. She herself seemed undecided as to the appropriate mode of procedure. The English band was playing a tune I recognized as an American song, a noxious, saccharine ditty called "Blue Skies," and a mister-man of about my own age who professed to be a boy but looked like a girl was mooing into a microphone:

> "Blue Skies
> Smiling at me
> Nothing but blue skies
> Do I see . . ."

I smiled optimistically at my lady and she smiled back at me with a speck or two less optimism. The dancers meanwhile were cutting their figures around us. Standing there, I came to a decision. Since I did not know how to do the fox trot, and it seemed in any case an unimaginative and repetitious

form of dancing, I would "play mas'." I would adapt the carnival dance form with its calypso rhythms to the music of
"Blue Skies." I would "jump up." So my arms ascended
heavenward, my body began to sway like a young green
bamboo in the breeze, my backside cocked itself seductively, and my feet commenced to chip, drag, and shuffle in
preparation for my executing a series of leaps to the moon
and back to the earth in perfect consonance with a calypso
beat. My partner, displaying a most spirited faculty of invention, tried to improvise corresponding movements. "Play
mas'!" I called to the world at large, not wishing selfishly to
give myself alone—and of course my partner—this most exquisite of all pleasures. "Play maaaasss!" she gallantly supported my appeal. The rigidity of her spine—an anatomical
peculiarity of the English that extends as well to the upper
lip—did not permit her bottom the freedom of bounce, re-
bound, and maneuver a Trinidadian backside commands.
Yet within her ethnic limitations, there was no question that
she was putting on a damn good show. At one point, indeed,
the old girl went down on all fours, baying like a hound,
"Play maaaasss!" When she came upright again, she dispatched her behind in one direction while the rest of her
body took the opposite tack and her uplifted arms sema-
phored to the heavens the immortal Nelsonian message:
"England expects every man to do his duty." She was certainly doing hers, and I, desiring neither to be insensitive to
her efforts nor unworthy of my Trinidadian heritage, shook
my backside like a knight of the Round Table brandishing
his plume at Camelot.

The musicians did not at first know quite what to make of
this development. For a while they persisted in their sedate,
two-four rhythm, doubtless hoping that my intrusion would
soon end for lack of encouragement, if not by some more direct form of intervention on the part of the other dancers.
When on the contrary, however, these one after another
abandoned their hitherto servile adherence to the restric-

tive forms of the fox trot and, striking off their shackles, "played mas'," the musicians threw in the old starched shirt. They modulated the Pollyanna measures and soporific rhythms of "Blue Skies" into the rapturous pulsations of a calypso beat. At least, they did what they could to attain a state of such divine grace. If they did not quite succeed, it was in no way to be attributed to want of aspiration. It is simply a fact that the English are better colonial administrators than they are calypsonians. This is no fault of theirs. In this respect, they have been disadvantaged by nature. There is no reason to look down on them. They are not to be thought racially inferior merely because their backsides are held too firmly in place by an inelastic vertebral column. They did not design their own anatomy. They were obliged to take what was given them. It was theirs not to reason why, theirs but to do the best they could with their frozen bottoms when they found themselves among tropical peoples whom nature had unfairly provided with self-lubricating ball bearings in centrally heated backsides. I like and respect the English despite this sad physical handicap of theirs, and never at any time have I disparaged them for it on racial grounds. Would the Charge of the Light Brigade into the Valley of Death, with the proto-communist guns of the enemy volleying and thundering, have been accomplished by Six Hundred freewheeling black backsides? I ask you.

With the whole company of dancers and diners now shouting in and out of unison, "Play mas'!" the musicians launched into calypso expositions of "Tiptoe Through the Tulips," "Five Foot Two, Eyes of Blue," and "I've Got a Feeling I'm Falling." Under the mistaken though flattering impression that my attire was a carnival costume, many of the revelers returned briefly to their cabins and then reappeared in various states of dress and undress, adorned in some instances by varicolored ribbons and improbable headgear, simulating carnival disguises. Everyone was

93

"jumping up," the alternative Trinidadian expression for "playing mas'." A forest of arms groped toward the ceiling of the dining salon, and coveys of European backsides wheeled with the agitation of startled birds flushed into the open by a predatory hawk that had landed on a branch of their favorite tree. Amidst the merry tumult, the African, Dr. Schwanz—or, as he eccentrically preferred to call himself, Marcellin Gros-Caucaud—achieved great distinction by his elegant performance of one of his native dances, in the course of which, following the requirements of the dance, he stripped off most of his clothing until, so awesome in size were his private accouterments, he appeared to be dancing on a tripod of three members consisting partly of two legs. His "person" (to employ my mother's refined usage) seemed, if anything, to be larger than all the rest of him, even including his massive thighs. He was every inch an exceptionally well-hung elephant at large in a nudist colony of mice. Nor were the ladies unappreciative. They took turns kneeling in a circle around him, gazing at his midpoint after the fashion of devotees in a trance of religious ecstasy. It was as if, by an unfortunate error on the part of the executioners of John the Baptist, he had been depricked rather than decapitated. Herod's consequent gift to Salome might then have inspired in her much the same response as the female merrymakers in the dining salon of the *Frederick of Prussia* were exhibiting at the sight of the African's "pencil" (in Aunt Jocasta's playful yet reserved phrase). Kneeling in adoration while Dr. Schwanz danced, they sang "Five Foot Two," their collective gaze focused in enraptured concert on the African's "boutou" (a vulgar Trinidadian patois synonym for "penis," of which both Aunt Jocasta and my mother disapproved. I myself shared their disapproval of this usage, as well as of "totee," another vernacular term for the male organ much favored by ill-bred Trinidadians). The carrot-faced Englishman was by no means insensible to the ritual of phallus worship that was taking place. But he was English to the kernel. He had changed into a fox-hunting costume, and after an initial cry of "Tally-ho!" in sheer wonderment that even so powerful a locomotive as the African could pull so stupendous a train, he sternly disciplined himself. Thereafter he marched up and down the dining salon like a dehorsed fox hunter whose backside in wistful nostalgia was imitating the pendulumlike motions of the tail of his runaway steed as it repelled from its haunches the sexual advances of rapist flies. He was as much admired for the glacial immobility of his upper lip as for the correct though unemancipated movements of his bottom. By way of a special tribute to him, the band played a rousing calypso version of "Rule, Britannia." It was under the spell of this splendid musical invention that my partner, from whom I had seldom been parted during the whole of this interlude, proposed marriage to me. I was obliged to decline the honor. As a virgin, I said, I could not marry: while, if I were to marry, I feared I would not long remain a virgin. With true English tact and imperial delicacy, she conceded the insoluble nature of the classical problem I confronted. Yet her attentions to me were rapidly assuming the character of gunboat diplomacy. The native, having rejected the Christian Bible as a fair exchange for his raw materials, must be made to suffer the consequences of his backwardness. The look in her eyes, together with the colonialist forays of her hands toward my "person," left me in no doubt of her imperial design. Cecil Rhodes and Lord Milner were written all over her. I feared the worst. My maidenhead was in peril.

Happily, however, she was deflected from her devirginating purpose by Dr. von Buffus, who, goose-stepping with all the elegance of Frederick the Great engaging in a minuet with Voltaire at Potsdam, seized her masterfully around the waist. He then drew her to him with the disciplined force, precision, and military élan that had carried the Prussian monarch successfully through the Seven Years' War. His whole bearing and his movements, liltingly accommodated to the calypso pulse of the music, were those of the triumphant prince who was, by his own preference, "not absolute master, but the first servant of his people." She, for her part, showed no lack of ardor in her desire to be served by so irresistible a prince.

Now, when you're "jumping up," you don't just stay with one partner all the time—you diversify the portfolio. You buy this stock and sell that, you change this utility for that municipal, and so on. A girl might start jumping up with the Frog and end up with Prince Charming. Or a boy, starting out with an Ugly Duckling, might finish up with a Beautiful Swan. You never can tell. Playin' mas' is a lottery. The only certainty is that you do not know what you'll get for a prize. Never could I have imagined that an old English lady—well, not so old, after all: older than my mother, yes, but not as old as Aunt Jocasta—would jump up like this. Thinking in this way, I leaped so high that my head nearly bumped against the ceiling, which was about twenty feet above the floor. When I came down again and looked for my partner so as to be sure that she had seen what I had done, she wasn't there. Just out of curiosity I looked around for her. Yes, there she was, an'—Je-e-e-e-sus Chris'!—I could not believe my eyes. My partner, together with Dr. Schwanz and Kapitän Gebumst, was dancing the "Dame Laurine"—a salacious dance, lustful and obscene, that Trinidadians traditionally performed in tents and carnival halls the night before *"jour ouvert,"* the early-morning celebration of the first day of carnival. She had evidently undergone a period of apprenticeship to those two experts during her absence from me. While her bottom did not speak with the inspired eloquence of Trinidadian backsides on such occasions, it was nonetheless making statements that any Speaker of the British House of Commons, however indulgent, would have ruled out of order. I was obliged to intervene, when, at the climax of the "Dame Laurine," Schwanz and Gebumst, having sandwiched her front and back between them, began a

96

graphic choreograph of the joyous possibilities of sexual intercourse à trois. I did not think that the rakish old Empire in its declining years should be put to such carnal exertions by subject persons to whom, at great imperial sacrifice, it had brought the Christian Bible while so charitably relieving them of the oppressive burden of continued possession of their tribal lands. It was, I thought, less than grateful to debauch this noble heritage by orgiastic excesses of colonial backsides spinning and wheeling lubriciously out of control. Playin' mas', my rotating behind keeping me on course like a gyrostat and my exultant heart singing "God Save the King," I made my way toward them and rescued the lady.

At the conclusion of the revels, as the dawn was coming up, I was on my way to my cabin when in one of the ship's corridors somewhat off the beaten track I saw the German stewardess trying, it seemed to me, to climb up Dr. Schwanz (I mean, of course, Marcellin Gros-Caucaud, as he foolishly chooses to be known). He was flattened against a wall, as though he were a tree. She was literally clambering up him like a native shinning up a coconut palm. I thought I should withdraw as discreetly as I could, unless the lady or Dr. Schwanz called for help, which, to be sure, neither of them appeared likely to do. Before I could make a decision in the matter, they both became aware of my presence. She made some scant pretense of protest, directed more toward my untimely happening upon the scene than toward anything she was attempting to do to Dr. Schwanz. But he was elemental in his rage. He accused me of the vilest forms of sexual espionage, calling me *macco*—an odious reproach, indeed—and *voyeur* (but Dr. von Buffus said I should be proud of having this epithet applied to me) and *sale* (which the professor translated to mean "dirty"). Imagine: me— Johnny de Paria—"dirty." Me, who am in the habit of bathing myself five times a day. Me—"dirty." An' look who's callin' me that, nuh? Man, but you ever see t'ing so? I's a true sayin', yes: people always takin' trick to make luck. O God, boy! Jump high, jump low, people always ... But jus' look, nuh ... Anyway, as the professor told me, don't worry, every hippopotamus in the zoo in Schwanz's home town refuses to bathe in the same mud with that mister-man.

I thought of the professor, with his odd look of having strayed from his duties as the perennial keeper of a pigeon run whose feathered occupants had mistaken him for a communal lavatory. Strolling along the corridor, I recalled him as he had disported himself on the dance floor, playing mas', tossing his arms skyward like Alexander von Humboldt enraptured at observing the transit of Mercury. I could not help noting, however, that the transports of his bottom owed more to the art of horsemanship than to the license of carnival. There was a scholarly tentativeness about the choreographic assumptions of his backside that, in a transfigured image of speech, could well suggest the movements of a show horse performing the evolutions of dressage. And when he shouted, "Play mas'!" it was with the high timbre and vaulting tenor of a *Kapellmeister* insisting on a more liberated C-sharp from his choristers. But from time to time his hands, by some unscholarly impulse, would be diverted to his private parts and then he would seem to be making a gift of carnal life and sensual largesse to the universe. The professor ...

A duet of laughter in what I thought might be an impromptu concert of mutual pleasantries between two friends halted me. The cabin door (the room, I knew, was the professor's) was hospitably half open. As I was standing there, undecided whether to continue on my way to my own cabin or, briefly, to join Dr. von Buffus and his companion, the duet grew more rapturous. I hesitated no longer. Tapping on the door with no more than the bare formality required by good manners, I entered. There—there— mounted on the professor, who was on his hands and knees, crawling on all fours around the cabin, was the English lady. They were both as naked as Job's turkey cock. To say that I was transfixed would be putting it with something less than complete exactness. I had suddenly sprouted roots, which had proliferated to such a depth that a volcanic upheaval could not have dislodged me from the spot.

"Giddyap, you old devil!" my partner in the revels just ended was exhorting Dr. von Buffus as she spurred and roweled his naked flanks with her heels. "Giddyap!" She slapped him vigorously on the hindquarters.

Neither took the slightest notice of me. I thought that I should withdraw from the scene as soon as I could succeed in uprooting myself.

"*Ach*, so," the professor now said to the equestrienne astride him. "*Ja*. It is time. I ride you."

Sporting as always, the English lady assented. The game was the thing. "D'yew mind if I buck?"

"*Nein, nein*. I like that."

She dismounted and now in her turn got on her hands and knees. The professor, crouching, positioned himself strategically behind her haunches and, placing his hands on their sloping, ivory-pale expanse, prepared to mount her.

"Not that! Not that! You bloody bugger!" she objected. "Off with you!" Her tone, however, was freighted with something less than absolute conviction.

The professor directed a series of brisk, unicornlike thrusts at her hindquarters. "*Einmal ist keinmal*," he reassured her. (By discreet inquiries I afterward learned that this expression means "Once is nothing.") He was short of breath but resolute. "*Einmal ist keinmal*." He thrust again—

With a heroic effort, I displanted myself and, still unnoticed by the preoccupied equestrians, took my leave.

How strange, I thought. What a night. And what a far cry, after the fleeting passage of a few days, from my hammock, my guitar, my calypsos, my rum punch, and—

"But w'at the hell is this I'm seein', man? Don't talk foolishness—I mus' be crazy. Je-e-e-e-sus-s-s-s Chris-s-s-s'!"

This is what I am saying to myself because of what I am seeing right there in front of me. Balgobin Maraj (or Kapitän
Gebumst, as the professor calls him) is struggling with the
Englishman whose lady I have just left playing horsey-hors-
ey with Dr. von Buffus. And the East Indian is saying to the
Englishman, "No, no, sahib! I can't do it, sahib. O God, leggo
me totee, sahib! Leggo me totee!"

The Englishman, panting and red-faced with exertion, is
trying alternately to maul and cajole the East Indian into
compliance with his wishes. They are both clad only in their
underwear. The Englishman, who has a firm grip on the
East Indian's penis, executes a swift, acrobatic maneuver
and gets into a kneeling position before him.

"O God, sahib!" cries the East Indian. "Leggo me totee!
Leggo me totee, sahib! Leggo! Ah beggin' you, sahib!"

With true bulldog tenacity, however, the Englishman re-
tains his grasp of the East Indian's "person." On his face
there is an obdurate look that plainly suggests his adherence
to the ancient maxim, "What I have, I hold."

On seeing me, the East Indian exclaims: "Sahib, people
watchin' we. Dey watchin' we, sahib—"

The Englishman, still retaining his grip on the East Indian's "pencil," turns his head in my direction. Even having
seen me, he only reluctantly releases his hold on the East Indian's penis. This, I later reflect, this is the spirit that built
the British Commonwealth and Empire Beyond the Seas.

The Englishman gets up from his knees with creaking, ar-
thritic difficulty and levels at me a look of deep distaste reserved especially for "the lesser breed without the law"
whenever they get beside themselves. I should like to explain—to apologize—for my untimely blundering upon so
intimate a scene. But he gives me no chance to do so. He
merely grunts his disapproval, hardly deigns to glance at
me, enters his cabin, and slams the door.

"What's the matter?" I ask the East Indian.

Plainly, he is overwhelmed by this shipboard encounter

100

with the Spirit of Empire in acquisitive action. When he re-
covers his tongue he replies: "The sahib want *me* to put *my*
totee in *his* mout'." But this, it seemed, was not a hazard to
which the East Indian was eager to expose his penis. No
doubt he counted among the risks the possibility that, carried away by imperial ardor, the Englishman might have
bitten it off.

I wondered, though, how he would have responded if it
had been the Prince of Wales—or the King-Emperor himself—who had expressed such a wish. As an obedient servant
of the Imperial Crown, would it not have been his bounden
duty to accede to it as a royal command? The question engrossed me. There was a certain constitutional nicety about
it. I sometimes speculated in my own mind as to what my
proper response should be were His Imperial Majesty the
King-Emperor to summon me to Buckingham Palace. I
would of course make my humble duty to my Sovereign by
prostrating myself at the foot of the royal throne and, my
forehead pressed against the carpeted floor, await the King-
Emperor's command. "De Paria," he would say to me, "I
know you are puzzled that I have bidden you instead of
your aunt Jocasta here. It is because I desire my daughter on
her impending birthday, when she comes of age, to have the
supreme happiness of sanga-wanga-in' with a Trinidadian
boy." Would it then be consistent with the duty of loyalty I
owe the Imperial Crown to respond: "Sire, I am a virgin"? I
am much troubled, and my sleep is often disturbed, by this
knotty point of colonial etiquette, not to speak of its constitutional implications.

Hardly less disquieting to me, however, had been the
spectacle of a colonial subject resisting, as Balgobin Maraj
had done, the express wish of an Englishman. There was
something enormously disenchanting to me about that
scene. I was afflicted with a sense of decline and of melancholy, deeper still when I recalled that the day—this day on
which it had occurred—was the twenty-fourth of May: Em-

pire Day. This was the day when, each year, we, the loyal people of Trinidad and Tobago, foregathered on the Queen's Park Savannah and elsewhere in borough, hamlet, and village to sing, "Rule, Britannia! Britannia rules the waves/Britons never, never, never shall be slaves!" We also sang "God bless the Prince of Wales." But that was before he found the burden of reigning over us to be insupportable unless he were allowed to have, propping him up as it were, the woman he loved. He needed help. All the damn battleships—*Hood, Repulse, Renown*, and the rest of them—were not enough for him. So we in Trinidad and Tobago, partly in wonderment and partly in derision at the weakling ways of pampered monarchs, sang:

> "Is love, *is love ah-lone*
> Dat cause King Edward to leave his t'rone!"

Sanga-wanga is hell, yes. O God, man!

Suddenly recollecting that he was almost nude, Maraj points to the Englishman's cabin. "He got all me clothes in there." He goes to the door and knocks gently. "Sahib? Sahib? Sahib?" In his voice there is profound entreaty, the loyal pleading of a dutiful colonial subject. But there is no answer.

"Wey Ah go' do?" Maraj asks, less of me than of the universe as a whole. He stands there, and I with him, aghast and bewildered at the ways of the Builders of Empire. "Wey Ah go' do?"

Abruptly, the Englishman's cabin door is thrown open. A bundle of clothing is heaved at the East Indian. The door slams shut again.

Balgobin Maraj (or Kapitän Gebumst, as the professor refers to him) stoops and gathers up the scattered garments, piece by piece. When he has recovered them all, he straightens up and with reverence addresses himself to the Englishman's cabin door. "T'ank you, sahib. T'ank you." He performs a salaam—a ceremonial act of obeisance—with the deepest respect and humility, bowing so low that he almost topples over.

His gratitude astonishes me. I consider it misplaced. But I say nothing. Yet I do not think he should be wandering about the ship clad only in his underwear. It is prison-striped and bell-shaped, and it balloons with a marked resemblance to a bathing costume fashionable at the turn of the century. His appearance is inelegant and unbecoming. Nevertheless, I invite him into my cabin so that he may put on his clothes. He takes more than an hour to do so. Much of the time is occupied with a self-pitying recital of his marital woes. Nothing is too intimate to be confided in me, an almost total stranger. "Me an' she was so nice, man. We 'n' use' to sanga-wanga every day—two, t'ree times." Recalling his vanished joys, his face lit up like a funeral pyre on the banks of the Ganges. "An' w'en de rain fall"—remembered ecstasy was liquescent in his eyes—"we 'n' use' to play 'goat.' 'Beh-h-h-h-h-h-h!' I 'n' use' to tell she w'en I feel like somet'ing—" His hands gravitated toward his "person." "'Beh-h-h-h-h-h!' An' she 'n' use' to tell me: 'Beh-h-h-h-h-h!' Den we sanga-wanga all night long." His face was enrapt with the bliss of memory. "We was nice, man. But now—" He spread his hands infinitely wide in a vain attempt to measure off the endless moons of his conjugal abstinence. "Ah don' know w'en las' Ah get on top o' she. But still an' all—" The nobility of the man's character shone through his sadness and despair. "Love is not love," he seemed to be saying with a poet somewhat better known in the colonies than Rabindranath Tagore, "that alters when it alteration finds." He clasped his hands together, interlacing the fingers in meekness and submission. "Ah'm carryin' she to England wid me—she an' Sita, me darter—because, jump high, jump low, she's me wife, an' w'en you married, boy—"

Hitherto, Balgobin Maraj had spent a good deal of the voyage informing all who listened that he invariably traveled "in style." By now most of the first-class passengers were aware that he had made fourteen crossings by ship between Trinidad and Tobago, an epic journey of less than thirty miles. But this was his first trip outside of the West Indies, and since his destination was England its importance to him from a social point of view could not be exaggerated. He foresaw a revolutionary change in his personal status. On his return to the island, he would take his place in an élite group who, like himself, had journeyed to England. By various ruses he had succeeded in obtaining the home addresses in England of some of the English bankers and merchants who resided and did business in Trinidad. A sample of the vital data he was interested in compiling for comparative purposes was, for instance: the size of their homes in England, how many servants they employed there, and so on. Armed with this information on his return, he would then be in a position to remind them that, for all the airs they gave themselves as colonial masters, they really did not amount to much "at home." "I'm going right into their bedroom in England," he had confided to his friends. "And another thing: I no sooner arrive in London than I want my shoes shined in Waterloo Station or Paddington—wherever the train comes in—by an Englishman. I hear they shine shoes and sweep the street there just like we do over here in Trinidad. I want to see it for myself."

Maraj also entertained political ambitions. "One of these days I'm going to be a big man in the legislature." For the time being, however, he was wholly intent on elevating his social position. His wife and daughter were traveling with him, but few of the other passengers had seen them since the beginning of the voyage. Maraj had explained this circumstance to the ship's company, without his having been asked to do so, by disclosing that his wife was prone to seasickness, and that his daughter had chosen to stay in the cabin and look after her. "And an ole white man—a German doctor—is looking after her, too." For some reason or other, whenever he imparted this information, he would clutch by the arm whoever it was he happened to be talking to and, leaning on his interlocutor for support, would collapse helpless with laughter. And when he had managed to subdue his enjoyment of the state of affairs he was describing, sufficient at any rate to regain a measure of coherence, he would exclaim: "But I know what I'm doing. Balgo"—his pet nickname for himself—"ehn't no coonoomoonoo [meaning "foolish"]. Balgo know de man is a capon. He keah do a damn t'ing."

Despite Dr. von Buffus's disclaimers, Maraj had decided that the learned man was a doctor of medicine and had insisted on consulting him about Mrs. Maraj's indisposition. Unable to get Maraj to understand that his four doctorates did not include a degree in medicine, the professor made suggestions about treating Mrs. Maraj. "Balgo" led him, well-nigh by main force, to visit Mrs. Maraj for clinical purposes. The professor's experience on entering the suite had caused him to prescribe that the portholes be opened at once and kept open. Mrs. Maraj began to make a rapid recovery. This further convinced "Balgo" that Dr. von Buffus was indeed a medical practitioner. As a result, the latter was spending much of the voyage in Mr. and Mrs. Maraj's suite, ministering to Mrs. Maraj and counseling her daughter, a beautiful girl of eighteen on whom filial duty had imposed a heavy weight of boredom.

The professor was also taking advantage of his shipboard leisure to work on a treatise that had occupied him intermittently over the last forty years. He was engaged in a consideration of the Hermetic philosophers and their influence on medieval and Renaissance thought. It was in particular his intention to reveal the intellectual affinity between Albertus Magnus and Hermes Trismegistos. This had involved him in close and comparative studies of Greek rationalism and Arab mysticism. He was slowly groping his way to the conclusion that the Western world, as a whole, was less indebted to the former than to the latter. That of course was contrary to the accepted view of Aristotle's two-millennia-long suzerainty over the thought of the Western world. As Dr. von Buffus saw it, the religious inspiration of the Western Church, especially in its more arcane aspects, derived a good deal more directly from Trismegistos than from Aristotle. An important proof of the correctness of this thesis was the doctrine, central to the belief of the Western Church, of divine revelation. It was completely unscientific and in stark opposition to the obsessive concern of Greek rationalism with systematic inquiry conditioned by a priori constraints. According to Dr. von Buffus, all a priori thinking was, inevitably, an exercise in the fallacy of *petitio principii.* He was therefore an impenitent anti-Aristotelian. The task he had set himself was nothing less than the intellectual rehabilitation of Hermes Trismegistos. He also hoped to show that the Christian dialectic of God the Synthesis—the Divine Reconciliation of the Thesis of Good and the Antithesis of Evil—was the natural parent of its Hegelian offspring. Mainly, however, Trismegistos preoccupied him. Much of his time these past decades had been spent in sometimes cloistered contemplation of the hermetic writings ascribed to Trismegistos, the Thrice-Greatest.

His lifelong absorption in arcane studies had given him something of the look of a medieval alchemist forever on the verge of achieving the fabled transmutation of base metals into gold. The same eager hope, the same wistful expectation, the same bemused frustration had contrived a suggestion about him of an old, dog-eared book whose pages had been turned with greater frequency than love. Yet this resemblance of his to a well-thumbed volume did not detract from the dignity, evident though not assertive, with which he carried himself as a man of learning. Short of stature and slight of build, his attenuated neck seemed to provide as insubstantial support for his great, magisterial head as did the fragile plinth of his stooped and narrow shoulders. As might indeed be expected of a man so immersed in the recondite, he gave little thought to outward adornment. His habitual dress consisted of a moribund green velvet jacket and trousers of tropical twill once, a generation ago, dark blue but now the despairing color of the last wisp of smoke before the fire goes out. And always he wore carpet slippers, indoors and outdoors, whatever the occasion.

On the first day at sea, Maraj had seen the professor leaning against the ship's rail in all his dog-eared decrepitude. His immediate impulse was to be helpful. For surely anyone looking like that must be in need of some assistance. The appearance the professor presented was that of a drooping, tousle-haired old hound no longer fit for any chase. It was impossible to imagine such a decayed old hound baying even the most cowardly of quarries up a tree. The professor had seemed collapsed rather than leaning against the ship's rail. Maraj knew that he was in some way connected with "that big-bam-bam woman in San Fernando," as he described Aunt Jocasta. Occasionally he had seen Dr. von Buffus from place to place about the town, yet they had never met. Recognition now reinforced in him an impulse of benevolence. He went over to Dr. von Buffus. "My name," he said, "is Balgobin Maraj. I am from Trinidad—from San Fernando. I am the sole proprietor of 'Balgobin Maraj: The Emporium: Dry Goods and Hardware.' I am traveling to England with my wife, Mrs. Maraj, and my daughter, Miss Sita Maraj."

The professor extended his hand. "Buffus zu Damnitz."

"May I offer you a drink, my good sir?" Maraj led the way to the ship's bar.

During the course of that evening and the progress of the next several days, Buffus zu Damnitz and Balgobin Maraj, in the long-established tradition of shipmates, became—from the latter's point of view, at any rate—"bosom friends." Maraj would muse, reflecting upon the swift evolution of their personal intimacy, "Man, I never see anyt'ing like this. Me an' the ole man 'come *so*—" And he would superimpose his middle finger on the index finger of the same hand to illustrate the closeness of the relationship that had developed between himself and the professor. Moderation is alien to the ethos of fellow passengers aboard ship. They either love or hate one another, extreme as bow and stern. Amplifying the point, "We're jus' like farder an' son," Maraj would announce. An equally close friendship between Mrs. Maraj and the professor also took root. At this point, Maraj was wont to declare to all and sundry that Dr. von Buffus was a "member of the family." To this Dr. von Buffus did not take exception. He obtained seasick pills from the ship's doctor and administered them to Mrs. Maraj. "Balgo" was profuse in his thanks. However, the professor declined the "fee" the grateful husband pressed upon him. He had wearied of reiterating that he was not a doctor of medicine. There was on this score an obstacle in Maraj's mind insurmountable by the idea that a man might indeed be a doctor though ignorant of medicine. The professor accepted his fate with the resignation of a scholar and the opportunism of an entrepreneur. There was a dramatic improvement in Mrs. Maraj's health. No one was more pleased than Maraj—except, of course, Dr. von Buffus himself.

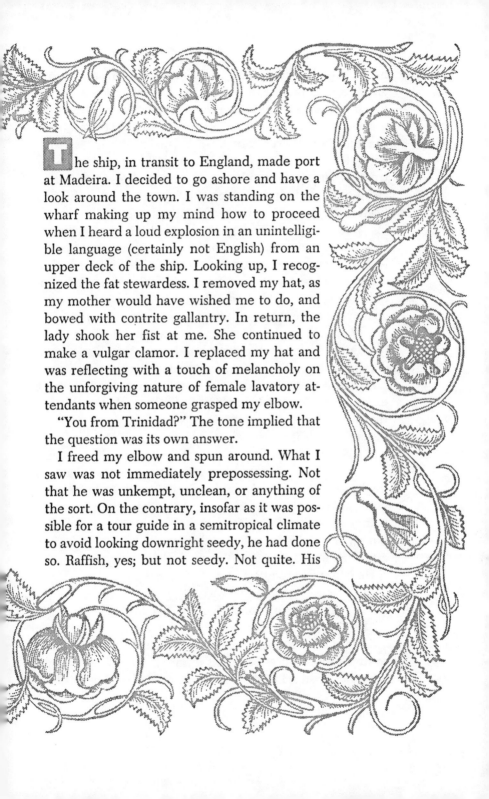

The ship, in transit to England, made port at Madeira. I decided to go ashore and have a look around the town. I was standing on the wharf making up my mind how to proceed when I heard a loud explosion in an unintelligible language (certainly not English) from an upper deck of the ship. Looking up, I recognized the fat stewardess. I removed my hat, as my mother would have wished me to do, and bowed with contrite gallantry. In return, the lady shook her fist at me. She continued to make a vulgar clamor. I replaced my hat and was reflecting with a touch of melancholy on the unforgiving nature of female lavatory attendants when someone grasped my elbow.

"You from Trinidad?" The tone implied that the question was its own answer.

I freed my elbow and spun around. What I saw was not immediately prepossessing. Not that he was unkempt, unclean, or anything of the sort. On the contrary, insofar as it was possible for a tour guide in a semitropical climate to avoid looking downright seedy, he had done so. Raffish, yes; but not seedy. Not quite. His hair escaped in marcelled waves and ringlets from beneath an official-seeming cap. And indeed it was official, for on closer inspection I saw that it bore a number engraved on a metal badge attached to the upper surface of the green-shaded visor. His uniform of dark material (unseasonably heavy for such a warm climate) was not freshly pressed—the trousers drooped seamless and disconsolate—but it was clean in a rough-dried fashion. I mean, it looked as if it had been washed and then hung out in the sun to dry before being put on again. The general effect of him—with his beaked nose convex in aquiline bas-relief against a round, leather-brown, Lusitanian face, and an obtrusive smell of cheap pomade, his uneven, tobacco-discolored teeth, his inquisitive ears beagling forward, his cowled, metal-gray eyes conveying surreptitious hints of tales to be whispered and horrors to be concealed—all this, in its general effect, while it did not repel, nonetheless created in me very distinct reservations about him. He was at once respectful and overfamiliar, and I was sure that if I ever became careless about exacting the former I should soon find myself subjected to the latter. There was something else, too, that increased the distance I felt it necessary to maintain from him, and that was the mirrorlike gloss of his needle-toed, Italian procurer's shoes. They shone with ostentatious polish so that one might almost see one's face reflected in their indecorous glitter. No gentleman, I thought, would be caught dead in a pair of shoes like those. Besides, there was a hoarse, sub rosa quality about his voice—a timbre of dubious, ingratiating, and even improper suggestiveness—that put me off.

He continued to question me. "From San Fernando?"

"Yes."

"You know the Black Cat Bar on High Street?"

"Yes."

"I used to work there." This piece of information was not so much disclosed as confided to me. I did not understand why, yet I had no interest in pursuing the matter. His face wore a curious approach to a smile—that is to say, more than a mere suggestion, but not quite a preliminary statement, of an intention to smile. "My name is Joe Caldeira." He said this as if it were the sort of intelligence that would, whenever communicated, result either in his canonization or his coronation. But as I did not seem to be aware of its earthshaking significance, he resumed his grip on my elbow and began to propel me along the quay.

With the renewal of his hold on my elbow, remembrance was rekindled. "Joe Caldeira ... ?" I stood still while embering memory flickered. Quickly it flared into a blaze of vivid recall. Joe Caldeira ... the Black Cat Bar ... High Street ... ? He too had paused and was regarding me with a smirk of triumphant self-satisfaction.

He brushed aside my astonishment. "Come," he told me. "Leh we go. We don' have too much time." He said this beneath his breath, lest, as it were, respectable people should overhear him. "I want to show you everything." And he once more took me by the elbow.

I felt an urge to resume possession of my elbow, but I wished to avoid giving him offense. At the same time, I did not care for the appearance I might convey to my shipmates of being under arrest.

"First we drink some wine. I take you to a factory." He examined my profile. "Then we see the town." His examination of my profile continued. At length, as if he had acquired data with which to warrant the inference, "You like girls—ha! You not from Trinidad for nothin'."

Then and there I decided that the fellow was inclined to be overfamiliar. Nothing in our acquaintance could justify the liberty he had just taken. I debated with myself whether to make this plain to him at once, but settled instead for the liberation of my elbow from his grip by a deft maneuver I had learned from a Syrian strongman in San Fernando with an expert knowledge of judo. Thereafter his tone grew respectful and, having taken the trouble to make certain of

111

my name, he called me "Mr. Johnny." This was more like it, I thought. I have never cared for excessive familiarity.

He conducted me on a wine-tasting tour of one factory after another. At the end of two hours or so, we had sipped three or four gallons of the choicest Madeiras and, as he judged it, I was ripe for the suggestion he now made.

"So now we go see the girls, eh, Mr. Johnny?"

I did not demur. I knew what was on his mind, but I was determined to set foot in England as I had departed from Trinidad, an honorable and unsullied male virgin. My virtue would be proof against any and every assault.

He led me into a short and reticent street lined with modest-looking houses, each having a small, exterior balcony. It was the hour of the midday siesta and the houses were shuttered against the afternoon sun. He knocked at a door that was indistinguishable from other doors on either side of it. The door was opened by a manservant and we entered into an atrium. It was cool and there was a sequestered air about it. The manservant indicated that we should be seated. He made us a formal bow and retired.

"Nice girls, Mr. Johnny. You see." My guide gave me a complicit look that I found distasteful. He had spent some time during our excursion to the wine factories advising me, in the fawning, confidential tone he employed, on the most effective ways of seducing respectable ladies. "But lissen to me, nuh," he had observed from time to time, giving me a sly, insinuating look, "tryin' to tell a Trinidad man how to sanga-wanga a woman. But you ever hear t'ing so?" This would be followed by a burst of laughter that could only be described as lewd. Since, however, he was being good enough to show me the sights of the town (even though for a fee), I did not think I should be severe with him. Unless, of course, he went too far, as often, it seemed, he was prone to do. As when now, for example, he was sketching in the air for me, quite unbidden, the voluptuous forms of the girls I should presently meet. I ignored him as politely as I could and pretended to be engrossed in the copy of Homer's *Odyssey* I was carrying with me.

"W'at you readin'?" Again, that repulsive laughter of his. "But Mr. Johnny, you's a funny one, yes." Before I could reprimand him, as it had begun to seem that I should be obliged to do, a lady materialized before us.

She was tall and thin and elderly, the very archetype of a maiden aunt or of a governess in retirement after a lifetime of devotion to children of the best families.

"The Madame," my guide whispered to me. Understanding him to mean that this dignified lady was the chatelaine under whose roof we were to be entertained, I arose, bowed, and took her proffered hand, saying courteously: "I am pleased to meet you, Madame."

She smiled, although her features retained their severe respectability. She reminded me so much of Aunt Jocasta that I began to feel homesick. My guide drew her aside and for a moment or two they held a low, whispered conversation. Because I did not altogether trust him, I strained to hear what he might be saying to her. I thought I detected his use of the words "rich" and "cocoa estate" in some obscure connection that could have had, of course, nothing to do with me. When, however, Madame next smiled at me, which was almost at once, I noticed that her features had lost a good deal of their initial severity.

"The Madame would like you to take a glass of wine with her." My guide winked at me.

She was seated now, and I was noting again with deepened nostalgia her resemblance to my aunt Jocasta when the manservant entered with a tray on which there were three glasses filled with what I assumed to be wine.

When I had been served, I arose and, with a bow to my hostess, pledged her health.

"You see w'at Ah was tellin' you?" Caldeira informed her. Not only did his remark seem to me gratuitous, but I did not understand how it was that they were able to communicate with each other, apparently about me, by means of a private code. Madame began to look rather less like my aunt Jocasta than I had originally supposed. Yet the resemblance remained sufficiently close to be startling. So, "Madame," I said, "you remind me of my aunt Jocasta."

It was an unfortunate remark. For Madame somehow understood me to mean that my aunt Jocasta was engaged in a business enterprise similar to the one, whatever it was, that she pursued. It was still not clear to me exactly what, if anything, my chatelaine might be engaged in, and I am disinclined by temperament to form precipitate conclusions. But whatever the nature of her business, at my disclosure of her resemblance to my aunt Jocasta, Madame became a great deal more animated, her features lost almost all of their severe respectability and she summoned her manservant to replenish our glasses. Her impression that she and my aunt Jocasta were in the same line of business was reinforced in covert ways by my guide. In order to avoid any misunderstanding on this point, I tried to explain that my aunt Jocasta was an extensive landowner in southern Trinidad, that she was a latter-day relic of colonial feudalism, and that she was a profoundly Victorian lady. "Rather like you," I told Madame, bringing the familiar to the illumination of the unknown. In response, Madame and my guide both indulged themselves in wheezing gusts of immoderate laughter. "You see w'at Ah tellin' you?" the latter repeated to the former. "Dis Mr. Johnny is a hell of a boy, oui!" The chatelaine wheezed again with pleasure and in obvious agreement. Enchanted, she shook her head.

"Bottoms up!" Caldeira exclaimed, raising his glass. Full of self-congratulation on having introduced so pedigreed and mirth-inspiring a guest to Madame, he signaled to me with an elaborate flourish of his upraised glass an invitation to drink with him.

I grew more and more displeased and I was considering

whether or not to "show my displeasure," as my mother would have said, when Madame spoke to me.

"How many girls has your aunt?"

I was taken aback by this question, for I had been at pains to make it clear that my aunt was a landowner and, moreover, that she was a maiden lady and, therefore, childless. Evidently, there was a misunderstanding. "My aunt Jocasta," I said, "has no children, Madame."

To my extreme bewilderment, she and my guide were once more afflicted by asthmatic and excessive laughter. As soon as he could get the words out between the intervals of his labored, guttural breathing, he again said to her: "You see w'at Ah tell you?"

Madame replied to him in what I thought to be Portuguese, a language I did not understand. Then, still somewhat convulsed with amusement, she inquired of me: "She has boys, then?"

If, previously, they had displayed signs of vast happiness (despite their respiratory difficulties), they now appeared to be ecstatic. Caldeira bounded up from his chair, held his head between his hands, slapped himself on the thigh, collapsed onto his chair, spread his arms wide, his legs doing their utmost to follow suit, while he gasped, rumbled, and stuttered in a more or less unsuccessful attempt to repeat Madame's inexplicable query. Madame herself was so transformed by her own delight that she no longer seemed at all severe and, had I been captious, I should even have thought that her features had lost most of their respectability. She no longer looked at all like my aunt Jocasta. Though, to be sure, she was as tall as Aunt Jo, wore her straight, black hair parted in the middle and constrained into a tight, formal bun at the back of her neck (just like my aunt's), had the same gray-blue eyes and sun-browned skin, and was dressed in an ankle-length black frock buttoned at the throat, in the fashion once made popular by her Imperial Majesty Queen Alexan-

115

dra of Great Britain and Ireland and loyally adhered to by Aunt Jocasta of San Fernando, Trinidad, long after the flapper couture of the 1920's.

It was, in fact, extraordinary and, now that I no longer approved of her, disturbing how much she still continued to resemble my aunt Jocasta. As for my guide, it was plain to me that he had been corrupted beyond redemption by his former employment at the Black Cat Bar in San Fernando and that I should be wise to keep a sharp eye on him. Madame, however, was directing another question to me. "How much does your aunt pay the chief of police?"

I saw now that uncommon patience would be required of me. While it was unthinkable that I should give way in any circumstances to the unrestrained glee exhibited by Madame and my guide, I thought a reserved smile would reassure them that, whatever the joke, my superior station in life did not altogether preclude me from sharing it with them. I also took the opportunity to reply to Madame with formal and resolute courtesy: "My aunt Jocasta does not employ our chief of police. He is a public servant and, I may say, one of the most upstanding of our townspeople."

This simple, straightforward statement increased, if possible, their already immense elation. There was more of "You see w'at Ah tellin' you?" on the part of my guide, addressed to Madame, and by this time not a particle of respectability lingered on her face. I thought I would be well advised to leave. My aunt Jocasta had expressly warned me against having anything to do with people who were prone to undue relaxation in their personal conduct. It was one of the last things she had said to me as I was bidding her farewell. "Always remember," she had enjoined me, "evil associations corrupt good manners." And here was I—

Madame brought the palms of her hands together with a subdued yet penetrating sound. This simple action had the most astonishing result. Into the room came a procession of young ladies, about a dozen of them, naked as the day they were born, though of course bearing visible signs of the wondrous changes that had taken place in their bodies since that initial event. Until now, peep as much as I might, never in all my life had I ever succeeded in seeing a bare-arsed lady. Here, all at once, only a few days' sail from Trinidad, I was half-surrounded by a dozen of them, for they had formed a semicircle in front of me. Whatever the depth of my surprise or the extent of my shock, I was prepared to be courteous. I rose to my feet and, carefully averting my eyes after a swift, all-seeing glance, bowed to the ladies. I remained standing. My head was uplifted and my eyes trained upon the remote distance. The circumstances were novel to me, to say the least, but I certainly did not intend to be deficient in good manners. As my mother had so often said to me: "Manners makyth man."

"Buy the girls a drink, Mr. Johnny," my guide suggested.

"By all means." I was as gracious in my response as my aunt Jocasta when the Roman Catholic priest had come to call and she was expecting the Anglican canon of her parish. "Please ask the ladies what they will have." I studied the stained-glass window at the far end of the atrium with all the concentrated interest of an archeologist at a new and unexpected find of vast historical significance.

One or two of the ladies had been giggling, but something like a general titter of approval now arched across the semicircle.

Caldeira interpreted it for me. "They like you, Mr. Johnny."

"They are most kind," I replied. If there was a certain stiffness, there was also a manly firmness and resolution in my tone. I knew what my mother would say of my conduct in the circumstances. She would be pleased and she would quote a favorite couplet of hers:

"He nothing common did or mean
Upon that memorable scene."

117

My aunt Jocasta would be less literary, but, I felt, no less commending of my behavior.

"Which one you like, Mr. Johnny?"

Diplomacy seemed to me to be essential to a correct solution of the problem with which I was confronted. So I said to my guide: "I like them all."

What had been a titter among the ladies now enlarged into laughter. This was augmented by the asthmatic delight of Madame and my guide. "You see w'at Ah'm tellin' you?" he called out to her. "Ah know w'at Ah sayin', yes."

The manservant entered with drinks for everyone. As he was proffering the salver to Madame, and I was experiencing an incorrect urge to inspect the nude ladies rather than study the bare ceiling, my guide remarked to me: "But you don' have time for all o' dem, Mr. Johnny. Only one. You' ship—"

Here indeed was a predicament. I had supposed that there would be "safety in numbers," another of my mother's favorite sayings. If, however, the field were narrowed down to one, I should have, inversely, less room for maneuver. "There'll be time enough for everything." I tried to impart to my voice a seasoned, man-of-the-world ring of assurance.

"O God, Mr. Johnny! But you's a real Trinidadian, yes. Not all o' dem, Mr. Johnny. Not all o' dem. Take one." He demonstrated a single digit with a stunted forefinger. "You got— lemme see—two, t'ree hours befo' you eat dinner. But yo' ship ain' leavin' 'til nine o'clock tomorrow mornin'. Yo' know dat?"

I knew that.

Madame demanded attention. She wished to propose my health. With an erudition that would have done credit to my aunt Jocasta, she likened me to Paris confronted with the necessity to choose one woman as being the most beautiful of all. (Her statement was not excessive in its implied universality, for the ladies were of all races under the sun, as it had seemed to me when they marched in and I, for an un-

118

gentlemanly moment, had found myself unable to divert my gaze from their unconcealed midriffs.) She could assure me, however, that my choice would not be fraught with those consequences that had given the judgment of Paris its momentous and not wholly mythic outcome. Her establishment was fortunate, she said, in the agreeable harmony of my personality and intentions with its character and resources. So that, however I might choose, only happiness would ensue. She considered herself honored by my visit and flattered by the knowledge that my distinguished aunt was also engaged in the business that had occupied her now for fifty years. She would look forward with a sense of the utmost distinction to meeting my aunt, between whom and herself there were such intimate links of personal taste, as well as professional interest and experience. She wished me robust and unvarying health my life long, and happiness not only for the next succeeding hours under her roof, but for all eternity to come, between whatever banks of destiny the river of my life might take its splendid course.

I have since heard many great orators. I have listened to speeches whose verbal tapestry was woven out of the transcendent stuff of some high historic hour. But Madame's toast to me survives in my memory as the very greatest of them all. I admit that she misconceived the nature of Aunt Jocasta's occupation and mistook my aunt's profession for her own. It was the unintended result of an honest misapprehension. The greatness of her inspiration and the apposite expression of her sentiments remain unequaled and unsurpassed in my judgment.

She raised her glass and the rest of the company drank with her.

In reply, I said that I deeply regretted the absence of my aunt Jocasta, between whom and my beautiful and gracious hostess (I bowed to Madame) a meeting would provide an instructive degree of mutual illumination. I expressed the conviction that Madame would find Trinidad much to her taste, especially if she were accompanied there by her love-ly "children" (as I referred to the ladies) and escorted by my generous guide, Mr. Caldeira. (The last-named person here interrupted, exclaiming: "W'at Ah tell you? You see w'at Ah tell you? This boy can talk like hell, oui! He does talk jus' like co'beaux [carrion crows] does shit." The fellow's coarseness, especially in the presence of Madame and the ladies, revolt-ed me. At any rate, I continued.) My visit to Madame's gra-cious abode was, for me, an experience as unprecedented (much to my chagrin, I mispronounced that word) as it was fascinating. (At this point, my guide interjected: "O God, Mr. Johnny! Lang-widge, boy! Buh lissen to 'im parlez, nuh. Lissen to 'im parlez. Lang-widge, boy! Lang-widge!") I wished to assure Madame and her exquisite "children" that they would always be as welcome in Trinidad and, in partic-ular, among my family as I ventured to hope that I should be in Madame's hospitable residence on any future occasion when I might have the happiness of retracing my footsteps to her door. (Madame nodded several times in pleased and vigorous affirmation.) Might they all, I ended, enjoy many years of joyous consecration to their high calling, and at its close might each and every one of them be crowned with the matchless diadem of jeweled and protracted ease.

I raised my glass. As I did so, I was aware of the general admiration with which my remarks had been received. Ma-dame had been incomparable, yet I felt that I myself had not fallen far short of the sovereign majesty of the occasion.

"Bottoms up!" cried my guide, tossing his head back as the glass traveled upward to his lips. He gulped the wine down and then said to me, as he had earlier done: "Which one you want, Mr. Johnny?" With one hand he indicated the irregular arc of naked girls who stood there sipping from their wineglasses and whispering to each other.

Madame settled the matter for me. Had the goddess been as thoughtful in the case of Paris, the Greeks would have been spared much dissension and Homer would have had less to lament. My chatelaine moved with slow and spacious dignity up and down the rear of the line. Then, pausing behind one of the ladies, she smacked her smartly, though not unkindly, on the backside. The chosen one took a step forward. The other ladies bowed to me, I to them, and they withdrew.

My guide said to Madame, "We better leave them alone, eh?" And as they too went off, he remarked to her: "I have to go back to the ship to pick up a ole frien' o' mine. 'E's a professor."

The young lady and I faced each other.

Now it is a fact, conceded the world over, that all of the ladies of Trinidad are both beautiful and kind. There is a civilized fragrance of character about them that has attained its essential expression in the calypso:

> "Me Mooma tell me don' ride wid strangers
> In deh moto'-car
> An' though you look like a decent stranger
> You might go too far.... "

Observe the sense of filial duty, the respectful inclination to obey. At the same time, consider the delicacy with which she hints that an exception might be made in the instance of a "decent stranger." To such an exception, surely, no reasonable parent could demur. Finally, regard the cautious apprehension tempered by the wistful hope that such a "decent stranger" yet "might go too far." No man who has ever lingered on Frederick Street in Port-of-Spain at four o'clock in the afternoon, when the shops and other business places release their female captives at the end of the working day, has ever afterward been able to leave Trinidad without weeping great salt lakes of tears for a lost Paradise. This is also true of Kingston, Jamaica; Castries, St. Lucia; Bridgetown, Barbados; St. George's, Grenada; and the capital city of every former Caribbean jewel of the British Imperial Crown. A group of touring Russians from the High Cauca-

sus, dedicated communists all, renounced forever the celebrated charms of their Circassian women and sought political asylum in Trinidad after having stood on Frederick
Street in Port-of-Spain at four o'clock in the afternoon. During the old colonial days, whenever a Royal Commission was
sent to Trinidad and Tobago to investigate the local state of
readiness for freedom and independence, thereby wasting
everyone's time and their own (not to speak of the very considerable expense to the island's taxpayers), a proven method of handling such intrusions was readily available. The
Royal Commission used to be taken en masse to Frederick
Street at four o'clock of an afternoon. Thereafter they never
bothered anybody. When they were eventually persuaded
to go home after having exceeded their prescribed stay by
several weeks, they would report their unanimous finding
that Trinidad and Tobago would not be ready for freedom
and independence for at least another hundred years, and
that meanwhile a Royal Commission should be dispatched
to the colony every year for a tour of inquiry lasting from
three to six months in order to keep in touch with native developments. In fact, about one hundred and fifty years ago,
an entire Royal Commission defected and took up residence
in Port-of-Spain. Their descendants now comprise a thriving
and industrious community. They are among the island's
most exemplary capitalists. They own and operate with impressive success all the brothels on Wrightson Road where
the Gulf of Paria forms a western moat that, unfortunately,
was inadequate to deter that poxy adventurer, Christopher
Columbus.

So I shall be taken with exact and scrupulous literalness, I
trust, when I say that even by the peerless standards of my
native Trinidad, the young lady now standing before me
was of superlative loveliness. Her skin was the color of the
heart of a sun-ripened sugar cane. While my good manners
would not permit me to subject her to detailed scrutiny and
minute inspection, a glance was sufficient to assure me that

I was in the presence of the equal of any of the magnificent four o'clock flowers of Frederick Street. To be sure, I had never encountered any of those young ladies in quite the present circumstances. Yet after making that allowance, I was bound to conclude that there, too, on Frederick Street in Port-of-Spain, she would have held her own.

"You want to come with me?" It was difficult to say which was more deeply ravished—my eye by her loveliness or my ear by the lilt of her voice. She spoke in imperfect English accented like a musical chant. Trinidadian girls are worshiped in every quarter of the globe for the liquid melody of their speech, among other things, but this young lady's voice cast over me a spell at least as potent.

"May I?" I said, taking off my coat and offering it to her. She declined it with a gesture of such ineffable innocence and grace that I felt as though I had committed an unpardonable breach of the code of good manners which my mother and Aunt Jocasta had inculcated in me. I followed her out of the room. Walking behind her, I at first kept my head tilted toward the ceiling out of modesty. No well-bred Trinidadian would ever survey a lady's backside without her explicit invitation. But fearing lest I should stumble and thereby alarm her, I lowered my head. "Carapichaima!" I exclaimed under my breath. "This girl is nice, man." (For the benefit of those readers unacquainted with the geography of my native land, Carapichaima is an ancient Carib place-name for a rural settlement in Trinidad.) She glided forward without the slightest tremor of her pneumatic bottom. Observing this moving spectacle, I recalled that for "bottom," my aunt Jocasta often employed the word "hillocks." Depending on the circumstances, "If you do (or don't), I shall spank your hillocks. . . ." The young lady preceding me was neither slender nor plump. She could have run at record-breaking speed and there would have been no jouncing movement of her full, sculptured breasts nor the merest quiver of her taut behind.

123

Her room was severely functional. There was a chair, a bed. There was also a screen behind which she now retired for some esoteric purpose. When she emerged, she was wearing (such was her modesty) silken drawers. But her breasts remained innocently uncovered.

She reclined onto the bed with all the grace of a deer in a forest glade in Trinidad going to sleep at nightfall. She invited me to share it with her.

I took a firm hold on my copy of Homer's *Odyssey*.

"Take off your clothes," she suggested. A sweet and artless courtesy reaffirmed her innocence.

"Thank you," I replied. "I'm not warm."

"You not?" She turned over on her side and considered me. I had remained standing. "You don't like me?"

"O, indeed, I do. You are"—I fumbled for the complimentary phrase I wanted—"most charming."

"You think—?"

"O, yes. Most charming. I do think so. I assure you."

"Why you not take your clothes off?"

The question presented me with a difficulty. I could not very well explain that I had never previously undressed in the presence of a lady without perhaps implying that she was immodest to have made such a request of me. Neither could I disclose the fact that I was a virgin without perhaps imputing some moral reproach to her. Good manners alone required that I do everything possible to refrain from impugning her in any conceivable way. "Manners makyth man." Whatever I should do or say, I was resolved to observe good manners. I therefore launched into an extended disquisition on the difference between the climate of Trinidad and that of Madeira. I spoke of their relative latitudes, their distance from the equator, the Trinidadian rain forest and the absence of similar forestation in Madeira and its consequent influence upon the climate. I spoke of the danger of pneumonia from unwise exposure and, granted only a constitution that was less than robust, the peril of decline into tuberculosis and the risk of my infecting her with that distressing ailment. I should never forgive myself, I said, if by any selfish want of restraint and, above all, an absence of good manners, I were to expose her to a hazard so dreadful in its probable consequences.

Somehow or other, despite my discourse on comparative climatology (or perhaps because of the exertion it had entailed), my hands were growing clammy, so that the copy of Homer's *Odyssey* almost slipped from my grasp. My breathing was also growing shorter, with an irregularity that I had never before experienced. Other unusual phenomena were manifesting themselves and I tried, surreptitiously, to lengthen the front of my jacket. I was obliged to cross my legs, for my "pencil" (my aunt Jocasta's polite euphemism) was asserting a powerful urge to do some illicit writing. Altogether I was most uneasy. Only a few days' sail from Trinidad and I was already a different person. I decided to concentrate on the excellence of my upbringing and to tighten my hold on the *Odyssey*.

"Take it off," she whispered in a voice lutelike with entreaty.

I began to feel as if I were in the grip of a hypnotic spell, and in the most curious fashion I was actually perspiring, though the room was by no means hot.

I managed a courteous smile in response to her entreaty, and when she whispered again, "You don't want to lie down?" I thanked her, saying that I was not at all tired.

"What is your name?" she asked.

"John Sebastian Alexander Caesar Octavian de Paria," I said. "But everyone calls me Johnny."

"Johnny? I's nice name. And you nice, Johnny. Gentle. So gentle." What I would interpret later on as a spasm of anguish zigzagged across her face. "Not like—"

I was a trifle embarrassed by her good opinion of me. "You are most kind," I said. "May I ask your name? Please forgive me"—I searched the expression formulated in the

125

space between her eyes, endeavoring to be certain that I was maintaining a correct restraint—"if I'm being presump—"

"What mean you? My name? I have no name."

"Ah, but you must! Everyone has a name."

She shook her head, looking at me with a sort of unbelief in her eyes and a suspicion of amusement, too.

"Come," I said, "you are teasing me. Tell me—" But I could see that she wouldn't, at least not yet. So I altered my approach. "I shall guess it. How many guesses do you give me?" She, however, would not enter into the game. Instead she covered herself with a portion of the sheet.

"Since you won't tell me your name, I shall give you one. Let me see, let me see...." I sought to achieve the necessary inspiration by raveling up my brow. "Yes, yes—I know: Dorothea—Dorothea—I shall call you—"

"Dorotea?" She frowned and smiled. "What mean it— 'Do-ro-te-a'?" Her frown deepened. "Do-ro-te-a?"

"It means 'Gift of God.'" I knew this because I had once heard Aunt Jocasta say that it would have been my name if I had been a girl and that the name meant, as I had just exhausted the entire sum of my erudition in explaining to Dorothea, "Gift of God."

"Gift from God? Me? Gift from God?"

"Yes. You. 'Gift of God.' You—Dorothea—"

She smiled. "You sweet." Her gaze alighted softly on me.

"Dorothea—?"

Her smile indulged rather than accepted the play of my fancy in so naming her.

"How old are you—Dorothea?"

She laughed. "Do-ro-te-a," she repeated. She laughed again. "I have sixteen years." Her voice was the murmur of a seashell bringing distant tidings in the fleeting hush of midday.

"Were you born here—in Madeira?"

"No. I come from Azores." She was studying me intently. "You t'ink I crazy, no?"

"Crazy?"

"Funny, no?"

I, however, would not be turned aside from my pursuit of more information about her. "And why—how—?"

I suddenly realized that I was on the point of prying. Very bad manners, indeed. So I was silent, and in order to restrain myself from further grossnesses, I opened the *Odyssey* without intending to peruse it, for that also would have been bad manners, of course. I merely wanted to keep a careful rein on myself. For aside from the risk of bad manners, my "person"—in my mother's phrase—was growing quite restive. I had begun to sweat again and I was aware of an ungentlemanly desire to remove the sheet that Dorothea had pulled over herself. This was all very unusual. At the same time, I could see that Dorothea was experiencing similar sensations by the way she was looking at me without saying anything, yet achieving the most explicit communication.

She shifted her body, and for some reason or other, I found it necessary to stifle a groan. But she did not remove the sheet. "What you want, Johnny?"

I sighed. "O, I don't know, Dorothea. I wish I knew—"

She shifted her body again. It was curious how disturbing an effect so innocent a motion was having on me. I was not at all myself.

"Johnny? You no want me?"

"O, Dorothea. Want you?"

"Yes, Johnny. Come. Take off your clothes. You so sweet." She threw aside the sheet.

The *Odyssey* fell from my hands. The clatter of the book against the floor broke the spell and I saw now, clearly, that it was my duty to protect this enchanting girl against my lamentable weakness, as my mother would have said. That was my plain moral duty, as Aunt Jocasta too would have said. So, having retrieved the *Odyssey* from the cool, checkered floor, I suggested to Dorothea: "Let me read to you, may I?"

She replaced the sheet over herself. "What you read?"

"The *Odyssey* of Homer."

"Ho-ma?"

"Yes. Homer. A Greek poet. The professor says, one of the greatest of—"

"An' you, Johnny? What you is?"

"Me?" Just a good calypso man, I thought. "I'm on my way to London—to read—for the bar." I felt somewhat foolish saying this.

"Bar? You like get drunk, Johnny?"

"Get drunk? O, I see. No. What I mean is, become a lawyer."

"Same thing, Johnny. Lawyer like get drunk. Much lawyer come here."

"Here? You know lawyers, Dorothea?"

"What you mean? Sure I know lawyer."

A vague dissatisfaction stirred in me. Surely I was being inquisitive. It occurred to me that, for the sake at least of good manners, I should abandon this indelicate line of questioning. After all, what... "I mean—" I wavered halfway between retreat and persistence.

"I know what you mean." It was plain that she was trying to be helpful. "I make business, Johnny."

"Business?" I pretended to be groping for the truth that was crystal clear to me.

The pride of vocation uplifted Dorothea's head. Her eyes met mine directly. "I am businesswoman."

"Ah, I see." I pondered the matter with as much a man-of-the-world air as I could command. And it was precisely at this point that I realized it was my duty as a gentleman to marry Dorothea because of the compromising circumstances in which I had placed her by being closeted with her, as I was, while she reclined in a state of partial undress. I had been gravely derelict in my manners, and only by marrying the victim of my unspeakable lapse could I restore myself to the status of a gentleman. I felt, however, that admirable though my intention, it yet required further consideration. It was the first responsibility of a gentleman, I had often heard Aunt Jocasta say, not to be a damn fool. In order, then, to return myself to a condition that I might recognize as one of solid and familiar common sense, "Let me read you something from the *Odyssey*," I told Dorothea.

She weighed my suggestion before replying, "Read me, yes."

As I read, she grew more and more intent, and her eyes never left my face. Her eyes: have I said that they were soft and apple-green, deep inset and lambent against the olive-brown of her skin? She lay on her side, supporting her weight on an elbow with her head resting, a proud and beautiful trophy, on the plinth of her open hand. I would sometimes pause and ask, "Shall I stop?"

"No. Read me. What you read—I know it. It happen."

So I continued. When at length I came to the end of the third book: "Now when the sun had set and darkness was over the land . . ." she interrupted me for the first time.

"It get dark, Johnny."

I saw now, indeed, that she was right. I had been so absorbed in the music of the *Odyssey*, I'd not noticed that the sunlight was retreating from the room. It would soon be night. I should have to think about dinner. The ship was not sailing until nine o'clock the following morning, and I could either return and dine on board or stay ashore and have dinner at a restaurant. In either case, I thought, with Dorothea as my guest.

"Will you dine with me this evening? We could go to the ship or, if you prefer, a restaurant somewhere in the town."

She slid her supporting arm beneath her body and laid her head on the pillow. "I have to work."

I knew what she meant. What a pity, I thought, looking at her and feeling suddenly swamped by huge sea swells of anger at the maladroitness of the universe.

There was a knock on the door. Dorothea sighed and sat up. "I's you' frien'." She drew up her legs and rested her head on her knees. "You have go," she told me.

"Certainly not. Unless you—"

"No. I want you stay. But you have go."

There was another knock, twice repeated.

"Go say, Johnny, you go."

I went to the door, opened it with care, holding it narrowly ajar so that my guide (for it was he) could not see into the room.

"Mr. Johnny," he said. "You had a good time?" He was grinning as if he and I were complicit in something that may have been nasty but was also enjoyable. I was furious. But I replied calmly: "Very nice. But not what you think. We're going out to dinner. Not you," I disabused him at once. "We—" I looked back into the room and saw that Dorothea had disappeared behind the screen.

"You mean you goin' to keep she for the whole night? It go' cost you—"

"I don't care what it costs." The whole night? That had not occurred to me. However, why not? I could go on reading the *Odyssey* to her after dinner. It would be fun. She was clearly enjoying the story. "Yes. I shall keep her, as you say, the whole night."

"But Mr. Johnny, you's a hell of a boy, oui. You jus' leave home—an' look at you." He stepped back the better to survey me. "You's a man already." That repulsive laughter of his shook him. I felt an acute distaste for the fellow. He reminded me of exactly those people in Trinidad of whom Aunt Jocasta was accustomed to say: "Evil communications corrupt good manners."

But I was resolved to remain courteous to him. "I am prepared to pay whatever is required."

An ectoplasmic figure floated along the unlighted corridor and presently became corporeal in the person of Madame. "Good evening," I said, bowing to her.

"Mr. Johnny want she for the whole night," my guide informed her.

"Ah, youth," she sighed. A fluttery wisp of a giggle escaped her. She went in search of it with a self-conscious smile, failed to recover it, and resumed her formal, business-like manner. "My choice pleased you?"

It is impossible to convey my disgust at this trafficking that was taking place between us. Nevertheless I replied without, I think, the slightest hint of discourtesy in my tone: "Indeed, Madame, I have been very happy in your choice." The only exception my aunt Jocasta might have taken to my conduct would have been, perhaps, on the ground of my somewhat less than complete aloofness. I could also hear my mother's voice: "Always maintain your distance, my son." I decided to conclude matters without stooping to bargaining in any form whatever. I would not sully my companion by huckstering. I refused, accordingly, to ask, "How much?" Yet I knew what the circumstances required of me. There was a price on Dorothea exacted by the nature of the business she was obliged to engage in. I took out my wallet and handed it to Madame. Even in the dusk of the lightless corridor I was able to see the look of astonishment that swept over her face. My guide himself regarded Madame with an expression on his face that plainly said: "Do you see what sort of clients I bring you?" His triumph was evident, if also vulgar. I do not care for exultation in any form. At Aunt Jocasta's insistence, I had learned by heart a line or two of a bathetic poem by a posturing Anglo-Indian:

> "If you can meet with triumph or
> disaster
> And treat those two imposters both
> the same . . ."

131

If I were to spend more time with my guide, I should certainly find it essential to impress upon him, as my mother would say, "a becoming reserve in sunshine or in sorrow."

Madame stood for a few moments with my wallet in her hand held at the level of her chest while she gave me a long, appraising look. She returned the wallet to me, unopened. "I am honored to have you under my roof," she said. "Before you leave—tomorrow morning—should you care to make a gift to the house—" I noted the respect in her eyes. "I believe that this is how your distinguished aunt would act in similar circumstances."

I was aware of a recurrence of my original unease at her misconception of Aunt Jocasta's business. Yet since the latter had always impressed upon me that a gentleman never argues with a lady, I refrained from making the necessary correction so as to avoid the risk of involving Madame in an exchange at cross-purposes. Caldeira was viewing me with all the pride of a debauched uncle in a dissolute nephew and fondly exclaiming over and over again to Madame: "W'at Ah tell you? W'at Ah tell you, eh? You see w'at Ah tell you? Dis boy is hell self, oui!" Then addressing himself to me: "You' ship sail nine o'clock in the mornin', Mr. Johnny. Eight o'clock I will come fer you." He launched into a well-known Trinidad calypso, throwing his arms upward and singing in an astonishingly fine calypso voice a lisping girl's anxious warning to her "sweetman" as they lay together in bed, taking their ease after an hour of love, that her grandmother would be returning any moment now:

"Lord Invader, det up!
Gwanmudder tomin' twelve o'clock. . . ."

He rotated his hips, swiveling and sometimes jerking them backward and forward with a vile, lubricious dexterity. His pleasure at his own performance exploded into a shout of revolting laughter. "Sleep good," he told me, and winked and leered. I was relieved that he could no longer claim Trini-

132

dad (in particular, my home town of San Fernando) as his place of abode. Even by the somewhat relaxed standards of the southernmost Caribbean, he was, I thought, an extraordinarily common person. His years at the Black Cat Bar on High Street had done him little good. I was careful, however, to keep the least trace of censoriousness out of my voice as I thanked him and confirmed that I should expect him to call for me at eight o'clock in the morning. The contrast between his knowing familiarity and Madame's correct reserve was a precise illustration of the wisdom of my mother's oft-repeated injunction that "Manners makyth man."

This man, Caldeira—my guide—was almost entirely without manners. How sad. If I were going to be here only a little longer. . . .

"Would you care to have breakfast served in the morning?" Madame assumed rather than awaited my reply. "At seven?"

I bowed acceptance and thanked her.

Whereupon my guide made a fist of his right hand, and shaking his lower arm to and fro on the hinge of his elbow, he said to me: "Don' spare she, Mr. Johnny. Gi'e she de 'number-ten'! Gi'e she de 'number-ten'!" His fist descended toward his privy member and there continued its obscene, pumping motion. He laughed again in that repellent fashion of his, and even in the darkness I could see the disgusting leer on his face. "W'en de mango ripe, eat it!" he counseled me.

At this point, I was of two minds as to whether or not I should announce forthwith my intention to marry Dorothea. But I restrained myself. As I shut the door behind me after they had gone away, I couldn't help reflecting that whatever they might fear as to my substantive purpose, neither Aunt Jocasta nor my mother would disapprove of my manners. And there, sitting on the edge of the bed in the dusk of the room, was Dorothea.

"They've gone," I told her.

"I go, too."

"O, no. You needn't. You mustn't. Unless—" I thought to strengthen my case by invoking authority. "They said that we could have dinner together—and breakfast in the morning."

"I hear them."

"Well, don't you—wouldn't you—care to dine with me?"

"I like, yes. But maybe is not good for you."

"For me?" I was incredulous.

"Yes. For you. For me, is nothing. For you—"

I now saw that she was fully dressed. She moved to the window and stood there looking out on the night. Something odd was taking place in my throat. My breath seemed to be impeded on its way out. She turned around and her eyes were aglow with their strange chalcedony. "Johnny," she said, "come here."

I went to her.

"You know what you doing?"

"Doing? Why, yes. Taking you out to dinner, and reading to you, and talking with you, having breakfast in the morning."

"Yes?"

"Yes." I smiled at her, but she did not return my smile.

She resumed her scrutiny of the night while I went to a small, oval wall mirror in the room to make sure of the set of my tie and the hang of my coat. As I was maneuvering the knot of my tie into a neater relationship with my collar, she came over to me. "Kiss me, Johnny."

I laughed to conceal my embarrassment. It was an awkward effort and it sounded, to my ears, hollow. I was uneasy.

"You never kiss girl?"

"No." I felt extremely callow and unfledged. "Never."

"Never? You funny, Johnny. So funny. How you never kiss girl?" She regarded me with the look of a child who has discovered a strange though harmless insect. "You is how much years?"

134

"Twenty-one—last February—the twelfth."

"Twenty-one. You have years more than me. And you never kiss?"

I began once more to experience that curious sweating sensation I've already noted, accompanied by other clinical manifestations involving my "person"—as, I reminded myself, my mother would say. But the thought of my mother struck me as a quite unnecessary intrusion at that moment. As she herself would have observed, "There is a time and place for everything." I thrust aside the memory of her.

"Kiss me, Johnny."

"Well," I faltered, suspended between inhibitory moral precepts and the insurrection of my "pencil"—in Aunt Jocasta's phrase. Aunt Jocasta—I was quite unexpectedly irritable at the thought of her at just this moment. There is a time and place . . .

"Kiss me, Johnny." She placed her hands on my shoulders. Her breasts caressed my chest and her face rose toward mine, making me a free and compelling gift of her exquisite lips.

I kept a firm grip on myself. "Let me think—"

"You no t'ink, Johnny. You kiss."

I was in a state of some befuddlement. If I were to kiss her, would I not as a result of my "lamentable weakness" (in my mother's words—I was again irritated by this inconvenient remembering of my mother), would I not—? There was, I noticed, a delicious little mole a fraction of a millimeter beyond the corner of one side of Dorothea's lips. I breathed in the fragrance of her, my senses whirling about in a violent hurricane of wanting, my person "weeping" passionately under the stress of my iron resolution to be a gentleman.

Dorothea had closed her eyes, certain of the arrival of the magic carpet that would transport her to bliss. It was a moment or so before she realized that her departure would be indefinitely postponed. She sighed and opened her eyes.

My head had spun off into outer space and was orbiting there weightless, emancipated from gravity.

"Tonight—later, Johnny—you kiss, yes?"

I knew that I was in the throes of a last-ditch struggle to maintain my standing as a gentleman. The outcome was gravely in doubt. "Let's have dinner," I said.

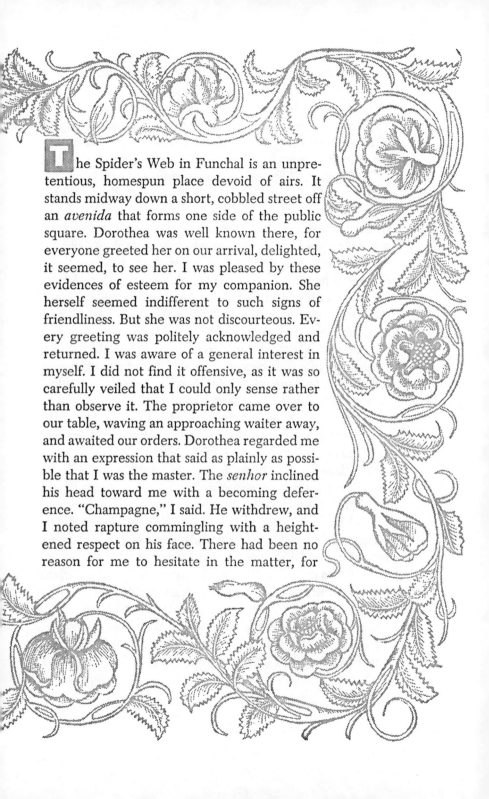

The Spider's Web in Funchal is an unpretentious, homespun place devoid of airs. It stands midway down a short, cobbled street off an *avenida* that forms one side of the public square. Dorothea was well known there, for everyone greeted her on our arrival, delighted, it seemed, to see her. I was pleased by these evidences of esteem for my companion. She herself seemed indifferent to such signs of friendliness. But she was not discourteous. Every greeting was politely acknowledged and returned. I was aware of a general interest in myself. I did not find it offensive, as it was so carefully veiled that I could only sense rather than observe it. The proprietor came over to our table, waving an approaching waiter away, and awaited our orders. Dorothea regarded me with an expression that said as plainly as possible that I was the master. The *senhor* inclined his head toward me with a becoming deference. "Champagne," I said. He withdrew, and I noted rapture commingling with a heightened respect on his face. There had been no reason for me to hesitate in the matter, for

Aunt Jocasta always insisted that when entertaining a lady, a gentleman naturally ordered champagne.

"Dorothea?" I began, and for some reason could not go on. In all my life I had never suspected myself of a stammer. But now something like it, slight perhaps yet distinct, was impeding my speech. "Dorothea?" I said again.

"Yes, Johnny?" She sat with her hands in her lap and her head bowed, smiling. Her voice was very soft, almost a whisper. I would give my life to protect her, I thought, and I wished, inwardly, for occasions to prove my attachment to her. Our eyes kept tryst, and when I suddenly looked up, the proprietor was standing there, his manner suffused with respect as he held a bottle of champagne toward me for my approval. I noted the vintage, as Aunt Jocasta had told me I should always be sure to do. "Nineteen thirty-three," I remarked. "Was that a good year?"

"One of the best, *senhor.*" He cradled the bottle with the tenderness of a connoisseur. This was one of the signs Aunt Jocasta had told me to look for. I was satisfied. The realization that I was actually ordering champagne for a lady quite overcame me. Time and again had Aunt Jocasta raised this possibility in her lectures to me on the manner in which a gentleman conducts himself. I felt certain that so far I had in no way been unworthy of the principles she had instilled in me. Dorothea plainly was of the same opinion, for though her hands were still folded on her lap and her head still bowed, there was an air of modest pride about her as she observed the easy skill and masterly address with which my behavior proclaimed me a man of the world. To tell the truth, I was not at all displeased with myself. The proprietor made a point of tacitly drawing to the attention of the other customers my preference for champagne. I could see by the respectful looks they gave me that they appreciated my demonstration of good taste. Nor, to judge by their admiring regard for her, had Dorothea declined in their estimation.

The proprietor poured the champagne and I raised my glass to Dorothea. The eyes of the whole room were upon me and I was more than ever conscious of my duty to live up to Aunt Jocasta's precepts. I rose from my seat, bowed to Dorothea, took a sip from my glass, and resumed my seat. A low murmur of approbation rustled through the room. With an imperious gesture, the proprietor directed a waiter to my table. The latter came posthaste, bearing the *cartas* on a salver. I motioned to him to give one to Dorothea while I removed the other. We studied the menu and consulted together. I possessed a bare smattering of Spanish, which was helpful in enabling me to decipher the dishes offered, though the menu was in Portuguese. I remained in doubt, however, as to my choice of the main course. When in doubt, Aunt Jocasta had said, always consult the waiter. I did so. Part of the reason for my hesitancy was due to my passionate fondness for *bacalhao*, otherwise known as saltfish, a plebeian dish that was featured on the menu. I was in the grip of a stern inner conflict over this dish, for Aunt Jocasta, reinforced by my mother, always maintained that no gentleman ever ate saltfish in the presence of a lady. Yet not only was saltfish a great favorite of mine, but it was also the theme of an especially melodious calypso.

> "O, gimme de raw sal'fish,
> I don' warnt no calaloo!"

("Calaloo" is a dish derived from the West African cuisine. It is concocted of boiled vegetable leaves fortified with crab, salt pork, and other meats. The dish is commonly served in the form of a rarefied puree.) At the thought of that calypso I began to feel homesick. The sensation was unmanly, so to suppress it I said with some haughtiness to the waiter: "What is this?" I pointed to *bacalhao* on the menu.

"O, very good, sir, very good." He made a circle of his thumb and forefinger and winked at me. "*Bacalhao*, very good." Had he said anything else, I would have broken his damn neck.

I looked across the table at Dorothea, implying that she would have to endorse the waiter's judgment before anything so unfamiliar as *bacalhao* should cross my lips.

"Is good," she said.

What a wonderful creature, I thought. What exquisite taste. "Very well." I nodded in the waiter's direction. "And—another bottle of champagne." This relieved me of the feeling that I was about to betray Aunt Jocasta by eating saltfish in the presence of a lady. The second bottle of champagne would bear witness to my loyalty to her teachings.

As Dorothea and I were concluding the hors d'oeuvres, someone began to sing, accompanying himself on a guitar. The music was strange to me, and I must have revealed this fact by my reaction, for Dorothea said to me: "Is fado."

Ah yes. Fado. I'd heard of it. A melancholy brooding upon the cynical irony of human existence and the resolute despair summoned up in defiance of it.

> "You may destroy me, O my life,
> Make me old and ugly,
> Enfeeble me and cause the beautiful women
> Who once languished at my glance
> To mock my weakness with their contempt.
> Yet I defy you, Illusion—
> For since you are no more, and even
>   less than that—
> You shall not overcome my despair."

Beautiful. Haunting. As a West Indian from Trinidad and Tobago, I should have expressed the matter differently, with at least a certain ribaldry. My despair would have been no less profound, but I should have celebrated defiance in irreverence and mockery. Every Trinidadian carries Vol-

taire in his soul. Calypso replaces fado. I should have sung—
indeed I had begun to feel like singing:

> "Bad woman, aie-y'aie-y'aie
> Bad woman, oie-y'oie-y'oie!
> Bad woman make sweetman hold 'is t'ing
>   in 'is han'!"

I was in fact finding it necessary to restrain myself from demanding the guitar and singing to my own accompaniment
a selection of calypsos. One that insistently urged itself upon
me was in the form of an appeal by a young lady to her beloved to "water me garden." Aunt Jocasta would have regarded this, however, as in extremely bad taste, and I myself
felt that the sentiments were inappropriate in Dorothea's
presence, as well as to the existing circumstances. "Can you
sing fado?" I asked of her.

She hesitated briefly before replying. "My life is fado. Jus'
like fado. I no have sing it."

I poured her more champagne before the waiter could
anticipate me. The proprietor gave him a dark look, as if to
say: "On your toes, you peasant!" Then he smiled at me
apologetically. I inclined my head in his direction, being
careful to avoid the slightest semblance of undue familiarity.
Aunt Jocasta, without the least question, would have approved of my dignified reserve.

The singer grew more and more impassioned. His voice
descended into a deeper timbre even as it soared into a
more pulsating despair. A sense of identity with the singer
took possession of me. It was as if he had discovered some
secret recess within me in which I had hidden my most private thoughts and was now revealing to me some of whose
existence I myself had remained largely unaware.

> "And now at last what is your triumph?
> To have stolen my fictions,

The rags in which I dressed myself
To make believe I was a king.
Take them; they are yours to keep:
Life—ragpicker."

When I raised my head, Dorothea's eyes were luminous
with profound resignation. I glanced across at the waiter,
who was leaning against a timbered post with an air of bemused melancholy. He came to me at once. "Ask the singer
to accept a bottle of wine with my compliments," I told
him.

The singer strolled over to my table to pledge my health.
When he had emptied his glass, he handed it to the waiter
and began to sing to Dorothea and me. She afterward translated the words of the song. They went like this:

"Youth is the sacrifice that love makes to life.
Except for life, there are no monsters,
And love is the sorcerer that does its bidding.
We yearn for love, knowing that it will pluck
    from us
The spring flower of our years,
Then cast us off to wither and die.
But who does not wish for love?"

He toasted my health again and asked my permission to
pledge Dorothea's. His good manners made a very favorable
impression on me.

By now I was feeling stirred by all the circumstances:
Dorothea, fado, and champagne, together with the excellent *bacalhao* I had eaten. More than ever, I wanted to sing
calypso. At last I could restrain myself no longer. It would be
selfish of me to deprive these warmhearted people of acquaintance with the famous folk music of Trinidad. So I
summoned the waiter. He in turn communicated my wish
to the musician, who brought his guitar over to me and sur-

rendered it with a courteous bow. I took it from him, tuned it to my taste, and began to sing. The natural range of my voice is within the key of C minor, one of the authentic modes of the calypso. In order to celebrate the superb saltfish I had dined on, I first sang, "O, gimme de raw sal'fish!" and, even if I myself say so, sang it well. By the time I came to "Nora," whose lover was plaintive on the subject of her "badness," I was so moved by the melodious lilt that I did a carnival shuffle up and down the room. There was much applause. I ended with a spirited rendition of "Ah jump, Ah jump, an' Ah jump on she bel-lee!" I do not at all exaggerate when I say that the customers erupted with sheer delight. The fado singer suggested then and there that I cancel whatever plans I might have and remain in Madeira, where, he was certain, I had a great future. He himself would undertake to instruct me in the art of the fado, although with such natural genius as I clearly possessed no prolonged instruction would be necessary. I ordered wine for the house. Dorothea was enchanted with my performance, not only as a singer, but, as I could easily see by the pride with which she regarded me, as a man capable of holding his own on any terms. I knew that I had so far acquitted myself commendably, though perhaps Aunt Jocasta would not have approved of my choice of the final calypso. It is possible that she might have thought it indelicate. Yet she need have had no fear. Even if I was in superlative spirits, I was maintaining at all events a sensible and well-balanced dignity. Above all, my manners were unassailable.

Dorothea had flowered, miraculously. It was as if she were a lovely plant in my mother's garden that had been neglected by the early rains. But now, with the full onset of the rainy season in the person of myself, John Sebastian Alexander Caesar Octavian de Paria, she had bloomed. I became conscious of ardent stirrings within me. Her décolletage in her room back at Madame's suddenly seemed infinitely correct to me. I wondered if I should ever again be privileged to read to her in such circumstances.

"What you think, Johnny?" Her voice was a sweet reproach to my self-absorption.

I wished to say, "Of you." But all I could manage was, "O, everything."

"You no think of me, Johnny?" She smiled with the assurance of a woman from whom the man she loves has no secrets.

There was little point in dissembling. I admitted that I had been thinking of her.

"An' what you think of me, Johnny?"

This, however, I could not bring myself to tell her. Indeed, I hardly dared admit it to myself. So I hung my head, and when I looked up, someone was standing at my table and the room had become still. I glanced across at Dorothea and noted with surprise and alarm something like terror on her face. Then my glance shifted to the man standing there.

He was of medium height with wide shoulders, and he was handsome, I thought, in a brutal way. Overdressed with exaggerated elegance and his hands on his hips—obviously not a gentleman—he just stood there looking at us. For some reason or other, I had a feeling that this mister-man was formulating an intention to do me grievous bodily harm. He said something in Portuguese to Dorothea, which I could not quite understand, but sufficiently at any rate to know that it was a brusque command.

I arose. "Do you speak English?"

He did not reply; only looked at me.

"What do you want?" I demanded. It was impertinent of the fellow to behave in this fashion. Must be one of the local lunatics, I surmised.

But he simply repeated, so far as I could judge, his original remark to Dorothea. She remained seated, never looking at him, but with a troubled expression on her averted face.

144

"Who are you?" I demanded again.

As an answer, he attempted to take Dorothea by the shoulder. But he had reckoned without me. "Always remember," Aunt Jocasta had said to me as I was leaving home, "always remember that you are a de Paria. Never forget that."

So before the mister-man could soil Dorothea once more with his touch, I'd spun him around so that his back now was to our table and, applying my knowledge of jujitsu, in which I was expert, I placed my foot in the center of his back and sent him flying toward the door. He slammed into it and whirled with an open knife in his hand.

"Come," I taunted him, as a matador with a bull, beckoning him to me. "Come. I have something more for you." My temper was up. I remained outwardly cool, however, cool as a coconut with the early-morning dew on it. A de Paria facing danger never loses his head. I folded my arms across my chest. "Come," I beckoned him with one finger. "Don't be afraid." (Privately, I was saying to myself: "Yes, come. I only want to kick your arse." But my good manners would not permit me to employ such language in public and, above all, in Dorothea's presence.)

He turned and went out the door.

As though released from a maleficent spell, the room came back to life. There was a low, susurrating sound like a collective groan, followed by a scattering of applause, which I ignored because I had done nothing of any consequence. I had merely given an ill-mannered lout his deserts. I ordered more wine for the house. My spirits now rose above even their previous height, which had been considerable. I was aware of an urge to sing some more calypsos, and I would have asked for the guitar but for the fact that the fado singer broke into a dirgelike melody, full of that vibrant despair which, by reason of its very purity, its irreducible hopelessness, provides a negative triumph over the illusion known as

145

life. As Dorothea presently translated for me, the words of the song were these:

> "Life is a lie
> And Death the only truth.
> Who, then, would fear to die,
> Scorning to cling to a lie?
> Life is every man's betrayer
> And Death the universal mother."

As the singer concluded his song, it became plain to me that Dorothea was no longer enjoying the evening with the same unreflecting happiness as she had earlier done. From time to time she would glance at the door and her lovely face would grow grave. She now said to me: "You want go, Johnny?"

I summoned the waiter to settle the bill. Instead the proprietor himself came forward and presented it. He made me a courteous speech in which he thanked me for the honor of my patronage and expressed the hope that this evening would always remain graven upon my heart. He apologized for the interruption to which we had been subjected. But (he glanced in a veiled manner at Dorothea) he was sure that the *senhora* would understand. His humble establishment would always be at my command, and he could hope for no greater happiness than my frequent presence under his roof.

I was not unworthy of the occasion. I responded briefly but, I thought, not without eloquence. The waiter flung the door open for us with a grandiose flourish. As he did so, he said something under his breath in Portuguese. I did not know what he meant, nor did I care, but Dorothea of course understood. She said to me: "You go back ship now, Johnny."

"Certainly not," I told her. "The evening has just begun. We've the whole night before us, with nothing to do but

146

make fête." Then, thinking that I might be inconsiderate, I asked: "Are you tired?"

"Tired? Ah, no. No tired."

We were at the end of the street and rounding the corner into the *avenida*. An ox-drawn cart, festooned with flowers, came along. The driver signaled to me and called out an invitation to go riding with him. This seemed to me in my present temper the perfect thing to do. My spirits were at a peak, a beautiful girl at my side, and the evening was as lovely as a moonlit night in a Trinidadian cane field at harvest time. "Did you like my calypsos?" I inquired of Dorothea, taking her with me toward the cart. "Let's go for a ride."

As we settled ourselves on the cart, she said to me, "You sing good, Johnny. Very nice." She also said something to the driver in Portuguese. He touched his whip to his hat and then lightly to the ox's rump. We moved along the *avenida*. This is life, I thought. Only a few days away from Trinidad— and look at me! Riding with Dorothea behind a big old bull right in the middle of Madeira. Jeez-Chris', boy, but life is funny, yes! The bull's tail swished from side to side at the flies dive-bombing his backside.

Dorothea had done me the honor of placing her hand in mine and I held it with cherishing protectiveness. A lady who places her hand in yours places her trust, I had once overheard Aunt Jocasta say with some severity to a gentleman who had called on her to ask, it seemed, for advice in a matter that troubled him. People were always resorting to her for counsel. I wished so much that I could take Dorothea to Trinidad, where she would stay with Aunt Jocasta and have the benefit of her advice. Thinking in this vein, I glanced at Dorothea and was astonished to see that a certain sadness had taken possession of her. While I had been inwardly celebrating the evening with all its invigorating store of events, Dorothea was clearly anything but happy. I

asked her why without, I hoped, prying or otherwise showing any lack of good manners.

"True. I not happy," she admitted.

A profound alarm seized me. "Why, what have I done?
Have I—?" I stopped, hardly knowing how to speculate as to
the possible cause of my wrongdoing.

"Not you, Johnny." She gave me a sidelong look of ineffable sweetness.

"Then what?" I stopped again, uncertain and confused.
"Can I—?" We began to descend from the crest of a hill
along a cobbled incline. All at once I saw the funnels of the
Frederick of Prussia. We were on the wharf. "What are we
doing here?" I said to Dorothea. It was plain that the driver
had blundered. The silly fellow. "Driver!" I called to him,
and Aunt Jocasta would have approved of my imperious
tone. "Driver!"

He turned and looked, not at me, but at Dorothea, in a
mute appeal to her, as it were, to supply me with the necessary explanation.

She complied. "Johnny—" Her hand parted company
with mine. "You go back ship."

"But we don't sail until nine o'clock tomorrow," I told
her.

Her surprise and skepticism were evident. It was obvious
that she did not believe me. I should have to convince her.
"All right. *We*—you and I—will go aboard the ship and ask
the captain. Then you will see that I am telling you the
truth." By this time the oxcart had come to a stop. I got off,
preceding Dorothea in order to offer her the support of my
hand as she in turn debarked. I now understood the nature
of the colloquy in Portuguese between the driver and herself as we had boarded the conveyance after leaving the restaurant. She had given him instructions to proceed to the
ship. "Come with me," I said, turning to her with my hand
outstretched. She sat still, however, and gave no sign of an

148

intention to leave the cart. "Dorothea?" My voice contained a query as well as a plea. Our eyes held a negotiating session.

"Johnny," she told me. "Goodbye." She averted her face.

My heart dropped like a fishing boat in a rough sea. "Dorothea, you jokin', man." Under the unexpected stress of the situation, I had lapsed into my native dialect. The correct English I had been employing, and which Aunt Jocasta would have been delighted to hear, deserted me. "O God, man, you keah do me dat. No, man." I was deeply shaken.

"Goodbye, Johnny." She held out her hand.

"Dorothea." I looked away from her hand, though intending her no discourtesy. There she sat, lovelier than starlight in a coconut glade, and I was standing like a tree on a windless day, with my heart pounding as the surf on a rough afternoon at Mayaro beach in Trinidad. Then I leaned over, picked her up in my arms, and started toward the ship. She didn't struggle. All she said was, "Johnny." I carried her as easily as I would have done a sack of mangoes I had stolen as a boyhood lark from someone's orchard. She was the most delectable burden I had ever borne. But the driver of the oxcart began to make a considerable din, shouting after us, and attracting the attention of onlookers.

"He want money," Dorothea explained. So without pausing in my stride and without releasing Dorothea from my embrace, I flung some money over my shoulder at the fellow. I was angry at the row he was making, as though I were a common thief absconding with his property. Otherwise I would have treated him with better manners. But I felt that I should show my displeasure, as my mother would have said. A de Paria could do no less. His outcry subsided, only to be succeeded by a shout in a voice I recognized at once. "O God, Mr. Johnny!"

It was my guide, Caldeira. "I been lookin' ev'ryw'ey fer you. I have good news fer you, man. De ship"—he indicated the *Frederick of Prussia*—"dey ain' leavin' 'til day after to-

149

morrow. De injin have to fix an' it go' take two days. Maybe t'ree—"

With a mixture of reluctance and relief I deposited Dorothea. "You see?" I told her, spreading my hands, palms upward, and my arms outstretched. I was so happy at having persuaded Dorothea to accompany me aboard that it never occurred to me to ask Caldeira why on earth he was following me about.

Dorothea was enchanted with the ship. I showed her my cabin and she remarked on its size. "Is for a little Johnny. No big one."

True. But I welcomed the restricted size of the room. With Dorothea there, it was like a cozy hutch for a pair of congenial rabbits. I opened the porthole so that she could see the moonlight dancing on the water. We sat on my bunk, my feet resting on the edge of the brass-bound box, which the motion of the ship apparently had thrust out a bit. Its presence beneath my bed had escaped me; I had given no thought to the matter. But now I told myself that sometime I'd have a closer look at it. Dorothea also remarked its presence. "You' clothes?" she asked.

"No. Not mine. I don't know—" I got up, stooped, and tugged at the box. It was difficult to move, but I succeeded in pulling it out. There were tiny holes, evidently to permit the passage of air, drilled through the cover. A key had been left in the lock, and a companion key dangled from a short string attached to the other. An impulse of curiosity urged me to open the box and ascertain its contents, but propriety restrained me. After all, it was not my property and I should not yield to coarse inquisitiveness.

Dorothea noticed the key. "You open it, Johnny?"

"No. I don't know who it belongs to. And—" I had a distinct impression of a sound as though of movement inside the box. The impression was so strong that I bent over and placed my ear against one of the holes perforating the cover. I listened but heard nothing.

150

"What's wrong, Johnny?" Dorothea's face wore a look I would remember all my life as that of one of the Fates, a goddess supremely indifferent to human destiny. "You want me open it?" She gestured toward the box. On her face was an expression of remote, occult abstraction. Purpose now assumed a clearer contour, the outline, no longer impalpable, of an objective. "I open it—for you—?" Her hands made disembodied gestures, groping, fluid, and formless, toward the box.

"No," I told her. It was curious how vast an effort of will so simple a declaration entailed. "Don't."

The unearthly luminescence vanished from Dorothea's eyes. She sat for a moment an infinity away in another sphere of being. Then, drawing a deep, prolonged breath and exhaling with an air of profound preoccupation, her hands conjoined and composed themselves in a token of resignation.

With a sense of resurrection, I cast aside, as it were, the cerements of the grave and, my strength renewed, I thrust the box back out of sight beneath my bed.

"Tell me about yourself," I said to Dorothea. I resumed my seat beside her. I was careful to leave the door of the cabin wide open. I did not wish to compromise Dorothea any more than I had already done when I had been so incorrect as to closet myself in a room with her at Madame's while she was clad only in her drawers. Aunt Jocasta always emphasized that no gentleman ever entertained a lady behind closed doors, unless at the risk of besmirching the lady's reputation.

"What I tell you, Johnny?" And she looked so at me that I felt as if I were eddying away from myself, far beyond my reach, on a current too strong, too swift, for good manners. I wanted to seize hold of Dorothea and cling to her and never let go of her, floating face downward on the stream of her and merging with her until with a wild deliquescence she and I dissolved together to form a tranquil pool of confluent

151

and perennial rapture. The percussive rhythm of my heart would have stirred the interest of a seismologist. My shoes scraped on the floor of the cabin, and, of their own spontaneous choice, my hands groped in a blind and sensory anarchism toward Dorothea. I knew that I must either break this carnal spell that was overcoming me or irrevocably forfeit my standing as a gentleman. I crossed my legs, ruthlessly suppressing my "pencil," breathed as deeply as I could, and struggled to secure a firm grip on myself. "Let's go up on deck," I said, uncrossing my legs. As I did so, my "person" flew up from confinement as though released by a mechanical spring.

I was able to walk only with difficulty, so impeded was I by my insurrectionary "pencil." Dorothea and I made our way around and across accumulations of ropes, blocks, and stanchions scattered about the ship's deck toward a space recessed in the area of the bow by a number of packing cases. I chose one that would seat both Dorothea and me. Flicking at its surface with my pocket handkerchief, I made certain that Dorothea's dress would not be soiled when she sat down.

"Is clean, Johnny," she told me. I replaced my handkerchief and remained standing until she had seated herself. Then I sat beside her. Once more, however, the disturbing symptoms that had impelled me to leave my cabin manifested themselves. I was again obliged to cross my legs and again had enormous difficulty in doing so. This simple act, normally accomplished with unthinking ease, had now become a painful process of the most delicate strategy. Dorothea looked at me. The moon, holding its candle to her eyes, enabled me to read by its light a message whose import I was well-nigh powerless to resist. My good manners were tottering on the very brink of deserting me. It was all I could do to keep my legs locked together. Something like a groan escaped me.

Dorothea took my hands in hers. "What'sa matta, Johnny?" The cloud-shadowed moon partly obscured the smile on her lovely face. Whether because of the moonlight or some trick of the atmosphere, her eyes were ablaze with a mysterious effect of Saint Elmo's fire. The moonlight listed across her cheek, illuminating that side of her face and leaving the other in shadow, so that she seemed like some beautiful creature of the dawn entrapped by night. "You know Santa Maria? Santa Maria—I come from—" The slap of the tide against the ship's keel spurred her memory. A landward odor, faraway in its texture, faint and effluvial in its essence, floated across the bow of the ship and expired as it collided in its dying moments with the entrenched malodor of the seaport. Dorothea drew a deep breath and exhaled it slowly with a sigh. "Santa Maria—" she said. "Azores—just so it smell."

It also smelled like San Fernando, I thought. But as in these later years I have come to realize, it was the smell of all faraway places experienced when memory, haunted and fugitive, rekindles some embering incident to warm and protect itself on desolate nights menaced by loneliness and terror. The whistle of a tugboat in the harbor soared up to us, loud and braggart, triple blasts proclaiming its lordship of the coastal waters.

"Three, four days from here—Santa Maria. Is beautiful, but no money—" Remembering, she was silent for a moment. From way down at the bottom of the ship came a sound as of hammer blows, an abrupt and ringing sequence of noises followed by silence. Overhead a shooting star coruscated across the sky. The nostalgic smell of remote places returned, exhumed and freshly linened for still another tryst with the odor of Funchal. A covey of seagulls, disturbed by a renewed sequence of hammer blows exploding from the belly of the ship, shrieked, fluttered, and settled down again.

"Dorothea—?"

Her head swiveled toward me, then her body followed so

153

that we were sitting face to face. I reached out with the index finger of my left hand (I am left-handed, a congenital condition that Aunt Jocasta had tried to correct but then had given up as hopeless). Gently touching the point of her lowered chin, I raised her head until her eyes and mine refracted the moonlight from the one to the other and our faces were close and our breathing came and went in the same intense, arrhythmic unison. A seagull drew a circle around us and returned to its perch. "Dorothea—?" I said again. "Will you marry me?"

The seagull uttered a hoarse, monitory cry.

I was suddenly seized by the lapels of my jacket. "Aha. Aha." I looked up.

It was the Amazonian stewardess. She lifted me to my feet. "I have you."

Now, a gentleman never struggles with a lady. I could easily have broken her hold, as I had been trained to do by my jujitsu teacher in San Fernando. But except in extreme circumstances, only the most restrained conduct in dealing with a lady is permissible on the part of a gentleman. To illustrate this standard of conduct, which she firmly endorsed, Aunt Jocasta often spoke of Mr. Ching Po Lee, whom she held up as a model. This dealer in imported silks was married to a termagant wife, who, to crown it all, was addicted to physical violence. Not only was she a relentless scold, but she habitually subjected her husband to cuffs, slaps, and kicks, even—indeed, especially—in public. Never once did he retaliate. With a forgiving smile he would passively defend himself against her, warding off her blows and gently remonstrating, "But behave yo'self, nuh, doux-doux. Look how yo' rumplin' up you' hair an' spoilin' you' nice new dress." He would murmur other admonitions of a similar nature while she raged and scratched and clawed and called him vile names. Every afternoon after this saintly man had finished his day's work, he would repair to a small orchard that he tended at the margin of the town. When he returned home at nightfall, it was always with the look of a man in possession of a return ticket to heaven valid for eternity. As I later discovered, Aunt Jocasta was unaware of the fact that this noble paradigm of a gentleman cultivated only two types of produce in his orchard: papaws and banana trees. As Ah Sam, Ah See, and I could have told her, these were the great loves of his life.

I myself lacked the advantage of either of these indispensable aids to perfect knightliness. So it was necessary for me to rely on my mother's maxims and Aunt Jocasta's homilies to be certain of acquitting myself as a gentleman in the present pass.

With the stewardess maintaining a resolute grip on my well-tailored lapels, I was more conscious than ever of the need to conduct myself in a manner altogether beyond reproach. I was also aware that Dorothea had somewhat unexpectedly detached herself from my fate at the hands of my captor. I put aside this thought, for my immediate aim was to be freed from the clutches of this mountainous female without in any way whatever resorting to actions unworthy of a gentleman.

"Zo," she demanded of me. "Vot now say you?" There was no mistaking her disapproval of me. She pulled me briskly toward her, then thrust me forcefully away from her, and twice more repeated this maneuver while continuing to demand of me, "Vot now say you?"

Here, I thought, was a damn "calaloo" indeed. She began again to rock me backward and forward. "*Sie haben mich angeschissen, ja?*" But remarking with admirable sensitivity the look of blank incomprehension on my face, she very kindly supplied me with a translation. "You shitz on me, yes?"

I denied this as firmly and as politely as I could. But all to no purpose. "*Ja,*" she insisted, "*sie scheissen—*" And again she rocked me to and fro.

"*Sie haben keine Erinnerung.*" Which, once more, she translated for my benefit. "You remember not."

I disclaimed the recollection in the terms in which she had expressed it and I attempted to explain exactly what in fact had taken place and why, interlarding this with a courteous apology for the mishap. The point I took was that she had confused the contents of my upper with those of my lower intestines. There was, I urged, a distinct physiochemical difference which is usually visible on closer inspection.

"*Krank, ja?* Sick?" Her tone was not unsympathetic, I was glad to note.

I admitted that I had briefly been indisposed. Her grip slackened and she released me. She nodded in Dorothea's direction. "*Das ist deine Puppe?* You' 'oman?"

This reference to my fiancée did not wholly meet with my approval. But I was unwilling to risk injury to our new-found amity.

"Yes," I told her.

She gave Dorothea an intent though fleeting look. Then she turned to me. "*Vorsichtig*," she said. "Careful." She glanced again at Dorothea, then moved off with a cumbrous, purposeful gait and descended a companionway.

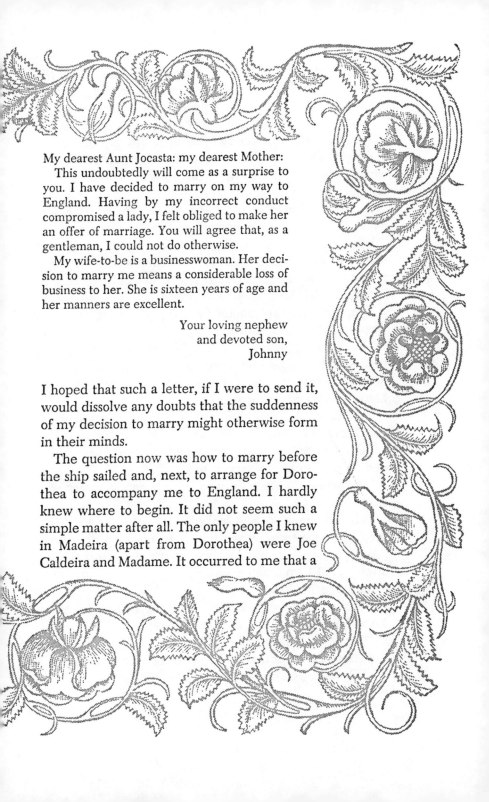

My dearest Aunt Jocasta: my dearest Mother:

This undoubtedly will come as a surprise to you. I have decided to marry on my way to England. Having by my incorrect conduct compromised a lady, I felt obliged to make her an offer of marriage. You will agree that, as a gentleman, I could not do otherwise.

My wife-to-be is a businesswoman. Her decision to marry me means a considerable loss of business to her. She is sixteen years of age and her manners are excellent.

> Your loving nephew
> and devoted son,
> Johnny

I hoped that such a letter, if I were to send it, would dissolve any doubts that the suddenness of my decision to marry might otherwise form in their minds.

The question now was how to marry before the ship sailed and, next, to arrange for Dorothea to accompany me to England. I hardly knew where to begin. It did not seem such a simple matter after all. The only people I knew in Madeira (apart from Dorothea) were Joe Caldeira and Madame. It occurred to me that a talk with either or both of them might be helpful. At my suggestion, Dorothea and I now left the ship and returned to the house where I had met her.

When we got there, I had a qualm or two about disturbing the chatelaine at that hour of the night. It was well toward midnight. Dorothea assured me, however, that Madame would be awake, for she never slept before sunrise. "Much business," said she.

Dorothea let us in with her key and went in search of Madame. She returned in a few minutes. "She will come."

When Madame appeared, I was seated where I had been earlier that day on my first visit to the house, but Dorothea now was seated next to me and her hand was in mine.

I arose as Madame came into view.

"Ah, *senhor!*" she greeted me with the most charming warmth. "What a pleasure!"

I held out my chair to her, but she declined it and instead took another. "And how have you passed the time? But I need not ask. I can see that you are very happy." She gave Dorothea an approving glance.

"Madame," I began, but found that for the moment I could proceed no further.

"Yes, *senhor?*" And as I remained tongue-tied, she continued: "How can I be of service to you?"

"Madame—I wish to ask your permission to marry your daughter."

"My daughter—?" She looked at Dorothea. "Ah. Yes. I see." Her face transformed itself into an inscrutable mask. "And you, *senhor,* wish to marry—my daughter? That is strange, but I am much honored."

"Strange, Madame?"

But she did not seem to have heard me. Instead she asked: "And how soon, *senhor,* do you wish to marry?"

"Tomorrow, Madame."

"There are other matters. You do not mind my asking?"

"Whatever you please, Madame."

158

"You are aware of the employment of—my daughter?"

At first I did not grasp her meaning. She realized this. Still she hesitated, looking from one to the other of us. Presently, in some bewilderment I replied: "Of course. She is a businesswoman." I glanced at Dorothea, who seemed detached and remote, hardly indeed to be listening. "She makes business." And in a cascade of candor: "I must apologize, Madame, for having compromised her." I hung my head.

At this Madame laughed with so much pleasure that I almost felt forgiven. It was odd how laughter transformed the severity of her features, so that she no longer appeared to be a retired governess but was actually girlish in her merriment. "Compromise? No. Not so—" She considered me with the air of a lepidopterist who, by the happiest of accidents, has ensnared a rare species of butterfly. "It is my duty to ask you to give yourself time to think of the wisdom of what you wish to do."

When I did not reply, she summoned a servant. "We will drink wine," she said to me, "in honor of the occasion."

While we awaited the wine, Madame appeared to be rapt in thought. There was, I felt, something that she wished to say. But the wine was brought before she could say it. She raised her glass. "Good health and much happiness," she proposed.

Madame thought that inasmuch as we were to be married that very day (for it was now past midnight), etiquette no less than my own scruples as a gentleman required that we occupy separate quarters until the wedding ceremony was performed. Her sense of propriety put me much in mind of Aunt Jocasta.

The matter of witnesses presented no difficulty. Two would be needed. Madame of course would be one of them, and the other could be recruited from among the ladies who acted as hostesses at Madame's establishment. For that was how Madame referred to them. She only regretted that more time was not available. A wedding gown of suitable el-

159

egance would have then been possible for Dorothea, and perhaps my aunt would have been present. The loss of this opportunity to become acquainted with Aunt Jocasta made Madame wistful. She and my aunt, she said, "could have exchanged many professional secrets"; and, warmed by her third glass of wine, she confided that there were many intimate matters of business that she could discuss only with someone like my aunt, who would undoubtedly have had similar experiences. What a meeting that would have been! She sighed. "Ah, *senhor!* Your aunt would know so well these things that I have learned. When she and I were hostesses, before"—her head became erect—"we were proprietors, we studied. We were pupils."

Erudition enwreathed Madame's didactic features.

"Then"—she held the wine up to the light—"when we had finished our study"—the smile of a graduate with the very highest honors contemplating her scholastic career alighted modestly on her face—"it was time for us to take the next step. We were at last *pro-pri-et-ors.*" The inflection she gave to the last word imbued it with a distinction that was deeply impressive. "After all those years"—she selected the next phrase as a lover of grapes chooses one that is especially luscious—"of study." She relished its exterior texture, teasing it between her teeth, nesting it beneath her tongue, rolling it around in her mouth before crushing it gently, ever so gently, and expressing the juice. Then she tilted her head back so as to allow the sweet, dense liquid to trickle with slow, passionate sensuality past her palate and along the runnels of her throat through her pharynx until, feeling it enter her esophagus in its passage to her large intestine, she could relax in the certainty that its epicurean destiny had been fulfilled.

"How long did your aunt study?"

I had not previously considered this question, and I was at a loss for an answer. Aunt Jocasta was extremely well informed. She read no newspapers. As for books, she considered the Old Testament of the Christian Bible to be porno-graphic, deploring its excesses of lust and adultery, its preoccupation with the pursuit of vengeance, and—with al-most the single exception of Isaiah, she said—its celebration of war and conquest. About the New Testament she had fewer reservations, though she was inclined to regard the Apostle Paul as narrow-minded and intolerant. She felt that the premature death of her Lord and Savior, Jesus Christ, was so much the more to be regretted for, in her view, He would have exercised a restraining influence on Paul's fa-natical tendencies. Aside from the Bible, she read and great-ly admired the poems of Alfred, Lord Tennyson, which, in many instances, she thought far superior in their religious inspiration to the pre-Christian barbarism of a number of the Psalms.

But Madame was pursuing her question about the length of Aunt Jocasta's studentship. I decided to hazard a reply. "Ten years," I said.

My chance response delighted her. "Exactly with me. The same." Her look of a governess embalmed, while still alive, into incorruptible respectability, all at once melted away. I was astonished at the degree of relaxation a lady, as a rule so formal and unbending, could achieve without apparent loss of dignity. "Three years apprentice; seven years student. Now let me see—" She gave me an arch look that in a less exemplary lady would have been thought by some captious observers to have been downright indecent. "How long as teacher?"

Since, as it seemed, Madame was of the avant-garde opin-ion that work was a virtue, and I had, naturally, no wish to diminish Aunt Jocasta in her view, I chanced another guess. For some obscure reason, my imagination clung to the pre-vious figure.

So, "Ten," I said again, holding up both of my hands and separating the fingers.

I'd scored once more. If, before, Madame was highly

pleased, now she was ecstatic. "We are together! Ten years teacher. Exactly. So, me." Dorothea's less-than-half-empty glass caught her attention. "You do not drink your wine, little one. Be happy. Today you are a bride. Your happiness, my child!" She brought her glass toward her lips, then paused in mid-course and included me in her toast. "And to you, *senhor!* Health, fortune, happiness, long life!"

She resumed her scholarly collation. "So I ten years teacher, and she ten years teacher." She savored the parallel careers whose extensions had been protracted to so fateful a duality in time and space. "And proprietors now, the two." Her prim bosom seemed, suddenly, unstayed and about to burst into an insurgent roundness, a rebel voluptuousness. In the very nick of time, her spinsterish mien reasserted itself. With much of her ordinary composure she now asked of me: "And how did your aunt like to be hostess?"

She did not stay for my reply. "Beautiful woman. Very busy. Much interest. Many patrons." She pondered this for a moment. "So, too, was it with me. Some days—I speak of nights—as many as six patrons. The highest gentlemen. Governor. Admiral. Ambassador. General. Commendatore. Effendi. And—sh-h-h-!" She put an index finger across her lips. "The archbishop himself. Ah, what a man! So passionate, so generous. And the next morning"—the memory irradiated her—"I would take holy communion from him. Sometimes"—her face was like a sunburst—"he heard my confession. Ah, what days! The English I speak, I learned from the archbishop. He was a great scholar. Twelve languages he spoke. And the most beautiful English. Although he was not English. He once told me that he would have been Pope if one of his daughters had not made public claims upon him. Of course, he was obliged to deny her. But there was much scandal, and from the Curia in Rome he came here to Funchal. I was very grateful to him—it was natural—and I tried to give him a son. But the child lived only five minutes, just long enough for his father to pronounce the blessing of an archbishop upon him. That night he wept in my arms for his lost son. I was ill and desolate myself, but I did my best to console him."

Dorothea put down her glass. The slow and measured intentness of the downward movement of her hand betrayed, even as it attempted to conceal, her inner turmoil. Her face in its very impassivity revealed to me the hurt she was so careful to hide. And always, of course, there was that gesture of hers—treasonous in the circumstances—that rallying of her right hand to the wrist of her left. Whenever this occurred, I observed how her eyes became hostages to some cruel and oppressive memory.

Madame, however, was a very different case. She grew more and more vivacious with every glass of wine, of which she had now drunk several. "But there are things"—a look that I can only describe as roguish, inappropriate as the word may be, came over Madame's face—"things I cannot speak of to you." She regarded me with a benign but scalpeling look. "Your aunt and I—what a conversation we would have! What memories! How sad that she cannot be present at the wedding. She would be my guest here. My establishment"—she indicated her domain—"would be at her disposal." A reflection of some weight reposed for a moment on her ivory-yellow brow and furrowed divergent channels in the shape of a watershed between her smoldering, smoke-hued eyes. In her sober, high-collared dress of black lace, relieved by a half bodice of fine cambric, Madame gave the appearance of Whistler's mother on a spree. "To her I could speak of the general—ah, what a rascal!" She put a silk handkerchief to her mouth to restrain her merriment within proper bounds. "What a—pardon me, my children— *maquereau!*" (This was French slang, further corrupted in Trinidadian patois to "macco," meaning a libertine given to officious intermeddling in sexual and other matters of a private and personal character.) Madame kept the handkerchief firmly in place, but this expedient dramatized rather

163

than diminished the difficulty she was experiencing in giving dignified expression to her mirth. "And the admiral—" This recollection threatened deep inroads into Madame's self-control. "Imagine—but I cannot tell you, I really cannot. What a pity! The admiral—" Here Madame came close to stifling herself in the attempt to moderate her glee. "The admiral—" She said something in Portuguese, and Dorothea blushed. "Pardon me," she begged of me, although I had not understood what she said. Then she shifted to another language: "*Au chien.*" And in English, possibly for my benefit: "Like doggie-doggie!" To contain her laughter for the sake of decorum, she again sealed her mouth with the handkerchief. When she judged her self-control to have been sufficiently restored, she pantomined the appearance of a man wearing a monocle. Then, "Wow! Wow! Wow!" she barked. I was mystified. A dog wearing a monocle! Madame must be pickled. "Englishman," she explained. "The admiral was English." For some reason or other, this reference to nationality came closest of all to divesting Madame of the restraint that at most times lent her such distinction. "Wow! Wow! Wow!" She mimed the affixing of a monocle, then discontinued the performance. A trifle wistfully she said, elucidating the matter for me: "The admiral—God rest his soul"—she crossed her bosom with a bejeweled forefinger—"he was only able if I let him be doggie. And I, myself, doggie too—" She barked again: "Wow! Wow! Wow!" A musing look of a lost paradise dimmed the light of recollection in her eyes. Briefly, however, it flared again. "What memories for us to exchange with each other, your aunt and I!" And without warning: "Your aunt has had many lovers. Perhaps goat, too? Dog? Cat?" She spread her hands in a gesture, at once elegant and world-weary, of infinite experience. "All the same." Once more I was astonished by the unexpected roguery of the look Madame directed at me.

"Lovers?" I repeated. My surprise was considerable. "Goats? Dogs? Cats? My aunt—? Aunt Jocasta—?"

"You do not know." She dismissed and forgave my ignorance with a generous wave of a symmetrical hand. The delicate tracery of veins stood out dark blue and reticulate on the dorsal surface. "But your aunt of course will tell me—when me meet." Madame twirled her wineglass, set it down, and withdrew into a reverie.

I smiled across the room at Dorothea, whose eyes lit up, soft and phosphorescent, like the glow of a firefly in the darkness of the Queens Park Savannah in Port-of-Spain before the advent of a new moon. Aunt Jocasta's "lovers." I could have burst out laughing from sheer incredulity. Aunt Jocasta. Lovers. It was like saying, the mountain and a banana tree.

It was true that there were gentlemen who visited Aunt Jocasta's home from time to time, but they were always accompanied by their wives. "Never," as she often said, would she receive "an uncorseted woman," let alone "an unconsorted gentleman." At first even the Roman Catholic priest, Father Maginot, had to be chaperoned by a nun whenever he called on her, though in later years—in his case and in that of the Anglican archdeacon of her parish, but only in those two instances—she had rescinded that requirement. Dr. O'Flaherty, the Anglo-Irishman who had been our family physician for God knows how many years, could not make a routine call to ascertain the state of Aunt Jocasta's health unless he brought a nurse with him. She was very formal in her manners. I once heard her disapprove of Queen Victoria's unduly relaxed relationship with Prime Minister Disraeli. She herself, she said, would never have conducted affairs of state without the constant presence of a lady-in-waiting. "If I had been in Her Majesty's place—" How often had I not heard Aunt Jocasta take the late Queen to task on this score. As for Her Majesty's unfortunate, unroyal tolerance of the overfamiliar attitude and impertinent address of her Scottish ghillie, John Brown, toward her, this was an imperial mystery insoluble to Aunt Jocasta. In her mind it

165

gradually assumed the theological nature of a theodicy, a question impenetrable to human understanding. But not so where Father Maginot was concerned. He spoke in seemly undertones of the "anarchy of the flesh," illustrating his thesis by examples drawn from the history of royal houses. One instance he often cited and appeared to regard as being sharply in point was that of the sovereign of France who showed an inexplicable preference for mating with unwashed peasant girls. The monarch was inconsolable when an officious courtier insisted on bathing an especially odorous young lady before permitting her to enter the royal bedchamber where the king was awaiting her. "You have spoiled her for me!" he wailed, bemoaning the absence of her passionately anticipated fragrance.

Father Maginot's great historical learning was, however, unequal to the task of persuading Aunt Jocasta that the sexual tastes of a royal sovereign of France were capable of explaining lapses from absolute regality on the part of Queen Victoria.

Madame's voice ended the short and silent film of my interior recall. "Tell me—"

I leaned forward with courteous eagerness to comply.

"Are you a virgin?"

Now, I have found life in general to be so unexpected that the only armor against its unheralded incursions is good manners. I believe in good manners. I have often thought: how would it be if, unsolicited, someone were to kick me in the arse? How should I, a gentleman as I am, respond? By making a vulgar row? Knocking him down? Spinning him around and returning the assault with compound interest? Or simply turn, bow to the fellow, and say politely: "Sir, you are in error." Or even, indeed, if he were a lower-class person, by ignoring the incident until I could dispatch one or another of my servants to kick a bigger hole in his backside with usurious interest. I am in the habit of considering such contingencies before falling asleep at night. Always, without

166

fail, the ideal response to the unpredictable humors of life has seemed to me to be good manners. As time and time again my mother has said to me: "Manners makyth man." Without the slightest question, I am inclined to think that she is right.

Aunt Jocasta is a great lady who has carried her Himalayan backside through life with all the dignity of an African colporteuse to whom an English missionary has entrusted a consignment of Christian Bibles for sale to the former's fellow natives. Yet how, I mused, would she respond if Madame were suddenly to put to her such a question as she had now addressed to me? How—not what, but how—would Aunt Jocasta respond? As can easily be imagined, I was shaken to the very soles of my feet by Madame's thunderbolt from paradise, so to speak. "Are you a virgin?" As if I could have been anything else.

But before I was able to reply—with good manners, of course, but still not without some self-respecting trace of indignation—Joe Caldeira appeared. He seemed to be in extremely high spirits. Since it was well past midnight, and Madame, Dorothea, and I had only been kept awake by the excitement generated by the prospect of my marriage in the morning, I was astonished at his turning up. Madame took it though as a matter of course. I remembered Dorothea's saying that Madame never slept before sunrise.

"Eh, bien?" Caldeira said to me in his Portuguese affectation of Trinidad patois.

"Wey yo' say, man?" I chose not to be standoffish with him. "Wey yo' say, nuh?"

He surveyed Dorothea as if to discover from her appearance some sign of what he believed had taken place between us. "Wha' happenin'?" he said to Madame.

"I am glad you have come." She clapped her hands, and a manservant came into the room. "More wine." When the servant had gone off to do her bidding, Madame nodded, first in Dorothea's direction and then in mine. Caldeira,

167

sensing something unusual, leaned forward, his sun-broiled face tinted a lighter mahogany by the chandelier overhead. Somehow he put me in mind of a corbeau on the wharf at San Fernando scenting a choice bit of carrion. Madame kept him in suspense until the servant had returned and refilled the glasses. When the latter had left again, she said to Caldeira: "What do you think, my friend?"

He shifted in his chair, stretched out his legs, drew them up again, but remained silent.

"Imagine."

He achieved an air of deep, knowing absorption while maintaining his silence. Once more his gaze made a fleeting tour of Dorothea and myself.

Dorothea was rapt in contemplation of the ceiling. I noticed how firmly pillared her neck stood upon her shoulders, how prettily the deltoid structure reinforced its base. I saw her hair aglow in the light diffused by the chandelier. I observed the elegant symmetry of her legs as they ascended from her ankles to their junction with her knees, which were decorously concealed by the hem of her skirt. (Aunt Jocasta set great store by the reticence of a lady's knees.) I saw her breasts like sapodillas ripening, though not yet ripe, and offering the promise of luscious, milky fruit, and stirring deep within me the remembrance of breasts past.

"The little one—" Madame contrived a delicate, descriptive hesitancy. "Our friend from—" Again she balanced the act of explicit recognition on the brink of a dramatic reserve. At length, however, "The *senhor*—" Again, now, Caldeira's glance made a rapid, speculative circuit of Dorothea and myself. Apparently concluding that I was sufficiently defined, Madame announced: "They wish to marry."

Caldeira was stupefied rather than astounded. The distinction is a subtle one. If one is stupefied, one is in a state of inertness. If one is astounded, one is in a state of kinesis. In the latter case, one tends toward action; in the former, one is deprived of motor volition, the sign of which is a certain pendency of the jaw and a marked inability to close one's mouth. Caldeira was in the former condition.

His partial paralysis was shortly remitted, and then he said something that I could have sworn was a vulgar, four-letter invocation to fecal matter. I was sure that I heard him say "shit." Conceding him the benefit of the doubt, it might also have been an appeal to Madame to "sit," for she had risen from her chair and was studying the contents of her glass, into which a beam of light had entered, revealing the curvature of the liquid, a smug meniscus, its consistency mellow, its glint mocking.

"Not here, my friend," said Madame. She carried the glass to her lips. "Especially not now." She took two sips before saying to Caldeira with prim severity: "Think, my friend, think."

This was an exercise uncongenial to my guide. The thinkers of this world, with the notable exception of Dr. von Buffus, have had on the whole little connection with the Black Cat Bar in San Fernando, Trinidad. Neither do they spend much time flitting from winery to winery in Madeira sampling the goods. I do not mean that solely for these reasons my guide was an unattractive or ungenerous person. On the contrary, by now I had formed a reasonably good opinion of him, despite his nauseating commonness. He was fond of procuring happiness for others, a warmhearted fellow and companionable, a man in whom anyone would confide in time of doubt or stress as he dispensed refreshment from behind the counter of the Black Cat Bar or some similar "safe house" for fugitives from life. With such a man I'd sing calypsos and play the guitar any evening. A melody lilted in my fancy. I was back home in Trinidad lying in my hammock in the cool of the vine-sheltered veranda at sundown. On a small table within easy reach, just a short swing away, was a bottle of rum. Next to it stood a thermos pitcher of ice.

To the right of the bottle a saucer of halved and quartered limes. Just in front of the bottle a bowl of dark brown sugar, thick and earth-sweet, only one granulated step away from molasses. To the left of the sugar, a bottle of Angostura bitters. Grouped in a polished crescent, three or four glasses, the arc of the crescent running transversely across the table. In front of them, precisely at the center, a single glass—the King—three-quarters full and sweating. And I—I am there in my hammock, stretched out, relaxed and easy, strumming my guitar. My ear catches a slight—the very slightest—dissonance in the middle string. I adjust it. Play a few chords. C major. I shift to F. I try A. Then the mood seizes me. I modulate into G minor and I begin to feel a calypso coming up in me. But before I sing, I reach out and take a sip. O God, man! This is rum, boy. Rum like rum-self. I sip again. I put the glass down, gently, with respect. I sound the chord again. G minor. Plangent, melancholy. The sun is lingering in the sky, waiting to hear my calypso before going down for the night. There is a hush over everything. The whole world is waiting for me, Johnny de Paria, to sing. Not a frog is croaking, not a cricket is calling, not a bird is chirping. The lizards on the wall are like people at a concert just before Horowitz, Jascha Heifetz, André Watts, or Jacqueline Du Pré begins to play. Neither tense nor relaxed; just suspended weightless in expectancy. The sun gives the signal, brings down a salmon-and-gold baton against the sky. And I, Johnny de Paria, the great calypsonian, begin to sing:

> "Why Iris kill Bosco, nobody don' know.
>   Why Iris kill Bosco, nobody don' know.
> He had a little grievance,
>   She had one also,
> But why Iris kill Bosco, nobody don' know."

The sun pauses, stands still, listens, lavishes polychromatic applause in the sky, and goes down. I sing two more pen-

trains. My voice is plaintive but vibrant with pleasure at its own carefree liquescence, a little rough, a trifle unrefined, but supple and true. A real calypso voice. I pause, take two more sips from the glass, and I sing again.

> "Tell me, wey yo' bin las' night,
> Caroline?"

That is the way to live. O God, man! But Trinidad nice, yes!

"I shall have to send for Father Goncalves and—" Madame announced to my guide without finishing the sentence. She arose and left the room.

Her departure seemed to release Caldeira from his stupefaction. His eyes grew lustrous with resuscitated interest.

"But Mr. Johnny, you's a hell of a man, yes!" He gave a short laugh. "Aie-y'aie-y'aie!" Turning to Dorothea, "An' you, too—" He pondered us both as if we were a Madeira wine of interesting body but uncertain vintage. "All-you know w'at you doin'?" When we did not answer, he said to me directly: "Married is big trouble, yes, boy." I remained silent, and he pressed me further. "Wey de hell yo' tan'-tan' go say?"

I permitted myself a slight shrug of my shoulders so as to avoid the appearance of ignoring him.

"You tell she?" he persisted.

"Not yet."

He said something to Dorothea in Portuguese, and she replied, her voice soft and rustling, neither apologetic nor assertive, and expository rather than explanatory.

"Aha," he said at last when she had done speaking. "I see."

His attention reverted to me. "Mr. Johnny, you go' have to tell you' tan'-tan'. You know dat?"

I knew that.

"De li'l gal is nice." He passed judgment on Dorothea.

171

"She is like Madame' daughter." He expressed, however, a certain reservation. "But all-you so young." The point was driven home. "You keah wait? All-you in such a hurry. An' you, Mr. Johnny—"

But before he could disclose what was in his mind concerning me, Madame returned. "I sent for Father Gon— He was here last week. You remember—" She spoke to Caldeira alone, excluding Dorothea and myself. "He used to come every night."

"That's when Esmeralda was here," Caldeira reminded her.

"Even before that." Madame was emphatic. "In any case"—the pride of recall came out to do battle for her—"I was here *before* Esmeralda."

"Father gettin' ole, too, you mus' remember. He ain' no spring chicken."

"We're all getting old." At this, my guide squirmed.

I noted the resplendent jewel pendent from a heavy chain of gold around Madame's neck. It must have been a ruby, judging from its color, the size of a seagull's egg, wine-dark and reveling in the light it pillaged from the chandelier. Madame took it between her thumb and forefinger, caressed it, then let it fall to repose again upon her bosom and resume its opulent wantoning with the light.

"The archbishop was eighty-nine going on ninety—and he was still a man." The memory made her carriage taut, her bearing proud. "He could have gone on forever if he had kept on his flannel undershirt." She was musing now and seemed hardly aware of her listeners. "I told him: 'Feliciano, don't take it off. Please, I beg you.' But he was a stubborn man and I could never do much with him once he had made up his mind. So there he was, with his flannel shirt off on a chilly night, and with the windows open, too. Not a thread on him. And I said to him: 'Feliciano, let me put something over you.' And he made a naughty joke when I said that. Ah, so risqué! '*I* will cover *you*,' he told me. 'And not with the Holy Ghost, either.' "

Caldeira coughed into her memories and interrupted their ruminant flow.

Madame returned to Dorothea and me. "There must be a wedding dress for the little one." She made the transition from reminiscence to present reality with no apparent leap-frogging. "One of the girls will see to that this morning. There must be food. Wine. Flowers. Music. Everything will be done. But *senhor*—" She addressed me. "You still have not told me: are you a virgin?"

The query clearly stunned my guide. His animation had on the whole been less than it was earlier in my short acquaintance with him. He had not precisely been subdued, but it would be accurate to say that he had been burning low. Now, however, he flared up. "A Trinidad boy! You arksin' a Trinidad boy if he—O God, Madame, but you funny, yes! A Trinidad boy—! Aie-y'aie-y'aie! You ever see t'ing so? Mr. Johnny, tell de Madame, man, tell she—tell she how you does sanga-wanga girls ever since you was two years—"

But when I did not flare reciprocally in response to his coming alight, he looked at me with amused curiosity. "Mr. Johnny playin' sly." The joke was so rich that my alleged dissembling only deepened its humor. "A Trinidad boy—! A—! O God, man. Madame, from the time dey is eighteen months old, dey's already—" The sexual precocity of the boys of Trinidad, Caldeira's bliss plainly intimated, was a perennial wonder of a world sluggish and slow to mate. "That's why," he concluded, "dey tamboo-bamboo is so big—" The universal demanded of him a crowning particular. "O God, man! You should see Mr. Johnny' tamboo-bamboo—" His hands defined a linear space of some eighteen or twenty inches.

Madame considered me, a newborn admiration agleam in her eyes. Perhaps I might prove, after all, to be heir to the

173

archbishop. I could see all this coursing through her, and my guide's insinuations were creating fresh tributaries to a watercourse in her mind whose flood tide had already risen to a conviction of my astonishing sexual endowments. So it was not at all surprising when Madame said to me: "Then you are quite experienced, *senhor*—"

Out of loyalty to my native land, I neither confirmed nor denied this, and I would have emerged from the matter without so much as a scratch if Caldeira, bent on extracting all the fun he possibly could from the incredible notion of my virginity, had not kept on taunting and rallying me: "Tell de Madame, Mr. Johnny, tell she you's a vo-jin—" He jackknifed his body in the chair, sepulchral laughter rumbling up from the depths of him. I could stand it no longer, and I declared in a courteous manner, yet with a clear undertone of proud defiance: "Yes, I am a virgin."

This avowal of mine only increased his amusement, but it caused Madame to regard me speculatively as if I might be a possible though extremely fanciful hypothesis. Suppose indeed I were . . . So she resolved to pursue the inquiry. A certain skepticism was apparent in the polite irony with which she probed.

"Naturally, *senhor*, I do not wish to be—how shall I say—bold, but"—she directed an admiring, frankly covetous look at my "person"—"are you saying—telling us—that you—?" Her intended query trailed off into her preoccupation with my "person."

Caldeira was entranced. "Aie-y'aie-y'aie! Tell she, Mr. Johnny, tell she—" And to Madame he exclaimed with that horrifying coarseness that the Black Cat Bar was responsible for: "But you ain' see w'at 'e got dere—?" With a gesture of the most explicit commonness he indicated my "pencil," then continued: "But look, nuh. Tonnerre!" (A vulgar French expletive.) Making a fist with his right hand, he brought his arm up parallel with his chest. Then, elbow first, he lowered his arm, his fist still clenched, until his elbow rested against his "person." And he began to flex his arm to and fro and to sing a Trinidad calypso:

"Me donkey warnt water
Hold 'im, Joe!"

As persuaded as I had hitherto been of the fellow's abysmal vulgarity, this latest exhibition of his appalled me. While I admired his calypso voice, which was remarkably authentic for a foreigner (and his phrasing and mastery of rhythm alike, I noted with genuine pleasure, were beyond criticism), the obscene charade he had engaged in put me off altogether. No gentleman would take such liberties in the presence of ladies. Nor did he end there. Breaking off in mid-song, which, because of his virtuosity, I greatly regretted, he told Madame: "I bet you any money dis boy fandangle [another synonym for "sanga-wanga"] mo' gee-uls [he meant girls] dan monkey in cage brush one anudder." (The verb "to brush," in its depraved transference to local idiomatic usage, is employed to mean sexual intercourse.) At this point, not the slightest particle of doubt lingered in my mind that Caldeira, though an admirable calypsonian, was not a gentleman. It was simply infamous and on no conceivable ground excusable to use such language when ladies were present. I must admit, however, that neither Madame nor Dorothea seemed at all disturbed by Caldeira's grossness. On the contrary and to my considerable dismay, they were delighted. Madame's preoccupation with my "person" grew more intent, and Dorothea herself was gazing at my "pencil" in a manner that I could not even describe as surreptitious. My love for her, in all its ardor, could not disguise from me the fact that she was scrutinizing my "tamboo-bamboo"—as that indecent Portuguese had referred to it in the Trinidadian vernacular—with all the adoring rapture of a Madonna contemplating the Child.

Madame resumed her ironic questioning of me. "Are we to understand, *senhor*—?" She toyed with the substance of the understanding she had in mind, turned it over and over, peered at it, inspected and examined it, held it away from her, brought it closer, looked at it askance, viewed it directly, surveyed its surface, searched its depths, but was never discourteous though unfailingly ironical. The whole episode was being conducted against an obbligato supplied by the guide's reiterated, "Tell she, Mr. Johnny, tell she—O God, man! A Trinidad boy! Aie-y'aie-y'aie! A Trinidad boy—!" He leveled his gaze at my "person." "Wid a t'ing like dat. O, God! Big like a lamppost. Wid a tamboo-bamboo like dat? An' 'e sayin'—'e sayin'—'e's a vor-r-r-jin. A Trinidad boy—a Trinidad boy—wid a t'ing like dat." Well, as we say at home, the mister-man gi'ein' me "picong" (a patois corruption of the French *piquant* that in its modified Trinidadian usage denoted a low form of badinage, akin to the obscene American slanging-match known as the "dozens"), but me eh takin' 'im on at-all-at-all. No, man. Though his derision of me, I thought, was beginning to hover dangerously on the margin of the offensive. In a moment I might have to show my displeasure, as my mother would say.

Madame took up again her restrained and incredulous questioning of me. "Are you sure, *senhor*—!" And the query would vaporize into a courteous mist of unspoken disbelief. "Perhaps in your sleep, *senhor*, you might have dreamed—and remembered on awaking—a delightful dream—?"

She trifled with the ruby pendent from the chain of gold around her neck. "Is it possible that there was an actual incident which you have forgotten—perhaps more than one incident—? Do you know what I am talking about, *senhor?* Or, perhaps, you call it by some other name—?"

Ah Sam, Ah See, and I used to observe with studious interest the sexual encounters of farmyard creatures—horses, cattle, dogs, fowl, sheep, rabbits, goats, guinea pigs, and others. From time to time we had also witnessed that some of the most respectable gentlemen in the town preferred sheep. For instance, Mr. Deschamps, the druggist, had carried on an exceedingly passionate love affair with an old piss-tail sheep whom he evidently regarded as Helen of Troy. Secreted in the branches of trees in a meadow, we often watched from our hiding places as Mr. Deschamps made love to his lady-sheep. Her bleating and his sighing were orchestrated by their mutual passion into a love duet of Wagnerian intensity. It was touching indeed to watch the tenderness with which Mr. Deschamps embraced his beloved, fondling and kissing her, babbling endearments, and presently, when his passion could no longer be contained, unbuttoning his sobersided trousers of dark-blue serge, extracting his "person," and introducing it with the precise metage of an apothecary into his darling's hindquarters.

Then there was the Anglican archdeacon, who, though more catholic in his tastes, preferred above all a compliant she-goat of promiscuous habits. The archdeacon's technique of seduction depended a good deal for its success on distracting his light-o'-love with an abundant supply of fodder long enough to enable him to effect entry by stealth into the caprine ark of the covenant. At the point when he managed to seize hold of his sweetheart's horns while simultaneously investing her from the rear, he felt sanctuaried in bliss on Mount Ararat. At least, so one would have judged from his uncontrolled tremblings and the spastic movements of his clerical backside. With the receding of the waters, his and his inamorata's, he would descend along the flanks of Mount Ararat. He stilled whatever doubts arose in his mind as to the religious propriety of what he was doing by reflecting, no doubt, that it was worthier in the sight of the Lord to love a goat than to slit its throat. The ancient Hebrews, he perhaps surmised, had missed this point. When in later years I considered some of these matters in the light of a larger experience and riper maturity, I did not find it difficult to concede the justness of the archdeacon's point of

177

view. But I never could listen to Johann Sebastian Bach's "That Sheep May Safely Graze" without feeling censorious toward Mr. Deschamps.

There were townsmen, not always of accredited respectability, who had abandoned their wives and paramours, preferring in the one instance or the other a banana tree or a melonous fruit called papaw. In the former case, they would bore a hole in the trunk of the banana tree at an accommodating height. They would then lavish upon the tree the loving and impassioned embraces they had withheld from their wives or other womenfolk. The sight of a reputable townsman making ardent love to a banana tree, showering it with devotion, was deeply affecting. And when this was reinforced by their unrestrained outcries of ecstasy, the high C's extracted from bassos and the low A's from tenors, the effect was that of solo performances by virtuosi of orchestral capabilities. Ah Sam, Ah See, and I once glued with an adhesive substance a banana tree much favored by a schoolmaster who, on the solitary occasion when Ah See's curiosity had lured him into school, had whipped Ah See for his inability at the tender age of twelve years to recite the alphabet. At a time when any respectable child would be just entering the kindergarten phase of his or her preschool years, Ah See was expected to know his ABC's. He found the experience repellent, and he, Ah Sam, and I held long conferences about it. So the schoolmaster's favorite banana tree became an object of considerable interest to us. We paid particular attention to the hole in the trunk of the tree that he was in the habit of plumbing three or four times weekly for his pleasure. We filled it with an uncommonly sticky mucilage. Then we secreted ourselves and awaited the schoolmaster's arrival. As usual he was punctual, and as always he was passionate. Embracing the banana tree, he engaged in sexual intercourse with it. In paeans of ecstasy he called it fond names—"Toy-Loy," "Sugarplum"—and referred to himself somewhat boastfully as "Papa Steel-Stump." From a purely aesthetic standpoint his performance was displeasing to us. There was also his insult to Ah See to be avenged. We had applied the adhesive substance unstintingly to the entire bole of the tree. Now at length, all passion spent, the school-master lay passively on his darling's bosom. With the going down of the sun he decided to part for the night from his beloved. He found he was unable to leave. He was stuck fast to her. "Steel-Stump" was embedded in "Toy-Loy." His struggle rose swiftly in intensity from irritation to panic to frenzy. All to no purpose. "O God!" he cried aloud. "What Ah go' do?"

Ah Sam, Ah See, and I emerged from our hiding place. Majestic as judgment day, Ah See walked slowly up to the banana tree. "Schoolmaster," he said to the captive lover. "Is me. How you duz say de ABC—in Chinee?"

Yet potent as were the charms of a banana tree, there was no rival so dangerous to the stability of a marriage or liaison as a green papaw. A ripe papaw was formidable, though more transient in its allure. But a green papaw was peerless in its sexual power to alienate husbands from wives and lovers from mistresses. Having once experienced a green papaw and the rapture of embracing it with bateless, priapic potency, dutiful men of spotless repute were known to turn their backs on their wives and, worse, to refuse to acknowledge their mistresses.

Ah Sam, Ah See, and I were aware of the siren bewitchment of papaws and banana trees, and resolved to resist them with all our might. We had also decided that when in some remote future we might find it necessary or unavoidable to engage in sexual intercourse, we would adopt the elegant posture of rearward mount that we had noted among the so-called lower animals. We felt that this would be the sort of equitation we should find it desirable to adopt vis-à-vis our partners, human, animal, or vegetable, as the case might be. But we had never gone beyond this abstract decision because of our conviction that sexual activity was enfee-

179

bling and only to be engaged in at the peril of surrendering
one's vital energies beyond recovery. Not for us, then, this
debilitating contact. We were content to leave it to those
human beings and farmyard creatures who knew no better.
As to human beings, no one of our acquaintance had ever
participated in sexual intercourse without appearing much
the worse for it: less proficient at cricket and soccer, less
fleet of foot, less skillful in boxing, less powerful in wrestling.
There even were reports, which we culled at second hand,
that sexual indulgence led to madness. There was one
chap . . .

"But *senhor*, you will forgive me—did not your parents instruct you? Your aunt, she—surely—" And then, as a kind of
inward reflection, "It might have even been interesting for
her—"

At this my guide simply could not contain himself. "Ah,
Mr. Johnny! You an' you' tan'-tan'—aie-y'aie-y'aie!" He was
evidently much taken with this vision of carnal nepotism.
Before adducing further proof of his credentials as an authority on the sexual mores of the youth of Trinidad, he
emptied his glass and then at once refilled it. He took a sip
or two, paused meditatively, and appeared to be conjuring
up some distant recollection.

I meanwhile diverted myself by recalling Mr. Ching Po
Lee, the Chinese admirer of Aunt Jocasta's bottom, wailing
aloud rapturously in the shade of a breadfruit tree as he engaged in sexual intercourse with a green papaw. "Ah, doux-
doux! Yes, dahlin'!" And since it was his custom to bestow a
given name on each of his papaw loves, "You so nice, Mabel,
sugarplum—!" He gibbered with delight, embracing the
green papaw as he cradled it tenderly in his crotch.

Caldeira had been staring into his wineglass as though he
were studying the auspices. "You 'member de time I was in
Trinidad, Madame?"

Madame dispensed him a tolerant smile. The smile lingered briefly in the calipered lines that enclosed Madame's mouth in skeptical parentheses. It then vanished into her renewed absorption in the interplay between her ruby and the light. She adjusted her chair so that the arms of our vision no longer converged in the near distance, as had been the case with Dorothea and me, but hers bore directly upon me, while I, from the angle of my chair, met her three-quarters face. "You, *senhor*, are a virgin. My little one is not. You know this?"

I strove to conceal my embarrassment at the question. But before I could reply, Dorothea began to speak to Madame in Portuguese. I made out only two words—"Ho-ma" and "Oo-lee-see."

Madame listened with an astonishment that was gradually transformed into undiluted pleasure. She interrupted Dorothea from time to time so as to clarify, I thought, some point on which she was doubtful or concerning which she may have desired reassurance that her hearing was not impaired. She sometimes clapped her hands to her ears and inclined her head from side to side, laughing meanwhile until the tears ran down her face. "Ho-ma! Oo-lee-see!" she exclaimed again and again. "Oo-lee-see! Ho-ma!"

I realized that these were the names by which Madame would hereafter think of me and by which, privately, she would refer to me. But I was not displeased about this, for as between Madame and myself a mutual liking had taken root and I could in no way feel myself offended by what, in someone else, would have been excessive familiarity. So without understanding the literal text of Dorothea's disclosures to Madame, I was able to guess at their import and share without pretense in the hilarity they produced.

"You are fond of reading, *senhor?*" Madame began to laugh once more. I found myself laughing with her. A frown suddenly crisscrossed her forehead with a network of rivulets. "But what has happened to Father Goncalves?"

"What should have happened to me, Madame, at two o'clock in the morning, unless I was at my prayers?" A short, circular man, plump as a parish priest tended by a devoted flock, advanced toward Madame, accepted her hand, bent in a courtly fashion over it, and drew it to his lips. "Madame is well?" The query seemed to be exhaled, rather than spoken, in a sigh composed of equal parts of worldly interest and clerical concern.

"What shall I say, my dear Father?" Madame's indeterminacy had thrust her lower lip outward. But almost at once she retracted her lip, which in its brief protrusion had assumed—I do not know how—the appearance of a sugared macaroon, artfully colored and contrived for nibbling. An interesting woman, Madame. Forever suggesting by unspoken nuance or implicit gesture aspects of Aunt Jocasta hitherto unrevealed to me. Without actually resembling her in any physical sense, Madame seemed to contain Aunt Jocasta. From time to time at the constraint of incident or some other need she would distill, so to speak, an ingredient of Aunt Jocasta's essence, so that my awareness of my aunt was momentarily heightened. As now when she motioned Father Goncalves to a vacant chair and in the same instant signaled a servant to fill up the glasses, the courtesy of a gracious hostess blending elegantly with the hauteur of a grande dame. In the barely perceptible ascent of her eyebrows and the almost invisible semaphore of a sovereign hand, I recognized in Madame certain of the characteristics of my aunt Jocasta.

It is strange how from place to place people repeat themselves in other people. Father Goncalves, plump as a pullet ready for market, studied the solferino-red of his wine with an air of rapt absorption, his head a trifle to one side, the glass held at the level of his chest toward the heart. An episcopal ring on the little finger of the hand holding the glass refracted the light with a somber, cathedral effulgence.

I saw, too, that Caldeira was whispering something to

Dorothea, who had her hand under her chin and was shaking her head. And I saw a spot on Father Goncalves's trousers at the knee where some needlewoman in his congregation had darned a break in the fabric. I noticed, too, that the Father was turning and twisting his foot from side to side, not as if he were agitated but rather as though collecting himself to concentrate on an important matter that he would shortly have to consider.

Madame gave a little laugh. She sounded like an alarm clock that on being taken up to be wound and set, first clears itself of a leftover tinkle. "I thought you were on your knees, Father." She sped him a look encoded in cypher. "At this time of the night."

Father Goncalves coughed in a gentle, subdued fashion. One might think that he wished to deprecate Madame's remark without necessarily denying it. But otherwise he did not reply. Except if his nestling his glass against his beard could be construed as a reply.

Madame smiled. At that instant I remembered the expression on her face as she had looked at me in that brief interlude before she presented me to the naked ladies on the preceding afternoon. "We can never tell what the future will bring, can we, Father?"

A cloud of wisdom in the form of smoke issuing from the cigar he was lighting enveloped the russet-bronze of Father Goncalves's quattrocento Italianate face. He tilted his head at an angle of cogitation. "We are hardly aware of the present, Madame, let alone the future." His magnificent, diamond-studded pectoral cross glowed like the faith of the early Christian martyrs against his black grosgrain cassock. With his white hair and youthful face, assertive belly and overstuffed bottom, foreshortened legs, elongated torso, and wrestler's neck pillared on massive shoulders, his patrician's head and artisan's hands, Father Goncalves appeared to have resolved the complexity of his personal contradictions by emphasizing them. He peered out from behind the intri-

183

cate scrollwork of cigar smoke and sighed as if he would speak again but despaired of the treacherous role of words as an instrument of human utterance.

Dorothea had turned her head away from Caldeira, replacing her previous attention to him by a carefully angled withdrawal of her shoulder. "Excuse, please—" she said to Madame.

"Yes, my child." This distinguished lady and my aunt Jocasta might have been one and the same person, so alike were they in speech and bearing. Father Goncalves assumed an ironic mask behind a cloud of cigar smoke. Only Caldeira seemed insensitive to the legendary quality of the moment. In an hour when high resolutions were afoot, he sat there with a tapster's smirk on his circular, splay-nosed face, looking from one to the other of us as if we were all actors in some rustic comedy staged at the back of a low village tavern to tickle the ears of yokels taking their ease on a festive day. I decided to ignore him. He irritated me. That smirk . . .

"I not want go 'way from you," Dorothea said to Madame. Her hands interwove with each other, tying her declaration into an invisible knot of firm resolve.

"Aie-y'aie-y'aie!" Caldeira exclaimed. His tone was one in which I noted that surprise was scarcely present. And judging by the expression on Father Goncalves's face, there wasn't much difference between them.

Madame's expression did not change in the slightest. She spread the fingers of her left hand, fanwise, in front of her with an elegant gesture. Then she inspected the fingers of her hand, subjecting each to particular scrutiny. That was the only sign she gave of her feelings.

There was the remote tinkle of a bell beyond the room. Father Goncalves cleared his throat and returned his cigar to his lips. Madame threw her head back, her eyes narrowing in unspoken inquiry. Customers came at all hours, of course, but Madame was aware of an intuitive feeling that while this might be a customer, whoever it was would also turn out in some curious fashion to be an agent of the unforeseen. Something was in the wind. Madame's psychic receptor registered a warning, as yet indistinct though unmistakable. I could see by the way she got up from her chair at the sound of the insinuating though authoritative knock on the door that a situation had arisen. The expression on her face was that of a resolute general about to take command of an army made up of half-trained reserves. My aunt Jocasta sometimes looked like that, too.

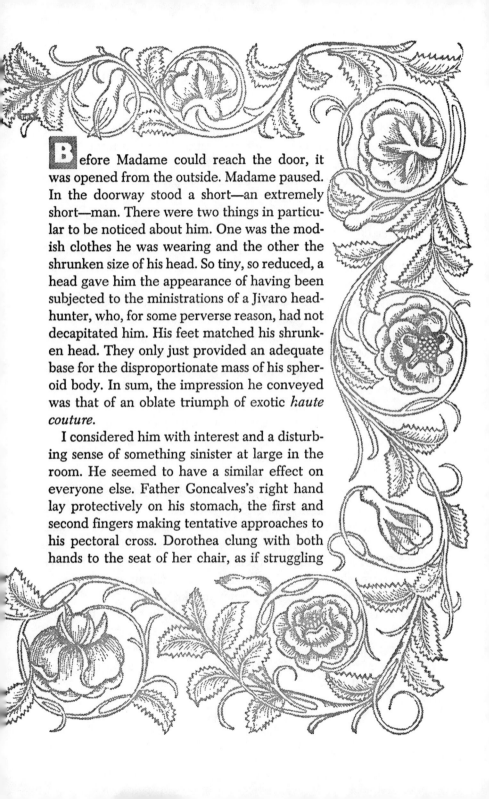

Before Madame could reach the door, it was opened from the outside. Madame paused. In the doorway stood a short—an extremely short—man. There were two things in particular to be noticed about him. One was the modish clothes he was wearing and the other the shrunken size of his head. So tiny, so reduced, a head gave him the appearance of having been subjected to the ministrations of a Jivaro head-hunter, who, for some perverse reason, had not decapitated him. His feet matched his shrunken head. They only just provided an adequate base for the disproportionate mass of his spheroid body. In sum, the impression he conveyed was that of an oblate triumph of exotic *haute couture*.

I considered him with interest and a disturbing sense of something sinister at large in the room. He seemed to have a similar effect on everyone else. Father Goncalves's right hand lay protectively on his stomach, the first and second fingers making tentative approaches to his pectoral cross. Dorothea clung with both hands to the seat of her chair, as if struggling against invisible abductors. Her face was overcast. Caldeira was unsmiling.

The new arrival bowed to Madame without lowering his eyes. They remained fixed on her despite the inclination of his minuscule head. And without awaiting an invitation to enter, he came into the room, moving slowly, his gait deliberate and controlled, an ovoid blob spreading inexorably toward an empty chair.

Madame closed the door. She seemed at length to collect herself and to resume her customary air of easy command. Yet a sort of deference had crept into her manner. It did not predominate, but it was present now where hitherto its absence had been the sign of a certain regality. One would not say that this intrusion of deference contained the merest hint of servility; but that it was, rather, a thoughtful, a self-regarding prudence. By her attitude toward the new arrival, Madame transmitted an impression that she was handling a deadly serpent that, inexplicably, had escaped from her private zoo.

"May I present," she said to the company in general, "His Excellency Dr. Luis Camoens"—she paused, then slightly quickening the pace of her words, completed the introduction—"the prefect of police."

His Excellency made formal acknowledgment in semicircular progression, beginning with Father Goncalves, who was nearest him, and ending with me. To each segment of the semicircle—to Dorothea, to Caldeira, to Father Goncalves, and to me—he directed a courteous nod. Except that in Dorothea's case, his nod might have been thought to have approached, although distantly, the declination of a bow.

"What will Your Excellency drink?"

The prefect of police seated himself, interlaced his hands across his stomach, and pondered Madame's inquiry. But before he could reply, if indeed it was at all his intention to do so, Madame said: "Ah, yes. Of course." And she rang for a servant.

188

But she had no sooner sat down than she was once again summoned to the door. When she returned, she was accompanied by a young man of medium height, broad-shouldered, who might have been either a Cretan bull-dancer or a Portuguese pimp, and was in fact the latter. I recognized him instantly as the person with whom I had had a brief altercation at the restaurant where Dorothea and I had been dining earlier that night. I gave him a hard, challenging stare, but the pimp withheld from me the slightest sign of recognition.

Madame did not introduce the pimp to the company. She merely indicated him. "Ferdinand," she said. With the same gesture of her hand, she bade him be seated. He hesitated in the manner of someone who continually found it necessary to regard his surroundings with suspicion. When he sat down, he tugged at the legs of his white duck trousers and pulled them an inch or two above his ankles. Then he placed his elbows on his knees, cupped his upturned hands, conjoined them at the wrists, and, leaning forward, concealed with them the lower portion of his face. So doing, he looked from Dorothea to me. His eyes then traveled in the reverse direction, from me to Dorothea, and rested in a proprietary fashion on the latter. It would be only accurate to say, however, that his gaze did not so much seem to assert actual ownership as the prospect of it. While, on the other hand, as he looked at me, there was a distinct suggestion in his black eyes, the color of his knitted shirt, of a raging, barely controlled hostility.

For his part, the prefect of police was taking a particular interest in the pimp behind the curtain of smoke his cigar had drawn across his face.

A servant entered carrying a tray of refreshments. Although Madame had not offered him one, and he himself had not asked for it, a drink was served the pimp as a matter of course, it seemed, and he accepted it as if the household were merely acknowledging his privileged position. His

189

manner was relaxed, slightly supercilious, and preoccupied. One would perhaps be correct in assuming that he had other things on his mind. And there might be additional evidence in support of this assumption to be derived from the occasional covert glances he directed at the prefect of police.

Furtively, and as if by stealth, Caldeira slipped, almost unnoticed, out of the room.

The prefect of police, looking straight ahead, and lodging his cigar in a beak-shaped grip between his thumb and index finger, said to Madame: "That little piece—over there"—he pointed to a piece of statuary, a figure of a snow-white falcon sculpted in marble and mounted on the wrist of a magnificent black hand carved out of ebony—"is superb." And without waiting for Madame to reply, he said to Father Goncalves, inclining his head toward the latter: "Do you not agree, Monsignor?"

Father Goncalves studied the figure briefly before replying. A shade of demurral, a fugitive dissent, flitted across his face. "A trifle theatrical, I think. But beautifully executed." He considered it again. His left hand traveled slowly along his thigh and stopped at his knee. "Yes. Beautiful."

The prefect of police pivoted in his chair, so that the mass of his body was brought to bear upon Father Goncalves. He had not fully given his back to Madame, but the rear of his head rather than his profile now was the object of her scrutiny. "You have reservations, Monsignor?"

Madame seemed to be inwardly exhilarated by the thought that she was, in more than a manner of speaking, presiding over a salon where Church and State confronted each other. That she, Hortensia Calderón, should have risen to such a station was a proof to her of the sublime goodness of God. She had employed scores of girls in the course of her business after her retirement from active duty. She had treated them as well as the pressure of circumstances allowed, and often better. Father Goncalves had been one of

190

her first patrons and had remained constant throughout the years. But it had been the prefect of police himself who had suggested to her that she enter the business. He had set her up in her original house, he had acquired a lease of the premises in his own name and endowed her with the services of some of his former mistresses to get the enterprise started. These two men were her best friends. She knew them as intimately as a woman could know men to whom for many years her bed was, in the one case, a confessional and, in the other, an oral archive for police dossiers. Yet until tonight the priest and the prefect of police had never met. Naturally, they had been aware of each other. But as far as she knew there had never been personal contact between them. At least, not in her house. It was one of her professional verities that the best place to discover and evaluate anyone's character was in bed. Her canopied four-poster was a magnificent specimen of antique opulence, as well as a pitiless revealer of character. The prefect's generosity to her, his loyalty, his friendship, were matters of the utmost public discretion and unshakable private certainty. She owed everything to him. And yet as she scanned his profile—his curiously Eskimoid features—she was all of a sudden seized by a cold tremor. This reaction to the presence of the prefect of police was not unusual with her.

"A matter of taste." Father Goncalves took his pectoral cross between his thumb and index finger. "Yours, Excellency, is a highly—"

The prefect of police was studying him as though he were intent on establishing the identity of a suspect in a police lineup.

Madame looked from the one to the other of the two combatants. For this was what she felt they were, instinctively, quite apart from the conflict in which they were now engaged. For the first time she formulated in her mind the reason why throughout all these years she had been so careful to prevent their meeting. These two men were natural

enemies. What emanated from them was less a mutual disesteem than a polar dissimilarity. Over the vast distance of essential character that separated them, there was not the mi-
nutest area that permitted them a meeting place for
harmonious discourse. They were doomed to antagonism.

I myself was put in mind of similar encounters in my
aunt's home between Father Maginot and the family physician, Dr. O'Flaherty, who when asked point-blank by Father Maginot, "Do you believe in God?" answered, "I believe in Aesculapius," and then threw his head back, his eyes
flashing like lightning to herald the thunder of his laughter.

Madame was inwardly moved at this point to reflect upon
the arcane usages of chance. It was true that, given the infinite reach of probability, its disinterested, cosmic omnipo-
tence, anything was possible. Her entire life had however
been devoted to the art of avoiding denouements in any
form whatever. Climaxes, vertices, culminations, were often
unpredictable, yet they were free of the unsettling drama-
turgy inherent in every denouement. Disorder and decom-
position, tragic or comedic, always marched in the train of
dramatic resolutions. A film of memory curtained off Madame's eyes, veiling her contemplation, turning her vision
inward. The archbishop . . . The filaments of recall became
lambent with remembered incident. Nothing had pleased
the archbishop so much as her occasional strayings from
grace. This was understandable enough, since they enabled
him to exercise his vocation. What is the point of salvation if
there are no sinners? In the archbishop's case, however, the
matter was somewhat more complicated. Madame was
aglow with recollection. A secret, musing smile was fugitive
at the corners of her mouth. The fact was that the archbishop was capable of sexual performance only with her; and
then, only after she had confessed the full and explicit
record of her congresses with the patrons of her establishment. Passion and tenderness mounted in him as she recited
her sexual transgressions. "My dear child! My dear child!" he

would exclaim with deep suspirations of pity. Then he would be convulsed by a divine ecstasy as the whole earth erupted like a cosmic volcano at the very epicenter of his being. When his tremors had subsided, he would make the sign of the cross, blessing her and absolving her of evil, remitting her sins and wickednesses.

She remembered his urgent catechisms, the intensity of their religious impulse: "And what did he do, my child?" She recalled the accelerated pace of his breathing, its low, labored procession through his distended nostrils, the malodor of decaying food in the rilles of his yellowing dentures: a holy halitosis. In her reverie she could hear again the sound of his artificial teeth clicking together like castanets. Click-click. "Ah, my child!" Click-click-click. "My child! My child!"

But while Madame was momentarily lost in abstraction, the prefect of police continued to bait Father Goncalves. "Of course, your God is omniscient, is He not?" The sneer on the prefect's face was altogether superfluous. "So it is possible for Him to resolve all oppositions in His mysterious dialectic. Freud and the Pope, Jung and Aquinas, Hegel and the Holy Ghost, all reconciled in the end by some miracle of antilogic—or, shall we say, supralogic—in a divine synthesis." The sneer on the prefect's face dissolved into laughter that gave off the sound of water thrown onto a hot metal plate.

So I'm listening to all this big talk and I'm thinking, Jesus Christ, man! I'm getting married in a few hours. I look at my watch. All this big talk between the monsignor and the prefect of police—if I had a guitar, I would ask everybody to excuse me and I would sing a song. Why the hell people like to talk so much when they could sing and play music? I look at Dorothea and I feel like a coconut tree in a high wind, all its branches singing and dancing with joy, and coconuts jumping down to the ground to get married to the earth and make more coconut trees. My mother always said that I was a poet—"like your poor father." But whenever she said any-thing about my father, especially when Aunt Jocasta was present, she would sigh and bend over her needlework or go out into the garden and cut roses, while Aunt Jocasta's face suddenly looked like a shower of rain. I had never heard of anybody singing a calypso at a wedding ceremony, but this was a special occasion. I was here, far from home, and I had to do something to remind everybody who I was. I wasn't some damn stray passenger on a ship, just any passen-ger who was getting married. I was Johnny de Paria from Trinidad. My aunt Jocasta's words came back to me: "Al-ways remember that you are a de Paria." Never—never would I forget that. Aha! You know what song I would sing? Back home, every time Father Maginot heard this song, his face would get red like a mango rose and my mother would make an excuse and leave the room. But my aunt Jocasta would stay and laugh like hell, especially when it was a fête and she had put away two or three shots of good Trinidad rum. Yet she never forgot that she was a de Paria. No matter what she did. The song went like this:

> "Entangle me not in thy mustaches
> Release me ere the old cock crows
> Dawn comes, and I come with it
> Release me ere the old cock crows."

According to Father Maginot, it was composed by the fa-mous English musician Walter Moorland, all the way back in the sixteenth century. As often as he said this, Father Magi-not would go on to say that songs like "Entangle Me Not" would never have been written if the Reformation had not reestablished the Dark Ages in Europe. Then he would talk about Henry VIII and of how it was a "plain medical fact" that at the time Henry changed his religion, his brain was al-ready damaged by the terrible disease (at this point Father Maginot would look mysteriously and respectfully at Aunt Jocasta) that eventually killed him. That was the reason, he said, that the English Tudors had died out and the Hanoverians—who were German—were able to succeed to the English throne. The Reformation in England had taken its moral color from Henry VIII. When he pronounced the word "color" he made it sound like mortal sin, heightening the second syllable and prolonging its accrescendo in an aggrieved, rising tenor. The poor Stuarts, he would continue, good Catholics all—every one of them—whatever their human frailties, had been robbed of their legal rights, first to make way for a half-civilized Dutchman and then—such was the vengeance of God—for a German who couldn't even speak a word of English.

By this time Father Maginot would be trembling with rage, his hands shaking, his voice quavering, his complexion no longer mango-rose but tomato-red. Aunt Jocasta would get up quickly and pour him another shot of rum. His indignation still persisting, he would swallow the rum in one gulp and then relapse, becoming gradually less tremulant, into a churchly, contemplative silence.

Aunt Jocasta would soothe him: "Jean-Pierre, if you want to find the white, look underneath the black." When the time came—I was nearing my fifteenth birthday—that I had to be weaned from nursing at the breasts of Indian ladies, I was given rum punch to console me. Some people told my mother it would be bad for me; it would make me a drunkard. But my mother explained to them that the choice was between my becoming, as they predicted, an adult drunkard, and my becoming, as she feared, a juvenile seducer. For I was never likely to develop such a fondness for rum punch, she thought, as I had shown for the mammary glands of Indian ladies. In this she was more or less right. Throughout all of my years at home, it is no exaggeration to say that rum punch was the staple of my daily life. Yet I never yearned for it, never at any time felt any imperative need of it. But this was certainly not the case with those milky fountains of Paradise at which I had spent the nutrient and enraptured years of my prolonged infancy. As Professor von Buffus was later on to inform me, I was afflicted with a "mammary fixation of Indo-Aryan provenience." I didn't understand just what he meant, but I gathered enough to know that he was talking about my "weakness," as he called it. "That is your Achilles' heel," he would sum up, shaking his huge, white-tufted head and looking for all the world like an omniscient Judge of a Final Court of Appeal. Profound understanding would suffuse his eyes with a tender mist of compassion.

As I was engaging in these musings, something singular and wholly unexpected occurred. The prefect of police, addressing Father Goncalves, yet speaking more directly, as it were, to Madame, said: "The girl is not getting married—to him." His attenuated head pointed toward me.

I leaped to my feet, then sat down again, feeling as though I'd just been dealt a violent blow in the stomach.

Madame determined her priorities after a moment's hesitation. Before making a full inquiry into the reason why I had been propelled from my chair, she went to the door of the room in response to a smothered knock that followed the sound of the bell.

When she returned, she was accompanied by the East Indian, Balgobin Maraj, and the African, Marcellin Gros-Caucaud, otherwise known to Professor von Buffus as Kapitän Gebumst and Dr. Schwanz, respectively. Maraj was in an expansive mood. He had scarcely been introduced to the other occupants of the room before he began an enthusiastic account of his experiences in Madeira since his arrival. There seemed to be no doubt in his mind that his listeners were bound to find the tale of his adventures every bit as interesting as he did.

"My wife an' my daughter—I hired a Po'tagee man to look after them." He emitted a long burst of laughter. "An' de ole pidgin-shit professor, too." This further amused him. "They will see the town. My wife is always sick. I do not worry about that any more. She is happy to be sick." An-

196

other access of mirth followed these remarks. "Woman is a funny nation." With this summary judgment of the female sex, he seemed briefly content to relapse into silence.

I was struck by his odd unconcern as to whether or not anyone was listening to him. It simply didn't seem to matter. He went on as if he were talking for his own delectation, rather than addressing at least a potential audience. "That woman costs me so much money. I do not know how I am still a rich man. The amount of money I have spent on my wife—all of her doctors are millionaires by now. If she coughs at night, I have a doctor's bill in the morning." Again the rumble of inexplicable laughter. This time, however, it preceded what can only be described as a cataclysm of mirth lasting, certainly, more than a full minute. When it began to subside, he confided in amplified tones to the room at large: "For three years I have not 'fugle' my wife. You know what it means—'fugle'?" His amusement attained a spastic intensity. "It means sanga-wanga." And as if that were not explicit enough, "Have sex." He rocked backward and forward in an autistic seizure of mirth. "But do not feel sorry for me. These three years I am not a virgin. My wife, yes. But not me." Once more he shattered the sound barrier with his supersonic gaiety. "Me, I always have substitutes for my wife. I am a very happy man." And speaking now directly to Madame: "Please be good enough to show me your 'jewels.' Mr. Gros-Caucaud said I might wish to buy one if the price is what I can afford." He stopped and looked around the room. "Where is that fellow—what's his name—? My Po'tagee pimp—ah, yes, I remember. I told him to go to the ship and take my wife and daughter—and his friend, that pidgin-shitted ole man, the professor—to see the town while I am here." He began again to quake with laughter. "My Po'tagee pimp—" And without awaiting a possible comment from any quarter, he went on: "It is true that I am a rich man, but I do not throw money away. I am very careful with money. That is why I am a rich man. Even

197

though I must purchase substitutes in place of my wife, I do not throw money away."

Madame forestalled in him another upheaval of delight. "If you would accompany me—" She arose from her chair.

With exuberant cordiality, however, he signed to her to be seated. "Let us *all*"—he included everyone in the room with a large, encompassing gesture—"have the pleasure of seeing your 'jewels.'"

As no one objected, perhaps because everyone was a little taken aback, Madame replied: "Very well, *senhor*, as you wish." She opened the door and clapped her hands, then remained standing at the door, which was ajar. In a few moments there was a soft sound of muted footfalls. Madame stepped aside to permit the entry into the room of a somewhat larger covey of nude young ladies than had greeted me on my arrival.

Balgobin Maraj put on a pair of brown horn-rimmed spectacles. Marcellin Gros-Caucaud, who had until now been silent and seemed only mildly interested in his surroundings, stirred and half-swiveled on his ample buttocks so as to conduct a closer inspection of the "jewels."

I found myself examining the young ladies with less abashed interest than had earlier been the case. Indeed, I was obliged to prevent myself from speculating as to which of them I would choose if, heaven forbid, anything should happen to Dorothea. As for the other men present, they all seemed to be on familiar terms with these ladies, greeting them like old acquaintances and making complimentary remarks of one sort and another. Father Goncalves was quite pleased with the contours of a lady he called Graciela, singling out her breasts for special mention. Presently he got up and stroked them with apostolic approval. The prefect of police also commented favorably on the breasts of another young lady, referring to them as "boobies." In Trinidad, a "booby" was a stupid person, and one did not lightly describe anyone in such offensive terms. At any rate, Serena—

for that was the name by which he addressed her—did not seem to mind.

The pimp displayed neither interest nor emotion, except insofar as the latter might have been evidenced by the cold connoisseurship with which he regarded them. He might just as well have been at an auction of yearlings whose points he was examining with a view to calculating their commercial value in terms of their probable potential on the race track.

But it was the black gentleman whose fascination was most visible. He was clearly ensorcelled by the spectacle before him. His protuberant eyes traveled from one girl to another in rapt, compulsive absorption. For him, the whole universe had contracted into two or three dozen mammary glands and a like number of plump backsides and hirsute vaginas. It was extraordinary. At the same time, I was glad that by having expressed a wish to marry Dorothea—despite that meddlesome mister-man, the prefect of police—I had saved her from being inspected and commented on in this manner. For the rest, I was careful—I was very careful—to exhibit no obvious interest whatever in the young ladies. After my initial inspection of them, which was very discreetly conducted, I did not so much as steal another glance at them except when I could do so undetected. Otherwise my attention was fixed solely on the reactions of the various gentlemen.

It was at this point that Marcellin Gros-Caucaud left his seat and went up to a sullen-looking, blonde young lady upon whom heaven, in its enigmatic providence, had bestowed rear and frontal charms of the most magnificent profusion. Despite heaven's munificence, the young lady wore an expression so aggrieved and resentful that one was tempted to wonder if, perhaps, she had discovered that, on any tree, predatory birds always pecked at the most luscious fruit.

At Marcellin Gros-Caucaud's approach, the blonde young

199

lady shrank back. Undeterred, Mr. Gros-Caucaud pressed
forward. The blonde young lady continued her retreat. Madame called out to her in sharp reprimand: "Amelia!" But
Amelia sidestepped Gros-Caucaud with surprising agility
and made off toward the pimp, who rose from his chair and,
taking a brisk step forward, placed himself between the
blonde young lady and her black pursuer.

The African drew himself up with all the bureaucratic
hauteur of a colonial civil servant of the middle rank. A certain outrage also informed his bearing, the outrage of an ambitious man on his way to the top who had been halted in
mid-career by an officious group administrator.

Madame recognized the need to reassert her authority:
"Ferdinand," she commanded the pimp, "sit down." She
waited until he had taken his seat. Then, "Amelia," she
called to the blonde young lady, "come here." Amelia
obeyed.

"What is the matter?" Madame demanded of her.

The African turned and stood watching them both, listening to the exchange between them, seemingly unconscious
of the embarrassment that pervaded the room on his account. He placed his hands on his hips and cocked his head
to one side, supervising the interrogation.

Before the blonde young lady could reply, Balgobin Maraj
observed to the company in general: "She has insulted my
friend. An apology is necessary. It is demanded. Such behavior cannot go on in civilized circles. My friend is a patron of
this establishment. Just as I am. Just as we all are. I do not
understand why this girl should insult my friend. An apology is necessary. It is demanded. Especially since my friend
is also worried about his missing luggage." But what this tan-
gential reference to "missing luggage" might have to do
with the present circumstances it would have been difficult
to say. It seemed to be the purest irrelevancy.

The blonde young lady whispered in an agitated under-

200

tone to Madame, who shook her head sometimes in demurral and sometimes in agreement. Ending the colloquy between the young lady and herself, Madame said to Gros-
Caucaud, whose demeanor—head inclined to one side and
arms parenthetical to his body—plainly was that of a man in
whom outrage was fast outstripping forbearance. "Amelia
is very sorry. She intended no offense. It is only that she has
heard—some things—" Madame paused and extended the
little finger of one hand upward in a delicate, confiding gesture. "Some things—" Again she hesitated, then decided to
make a swift, clean breast of the matter. "She is afraid that
you may be—well, sir, there are big ships and small ships,
but there are also huge ships that cannot pass through the
Suez or even the Panama Canal—you understand—?" She
sought to placate him with an apologetic smile.

The African was anything but mollified. "Big ships? Small
ships?" Furrows appeared in the taut skin of his forehead.
"What mean you? I no ship. She"—pointing to the blonde
young lady—"no canal. What mean you?" Despairing, apparently, of an adequate explanation from Madame, he
turned to Balgobin Maraj. "What mean dis woman? What
mean she?"

Balgobin Maraj had grasped the point at once. "Aha," he
began. "Aha." He seemed to be giving judicious consideration to the precise language he should employ. At length
he said, his manner as expansive as before and now, as well,
reassuring: "It is a great compliment to you, sir." He was
smiling as he addressed Gros-Caucaud. "I have never been
paid such a compliment. On the contrary, I have sometimes
been criticized. But you, sir, are highly esteemed. You
should be a very proud man. I envy you."

The African remained mystified, however, and Balgobin
Maraj went across to him and whispered in his ear. Gros-
Caucaud was transformed. He pressed his hands against his
incipient paunch, threw his head back, and directed a cack-

201

ling outburst of glee toward the ceiling. "True," he said between immense sea-swells of laughter. "True. Very many
say so. I know it myself." The waves of self-congratulatory
mirth became gigantic. He lapsed into his native French.
"*Oui. C'est vrai. Je suis formidable.*" The room and those in
it were swallowed up in his tidal glee.

"There is no problem," Maraj announced. "My friend is
very gentle."

But the pimp now got up and, going over to Madame,
confided something in a whisper to her ear, then returned
to his seat as Madame shook her head affirmatively. "Yes,"
she said aloud. "It will have to be done."

The young ladies, with the exception of the blonde girl,
were giggling and nudging one another. Madame appealed
to them to be quiet. Then she told the East Indian: "Your
friend must be measured. It is a necessary precaution. We
cannot run the risk of injury to our ladies."

"It is highly unusual," said Balgobin Maraj. "I have much
experience. But it is the first time I have heard of such a
thing. Many things I have seen. But this, never." He ap-
prised Gros-Caucaud of the situation.

The African roared with anger. They were all *racistes,* he
said, his rage flowing like molten lava over the others in the
room. He would remind them that these—he pointed rude-
ly to the young ladies—"are nothing but a bunch of whores.
And"—he turned on the rest of the company—"all of
you"—he made no bones about including Father Goncalves
and the prefect of police in his strictures—"a gang of pro-
curers." What, he inquired with scorching heat, what had
the size of his "*pé-pé*" to do with them? "*Mon pé-pé,*" he declared with the deepest emotion. "*Mon pé-pé est le mien.
Oui. Ni le vôtre. Ni le leur. Mais le mien. Oui. Mon pé-pé.
Complètement.*"

There is something about a man when he stakes an incon-
trovertible claim to his "person" that I find admirable. No

one, listening to the African at this stage, could have viewed him with anything but sympathy and respect. For a man, whatever his race, creed, or condition, is never more impressive than when taking a firm stand on the proprietorship of his "pencil." This was Gros-Caucaud's finest hour.

Madame had some command of the French language, acquired in the polyglot course of her professional career. Employing this tongue, she now sought to pacify him. In vain, however. It was well known, Gros-Caucaud informed them, that whites were envious of the *pé-pés* of blacks. That was why, in the United States of America for example, they were so much obsessed with black *pé-pés* and spent most of their time either cutting them off or preventing needy women from enjoying them. "*Salauds!*" he hissed in contempt. But before he could proceed further with his denunciation, the Indian gentleman put forward a proposal to conciliate matters. He felt sure that in the interest of harmony and fair play, his friend would not object to submitting to the required test if it were carried out in a manner that did not detract from his dignity and the honor of his race. "We colored people," he said, "should take every opportunity to demonstrate our superiority to our oppressors." In the present instance he regarded his African friend, Mr. Gros-Caucaud, as the standard-bearer of the colored peoples of the world. He was certain that Gros-Caucaud would rise to the occasion.

Whether he was persuaded by the eloquence of the Indian gentleman or impelled by personal vanity, it would be difficult to determine. More likely than not, it was a combination of both factors that induced Monsieur Gros-Caucaud to offer himself for inspection. And he did so with a spontaneity, an artlessness, in such contradistinction to his previous annoyance, that it was itself a tribute to the volatility and resilience of his ancient and distinguished race. As suddenly as moonrise in an African night he unbuttoned him-

203

self and there and then presented his *pé-pé* for inspection. Truly, it was an awe-inspiring sight and, truly, a credit to his race.

Envy ravaged the face of the prefect of police. He angrily considered putting this black bull—this nigger mule—under arrest.

The pimp fingered the knife he carried in his pocket. But as soon as he had recovered from his irritation, he began to make feverish calculations of the untold sums of money the African would earn for him if he could only be persuaded to accept the position of chief stud at this or any other whorehouse in Madeira.

Father Goncalves saw in the generosity with which nature had so wondrously endowed the black gentleman a divine proof of God's mysterious care for the earthly happiness of His much-abused Negroes. In an access of profound reverence, he made the sign of the cross. At the same time he wondered if it might not be as well to administer the last rites of the Church to the blonde girl, who was now kneeling before the black man, venerating his exposed organ and preventing the other young ladies from approaching too closely the sacred object of her adoring worship. Those young ladies, thus kept at a distance by their blonde colleague, were obliged to content themselves with soft cries and barely suppressed moans of approbation and desire. I noted, with some disquiet, that Dorothea herself was uttering muted cries of enchantment and had joined her colleagues thronging in reverential attitudes about the African. Rising to her feet, the blonde young lady took the black gentleman lovingly by the hand and led him away; the other young ladies followed them out of the room like a choir of angels attending Monsieur Gros-Caucaud in rapt and murmurous triumph to his heavenly consummation.

I found it necessary to restrain Dorothea from accompanying them. She gave me a look of the utmost displeasure.

Madame observed their departure with the air of a witness to Elijah's ascent into heaven. "What a man!" she exclaimed over and over. "What a man!" Then she told the company that in all her experience she had met only one other worthy of comparison with Monsieur Gros-Caucaud. He was a Turk who stood at stud in an establishment at Estoril and was a great favorite of a certain royal princess. On the unfortunate death of the Turk in an automobile accident, Her Royal Highness had had his penis removed at the autopsy and embalmed. Reports emanating from the palace were to the effect that, in this way, the Turk, though dead, continued to be an unrivaled instrument of happiness to his royal patroness.

The prefect of police shook off his brooding introspection. He had evidently come to a decision. "That nigger is a menace." He looked around the room, not so much seeking support for his view as making sure that everyone had heard him. Henceforward he would expect them all to act in accordance with his pronouncement.

Madame, however, entered an objection. "A man is not a 'menace'—as you say—because God has been good to him. Is it not so, Monsignor?"

The prefect of police restrained his impatience while Father Goncalves prepared to address himself to the question. The priest consulted his pectoral cross once or twice with an index finger and explored his gray-and-russet beard as if searching in its thicket for the answer to Madame's observation.

"God knows best," he said.

Madame pondered the ambient mysteries of a whorehouse: its capacity for weaving the most entertaining tapestries of exalted learning and low eroticism. While the pimp, studying Father Goncalves with a respectful air, thought: "The old capon—Graciela says he can barely get it up now." Father Goncalves's right index finger distracted him by a sudden lunge toward the pectoral cross.

The priest said: "My friends, the *pé-pé*—to use our brother the nigger's simple-minded expression—is the proof of God's surpassing love for us. As Adam discovered when God gave the woman, Eve, unto him."

At this Madame smiled and smoothed the bosom of her frock.

"For God is love, and therefore the *pé-pé*—the instrument of love—is itself a proof of God's existence." Father Goncalves flicked at his pectoral cross and his eyes shone with the self-satisfaction of a preacher in oratorical control of his audience.

Madame was always enthralled by the scholarly discourses of her client and confessor. She had great admiration for learning. Nothing—not even his resourceful eroticism—was so tenacious in her memories of Father Goncalves's religious superior and predecessor, the archbishop, as the range and profundity of his scholarship and the angelic eloquence with which he propounded it. He had often accused her, however, of being a female chauvinist. He used to make this accusation against her in their lighter moments as he took his ease in the sanctuary of her boudoir, his milk-white legs truant from his flannel nightshirt and his stubby toes affectionately tracing ecclesiastical designs on the ruins of her once-spherical backside. A point that he delighted to make, to Madame's unfailing amusement, was his view of Madame de Staël as a suffragette whose pen was a substitute for the male phallus she would rather have possessed in her own right. The archbishop was fond of stressing the etymological relationship between pen and penis. "Both derive," he would say, "from the same root."

Madame sighed. What a good and learned man!

So deeply was she engrossed in her recollections that she did not at first respond to the servant who had entered the room and was informing her that Caldeira had returned and was asking to have a word with her privately. She started, then arose and followed the servant out of the room.

Caldeira was lurking in the shadows at the end of the hall.

As she approached, he came quickly toward her. She noted at once his feverish animation. Something was up. She felt it. Caldeira's manner was that of a victorious pimp who had raided a rival brothel and carried off its most accomplished whores. "Come with me," he told her.

The fact was that he had been to the ship and met Dr. von Buffus, whose presence aboard—and that of Mr. Balgobin Maraj—he had discovered from his perusal of the passenger list. "If is the same Balgobin Maraj—" he thought. Vengeance took shape in his mind. The goodness of God had been made manifest. As yet, however, he could not be certain. Then, just past the ship's gangway, as he gained the deck on his way to surprise his old friend, the professor, he saw Balgobin Maraj, who was going ashore. With him was a black man. Giving no sign that he had recognized Maraj, Caldeira touched his cap respectfully and offered to be of service. In the shabby figure of the Portuguese guide who stood before him there was no semblance of the man who had been the debonair bartender at the Black Cat Bar in San Fernando. Maraj hardly looked at him, anyhow. He was canvassing with his African companion the prospects for spending a few hours with "the best whores in Madeira." Caldeira ventured to interpose an assurance that he was ideally situated to fulfill the gentlemen's wishes in this regard. He had all the necessary connections. But would they not first care to see the town?

"No—not right now. Don' bodder wid dat, man. Afterwards."

Caldeira took them to Madame's. He then returned to the ship. He renewed his acquaintance with the professor, who then introduced him to Balgobin Maraj's wife and daughter. It had been unnecessary for Dr. von Buffus to remind Caldeira of those events that had led to the latter's departure from Trinidad, or of the part that Balgobin Maraj had played in bringing this about.

"But Professor—" Caldeira had remarked to Dr. von Buffus at this *plaisanterie malicieuse*—this sardonic jest—of the gods, "but you ever see t'ing so? De rat walk right in de trap, an' de trap wasn' even set. An' it didn' have no bait—" He shook his head, uncomprehending in the face of the inscrutable caprices of the Supreme Deity, Randomness. "Not even a li'l piece o' sal'fish. Aie-y'aie-y'aie!"

The professor was pensive. " 'The gods arranged all this—' Do you know who said that, my friend? But it doesn't matter if you know or not. I mean, if you are *aware* that you know—"

Caldeira interjected: "An' you know somet'ing? De man even tell me to look after 'e wife an' darter—an' 'e even payin' me." The retributive purity of this ironic jape of the gods delighted Caldeira. The tapster's smirk he ordinarily wore on his chestnut-colored face was replaced by a look of unmixed felicity. "You ever see t'ing so?"

But the professor was unable to respond just then, for Mrs. Balgobin Maraj and her daughter, Sita, were approaching. At the sight of them, Caldeira put a silent query to the professor. Also without speaking, Dr. von Buffus answered, yes.

Careering along the streets of Funchal in an ox-drawn cart, Caldeira pointed out the sights of the city to his passengers. He waved his arms about and laughed, grinning like a monkey hidden in a coconut tree and hurling the big nuts down on the heads of people standing below. Man, that Babu—for that was how in his exhilaration he thought of Balgobin Maraj—that Babu was going to piss pepper sauce. He was so filled with glee at the denouement he planned to contrive that he misdirected the driver and, realizing his mistake only after several hundred yards, berated the man instead of reproaching himself for his incompetence.

Shortly, however, they came to Madame's. There was a legend on the lintel of the front door, inscribed in an elaborate, rococo script, cursive and curlicued: THE CLOISTERS.

On being introduced by Caldeira to Professor von Buffus and Mrs. Balgobin Maraj and her daughter, Madame managed to conceal her astonishment beneath an urbane mask of courteous sophistication. She betrayed neither surprise nor curiosity, but, inviting them to be seated, summoned a servant and then inquired of them what they would have to drink. They were sitting in a room that opened onto the end of the hall opposite the location of the other room where her remaining guests—the prefect of police, Father Goncalves, Ferdinand the pimp, Balgobin Maraj, and Dorothea and I—were gathered together.

"I can recommend some excellent wine," she said. "The finest Mateus." There was something strange afoot. She surmised that these people might have something or other to do with the East Indian and, perhaps, his friend the African. What might have been a frown in a woman less self-contained compressed itself between her eyebrows into tiny runnels of thoughtful concern. *That* Caldeira—he was capable of anything. Some *diablerie* like this would be just his idea of a good joke. But it was impossible. Even he—

"You have a nice place here," Mrs. Maraj said to Madame. "It reminds me of my own in Trinidad."

Mrs. Maraj had been brought up to believe that courtesy requires conversation and that silence implies hostility or else some form of social unease. People were to be considered polite and well disposed only when they talked. "I have my own business there—me and my husband," she confided to Madame. "My daughter"—she indicated the girl, Sita, with a brisk, businesslike motion of her head—"she has just joined the business." She grew more confiding as she felt the warmth of Madame's hospitable regard. "I have seventy-eight girls."

Madame reacted with the deference a medium-level entrepreneuse shows a tycoon of the first rank. "Seventy-eight—!" She brought her hands together in front of her chest, palm meeting palm, then with a quick backward flip directed them, conjoined, toward her chin, where they rested briefly before inching up to Madame's nose. Ah! But these Trinidadians were enterprising! First that young man's aunt, and now this! With slow and respectful inclinations of her head upward and downward, she tried to dissemble her astonishment at the chance that had brought these eminent and exotic members of her profession to her door this evening. But with her habitual caution in the face of the unexpected, she turned to Dr. von Buffus for confirmation—at the very least, a hint of elucidation. The professor made what might have been a concurring gesture with his head. Otherwise he appeared to be in full enjoyment of his customary state of surface bemusement.

Mrs. Balgobin Maraj was aware of Madame's heightened respect. She saw no harm in further improving her standing with her hostess. "And I have nine boys. To take care of special orders." She laughed, trilling high with a quick upward cast of her head as if at an insinuation whose covert meaning would be well understood between Madame and herself.

Madame rewarded her with evident signs of livelier appreciation. Not so much flustered as reduced in her own self-regard by Mrs. Maraj's superior attainments in the pursuit of her private enterprise, she deferred to the Indian entrepreneuse by impalpable nuances of manner and minute inflections of speech, all intimating the admiration a small shopkeeper might exhibit on meeting the founder and president of a great department store. With wistful self-reproach she disclosed to Mrs. Maraj that she had never had much success with boys. She had once employed two or three, but there had always been complications.

Mrs. Maraj responded with the sternness of a martinet. "I discipline my boys. I do not stand any foolishness. They are there to work." She produced a well-tried maxim for Madame's instruction. "Business is business."

Madame now wore a look, unfamiliar when one recalled the usual assurance of her manner, of modest self-deprecation. The reason for her relative failure with boys as employees had had to do with her beloved archbishop of lamented memory. His devotion to her had never wavered save in one regard, namely, his preference—even above her—the recollection clouded her eyes with a watery overcast of pardon and regret—his preference for boys. So, for the sake of her own self-preservation, so to speak, she had ceased to employ boys. Yet she could not bring herself to disclose that little sadness to Mrs. Maraj. A more successful entrepreneuse than she the distinguished Indian lady might be, but Madame was not going to relinquish every vestige of her self-esteem even in the face of so impressive an achievement as her guest's.

"And you also employ your daughter—do you?" She put the question tentatively, but was hardly able to complete it, for Mrs. Maraj supplied the required answer in a gracious display of courteous anticipation.

"Of course!" She bestowed a look of pride and affection upon her daughter, who in return was grateful to be included in these exchanges between her elders. "Sita is my star!" And as though impelled by an excess of cordiality or, it might have been, self-satisfaction, she gestured toward Dr. von Buffus. "Ask him," she invited Madame.

Madame turned to the professor, who smiled like Peter repudiating the suggestion that he was acquainted with Christ. Then he took Madame by the arm, led her aside, and in low whispers clarified for her, partially at any rate, the present enigmatic situation.

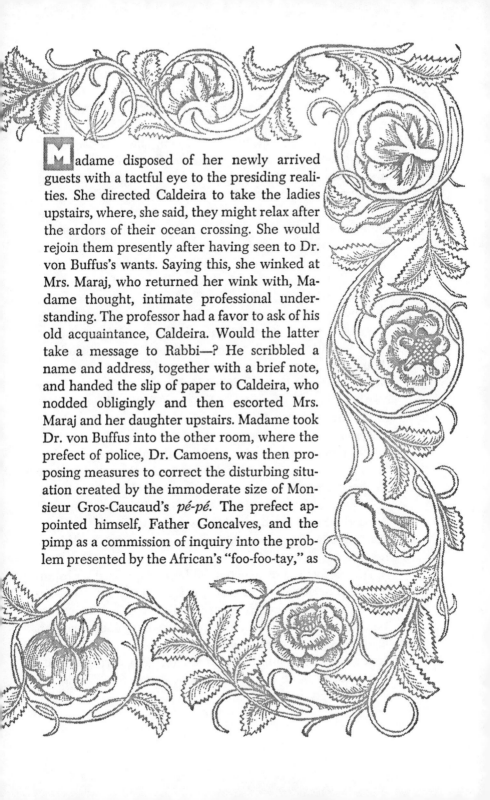

Madame disposed of her newly arrived guests with a tactful eye to the presiding realities. She directed Caldeira to take the ladies upstairs, where, she said, they might relax after the ardors of their ocean crossing. She would rejoin them presently after having seen to Dr. von Buffus's wants. Saying this, she winked at Mrs. Maraj, who returned her wink with, Madame thought, intimate professional understanding. The professor had a favor to ask of his old acquaintance, Caldeira. Would the latter take a message to Rabbi—? He scribbled a name and address, together with a brief note, and handed the slip of paper to Caldeira, who nodded obligingly and then escorted Mrs. Maraj and her daughter upstairs. Madame took Dr. von Buffus into the other room, where the prefect of police, Dr. Camoens, was then proposing measures to correct the disturbing situation created by the immoderate size of Monsieur Gros-Caucaud's *pé-pé*. The prefect appointed himself, Father Goncalves, and the pimp as a commission of inquiry into the problem presented by the African's "foo-foo-tay," as

Gros-Caucaud sometimes referred to his "person." He paused just long enough to permit Madame to introduce the professor before announcing that the commission was now in plenary session.

"You are very innocent, gentlemen," he told his fellow commissioners. "You have little experience of these blacks. If you only knew them as I do—" He hesitated, marshaling his memories. "I began my police career in Angola—Portuguese East Africa. Served there five years. Then Mozambique, seven years." The process of recall enfevered him. It was as if he were suffering from a recrudescence of tropical malaria. A burning sensation shot through him and he shivered. His bones ached with the recollection of endless, putrid swamps. Mosquitoes—huge, black, and canorous—sated with white men's blood, strafed him, machine-gunning his ears, to which he clapped his hands in futile defense against their relentless attack. "Mozambique," he repeated, as though the mere incantation of the place-name was sufficient to recount the horrors of his life there. Then he went off abruptly on a tangent of febrile recall. "I had some training in America, too. Special. Sent there from Lisbon. Police tactics in counterinsurgency." His extinct cigar lay at almost its full length, largely unsmoked, in the ashtray by his side. He summoned one hand to his brow and drew the back of the hand across its surface to dam the wavelets of sweat runneling from the roots of his ashen hair. "Harlem," he said. "And the South. Alabama. Mississippi. The Carolinas. Georgia. Virginia. Tennessee. Niggers. Niggers. Niggers. Always, niggers. Everywhere."

The prefect of police extended his arms toward his listeners, then deployed them after the fashion of a swimmer doing the breast stroke. He returned them to his chest and retained them there, directed outward, palms joined together, as he floated purposefully on the surface of his hearers' attention before taking the next stroke. "We Portuguese are the greatest of all colonizers. No other people—Gauls, Ro-

214

mans, Britons—have ever shown the consideration that we have done to our natives. We treat them like equals—even though, my friends, they are not. Race, color, religion—these things make no difference to us. To the Portuguese. It is we—we Portuguese—we who created the distinguished racial category *assimilado*, by which we gave explicit recognition to the ability of some blacks—some blacks, not all, not all—to become white in every respect except the color of their skin. As you well know"—he surveyed his hearers with the confidence, no more than an eyelash from arrogance, of a man having inalienable possession of an eternal verity—"there is no greater distinction." Pride suffused his bearing and uplifted his head. "My wife was a black woman. African. I married her"—he skipped a beat or two in the measure of his speaking so as to be certain that his freedom from racism did not pass lightly unnoticed—"in Angola. God rest her soul." He calculated the effect of this disclosure on his audience. But it had been received with no reaction of particular interest. Except on the part of Madame, who remarked: "And what a magnificent creature she was! How lucky you were, my friend! Everyone envied you—" She shook her head, freeing herself by that action of an unruly horde of recollections thronging into her mind. Father Goncalves, however, was more hospitable to his memories of the prefect's late wife. He had been her confessor and, aside from that, her secular confidant. She was critical of her husband, whom she habitually referred to as a "slave dealer." In actual fact, the prefect of police had purchased her from her parents during his service in Angola. She was then twelve years of age and he thirty-five years her senior. Her expectations of a normal African adolescence had been thwarted. Instead she found herself in the ownership of a Portuguese master and presently transported to a foreign land. She endured her unexpected state with remarkable guile and firmness of mind. Besides, her physical charms—even at that tender age—were so compelling that senior bureaucrats in

Lisbon, acting in the mistaken belief that the shortest route to her bed was by way of the quickest advancement of her husband's career, arranged his rapid promotion. Returning from Africa as a minor police official, he soon rose to a senior post at the Lisbon headquarters. After several years he was sent to the United States for advanced training in methods of detection. There were many among his colleagues who hoped that the reports of racial prejudice in the United States would induce him to leave his wife in Lisbon. But she was curious about America and bored by the continuous siege of her bedchamber. She decided to accompany him.

Once arrived in New York, the first stop on her husband's itinerary, she discovered Harlem. But her husband also made an important discovery of his own. He found that his wife, who was such an exotic adornment to him in Portugal, was a racial embarrassment in the United States. She, for her part, having been taken on a tour of Harlem, found the scene there so much to her taste that nothing could persuade her to return to the sterile hotel room in midtown Manhattan where she lodged with her husband. He himself was not altogether displeased about this, for he was shortly to leave for the southern part of the country and he had been advised that in view of certain peculiar circumstances existing there, it would be wise to leave his African wife in New York. This piece of advice was a relief to him and a delight to her. On his return from the South and other places on his training schedule, he would rejoin her for the journey back to Portugal.

For a lonely young African woman with a white husband engaged in studying police methods in the United States, what happier chance than to have found Harlem? So happy indeed was it for N'gawa that when her husband returned to New York at the end of his training program, he had a good deal of difficulty persuading her to accompany him back to Portugal. She had set up housekeeping in Harlem with a black man as magnificent as she from a physical standpoint who, moreover, viewed her as a gift from beyond the grave of the historic past sent to him by his African ancestors. He was therefore not disposed to return her to her "slave master" of a white, Portuguese husband. Neither did she wish to be returned. On the contrary, she asserted her right, in accordance with the polyandrous custom of her tribe, to a plurality of husbands. At this stage, however, she was opposed by her American lover, who, having been corrupted by the social conventions of the Christian West, was emphatic that one man should suffice for her needs, and *that* man of course was he. She succeeded in winning her Portuguese husband's agreement to her acquiring a "junior husband" in the person of her American lover. But the latter remained obdurate in his determination that she must have him and no other. It was true, he said, that he was a "nigger." But it was also true that his mother had taught him to be respectable no matter how black and poor he was. In addition, he was a born-again Christian, a Baptist in excellent standing and a lay preacher at a Harlem storefront church.

"You mean," she said to the American, "you think I am different—I am not good—because I sleep with another man?"

"Ah t'ink you is a hoo-er." The black Christian American minced no words in his moral righteousness.

"I not understand—"

"Hoo-er. Ho. Unnerstan'? Hoo-er." He launched into a vulgar elucidation of the meaning of the word. "It means you fucks—mo' dan one man."

"Oh," she said. "I see. Yes. Now I understand. But I am not 'hoo-er.' I am African woman."

At first her Portuguese husband had bridled at the prospect of a "nigger" as a permanent guest in his marital bed. Then he took with enthusiasm to the notion, envisioning all manner of alluring possibilities, calculating the highly varied permutations and combinations in which the anal

217

charms of the "junior husband" loomed as a factor of prepotent lure. He was hardly less disappointed than she when the American, outraged in his well-inculcated respectability, descended to common abuse, calling her "savage," "uncivilized," and other ill-tempered names, disclosing in effect the basest ingratitude to his remote ancestors. He had in fact not stopped at verbal reproach but in the midst of a discussion had produced a straight razor with which he threatened to chastise both the "hoo-er" his African ancestors had sent him and her Portuguese "slave master mother-fucker" of a husband. Whereupon the Portuguese displayed a gun and, apprehensive for his wife's safety no less than his own, pulled the trigger several times, much to the American's discomfort. The evidence of the razor satisfied the authorities that the Portuguese visitor had acted in self-defense and he and his African wife were permitted to leave the country while their assailant recovered at Harlem Hospital from his multiple wounds.

But the incident had soured the prefect of police especially because soon after their return to Portugal his wife had taken ill and died of pneumonia contracted when, in their haste to leave the Harlem apartment, she had fled scantily attired into the winter night and had then been obliged to endure prolonged exposure to the cold as they had awaited a taxicab.

The prefect now bore a grudge against all black men. He saddled them with collective guilt for the death of his African wife. Feeling as he did, he deeply sympathized in retrospect with the disapproving attitude toward blacks that he had generally noted in his travels throughout the United States. He also endorsed the old southern custom of castration of "uppity" black males. That African from the Côte d'Ivoire: he would be delighted to export him—to Alabama, for instance. But since that was not possible, he would deal with him here in more or less the same terms as would have obtained there. Every time he thought of that black mule

218

with the "oversized prick," as he inwardly regarded the African, he saw the black American in Harlem. They were all alike, these niggers; you couldn't tell one from the other.

"We should do something," said the pimp, but less in response to the prefect's representations than to his personal conviction that men talked only when they were incapable of action. "He's no good." A turbulent procession of black phalluses wended its way through the racial chaos of his mind. His eyelids performed a nictitating dance, blinking rapidly in a vain attempt to defend him against the black incursion. He employed black women in his business—they were his most lucrative source of income—but he drew the line at black men. This was in no sense the consequence of a sexist prejudice. It was simply a rule of business that he had formulated as the result of his experience. He had lost eleven of his white female employees after they had entertained black male clients. Indeed, one girl, rather better educated than the rest, had actually shouted "Eureka!"—and thereafter had absconded with her black patron, never to return. And that, in sum, had been his experience with the others. He had lost a good deal of business—and some very valuable whores—because of niggers. He was completely free of racial prejudice, but he was a businessman. What wasn't good for business wasn't good for him. In principle, he was opposed to castration. Also, he had nothing against the African. Yet, given the latter's genital endowments, it was undeniable that he could only be regarded as a threat to economic stability. What normal woman would not shout "Eureka!" at the bare sight of him? A few more like the African at large in Madeira and all the establishments would be emptied of their female staff. There would be nothing but vast and vegetating suburbs of contented housewives. This was an outlook as distasteful to the pimp as the spectacle of any of his girls appropriating to their own use the money they earned from the franchise of their bodies. In such cases, some form of mutilation was the required punishment. Castration was fair enough in the instance of the African. But the pimp was anxious to reassure himself that, at least, he harbored no racist animus toward the nigger. After it was all over and the latter had been rendered eunuchoid and harmless, he, the pimp, was sure that he would do anything for him. He would be his friend for life. He really liked niggers. Some of the finest black whores in Madeira worked for him. He was proud of it.

Looking across the room at the prefect of police, he experienced a disturbing sensation, which was only momentary, of peering into a mirror. Not for the first time had he remarked the strange physical likeness between himself and the prefect—a most curious thing. It was almost as if he were seeing a projection of himself thirty years hence.

Madame had caught his studied scrutiny of the prefect and, divining its meaning, sighed inaudibly. She decided that it would be prudent to deflect the pimp from his intent consideration of the prefect. So she took a hand in the proceedings. "And you, sir," she said to Mr. Balgobin Maraj in a clangorous tone that had the effect of scattering the pieces of the jigsaw puzzle which the pimp was trying to put together. "What do you think of—your friend?"

"I do not think anything. I do not know him. He is traveling on the ship. I have conversation with him. A whiskey. A beer. I try to help him find a piece of his luggage he has lost. But you cannot call him my friend. And I do not understand why they"—he looked from the prefect of police to the pimp—"do not like him. He is a quiet man. He does not bother anyone." He directed himself specifically to the prefect of police. "You say, my good sir, he is a 'nigger.' Well, am I not 'nigger,' too? I am Indian 'nigger.' I know. 'Nigger,' yes, I am." His voice took on the timbre of temple bells, plaintive at sunset. "Is it not?" Then, with a sudden defiant plangency, his head rearing up, his eyes at bay, he demanded: "Tell me."

Balgobin Maraj was at a loss to know what these "son-ah-

220

wah-bitches" (as he thought of them in the Trinidadian-East Indian vernacular) were up to. He himself was not especially concerned with God's color scheme. Privately, he felt that God often did not seem to know what the hell He was doing, anyhow. If you put a man in God's place and that man did some of the things that God did, everyone would say that that man was a damn fool. But if You are God, then You can get away with anything. No wonder there was only one God. If there were more than one, you could imagine what this world would be like. It was bad enough as it was, but with all those Gods doing whatever the hell They pleased, it would be an even bigger mess than it was. He was a Hindu and he had enough to do coping with his own God. So he didn't see why he should take on the Christian God, too. Let them—the Christians—worry about their God; he would look after his own God—his own Siva, his own Brahma, his own Vishnu—his own damn Cow. Until now he really had not taken these goings-on with very much seriousness. He demurred at the idea of interfering with the pleasures of the African, especially if this was to be encompassed by violence. He thought, and said as much, that violence was justifiable only if, as he expressed it, you caught a man "bam-bam-naked" in bed with your wife. If it should happen that you caught her in bed with a woman in a similar state of undress, then you would be entitled to take a whip to her behind—not to punish her with undue severity, but simply to chastise her for what he termed her "slackness"; if with a boy, you would be morally right to administer a damn slap to the young fellow (but not cuff, or kick, or otherwise mistreat him) and a strong verbal reprimand to your wife for being "so blasted idle."

Savagely, the tribunal turned on him and accused him of being a decadent Oriental.

"Our Hindu colleague," said Father Goncalves, "has made light of the chance of his respected wife's adultery with a member of her own sex—another woman." And here he paused to allow the enormity of Mr. Maraj's derelict code of morals to sink in upon his hearers. "But how, I ask you, sir, would you respond if a member of your own sex—a man like yourself—were to invite you to share his bed?" Father Goncalves looked intently at Mr. Maraj, and a sharp observer might perhaps have fancied, without malice, that he could detect a hopeful gleam in the eyes of the Reverend Father. Transferring his gaze to Madame, such an observer might have thought that he had seen her regard Father Goncalves with sly amusement, as if she were thus revealing her secret knowledge of his sexual preferences. But Madame's unspoken judgment was free of reproach. She had never permitted convention to interpose any barriers between herself and her equal—though not necessarily separate—enjoyment of both sexes. As the archbishop—that dear, good, civilized man—used to say: "Man cannot live by woman alone; nor woman alone by man." Amen, so be it, said she.

As became an intellectual, and with the situation regarding Monsieur Gros-Caucaud developing along the present lines, Professor von Buffus took flight into metaphysical speculations as to the Ultimate Necessity of the Human Phallus. His concern, unlike Balgobin Maraj's, tended to be abstract. He cleared his throat, following this by an audible smack of his tongue against the roof of his mouth. When the sound modulated into something between a snuffle and a whinny, he stretched out his legs and crossed his ankles and massaged them gently against each other. Only then—and this, more than anything else, betokened the greatness of the man—only then, and after isolating and elevating the middle finger of his right hand with an upward, thrusting gesture as a courteous request for silence, did he speak.

"The Human Phallus," he said, "is a long"—he reconnoitered his audience—"*histoire*. It is with great reluctance that I propose a difference with the learned monsignor." His respect for the eminent cleric was plain in the slight cough he sheltered apologetically behind the back of his hand. And his tone took on the gravitas of a Roman emperor's rescript as he continued: "In the beginning there was only Woman."

Father Goncalves started as if bitten by a Portuguese man-of-war while he was lying at ease in his bathtub. "You never can tell with these Germans," he thought. "They're either deposing Pope Gregory or standing barefoot and penitent outside his castle at Canossa." For the moment, however, he repressed the surge of disapproval of the professor cresting in his mind. It was the duty of a good Christian to suffer the heathen charitably.

Dr. von Buffus proceeded: "The male of the species had not yet made its appearance and indeed would likely not have done so but for one of those inexplicable genetic—" The professor sought—and with some difficulty at length located—the word: "conceits." He sucked in his underlip as though about to engage in an act of autocannibalism, then—not being hungry enough—extruded it. "Why is the penis of a jackass larger than that of a lion? Why do flowers pollinate, but animals copulate?" His eyes glistened with learning. "As Lartéguy-Pistier and my esteemed colleagues, Ernst Schüpthaus and Siegfried Henzelpüss, have conclusively shown as a result of their researches into the origins of the human penis, it was"—here the professor stretched out his arms, spread his hands apart, and rotated them in a scholarly fashion until they came to rest, palms down, before him—"a simple chromosomal accident." He mollified his hearers with a half-smile of dispassionate reassurance and repeated: "A simple chromosomal accident." He retracted his arms. Then he pulled his lips back across his dentures, which seemed to have been designed for a toothless horse and which gave him an impressive resemblance to George Washington.

Dorothea and I had more or less detached ourselves from the proceedings. I was whispering reassurances to her about

223

our future. But she turned her face away from me more often than toward me, and oftener still she cast furtive, sidelong glances at the pimp.

The professor meanwhile developed his disquisition. I noted that the prefect's cigar had expired. It now dangled indecisively and in insecure purchase between his lips.

"The Trinity in the Garden—Adam, Eve, and the Serpent—were thus joined by a new creature: Man, whom they named Lucifer." The expository rise and fall of the professor's voice held his hearers in thrall.

"Now Man quickly displayed his anarchic tendencies. For he had no sooner seen the two women bathing together at daybreak than, without even asking their consent, he straightaway mounted the two females one after the other, though one of them was his own mother. Thus he raped his parents, cuckolding one of them into the bargain. Not only was Incest born, but Jealousy as well. Strife erupted in the Garden. Until now, there had never been a cross word between Adam and Eve. But from this time onward, there was constant bickering between them. Eve would complain to the Man—Lucifer: 'You did Adam first yesterday; do me first today.' Then Adam would protest, saying that it was the day before yesterday, so it was her turn today. And they would begin calling each other names. Eve would call Adam a Capitalist who worshiped Profit even above God who had been so good to them. Adam would call Eve a Communist because she exploited Man. And so on. In the Garden, where at one time the loudest noise was the Serpent's hiss, there was now a constant din of quarreling, recrimination, and debate. Adam and Eve argued about the order in which Man should mount them before they went to sleep at nights. A compromise *à trois* was arrived at that was ingenious as well as gymnastic, and produced on the whole agreeable consequences. Yet it also gave rise to further disagreement on the question to be formulated billions of years later in theological terms in the fourth century. Under the rubric of the Nicene Creed it is subsumed as the 'homousian' as opposed to the 'homoiousian' belief. If Adam and Eve were of one substance (the homousian position), then could any argument be valid that denied that in the very act of mounting either Adam or Eve, Man at one and the same time mounted both of them? On the other hand, if they were essentially like each other yet not of the same substance (the homoiousian position), then was it not arguable that Man's Phallus was temporally limited and spatially restricted to serial rather than simultaneous functions? In other words," remarked the professor with a startling lapse into gross indecency, "Man cannot 'fick' and make pee-pee at the same time."

Madame's head jolted back. "The seedy old tomcat!" A smile danced across her face. In some odd way he reminded her of the archbishop. Enrapt in the professor's discourse, she did not at once notice that Caldeira had entered the room and was trying to get her attention. She now arose and went over to him. He whispered to her. Frowning with surprise and evident pleasure, she accompanied him out of the room.

She returned, preceding a bearded man who wore a skullcap and was dressed in a sober-hued suit of a cut that showed not the slightest regard for fashion, old or new. At the sight of him, the professor broke off speaking and came forward, arms outstretched. He and the newcomer embraced each other, Madame beaming all the while. Detaching him from Dr. von Buffus, she then introduced him around the room. "Rabbi Eleazar ben-Josephus."

The rabbi sat down and stroked his larch-silver beard that was trimmed to a scholarly compromise between a modest brush and a vaunting spade. His beard was an exegesis, a learned scholium, to the text of the self he piously cultivated as an inheritor of the ancient renown of the rabbinate.

Whatever the impulse or occasion that had brought him here at this hour, Madame's happiness at his presence was quite unaffected. That he was acquainted with the professor was natural enough, since learned men generally knew one another. "Please continue," she said to the professor with unexceptionable politeness, although she felt that he had talked enough as it was.

"I have just a little more to say." The professor grimaced with a wholly unexpected shyness that Madame found captivating despite his near-derelict appearance. He was developing his commentary on the parabiblical allegory of Jealousy in the Garden when, with a sound halfway between a whinny and a snuffle, the great scholar spread his hands apart and was silent. And with excellent reason. For into the room now came Monsieur Gros-Caucaud. The look on his face advertised his contentment. Smug and ineffable, it revealed the bliss of his ascension into heaven. There was an aura of postcoital ease about him, an air of having passionately skirted Gethsemane on his way to Paradise. He paused in the doorway, shifting experimentally from one foot to the other, making up his mind whether or not to rejoin these mortals below or shuttle back upstairs to heaven. His bemused rapture detained him a moment or two longer in the doorway before he made his way toward a chair and seated himself, hitching up his trousers, rearranging his tie, and smoothing the crisp hedge of hair away from his forehead with a gesture of his hand that intimated satiety and proclaimed triumph.

The blonde young lady, companion of his flight to Paradise, also reappeared in the doorway, much to Madame's astonishment, since it was against the rules of the house. Angels, like mere mortals, were required to know their place. Annoyance corrugated Madame's brow. Curiosity piqued the prefect of police. Father Goncalves sensed a Second Coming.

Before Madame could chastise the transgressor, who was standing there, her face aglow with the desire and expectation of an imminent return to Paradise, Monsieur Gros-Caucaud got up and started toward the door where his blonde houri awaited him. Wordlessly, in an ecstasy of nonverbal transport, they left the room together.

The effect on some of the occupants of the room was galvanic. They twitched, convulsed like frogs to whose legs a powerful electric current had been applied. As soon as he had sufficiently recovered, the prefect of police sought to put the informal court of inquisition back on its track. He threw all pretense aside, discarded the trumpery of dispassionate inquiry, and urged that the nigger be dealt with without further ado. The rabbi asked for clarification.

Meanwhile in one of Madame's *chambres d'assignation*, as she was fond of describing her upstairs rooms, Monsieur Gros-Caucaud and his blonde houri lay drowsy and sated on a furrowed bed. With one hand, trancelike, he stroked her corn-silken hair; with the other he played absently with the yellow-white switch of an electric cord suspended over the headboard of the bed. He contemplated her head at rest on his chest, as she lay partly asleep beside him. In profile, she was even more beautiful, he thought. But what especially riveted his attention was the contrast between the eggshell whiteness of her skin and the sloe blackness of his own. "*Cachou de Laval*," he muttered, withdrawing his hand from the electric switch and inspecting it minutely. Then, as if to dramatize the contrast between their respective pigments, he placed his hand against her stomach and kept it there. The starkness of the opposed colors brought a smirk of aesthetic pleasure to his capacious mouth. His hand commenced to explore the rubescent trail of silken down that began at her navel, and his fingers followed the trail downward. "*Cocquelicot*," he remarked of the color of the luxuriant undergrowth and noted again the contrast, which so fascinated him, between his near-sable and her off-white skin—or, as he observed to himself in his acquired French idiom, "*blanc de fard*."

She sighed and drew closer to him. A smile of eager accommodation replaced his air of satiety. His backside cocked in vaunting ecstasy, he bestrode the blonde young lady. As he did so, he remarked silently: "Those *salauds* downstairs should see me now."

The *"salauds,"* in Monsieur Gros-Caucaud's terminology, responded to the rabbi's request for clarification of the proceedings they were embarked upon by informing him in the words of the prefect of police that they were "going to take the nigger's balls." Dissenting, the rabbi cited a passage from the Old Testament: "He that is wounded in the stones, or that hath his privy member cut off, shall not enter into the Kingdom of Heaven. A eunuch shall not enter into the Kingdom of Heaven." Having thus revealed to the unenlightened the precise location of the Kingdom of Heaven, he then recommended circumcision.

Rabbi Eleazar ben-Josephus was a patron of Madame's establishment on the theory that the religious symbolism of the blowing of the shofar—the ram's horn—in Jewish synagogues had its secular parallel in the tide of human outcries that, night and day, rose and fell within the walls of the "Cloisters." In that vast diapason of ecstasy and lament, he heard the fugitive hope of triumph and the settled certainty of despair. There, he thought, in the ebb and flow of that dissonance, was the unmelodious, unorchestrated tone poem of the human condition.

Casting an appraising glance around the room, he noted again the various presences, and he remarked, too, a congruence, a symmetry, about the gathering, unprecedented as it was. Synagogue, Church, and State: God, Man, and the Devil. He explored the filaments of his beard, his fingers unconsciously forming themselves into an espalier to accommodate at need the hirsute, lush, and spreading tendrils.

Madame was intrigued by the complexities of the rabbi's persona, his hermetic urges contrasting so dramatically with his hankerings after the things of this world, an Essenian Jew at war within his spirit against the corruptions of the diaspora, to which he was every now and again in danger of succumbing. The Christian parallel of the rabbi's predicament was, she thought, the Temptation of Saint Anthony. She was aware that her friend the prefect, Dr. Camoens, did not share her view of the rabbi. "He'll weep like a saint as long as you've got your foot on his neck. But let him get his foot on yours and you'll see the difference. All that talk about loving mercy and doing justly and walking humbly with God—just wait and see. Wait. Just wait."

Take, for instance, the present case of the African: the prefect of police regarded the rabbi's position as a compromise of half-measures. He would have none of it. The rabbi stood firm, however, basing his stand, as he was entitled to do, on Jewish law and tradition. Speaking now, he trembled with the intensity that is commonly the mark of the illuminati. He focused himself as if for an earth-rending pronouncement from a Burning Bush. His entire aspect was that of a Prophet in possession of a Message delivered directly into his hands by the Ultimate Source of All Being. "When the Serpent, which is a form in which the Tempter often manifests himself, suggested to the First Man a *ménage à trois* with Adam and Eve, and Man accepted that suggestion, it led—as we know—to Man's exclusion from the Garden. For he had been lured by the Evil One into the acceptance of Tripersonalism—acceptance of the Trinity, that tragic falsehood, the threefold Diversity of which the Divine Unity is allegedly composed." The rabbi impaled his hearers with a look of penetrating sorrow. "Man Fell."

So here at last, thought Madame, was the reason for the rabbi's invariable insistence on two girls instead of one. He was what the archbishop used to call a "Crypto-Trinitarian."

Dr. von Buffus snuffled and nodded agreement with the rabbi, though remarking to himself on the capacity of Talmudic scholars for disemboweling a text of every particle of its intestinal significance.

Despite his regular diet of cream cheese and smoked

salmon, the rabbi's eyes were those of a man who subsisted solely on locusts and wild honey. This contradiction between his pampered body and his fanatical eyes was intriguing to Madame. As a favored customer, he was shown as a rule into one of her best rooms and supplied with two of her choicest girls. In accordance with his dietary laws, he strictly observed the kashruth and thus refrained from commingling dairy products and meat. In effect, this meant that the two girls he required for his pleasure had to be of the same skin color. Either two fair-skinned or two dark-skinned damsels, but never a contrasting pair made up of the one and the other. The girls reported that he also tended toward a certain orthodoxy in other respects. As, for example, at culminating moments of sexual ecstasy, he would cry aloud: "Hear ye, O Israel!" And at other times, "O God of Jacob!" A very pious man. At such moments Christians usually invoked the name of Christ or, among the more primitive of them, a four-letter expletive synonymous with fecal matter, while Muslims, in numerous instances, were given to uttering the plaintive, ululating cry of a muezzin in the minaret of a mosque calling the faithful to prayer.

The prefect of police ventured to interrupt the rabbi. "Pardon me—"

"In a moment, Excellency." The rabbi's right hand had returned to its inculcated reflex task of increasing the concavity of his beard while he meditated. A look of Delphic transcendence lit up his face. He seemed as if about to prophesy. But the inspiration faded, perhaps because of Dorothea's raising with disturbing candor a superbly sculptured leg and permitting it to linger in an unwitting act of intimate revelation before it slowly descended again until it lay, unquiet, across the other. Perhaps it was the mordant air of interior recall he felt exuding from Madame that suddenly put him in mind of carnal pleasures and uncovenanted delights. So he spoke instead of the Torah *she-be-al-peh* (the oral Torah) and the possibility of the textual corruption it may have introduced into the Torah *she-bi-kethabh* (the written Torah). Meanwhile he grappled inwardly with enticements of the flesh. He fought against the urge to investigate the present position of Dorothea's legs. The struggle was not easily won, for in the midst of it there intruded into his mind a rapturous vision of interminable grapplings with two delectable angels in one of Madame's upstairs chambers. Two identical angels, two identical ... In a fever of tropism his eyes sought Dorothea. He wondered when she would be available. Perhaps ... But, taking hold of himself, he yielded at last to the prefect's visible impatience and concluded: "As a people, we owe our earthly genesis to Abraham, but our miraculous persistence as the Chosen of God to Ezra. For it was Ezra 'who set his heart to seek the Torah of the Lord, and to teach to Israel statutes and judgments.' "

It was at this stage that I felt it might not be taken amiss if I were to intervene with a proposal of my own. I struggled a bit with myself before deciding on this step. My upbringing, which had been very carefully conducted, inclined me toward a certain hesitancy when it came to obtruding myself upon my elders. Young people should be seen and not heard. This was the primary rule of social intercourse between the respective age groups. Except in my instance, Aunt Jocasta brooked no deviation from it. I was therefore by training and habit unwilling to interpose myself in such a crisis as had arisen over the size of Gros-Caucaud's privy member. I should certainly have kept out of the matter altogether if I had not become aware that something extraordinary was afoot. For most people would agree that an uncommon event is set in motion when a proposal is laid on the table calling for amateur surgery on a man's private parts. I did not like the look of things. So, contrary to my inbred leanings, I ventured to make a suggestion. "You will pardon me, I—er—er—trust," I began in an apologetic tone. "But may I offer a proposal of my own?" There could be no mistaking the modesty of my reticence, the genuineness of my reluctance to intrude, or the deference with which I addressed myself to a gathering composed of people who, with the exception of Dorothea, were all very much my seniors. I took their silence as an indication of their willingness to indulge me. Thus I proceeded: "Inasmuch as your position in life, Monsignor Goncalves"—I meant the fact that he was a bishop of the Roman Church—"makes it"—I paused here, seeking the *mot juste*—"*unnecessary* for you to employ your privy member in the way that Monsieur Gros-Caucaud is obliged to do, would you perhaps consider"—I paused again, contemplating the precise word—"*sacrificing* yourself on his behalf? And you, sir," I said to the rabbi, being unwilling to risk by excluding him from my proposal an accusation of anti-Semitism, "would you?" And so as to show myself in no way hostile to the constabulary, I included the prefect of police on the grounds of his advanced age and the unlikelihood of his having any further sexual use for his "person." Finally, in order to make my impartiality plain beyond all question, I brought in the professor on the same grounds. Because of his relative youth, much as I disapproved of him, I excluded the pimp. While of course Balgobin Maraj was, like me, a Trinidadian whose "pencil" therefore possessed the sacred status of a religious object.

To my astonishment, my proposal was not well received. The profound silence that ensued was succeeded by a sanguinary onslaught against me. I was called a number of sordid names, repulsive in their sexual implications. Anal practices and obsessions of the most bestial sort were imputed to me. I bore all with the inborn dignity of a de Paria. Outwardly, at any rate. In my inner confusion and dismay, I noticed Madame whispering to the prefect of police, who thereupon threatened to place me under arrest on a charge of cruelty to my "person" by reason of my wilful refusal to allow it fresh air and exercise. The crime of "unnatural male virginity" was in his book a capital offense punishable by death on the gallows after a prolonged period of torture on the rack. Should I persist in my perversity, he would see to it that I either discharged my sexual duties as a man or paid the extreme penalty for my dereliction.

I was left in no doubt that he meant every word he said. Father Goncalves's crossing of himself and the rabbi's muttered "God of Abraham!" on hearing my proposal had not surprised me. But I was unprepared for the professor's reaction. For the first time in his tutorship of me, he betrayed distaste for my point of view. As before, he indicated his wish to address the group by isolating the middle finger of one hand and thrusting it vigorously upward. But despite his intention to direct his remarks to everyone present, he confined his digital gesture to me as a proof of the esteem in which he held his pupil. I was proud of his manifest regard. Strangely, however, he did not speak. With scarcely less unexpectedness, the other gentlemen whose spirit of self-sacrifice I had so eloquently invoked, each in turn repeated the professor's finger-probing gesture toward me. I was deeply moved by this sign of their good will, since I had only an hour or two earlier become acquainted with them for the first time. Wanting to give some sign of my own admiration for them, I thrust the middle finger of one hand upward as they had done. This token of my good opinion was greeted by a dissonant chorus in which only the words "Up yours!" were clearly distinguishable. They were all in a sudden dement, stabbing the air like frenzied assassins of invisible politicians. And, to my extreme perplexity, I was once again assailed with allegations of the coarsest character. It hardly seemed the proper response to my well-meaning gesture. I was all the more astounded when the prefect of police called me a "shit-eater" on his way to the door where he paused, half-turned, and shouted, "It's time for action!" All else aside, the prefect of police was, I thought, mistaken as to the nature of my diet. Within my certain knowledge, no de Paria has ever partaken of this Portuguese delicacy, ex-

233

cept perhaps unwittingly. I must remonstrate with that vulgarian. His manners are unsatisfactory.

The departure of the prefect of police had the momentary effect of reducing those of us remaining in the room to a state of seeming paralysis. Then, first the pimp, next Father Goncalves, and finally the rabbi and the professor followed him. This partial exodus might have been a signal for Caldeira, so quickly in the wake of their leaving did he now reenter the room. He beckoned silently to Maraj, who arose, looking perplexed and vaguely apprehensive. Taking him confidentially by the arm, Caldeira led him away. Dorothea and I were now alone with each other for the first time since our return to Madame's earlier that night.

As Caldeira was conveying Maraj upstairs, the latter asked: "What sort of woman is this you say you givin' me? You sure she—" He broke off and looked hard at Caldeira, obviously reconsidering the situation. Something about this man was obscurely familiar, he felt. It was as if he had seen—or met—him somewhere, sometime . . . "You sure—" he began again, and paused again, troubled by a tiny green shoot of memory trying to make its way toward the light. But how could he possibly be—? And yet . . . "I didn't hear your name," he said to Caldeira.

"My name?" Caldeira, one step higher, looked down at him. The sonofabitch didn't look a day older, he thought. Same shiny white teeth, same hook nose, same— "My—they call me—" He cleared his throat so as to gain time to decide if he should give his right name. Just in case—just in case— But what the hell, man, this "macco" never knew him so well that he could recognize him with any certainty in unfamiliar surroundings. But he'd better not take any chances. "They call me Brito," he said.

Maraj pondered the disclosure, baring his teeth with the effort of concentration, and running one hand through his hair in pursuit of remembrance. He sought a clue, a trail, a hint, a point of reference to aid recall. Whatever it was, he did not find it. Perplexed by the elusiveness of recollection, he resorted to whimsicality. He wished to tell Caldeira a joke. "You ever hear this one"—the disturbing sensation persisted, but he shrugged it off—"Brito?" Even now, however, a speculative doubt returned. Had he met this man before?

Though a step below Caldeira as they stood on the stairs facing each other, he was almost as tall as the latter. He smiled, hoping to put Caldeira at ease, conscious as he was of his own unease. But the thought of the woman to whom Caldeira was taking him obtruded into his mind. Eagerness supplanted uncertainty, and his loins, aiding and abetting the resurgence of confidence, warmed to the task ahead. He put both hands into his pockets and, so doing, assured himself of his instant sexual capability. He was ready. "Leh we go, man," he told Caldeira.

The latter did not move. He seemed instead to be studying Maraj. He must have been rather less than reserved in his exploration, for Maraj said to him with emphatic though good-humored impatience: "What's the matter, man?"

Caldeira terminated his study. He returned Maraj's smile. "Nothing, man. Ah was only—"

"Wey's de woman, man? Leh we go, nuh, boy—"

"You in a hurry, yes." He watched Maraj, apparently enjoying what he saw. "But business first, man."

"Buh how you mean—?"

Caldeira rubbed his index and middle fingers against his thumb in a smooth and rapid motion.

Maraj got the point. "Money?"

"Uh-huh."

"How much?"

"For a short time or a long time?"

"Ah go see, nuh, man. If she nice—"

"Long time, two dollars. Short time, one dollar."

In his delight at such a bargain, Maraj almost fell on Caldeira. "Two—" he gurgled. "One—"

"Yes, man. I wouldn't charge you nothing—ef it was me alone. But I got to pay the Madame something—"

"But you not chargin' me much, man. Two—"

"I know. But I like you, man. I can see you'se me frien'."

Maraj put his hand on the other's shoulder. "If you ever come to Trinidad, boy"—he amassed his prospective generosity into an impressive pile—"I'll buy you the best whore in the whole island."

"She couldn't be better than this one, man, this woman Ah got fer you upstairs. Every man come here—she is the first one dey arks for. Dey don' warnt *no*-body else."

"She mus' be good, boy."

"Champion."

"Yo' ever try she yo'self?"

"Plenty times, man. Ah'm telling' you she good. She good too-bad. She really good." He felt that he should adduce a concrete instance to support his encomium. "She does do anyt'ing you warnt. Wid dog, cat, monkey, mule—anyt'ing."

"Dog—?" His imagination exploded into a riot of erotic fantasies.

Caldeira nodded, feeding him a fresh stimulus. "Jackass, too."

"Jackass—?"

He nodded again. And so as to do full justice to the prowess of this eminent whore. "I see she one time with a horse, boy—an' you know, horse totee big—"

"O Gawd, man! You mus' be mekkin' joke. You mus' be— horse, you say? Horse?"

"Ah'm tellin' you, man. True-true." He made a cross with the index fingers of both hands and kissed it. "True-true-true. S'elp me Gawd." And so as to remove the least particle of doubt that might yet linger in Maraj's mind, "Two man try she out one night—one in front and one behind. All night long. Nex' mornin', bright an' early, she went to mass—as if nuttin' happen. Buh dem two—big, strong man—dem two, boy, dey sleep fer t'ree days, dey so tired. Dat 'oman nea'ly kill dem, she so good."

Maraj's hands returned to his pockets. Fired anew by the solid reassurance he encountered there, he was overcome by his impatience. "Leh we go. Ah keah wait, man."

Caldeira ascended two steps and stopped, barring Maraj's passage. He raised his hand in a detaining gesture.

"Wha' happen', man?" Maraj did not understand the delay. He explored Caldeira's face afresh and again was seized by the notion that somewhere, sometime . . . But his effort at recall was deflected by his hand's slipping back into his trousers pocket. "Ah'm ready," he said to Caldeira.

Yet the latter was unmoved—and unmoving. "Lissen, nuh." He wore an air of grave concern. "If you find out— afterwards—that she gi'e you—a clap—you go' blame me?"

Maraj indignantly dismissed the possibility either of contracting a venereal disease or of blaming Caldeira. "Clap—?" His voice rose and his eyes kindled. "Don' make joke, man."

"Clap eh' no joke." Caldeira pondered his aphorism as Maraj, ignoring its homely wisdom, tried to push past him. But Caldeira refused to give ground. "Leh me tell you, boy. She—dis 'oman—is a big ho', you know. She—an' she daughter—dey's two o' de biggest ho's—"

"Man, gimme de daughter, too. Wey de hell you tellin' me 'bout clap? Clap arse, man. Yo' tryin' to frighten me? Eh? Leh we—" He paused, his assurgent penis prefiguring for him visions of dual ecstasy. "De two o' dem, man. De mudder an' de darter. O Gawd! Ah go' gi'e dem lartee [a vulgar East Indian synonym for penis]. Yes, de two—" He pulled out his wallet. "How much?" His long, beautifully sculptured fingers probed the interior of the wallet and presently emerged with a number of fresh, virginal bank notes.

There was nothing—and no one—that money could not buy. "Look, man: how much you warnt—fer de two o' dem?" With deep satisfaction he relished the power his money conferred on him. The notes made soft and sibilant sounds as he rustled them between his fingers. The susurration of financial power enchanted him. The marketing of clandestine love allured him. And the blazing fire in his loins— "Here." He offered one of the notes to Caldeira, who gave no sign of acceptance. Instead he appeared to be absorbed in contemplation of Maraj, taking him in but at the same time spewing him out. In Maraj's febrile urgency to be conveyed to the women who awaited him, his breathing became quite audible. An ingratiating smile, enwreathing power with the grace of charm, emphasized the aquilinity of his nose and advertised the splendor of his teeth.

Caldeira, however, was unpersuaded. He seemed indifferent to the symbol of financial power that Maraj was dangling before his eyes. Indeed, he did not so much as glance at the money to make sure, at least, that he was not refusing more than prudence would approve. He disclosed his own teeth in pretended amiability. "O Gawd, man!" he exclaimed. "Ah keah leh you do dis."

Maraj winced like a man who had just been dealt a solid blow below the heart. But he recovered almost at once and, believing that he had diagnosed the cause of Caldeira's change of mind, increased his offer of payment. He was all the more puzzled when Caldeira declined it.

"No. All Ah warnt is—"

By this time Maraj would have cheerfully given him the whole earth and thrown in with it for good measure the highest prospects of heaven.

"You know somet'ing," said Caldeira, veering away from whatever it was he had begun to say, "dose two bitches might gi'e you somet'ing else, too. Ah'll be sorry fer you, boy." He appraised with a pitying look the object of his probable sorrow. "You ever hear 'bout a t'ing call 'buboe'?"

Maraj shook his head once, twice, up and down. Yes, he

had. But not all the plagues of all the brothels in the universe would deter him now. "How much you warnt, man?"

"Aaaa-right, boy. Don' say Ah didn' tell you. Dese two ho's is nasty, yes. Dirty too-much." He sighed with disgust.

"How much?" Maraj sensed the imminence of entry into Paradise. There was an orgasmic trumpeting about his ears and a blazing furnace in his loins.

Caldeira seemed lost in thought. "De darter is even wuss dan de mudder. W'en de darter gi'e you a clap, boy, it don' get better—she nasty so. But de mudder one time gi'e a monkey a clap, an' den—de monkey gi'e it to de darter. Den de darter gi'e it to a mule an' de mule gi'e it back to de mudder. Den de mudder gi'e it to a jackass an' de jackass gi'e it back to de darter. An' den de darter gi'e it to a big ole ram goat—beh-h-h-h-h! Beh-h-h-h-h! Beh-h-h-h!"

The effect on Maraj of Caldeira's imitation of the bleating of a goat was astonishing. He gripped Maraj by the arm. His teeth clattered and his eyes were live coals. He slid his free hand into a trousers pocket and his urgency grew ungovernable. "How much, man? How much? We was'in' time. Ah don' care if dey even have de syph—leh we go, man. Leh we go. How much?"

Caldeira removed Maraj's hand from his arm. "Ah tellin' you fer de las' time," he said to him, "don' blame me w'en yo' keah piss. Dem two ho's is so—" A simile to measure, to illustrate, their leprous, scabied state eluded him. "Dog 'self won' lick dem." He contemplated Maraj with pity and loathing as for a man about to dive headfirst into a cesspool crawling with the most repellent forms of life. "Gimme one dollar—fer de two o' dem."

"You foolin' me, man—"

"One dollar." The finality in Caldeira's voice cut sharply into Maraj's incredulity.

"Aaa-right. But Ah still t'ink—" The look on Caldeira's face curtailed Maraj's comment and put him in fear of the loss of Paradise unless he complied without further ado with the former's demand.

As Caldeira examined the one-dollar bill that Maraj had handed over, there was a look on his face that implied a suspicion as to its genuineness. When, apparently, he had satisfied himself that the bill was not counterfeit, he stowed it away with deliberate care in the inner breast pocket of his jacket.

Maraj, effusive at the completion of a much-sought bargain, confided in a waterspout of pride: "Life funny, yes. You t'ink, boy, you will ever see my wife an' daughter in a place like dis? No, man." They had reached the top of the stairs. He halted for a moment and placed his hand on the carved and ornamental top of the balustrade. "Befo' we leave dis place—I mean, Madeira—you mus' meet my wife an' daughter, man." He was eager to propose an occasion suitably to reward Caldeira for his friendship and munificence. "We mus' take dinner together. Eat some food, man. On the ship." He reached out and pressed Caldeira's hand. "Boy, you's a real frien'."

Abruptly, Caldeira withdrew his hand from Maraj's grasp. "Leh we go," he said.

They went along the corridor leading from the staircase to a series of rooms whose doors were tastefully decorated with individual and distinguishing insignia. "Flamingo," "Pelican," "Eagle," "Swan," and "Seagull" on one side of the corridor, and on the other, "Petunia," "Chrysanthemum," "Rose," "Gardenia," and "Lilac." At the end of the corridor, which was T-shaped, were the "Fruits"—five rooms in all, each designated by a chosen symbol of luscious fruit.

Caldeira halted at "Gardenia." He placed a finger against his closed lips as a gesture of silence. "Wait," he said to Maraj. "Ah'm goin' in to get she ready fer you." He entered the room. Maraj stood outside and waited.

"Jeesus Christ, man!" he exulted inwardly. Here he was in

a Po'tagee ho'house about to "tay-lay-lay" with one—maybe two—girls. Gratitude to Caldeira swelled and surged within him. Then a great wave of wanting crested in his loins. "Ah go' gi'e she good," he assured himself in a gloating whisper. "Ah go' gi'e she"—his hand in his trousers pocket tested the temper of his penis—"lartee." The indecent East Indian synonym for his "person" enveloped his face with a smile of pleasurable anticipation. But his leering expectancy was suddenly altered into a grimace of concern. He remembered now that that mister-man—Brito, as he'd said his name was—had earlier that night taken— No. He'd asked him to take them, his wife and daughter, to see the town. And he didn't even know the man's name. But the man had looked so familiar, and the professor seemed to know him. So he reassured himself that it was all right. In any case, by now—he scanned his wristwatch—they'd be back on the ship, fast asleep.

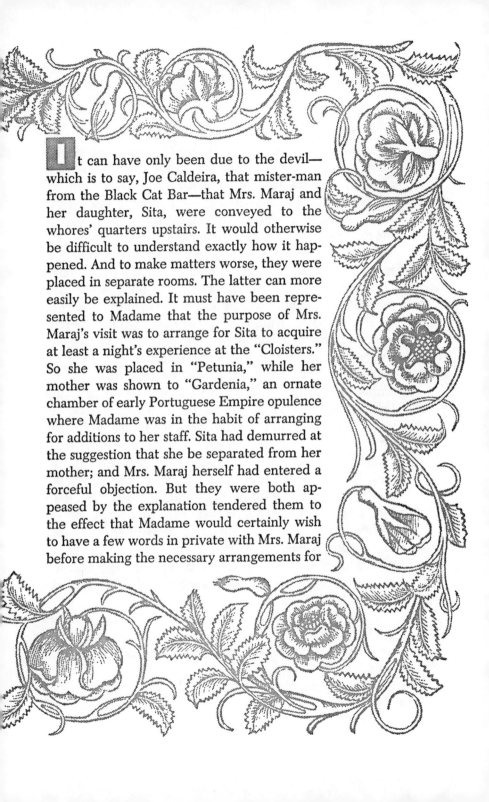

It can have only been due to the devil—which is to say, Joe Caldeira, that mister-man from the Black Cat Bar—that Mrs. Maraj and her daughter, Sita, were conveyed to the whores' quarters upstairs. It would otherwise be difficult to understand exactly how it happened. And to make matters worse, they were placed in separate rooms. The latter can more easily be explained. It must have been represented to Madame that the purpose of Mrs. Maraj's visit was to arrange for Sita to acquire at least a night's experience at the "Cloisters." So she was placed in "Petunia," while her mother was shown to "Gardenia," an ornate chamber of early Portuguese Empire opulence where Madame was in the habit of arranging for additions to her staff. Sita had demurred at the suggestion that she be separated from her mother; and Mrs. Maraj herself had entered a forceful objection. But they were both appeased by the explanation tendered them to the effect that Madame would certainly wish to have a few words in private with Mrs. Maraj before making the necessary arrangements for

Sita. It was a trifling matter of protocol and as soon as the required formalities were observed, the ladies would be reunited without delay.

"I hope my daughter will be safe," said Mrs. Maraj. They were, after all, in a strange land. She looked around the room, taking in its velvet-and-ormolu obeisance to the décor of a vanished era. Her friend Mrs. Mootisingh had antimacassars like those in her house in San Fernando. But she had never seen a coverlet like this. She got up and went over to the canopied four-poster. Running an index finger along the surface of the coverlet, she noted with admiration the knitted whorls in the variegated designs of contrasting colors. "It's like a rainbow on the bed," she told herself. The thought of a rainbow evoked for her the memory of a tropical sky after rain. Rain, batteries of rain, assailing the rooftops, fusillade after thunderous fusillade. So that one took refuge in bed, snug beneath the sheets, secure from the lightning though cowering at the thunder, apprehensive amidst the cool, reassuring linen of one's own inviolable bed, curling and uncurling one's toes until sleep shut out the sound of the thunder and snuffed out the threat of the lightning's vivid aggression. And once upon a time, if Balgo chanced to be at home, he would come into bed with her and the sounds of their rapture would commingle, dulcimer-sweet, in a duet for baritone and mezzo-soprano flute-piping against the growl and roar of the thunder.

Now, sitting here in this unfamiliar room awaiting—she did not know what or whom—Mrs. Maraj curled and uncurled her plump, silk-stockinged toes in the dagger-heeled, patent-leather shoes she was wearing. And she wished she were back at home instead of—

The door to the room was flung open after a preliminary rattling of the lock that in her deep abstraction sounded to her like thunder. She was startled and she sat up, her spine rigid.

Madame entered. "Welcome," she once more greeted

Mrs. Maraj. The scent of business imparted a quiver, a tiny, very tiny, quiver to her nostrils. She anticipated the recruitment of exotic additions to her staff. An expert eye took in Mrs. Maraj's charms at a glance and, remarking a brace of breasts, unconstrained, upspringing, outthrusting, and melon-sized, estimated her instantly as a potential asset of immense profit. She did not conceal her satisfaction at the prospect. How mistaken she had been at first. She had then thought that Mrs. Maraj was, like herself, a chatelaine. But Caldeira had put her right. "We shall get on well," she assured Mrs. Maraj. "Tell me all about yourself."

Mrs. Maraj's bewilderment was plain. She hesitated, groping for a clue to transparency in this opaque situation. She simply could not see what it was all about. Here she was, looking for her husband, and—

"Please take your clothes off," Madame told her.

Mrs. Maraj suddenly was unsure of her hearing. She cupped one hand and put it behind an ear. "Eh? What you say?"

Madame repeated her wish and, for the benefit of Mrs. Maraj, who evidently did not know English very well, she elucidated it. "Undress."

Mrs. Maraj's puzzlement reduced her to repetition. "Undress?" What the hell for? she thought. What was this damn woman up to? No sooner did you leave Trinidad than people began to act like blasted fools. She should have stayed home and let Balgobin go to hell about his business. All this England and England and England and London and London and London—and where was Sita, anyway?

The thought of Sita made a swift passage into an abrupt question to Madame, whose mouth folded, soothingly, into a little grimace of reassurance. "She's all right. Don't worry."

Madame appraised Mrs. Maraj in horticultural terms as a delectable fruit of the tropics ripe for plucking and lusting— simply lusting—to be eaten. She was particularly impressed by the size and symmetry of Mrs. Maraj's breasts. It was easy to see that in those twin treasure houses were rich cargoes of pleasure and handsome returns of commercial profit. To these dual prospects Madame was most sensitive. She could barely wait to explore these repositories of the sensual wealth of the Indies in all their nude, erotic splendor. For the first two or three weeks, she resolved, no one but she, neither man nor any other woman, would be permitted to love Mrs. Maraj. The razor-keen edge of her desire cut deeply into her patience. "Take your clothes off," she said again.

"But why?" Mrs. Maraj was half-curious and half-exasperated. She had heard about these people who lived outside of Trinidad, how strange they were, the things they did, the way they behaved. And this one— She began to curl and uncurl her toes as if she were in bed during a massive rainstorm. And this— But where the hell was Balgo? Everything was so strange, and the people so funny in their ways— And look at this damn room, man. She had never been in a whorehouse, but she should imagine that a whorehouse would look like this—would be something like this. With all this—this silk and satin—all this *"commerce"*—she felt Madame's gaze and heard Madame's voice. It was more insistent now, somewhat peremptory, with a hint of command. "Do as I say. Take your clothes off."

"But why?"

"It is the custom."

"What custom?" Mrs. Maraj curled and uncurled her toes. Man, you jus' leave Trinidad, an' everything is so damn—is like another world. She looked up at Madame.

"I shall help you," said Madame. She went straight to the point, attempting to remove Mrs. Maraj's underwear.

But Mrs. Maraj checked her with a stern forthrightness, an honest righteousness, that was a tribute to her Presbyterian upbringing in the fabled island of Trinidad, the adopted home of her grandparents. "Wey de arse wrong wid you, woman?" she rebuked Madame, thrusting her aside. Then charity—again, the legacy of her moral training at the hands of the Presbyterian ministry—coming to the fore: "Buh, lissen nuh, Ah warnt to arks you somet'ing." She eyed Madame with Christian disesteem, thinking to herself: "Buh jus' look at dis damn ole bitch, eh. She warnt to sanga-wanga me. Buh you ever see t'ing so? A ole, dry-up t'ing like dat." Aloud she said: "Somet'ing bodderin' me." Her eyes resumed their minute inquiry into the moral dilemma presented by what she saw as the contradiction between Madame's cambric-and-lace pretensions to respectability and her calico-and-burlap addiction to depravity. "Tell me de trut'." She made a cross with her index fingers and kissed it in an exemplary fashion. "So help you Gawd—tell me: you is a ho', eh? Tell me de trut'. You don' have to shame. God will help you," she promised on behalf of the Almighty. And with a smile of Christ-like forbearance from final judgment she reassured Madame, "Plenty people is ho'." But her eyes maintained their unrelenting inquisition. "Tell me de trut'. You is a ho'—you come in here tryin' to sanga-wanga wid me as if you is a man." She surveyed Madame in severe reproof. "An' you so damn ole—w'y de arse you don' go to church?" Her voice softened, though her eyes were no less Gandhian in their moral implacability. "You is a ho'. I know."

Madame showed no embarrassment. A brief titter of amusement was all that she permitted herself. In a moment she had again donned her habitual mask of composure and she was once again the poised and gracious hostess. "Quaint," she thought, "these savages." Yet instantly recalling her duty to the less advanced in the scale of civilization, she pointed to the bidet standing in a corner of the room and helpfully explained its purpose and mode of operation to Mrs. Maraj. Quitting the room, she made a mental note to admonish Caldeira to be more observant. Ah!—and this wedding—she'd almost forgotten. She went in search of Johnny and Dorothea and so missed Caldeira and Maraj as they came up the staircase.

Mrs. Maraj was reclining on the canopied four-poster in the room where Madame had left her, puzzling over the odd developments swirling around. She wondered about that broken-down old professor who was the cause of her being here. He and the Po'tagee—meaning Caldeira. She recalled the professor's habit of coming into her cabin every morning in order, he said, to make sure that the portholes were open and, because he was a doctor, always wanting to examine her—and Sita. She thought of his hands poking about their bodies, exploring their most intimate parts so as to find out, he told them, if they needed a prescription that he "could write but not fill." She remembered how he would sigh as he said that, shaking his head, which was as big as two ripe calabashes, and then laying it against her chest and on her stomach to listen for medical symptoms. He went through the same procedures with Sita and gave it as his professional opinion after having examined her one morning that when Sita became pregnant she would bear quadruplets. "Four," he predicted, illustrating the number with a show of fingers. His prognosis was based on certain indications that, thirty years previously—or perhaps twenty—or even ten—he would have explored more intensively. As it was, however . . . Once again a sigh that was more like a moan escaped him. It was when he demanded samples of their urine, though, that his medical services were terminated. His insistence that he was a "hydrological cabalist who specialized in urinometry" got him nowhere. The ladies were adamant in their refusal and began to question his professional credentials. For they could neither understand nor accept his demand that they urinate in his presence, else the samples would reveal nothing. He would also have to position himself so that he could actually *see* the ejection of the water, he explained.

248

"Wha' kind o' doctor you is?" Mrs. Maraj inquired with some vehemence, from which skepticism and incredulity were no longer wholly absent. "You look mo' to me like a w'ite obeah-man." A black obeah-man, she was implying, was one thing—and not at all unfamiliar. But a white obeah-man—?

Anyway, from that time onward she forbade him entry to the cabin unless her husband was present. He complained to Maraj, who then berated his wife for her suspicious nature.

"Ah don' suspec'," she defended herself and her daughter. "Ah know." And as an irrefutable warranty of her secret knowledge—and her daughter's—she told her husband in a tone cryptic yet as explicit as Eve admitting Original Sin to God in the Garden. "Boy, you damn lucky dat ole ram goat don' have no totee. You lucky 'is totee dead."

She wondered now what was happening to Sita in this damn place. . . .

Once again the door to the room was suddenly opened, and this time it was Caldeira who entered. He left the door unlocked behind him, and without a word began to undress.

Mrs. Maraj took immediate exception to Caldeira's behavior. "Wha' wrong wid you?" Bewilderment competed on more or less equal terms with indignation in her tone. "You goin' mad?" Her mouth hung agape as Caldeira removed all of his clothing. "Buh Jeez-an'-age! All o' you crazy so? De odder one—dat old dry-up t'ing—jus' come in here tryin' to make s'amie wid me. An' now, you—" She considered Caldeira with frosty disapproval, noting—among his other unattractive points—that he didn't have much of a "t'ing." It was shaped funny, too; like it had a little p'unch in the middle and t'in-t'in at the end. Her disapprobation heightened as she remarked the flabby state of his backside. Worst of all, from her point of view, he was covered from head to foot with a rank growth of weedlike hair—jus' as if he was a damn monkey. Ugh! De man ugly too-bad. Aloud, she said to

Caldeira, "Lissen, nuh, wey-ever de hell wrong wid you, boy, put back on you' clo'es an' get you' arse outa here."

Caldeira gave her an appealing smile and placed a forefinger against his lips, enjoining silence. But the effect on Mrs. Maraj was not disarming, and she showed every sign of being uncooperative.

"Ah'm goin' back to Trinidad," she announced. "Ah'm tired o' all dis foolishness. Ah jus' leave home an' look wha' happenin' to me—a ole squingy-up w'ite man playin' doctor come feelin' up me and me daughter. A old dry-up Po'tagee woman come in here tryin' to mek s'amie wid me. An' now you—you damn ole macaque" (a macaque being a species of monkey)—she eyed him with sharp distaste—"naked as you wuz born." She continued her appraisal of him, her estimate clearly being unfavorable. "An' you don' even have any t'ing—you damn ole capon." She left the bed and came toward him, bent on his extrusion from the room.

Sensing her intent, he began to dodge here and there in an effort to evade her. As he did so, he teased her playfully: "Leh we play Mooma and Poopa" (a Trinidadian euphemism for engaging in sexual intercourse), which only heightened her determination to be rid of him. Luring her near to the bed, however, Caldeira managed to trip her so that she fell on it. Whereupon he pretended to mount her. Furious, she heaved him off, but, laughing and shouting endearments to her so that anyone standing, as her husband was, directly outside the door must have heard, he succeeded in mounting her again, only to be heaved off once more and once more to remount, bellowing all the while: "Yes, doux-doux! Ah! But yo' so nice, dahlin'! Ah'll never leave you, sugarplum! Ah! Mo' by so, doux-doux! Yes, doux-doux! Yes, doux-doux!" She meantime was screaming, hoarse with anger, "Get yo' arse off o' me, you sonofabitch!" and reaching for his testicles in order to castrate him with her bare hands. But he had prudently hidden them between his closed thighs and, trying to imprison her hands and avoid her teeth, would whisper to her between his shouts: "It eh nutt'n, man. Is only a joke." Yet she, discerning no humor in the situation—not even an inquisitive appendage anywhere about Caldeira that might be described as probing—continued to scream, "Get yo' arse off o' me!"

It was at this juncture that Mr. Maraj found himself unable any longer to restrain his urgency. He was also intrigued by the orgiastic sound he could hear so much the more seductively by placing his ear against the door. So he entered the room.

He was at first winded, like a runner at the end of a long-distance race, by the spectacle that presented itself. There was Caldeira on top of a woman, alternately trumpeting and billing and cooing endearments to her. And there was the woman writhing and screaming in apparent ecstasy. He began to undress. Quite unexpectedly, however, Caldeira abandoned the lady's embraces. Pursued by her infuriated denunciations, in one swoop he gathered up his clothing and without even so much as a word of greeting or encouragement to Maraj, vanished naked through the door.

Whether from bewilderment or the sheer impossibility of conceding the stark actuality, it was a long, incredulous moment before Mr. and Mrs. Maraj identified each other. Recognition had come sooner. But it was the quavering disbelief, the paralyzing horror—on Maraj's part, and on hers—the shrill alarm, the terrified rejection of reality, that lent poignancy to their exchange.

"—Puthi—!"

"—O Gawd! Balgo—!"

At the sound of her voice, Maraj discarded his perplexity. Accepting the evidence of his own eyes, like the successful businessman that he was, he took a frenzied leap to an outraged conclusion. "So—" He surveyed her at a distance. "Ah ketch you." In his mind there was a single, uncontested certainty to which he now gave succinct utterance: "You's a ho'." His voice at first was low, his speech reined in and subdued despite its straining vehemence. "You's a ho'," he repeated. But overcome by his indignation, his voice rose and his speech grew comminatory. "You's a ho', Puthi. You mekkin' paccotee." ("Making paccotee" is Trinidadian patois descriptive of the sexual activities of a prostitute. "Paccotee" probably is a corrupted form of *pas couture*, the implication being that no lady ever entirely disrobed herself for sexual purposes; only prostitutes did so.) There could be no question about it. Maraj was displeased.

"I didn' do not'in'," she offered in self-defense.

"You didn' do not'in'? Is dat w'at you call it?" His tone was plainly sarcastic. "Buh look at you, nuh—you eh do not'in'. You dey wid you' clo'es rumple-up, de bed rumple-up— Ah hear you wid me own ears—you screamin', you like it so much. Ah see de man wid me own eyes—naked like a fowl-hen arse—on top o' you. An' Ah hear 'im wid me own ears— callin' you 'doux-doux,' 'dahlin',' 'sugarplum.' An' still an' all, you tellin' me you eh do not'in'. Don' make joke, man. Wey you call 'not'in'? You's a ho'."

"You wrong, Balgo, you wrong, boy. Lissen to w'at Ah'm tellin' you—"

"Ah don' warnt to hear not'in', man. Look—Ah leave you on de ship—Ah'm carryin' you to England wid me—to England, yes—an' w'en de mark bu's' [a vernacular reference to the winning number in a Trinidadian game of chance called "whé-whé"], Ah find you sanga-wanga-in' in a ho'-house. An' still an' all, you tellin' me—"

But Mrs. Maraj was annoyed by her jealous husband's impugning of her honor. In cold reproof she asked: "Wey youself doin' here?" And, giving him no time to recover from her unexpected thrust, she attacked again. "Why you come here? You stannin' up dey, playin' holy, wid you' drawers off an' you' piggie all expose'? Wey you lookin' for? A pot to pee in? An' de only place you could find one was a ho'-house? Man, you eh shame? Look at me—" She moved a step or two toward him, then stopped and lifted up her skirt, revealing her panties. "You see—I have on me drawers. So w'y you don' have on yours? W'y you stannin' up dey wid you' piggie? Look at you—dey—in you' merino in a ho'-house. You should be shame o' you'self—a big ole married man like you—"

Her husband, however, was not so easily overborne. Bitterly, his voice freighted with the knowledge of betrayal, he responded: "Kiss my arse, woman. You'se a damn bitch, man." In its way, his outburst was the equivalent of "*Sola. Perduta. Abbandonata.*" But Balgobin Maraj was unaddicted to operatic flights of mortification. "Ah gi'e you everyt'ing you warnt. Big house, plenty clo'es, de bes' o' food, de finest rum—everyt'ing. An' still an' all, Ah walk in here an' Ah ketch you mekkin' paccotee." He assimilated anew the enormity of her betrayal of him. "An' I—like a damn fool—I takin' you wid me to England. Not Barbados, nuh. Not Demerara, not Grenada, not Jamaica—but England. England 'self, girl. An' look wey you do me? You mekkin' paccotee—" He addressed her at this point with the earnest melancholy of a man whose pet rattlesnake has bitten him: "W'y you do me a t'ing like dis, man? Eh? W'y?"

"Ah didn' do you a damn t'ing, Balgo. Dat damn woman—de ole Po'tagee bitch—send me in here. Den she come tryin' to mek s'amie wid me. Den de odder one—de Po'tagee monkey you see runnin' out o' here w'en you come in—he come playin' he warnt to sanga-wanga me. Man—" Her face was upturned to her husband and her puzzlement extreme. "Wha' kind o' people is dis? Dey all de same t'ing. De ole broke-down w'ite man—de one playin' doctor—dat dry-up woman inside here—Ah know fer a fac' she's a ho'. An' dis one dat jus' was in here—he come in an' befo' I could even arks 'im wey de arse he warnt, he take off all o' 'is clo'es an' start runnin' about de room, t'rowin' me down on de bed and tellin' me, 'Leh we play Mooma and Poopa.' Man," she reproached her husband, "wey de hell you make me leave Trinidad for? Is de only decen' place in de world.

Ah warnt to go back home." She grew reflective, a thoughtful look on her face, a sense of the timeliness of an unexpected opportunity. "But wey you stannin' up dey like dat for,
man? Come in de bed, nuh. After all, you an' me is husban'
an' wife—"

Maraj frowned at the suggestion, and maintained, as he
hoped, a dignified reserve. "I eh mekkin' no paccotee." His
wit was a frequent source of delight to himself, and the present sally especially amused him.

"Don' talk foolish, man. Come in de bed."

He made a scarcely perceptible forward movement.

"Come, Balgo," she coaxed him. "Leh we play goat.
Beh-h-h-h-h-h-h! Beh-h-h-h-h-h-h-h-h!" Removing her panties, she positioned herself on her hands and knees, and presented her hindquarters to him. "Beh-h-h-h-h-h-h-h!" she
bleated. "Beh-h-h-h-h-h-h!"

Her husband went toward her, moving in ecstasy, the enraptured subject of an irresistible caprine spell. "Beh-h-h!"
he answered. "Beh-h-h-h-h-h-h-h-h-h!"

As Maraj mounted his wife, Caldeira, who was now once
more fully dressed, started in the direction of the living
room, where Johnny and Dorothea were seated. But suddenly in mid-passage he decided to return upstairs to "Pelican," where he knew that Monsieur Gros-Caucaud and the
blonde young lady were confronting their judges.

The African had been in a deep sleep, spent and fulfilled,
when a harsh thud on the door awoke him. He fumbled for
the electric switch, but before he could locate it the light
came on. His companion stirred in her sleep but did not
awake. Shielding his eyes, he looked in the direction of the
door. There stood the prefect of police, and there, shuffling
in his wake as he entered the room, was Professor von Buffus, followed by Father Goncalves, the pimp, and Rabbi
Eleazar ben-Josephus.

The blonde woman was still asleep in a posture of total
revelation. The light, committing treason against her, in-

vested her body with a graveyard hue, so that it looked waxen yellow. The pubic foliage, which in the more indulgent shadows of the room had seemed so luxuriant, now appeared sparse and scrubby. Saddest of all, its rubiate color had faded into a dull, fuscous cinnamon.

"What means this?" the African demanded.

The blonde awoke, blinked, and shielded her eyes against the unsparing light with both hands. Then she sat upright, drawing her knees up and encircling them defensively with her arms. She rested her head on her knees for a moment, closing her eyes against the light. When she lifted her head, one arm accompanied it so as to enable her to rub her eyes with the back of the hand. Before she could come fully awake and take in the unexpected situation, the prefect of police said to the protesting African: "It means, sir, that we wish to have a little talk with you." His manner was stern and official, but at the same time conciliatory. In dealing with blacks, he had always found that they responded much better if they were treated like children. The key to their successful management lay in one's being able to get down on one's knees and play with them on the floor—and yet, when the moment came, to have the firmness to refuse them any more candy. If it should become necessary, one also should not flinch at slapping their behinds and sending them to bed without supper. "There is something that stands between us." Involuntarily, his gaze traveled to Monsieur Gros-Caucaud's midsection. What it encountered there hardened his resolve. The fellow, he inwardly reaffirmed, was a monster. In all his experience he had never seen anything like it. The look he directed at the blonde woman was composed of equal parts of wonder, disapproval, resentment, compassion, and reproach. Before matters proceeded any further, however, he felt he ought at least to attempt to reassure and placate her. *Sympathie de race*, perhaps; but also in his mind was the prospect of her potential value as a material witness. When hereafter he might find it necessary to furnish collaboration of what he had seen and measured with his own eyes, her testimony would be conclusive. His police training and experience, indeed his entire professional life, emphasized for him the need to treat his principal witnesses with solicitude. So, from the contradictory welter of emotions the sight of the African's penis in all its awe-inspiring magnitude aroused in him, he carefully abstracted a semblance of compassion and directed it toward the blonde accessory. And in order to make more manifest his concern for her, he picked up a coverlet from the side of the bed where it had fallen and draped it around her knees. The African, suddenly aware of his own vulnerability, seized a corner of the coverlet and tried to conceal his penis from the fascinated scrutiny it was receiving.

The room itself was an unlikely setting for the sort of tableau that was unfolding. Aside from the bed, the sole furnishings were a chair, a small Pembroke table—one of its sides collapsed for lack of support—a wash basin angled asymmetrically into a corner, an unframed mirror perhaps twelve inches square attached to the wall above the wash basin, and, at the side of the wash basin, a bidet. The windows were curtained off by heavy mauve draperies, their bottom edges fringed with elaborate bell-shaped tassels, depending from the stuccoed ceiling to the sham mosaic floor. Directly over the bed a naked electric bulb was suspended, a harsh, unblinking sentinel, an unimpassioned observer at myriad rites of the flesh, exaltings and mortifyings of the spirit, frenzied journeyings to and fro between heaven and hell; an uncaring auditor of exultancy and despair, of murmurings, exhortations, and imprecations; the aloof, patrician censor of multitudinous reeks and fragrances.

The prefect of police held an inaudible conference with Father Goncalves and the rabbi. They gathered around the bidet, their backs to the other occupants of the room, and they whispered together, shaking their heads, grasping each other in turn by the arm, confidential, conspiratorial, their strategy taking shape in their sibilances. The prefect of police, with a final headshake to the rabbi and a reassuring squeeze of Father Goncalves's arm, went to the door of the room, opened it, peered outside, and then closed it again. Now, facing the African, he drew a gun. *"Eh, bien, Monsieur,"* he said. "Let us have a little talk." He seated himself on the sole chair in the room. "What is your name?"

Alarmed, the African did not answer at once. He looked from one to the other of those present, seeking confirmation for his belief that this was, after all, only a macabre joke in bad taste. "Marcellin Gros-Caucaud."

"You were born—?"

The African decided to humor this man by making a pretense of cooperation. "Abidjan, Côte d'Ivoire."

"How old—?"

"Thirty-six years."

The prefect of police balanced the number against the sum of his own years. The resulting equation displeased him. Thirty-six did not equal sixty-two; but, rather, in a non-arithmetical sense, exceeded it. The continuum of the years—it was a matter of integral value, he decided. One could be greater than two. The optimum was more desirable than the maximum. By comparison with his sixty-two, the African's thirty-six measured off an optimum. He felt within himself an insurgent anger. Until now his feelings had been dominated by professional calm amounting almost to serenity. There was a job to be done. It had fallen to him to do it. He would take the necessary steps.

If he were thirty-six . . . Despite his clinical habit of mind in the pursuit of his business, he could not help feeling that somehow, in relation to this black fellow—his gaze wandered off to the latter's genital area—he was at a certain disadvantage. At sixty-two even the best preserved of men— beneath the coverlet the blonde altered the position of her legs, arranging them now at an angle to each other, the soles of her feet effecting a temporary alliance while she considered the unheralded state of affairs that had come about—even the best preserved of men . . . The prefect's eyes hovered over the blonde's disposition of her legs. Sixty-two . . . thirty-six . . .

It was curious what an irritant these innocent prime numbers had become. They grated on his sensibilities, producing discordances and asymmetries that manifested themselves in the way he swiveled his neck like a peacock; and then, as if impelled by a subconscious urge to extend the resemblance, he got up and spread his hands outward behind his haunches. He rotated his neck again, inclining his head forward and punctuating the circular movement of his head with sporadic, pecking motions of his chin.

The prefect of police coughed, and the sound was discreetly swallowed up in the otherwise silent room. He coughed again, more emphatically—in protest, one might think, against the failure of the previous cough to achieve a more assertive expression of his self-importance. Some interior awareness of his need to loom larger, to impose himself more potently upon the present circumstances, acquired a critical edge and cut sharply into his self-esteem. Wincing, he produced a modest smile to correct the offending access of vanity, and did not cough again. But the internal scrutiny turned outward and focused itself upon Father Goncalves. There had been something in the nature of a truce between the two men after their initial encounter, a cessation of hostilities not so much negotiated as superimposed by the advent of the African and the necessity to deal, as civilized men, with the primitive menace that he presented. An ethnic closing of ranks had taken place. Yet this ethnic alliance was not only expedient but transitory. For a resurgence of hostility on Father Goncalves's part now threatened to embroil them once more. It was nothing explicit or apparent, nothing that you could put your finger on and say: "Well, these two cocks are at it again." Nothing of the sort. As a matter of fact, the prefect (to do him no less than justice) was, if anything, mollifying in his manner toward Father Goncalves. So the fault was not with him. He needed support and was therefore unlikely to reject allies. Nevertheless, he sensed the altered nuance of Father Goncalves's mood, suspected that it owed its origin to vocational ambivalences, and sought to soothe him. For the first time in addressing the latter, he employed the formal title of priestly respect. "Father," he said, "let's get this over and done with." He nodded at the pimp, who, in response to this signal, drew a knife. The blonde screamed and threw herself across the black, endeavoring to protect him.

Professor von Buffus stepped forward. "Allow me," he said, his manner courteous, his demeanor urbane, like that of a physician of extraordinary eminence intervening with all the weight of his authority and distinction in a diagnostic conference among his colleagues. "I am a urinometrist—a hydrological cabalist."

Perhaps because the profession was unknown to them, perhaps because of the universal feeling that whatever description the professor offered of himself was entitled to instant and unquestioning acceptance, everyone was silent. But whatever the reason, the professor went on: "I suggest that we submit Monsieur to Trial by Urinometry." His audience met his suggestion with indistinct murmurs of bewilderment. Thus encouraged, the professor continued: "Mine is the highest of all arts, the greatest of all sciences. On that exalted tableland where the paraphysical merges into the metaphysical and becomes the real—" He paused. What might have remained of the sentence was unarticulated because of his profound sympathy for the deficient mental grasp of his hearers. He would not tax them overmuch. His compassion consoled and absolved them. "Permit me—" he said.

No one presumed to interrupt him, so consummate was his aura of unchallengeable authority. "As a hydrological cabalist, I divine the *Existenz* and forecast personal destiny by means of urinometry." Percipient as always, the professor noted the general perplexity. "Fate," he enlightened them, "follows the flow of the pee-pee. I judge the flow, I determine the destiny. Any urinometrist could have foretold the outcome of the Battle of Leipzig. Napoleon was having much difficulty with his pee-pee, even then. By the time of Waterloo, in order that he should be able to piss, that impudent Corsican had to be milked—like a cow." He contemplated his audience in the manner of a great general lecturing his staff officers on advanced military tactics. "Had that upstart emperor of the French only consulted a urinometrist—" He smiled, sighed, shook his head, and spread his hands apart. "You may draw your own historical conclusions. Come." He invited them to be spectators at the clinical demonstration he was about to give. "I shall submit Monsieur to a urinometric examination." And to the African he said: "Make pee-pee."

Gros-Caucaud did not at once seem to take in the full import of the professor's request. "*Mais non,*" he objected. "*Pourquoi est-il mon pé-pé—?*" It was a thing *curieuse et singulière,* he thought, that this bizarre lot could not get their minds off his *pé-pé.* He had never experienced anything like it. And now—*cet vermoulu Boche-ci—*

"*Nicht,*" said the professor. "*Non. Pas pé-pé.* P-e-e P-e-e. *L'eau—de l'eau—*" He smiled after the fashion of a carrion crow reassuring a dying jackass as it was about to dine on the latter's entrails.

Caldeira had slipped unnoticed into the room and, catching the drift of the professor's purpose, tried to be helpful to Gros-Caucaud. "'E tellin' you to piss. So piss, nuh, man." And as if commending the soundness of his judgment to the world at large, "Is better to piss than have not'in' to piss wid." The elegant sophistication and palpable, self-evident truth of his aphorism gave him such intellectual satisfaction that he could thereafter only reflect in wounded silence upon the incapacity of ordinary people for plain common sense. If *he* had to choose between losing his "totee" and pissing when bidden to do so, O Chris', man! He'd piss like a river. He looked at the African, who was trying unsuccessfully to conceal his "foo-foo-tay" behind the curtain of his conjoined hands. "O Gawd, boy! But nigger foolish, yes! Dey foolish too-much, man." And, finally, with melancholy and regret, "Dey have no headpiece." His right hand journeyed upward to his own head on a mission of self-congratulation.

The argument might have proceeded indefinitely if the attention of the disputants and others in the room had not been drawn to the professor, who, lips pursed and mouth puckered, was hovering over the African's penis, wooing it with soft sibilances to make water. "P-s-s-s-s! P-s-s-s-s! P-s-s-s-s-s!" he cajoled the African's penis. Father Goncalves, the pimp, Caldeira, and the rabbi each in succession following the professor's example, bent low over Gros-Caucaud's "pencil" and courted its passage of water with the whispering sibilances: "P-s-s-s-s! P-s-s-s-s-s! P-s-s-s-s-s!" All in vain.

With an immense show of reluctance and distaste, the prefect of police took his turn. Stooping low and huddling over Gros-Caucaud's *pé-pé*, he sibilated with the tender murmurings of morning zephyrs. "P-s-s-s-s! P-s-s-s-s! P-s-s-s-s-s!"

As he was bending over the African's "person," his lips almost making contact with it, a powerful jet of urine, copious as a fountain-burst, struck him full in the face.

"Shit!" cried Caldeira. "Gros-Caucaud, man, you piss on 'im. Yes, boy, piss! Piss! Yes, piss!"

But Gros-Caucaud now needed no encouragement. He was urinating in an apparently endless geyser. Meanwhile, the prefect of police maintained his stooping position and on his face there was a look of supernal ecstasy as the African's urine foamed and cascaded over it. Gros-Caucaud was still micturating in the prefect's face when the latter collapsed on to the floor in the rapturous throes of an orgasm.

Dr. von Buffus, who had placed himself so that he might measure the parabolic arch and determine the urine's angle of inclination, was also the recipient of a considerable quantity of the overflow. For once he had been guilty of a miscalculation, having altogether underestimated the force and range of the gusher that pelted out of Gros-Caucaud's pipe. Like the prefect of police, he was drenched virtually from head to foot. But in contrast to the former, who had given every sign of drinking of the spuming stream with deep relish, smacking his lips and greedily poising himself open-mouthed over the African's penis, the professor, though nearly blinded by the acrid torrent, persisted in a heroic attempt to apply the principles of urinometrics. Dripping wet, he announced presently that in his next incarnation the African would assume the bodily guise of an animal hybrid, a cross between an elephant and a mule. Beyond that, however, he was disinclined to go, since he had not so much seen as felt the extraordinary parabola of the African's pee-pee. Nor indeed in these circumstances was his judgment necessary, for the proceedings had of their own volition summarily terminated themselves. Since they had all clustered around the African, everyone was in some degree saturated with urine, and, according to the rabbi, it is written: "They shall not tarry overlong in idle chatter who are smitten with piss, but straightway shall go forth and, repenting, cleanse themselves." So now did they all, except the prefect of police, who, piss-sodden and exhilarated, repaired to Madame's chamber. There, under the stimulus of the aphrodisia he had drunk, he submitted Madame to heroic exertions filled with novel and imaginative delights.

As for Marcellin Gros-Caucaud himself, as soon as he had resumed his clothing, he returned to the living room downstairs, where his strange adventures had begun.

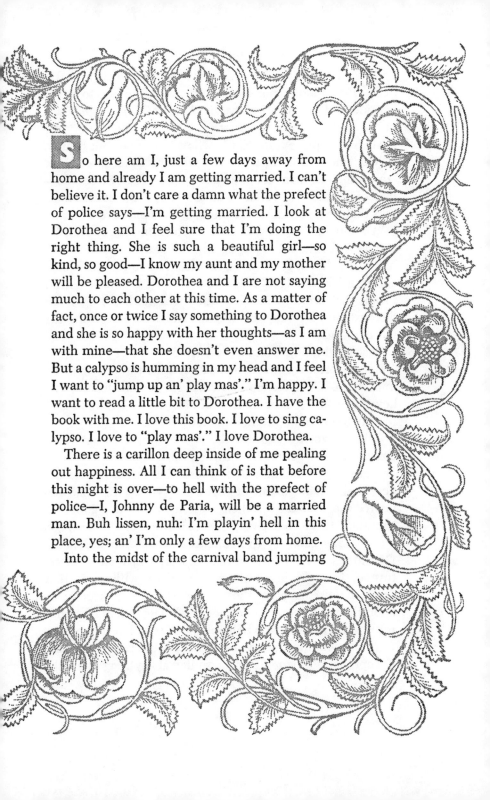

So here am I, just a few days away from home and already I am getting married. I can't believe it. I don't care a damn what the prefect of police says—I'm getting married. I look at Dorothea and I feel sure that I'm doing the right thing. She is such a beautiful girl—so kind, so good—I know my aunt and my mother will be pleased. Dorothea and I are not saying much to each other at this time. As a matter of fact, once or twice I say something to Dorothea and she is so happy with her thoughts—as I am with mine—that she doesn't even answer me. But a calypso is humming in my head and I feel I want to "jump up an' play mas'." I'm happy. I want to read a little bit to Dorothea. I have the book with me. I love this book. I love to sing calypso. I love to "play mas'." I love Dorothea.

There is a carillon deep inside of me pealing out happiness. All I can think of is that before this night is over—to hell with the prefect of police—I, Johnny de Paria, will be a married man. Buh lissen, nuh: I'm playin' hell in this place, yes; an' I'm only a few days from home.

Into the midst of the carnival band jumping

up in my head, the voice of the man from the Black Cat Bar in San Fernando intruded. "Eh, compère," he says to me in his adopted Trinidadian patois, "buh tell me somet'ing, nuh—you know wey you doin'?"

My first impulse is to tell the fellow to trot off. But I think, he can't help himself. He's only what he is: an interfering ma commère man" from a rum shop on High Street. So—matching patois for patois—s'affaire he (I mean, it's his business that he is as "macco" as he is, and I don't care a damn).

"Yo' tan'-tan' go' vex, boy." He's dragging in my aunt Jocasta. I feel I shouldn't put up with him any longer. So I tell him softly, like a gentleman, in a leashed voice with a cold and murderous edge: "Mind your fecking business." And I meant that literally, as well. But I was neither vulgar nor discourteous, for I had been careful to alter and refine the vowel sound.

"Aaaa-right, boy. Buh don' say Ah didn' warn you."

I considered further conversation with the fellow to be impossible. What did he know about my aunt Jocasta and how she would feel or think about anything? Irritation gritted my teeth and tightened my jaw. There was—

Caldeira got up and left the room, and, to my extreme consternation, Dorothea followed him.

I sat there, stunned, and at a loss what to do. I could not very well go in pursuit of them, nor—since they had not invited me—could I join them, wherever they had gone. Sitting alone there on the very eve, as it were, of my marriage, I eventually came to the conclusion that their absence—Dorothea's, at least—would be temporary. As soon as she returned, I would insist on our marrying without further delay. I must have sat there for perhaps a quarter of an hour, though it seemed considerably longer, when Dorothea returned. There was no palpable change in her manner toward me—nothing, at any rate, that I could put a finger on. Except that now whenever she smiled at anything I said, she appeared to be smiling beyond me, as if at some distant object to which I was only remotely peripheral. Neither, for the most part, did she respond in words to my queries and observations, but only smiled. I had an increasing sense, which I did my best to repel, of merely being humored. I found it impossible to account for this disquieting change in my love's demeanor toward me. I began to feel "en bas odieux"—"tout oublier"—to say it in the Trinidadian patois, as if an obeah-man had put something on me. I made the sign of the cross. "Dorothea—" I said.

"Go 'way, Johnny," she interrupted me. She was still smiling in contemplation of pleasant visions on far horizons.

I felt obliged, however, to refuse my beloved's request. There was a game of some sort afoot here, and I wanted to be in at the death. When the cocks are in the pit and feathers are flying, spurs flashing, and blood gushing, a man's place is there—right there—at ringside, not scurrying off somewhere or other to place a bet on a cock he doesn't know, has never heard of, and—what the hell—perhaps can't fight a damn. I could see that my love knew very little about cocks or she would never have made such a suggestion to me. But I could forgive her anything. Look at her, man. Just look at her—so beautiful. So sweet. So good. So kind. A treasonous recollection floated back to me, the memory of the manner in which she had looked at the African's—

I tried to blot out the recollection.

—at the African's—it was not his face that she had been staring at. There could be no mistake about that. It was true that the man had been forced to take off all his clothes. So, deprived of choice, he had sat there, bare as the bush. The hollow of my stomach had contracted each time Dorothea's gaze lingered on his "person," that monstrous threat to social stability. Why, I wondered, was she so taken with the sight of that hideous object? I thought of my own—pale

265

brown and slender, elegant in its symmetry, unmenacing, even—I dared say—beautiful. His couldn't match up with mine at all. Not at all, at all, man.

If it were only not such an ungentlemanly thing to do, I would have arranged to display myself to my beloved. She would then have seen something truly worthy of her admiration. Yet as Dorothea's gaze had grown more and more concentered, my stomach had become more and more constricted. Why, I had wondered, was she so drawn to that repellent object? There was nothing in the least attractive about it.

Perhaps these thoughts of mine had conjured up the African, for he suddenly appeared in the room, adjusting his clothing, which he must have put on with either haste or negligence. His necktie was askew, his shoelaces untied and—he seemed to be unaware of this—his trousers fly unbuttoned. The first two omissions were in no way menacing, and indeed he had set about putting them in order. But the last mentioned was, from my point of view, calamitous. For Dorothea now, as previously, at once became riveted, to the exclusion of all else, upon that horrendous appendage that had already been the occasion of so much discord. I did not know quite how to bring it to his attention that his "person" was partially unconcealed as a result of his ungentlemanly inattention to his dress. Neither, I feared, would Dorothea have been grateful to me for pointing this out to him, since the fascination of his undone fly had irradiated her lovely face with bliss.

I tried to get her attention, not because I wished to say anything to her but so as to distract her from her rapt fixation on the African, who was lolling back in his chair in a state of indecent exposure. She seemed to be hypnotized. I began to feel anxious. The same look now was on her face that I had earlier noted on that of the blonde woman—the look of a starving girl intent on biting into a large, ripe banana. A premonition of some sort assailed me. I fought it off—or thought I did. It returned, however, and this time made so deep an incision into my self-esteem that, to my own astonishment, I heard myself groan. In deepening anxiety, I searched Dorothea's face for some sign of reassurance. I discovered none. For some reason or other, I began to sweat. This outpouring of perspiration was accompanied by an unusual disturbance in the region of my loins. I could make neither head nor tail of it. Though when I gave the matter more thought, I realized that from the very instant of my meeting Dorothea at Madame's, there had been this tumult, this insurgency in my lower regions. It was all novel enough, yet there was no precedent whatever for the deluge of sweat that was inundating me. Not even when I had come face to face with the Most High Lord of All, the Imperial Emperor Mapepire Zanana, in Aunt Jocasta's garden. It was plain to me that something uncommon was taking place. But what? Aunt Jocasta often said: "When in doubt, do nothing." Remembering this, I felt relieved. The torrent of sweat diminished and the tempest in my loins subsided. For this I was extremely grateful. I silently murmured my thanks to Aunt Jocasta. Dorothea must have seen my lips moving. For she said to me: "What's the matter, Johnny?" And before I could reply, she added: "You no go—?" And she pointed upstairs. I saw now that the African was staring at me. Perhaps he doubted that I would sacrifice myself for him, as Dorothea evidently wished me to do. Yet I also noted that there was nothing at all suppliant in his gaze, but only a simmering impatience. That puzzled me. He had been threatened with grievous bodily harm—and worse—by the tribunal that had sat in judgment upon him. He had apparently in the end received a favorable verdict. Still, it would have been reasonable to expect that henceforward he would be at pains to be less assertive of his prodigious "person." Not, indeed, to hide it under a bushel—

though a ton perhaps would more adequately suffice—but at least to keep it out of sight—for discretion's sake, if nothing more.

While these thoughts were whirling about in my mind, Dorothea, it seemed, had edged closer to the African—or he to her—I could not be sure which, or preferred not to be certain. Meanwhile Dorothea and the African were whispering to each other, and Dorothea was smiling at him like an imploring subject in hopes of large benevolences from a king. Turning slightly toward me she said, speaking in half-profile, her eyes remaining fixed upon the African: "Johnny, go."

Not entirely sure that I should obey my beloved, yet not wholly convinced that I had any choice in the matter, and pausing only long enough to slip the *Odyssey* into my pocket, I left the room. I felt it would be discourteous of me to linger and ungentlemanly to look back.

As I closed the door behind me, hesitant and unsure of my destination, the sound of a footfall on the stairs caught my attention. Caldeira was descending. He had already seen me, and with his customary air of vulgar, slavering excitement, he was signaling to me. "Come with me," he said.

In the circumstances, I had no alternative. He turned and began to reascend the stairs. I followed. But at the top of the stairs I paused. There was a matter of some importance on my mind. It had not been easy for me to leave Dorothea. Indeed, I had only done so at her repeated insistence. But I was concerned about her being alone with that African. Out of her solicitude for all living creatures, she clearly was trying to comfort him in his predicament. That no doubt was why she had allowed him to place his head in her lap like a child entreating a parent's blessing. I had not been able to avoid observing this as I closed the door behind me when leaving the room. I could only hope that a gesture of such touching consideration as her stroking of his head would not go unrewarded. I attempted to convey some sense of my feelings to Caldeira.

"You say," he remarked to me, "'e put 'e head in she lap?"

"Yes."

"An' she pat 'is head, Mr. Johnny?"

"Stroked—"

"You mean—rub?"

"More or less. Yes."

"An' 'e head, you say, in she lap?" He clasped his hands, placed them against the side of his face, inclining his head and closing his eyes in a manner suggestive of someone asleep.

I confirmed the accuracy of his charade.

"Well, don' bodder 'bout it. Is a t'ing dat does happen to everybody—king, governor, priest, tout le monde [employing for this phrase the Trinidadian patois equivalent which, rendered phonetically, is "toot moon"]."

Plainly, the fellow had a foul mind. He stopped, facing me, and rested his hands on my shoulders. "'E head in she lap," he repeated.

I said again that that had been the case.

"Mr. Johnny, you see somet'ing else?" There was a look of earnest solicitude on his face.

When I did not reply, he said to me: "You didn' look, Mr. Johnny? Dat fella—an' wey you say she name—Doro-t'ea—?"

He may have seen the agony on my face, for in all the hours that had elapsed since our first meeting, he had never until this moment shown the tiniest spark of sensitivity. "O, don' mind dat, Mr. Johnny. Look: Ah got somet'ing nice fer you, boy." When he noticed my skepticism, he exclaimed: "O Gawd! Is true. Yes. Nice, Ah tell you. Nice, nice, nice. Come wid me, man. Come—"

Mrs. Maraj's daughter, Sita, fidgeted in the *clair-obscure* of a room that might have been elegant were it not for the pervasive overemphasis of its décor. It was a high-ceilinged room with pale-blue and eggshell-white draperies descending in soft velveteen folds to the Aubusson-carpeted floor. The ceiling itself was decorated with an elaborate, though not distasteful, *plafond* that featured leaves and tendrils in a pseudoclassical design suggestive of a vine-covered arbor. On the carved wooden bedstead, supported by six centipede legs of slender, polished brass, was spread a diamond-shaped, cream-white coverlet of Madeira lace threaded with blue ribbon. The ribbon crisscrossed the coverlet through the meshes of the lace in a diagonal, overlapping pattern.

Sita sat on a circular, satin-upholstered chair, imperial purple in color, and fretted at her unexpected and now prolonged—at least an hour long—separation from her mother. This was her first trip overseas, and, like her mother, she had had no special wish to come abroad. At her father's repeated urging, however, she had consented, but with the reservation that she would not go to Paris, as he also planned to do, for she had heard disturbing reports of the food preferences of the French. According to her informants, it was as dangerous to be a snail or a frog in France as to be a certain type of bird in England or a snake in Hong Kong or Singapore. For while the French and the Chinese ate everything that crawled, the English were ravenous for everything that flew. Sita was disinclined to choose between the two national groups, the French and the English. She had met some English people, at a formal distance, in Trinidad, and a few that were French or of French descent—French creoles, as they were known. As far as she could see, they were all alike: you couldn't understand a damn thing any one of them was saying. And they smelled funny. Sita had another reason for wishing to remain at home. With her mother and father out of the way, she would have been able to go out in the evenings, as most of her friends were able to do, without being chaperoned by a suspicious father and overseen by a mother with a hundred eyes. It was not that she was lacking in affection for her parents. Indeed, she was very much attached to them. But she chafed at the excessive care with which they supervised every aspect of her existence. She had heard exciting things from her friends, which they had found out for themselves because of their own relative freedom from the constant vigilance of their parents. No one would believe, she thought, looking about the room, that she had never been alone for more than a few minutes at any one time with a boy of her own age. And—her glance took in the pale-blue and cream-white bed—unlike so many of her friends, she always slept alone. Even when it rained and thundered in the hot afternoons. It was then, her friends related, that life could be at its most ecstatic. Except for her, who always slept alone. Just like a nun. And she thought: how could it be that at her age she had never even been kissed by a boy? The thought irritated her. All those nice boys she knew—from a distance—and not one of them had ever got close enough to kiss her. Because—and this was the only reason—her mother and father never let her out of their sight. Her reflections bred resentment in her, and her resentment in turn bred a resolve to do something about it. As soon as she returned to Trinidad. And sooner, perhaps, she told herself. Abstractedly, she tugged at the tasseled fringe of the pale-blue and cream-white coverlet. If she got the slightest chance. She felt like taking a nap. She began to undress.

Sita bore a marked physical resemblance to her mother. This was particularly true of the proportions of their long, deer-straight legs in relation to their narrow-shouldered, high-waisted, broad-hipped bodies, and of the manner in which their surging breasts flaunted an aggressive challenge to the world at large. But Sita also possessed her father's Buddha-like eyes and ardent, moist-lipped mouth. She also had an intense urge to experience for herself whatever it was that produced those keening outcries of rapture in her parents' bedroom at nights and during rainstorms in midaf-

271

ternoon. Those wailing assonances of bliss were less frequent nowadays than they used to be. In fact, she couldn't
remember when she had last heard them. But the pristine
recollection lingered with her. And if it was what her
friends told her it was, then why was such happiness forbidden her? Exactly as her mother might have done, she began
to curl and uncurl her silk-stockinged toes. A reverie of rain
absorbed her, torrential rain enhaloed, as it were, by foreknowledge of the incandescent late-afternoon sunshine that
would succeed the thunder's subsidence and the rain's exhaustion. So profound was her absorption that she was at
first unaware of a diffident knocking on the door. She
frowned and was mystified when in response to her invitation to enter there was only silence. I discovered later on
that it was Caldeira who had employed that ruse to ascertain which room she was in.

He now led me to a door inscribed in an elaborate, decorative calligraphy, "Petunia." The flower itself was depicted
above the inscription. In the discourteous fashion that was
in general typical of him, he opened it without knocking
and pushed me inside with such force that I stumbled. As I
was recovering my balance, I heard a soft scream that really
was more like a loud gasp. I turned in its direction and saw a
girl sitting up in bed while concealing herself as best she
could behind the folds of a coverlet. To my profound surprise, it was the East Indian girl whom, along with her
mother, Dr. von Buffus had brought to my cabin one day
during my seasickness. Recognition was instant and mutual.
My good manners came to the fore at once. "Excuse me," I
said. "There has been a mistake. I am extremely sorry." I
turned and went to the door, intending to leave the room. It
was locked. I shook the handle of the door, rattled it, turned
it this way and that, all to no purpose. The disgusting fellow
had locked me in. I would have to apologize to Miss Maraj—
for it was she—because of an intrusion that was, in fact,

none of my doing. Moving away from the door, I stood at a respectful distance from the bed. "I'm sorry," I began.

"It's all right." She corrected herself. "I mean—" She was holding the coverlet, I thought, rather negligently. "I don' know what's going on." She studied me with some closeness. "I'm looking for my mother."

What a beautiful girl! If I could only get out of this place, I'd certainly go in search of her mother. In fact, I'd do anything for—

"You come from Trinidad—like me. I see you—"

"Yes," I said, my eagerness heightening the pitch of my voice by at least two octaves. "I saw you, too—on the ship."

"Yes. But I see you in San Fernando. You belong to Miss Jocasta—"

"I am her nephew." I was conscious of the note of pride in my voice. I looked around the room. How on earth, I wondered, had this girl got here? An idea made its way into my head. Slowly, slowly, I deciphered it. At length I felt I could see through the whole thing. It was simply another of that—that—

"Come an' sit down," she invited me. "They boun' to open the door. They keah keep us lock-up here forever." She was holding the coverlet in front of her less negligently now. "You find it's cold?" She shivered slightly. "You know, we accustomed to hot weather." She shivered again.

I liked the sound of her voice. It reminded me of home. Listening to her, I could hear my mother speaking, and Aunt Jocasta. I could hear the birds singing, my dog barking, and the cocks getting ready to fight. I could smell the sea as it raced against the shore at high tide at San Fernando. And I could see the sleek brown girls in Aunt Jocasta's house moving slowly in the mornings to the rhythm of the awakening day. And all at once I wanted to go back home. I had had enough of these foreign parts—enough of foreigners. I was astonished to find that I did not wish to think of Dorothea; that the thought of Dorothea with the African's head on her lap, while she stroked his fleecy hair—

To my immense surprise, I detected myself shuddering. I, who was neither a fascist warmonger nor an atheistic communist, and—at worst—only by proxy a colonial exploiter or an imperialistic oppressor, I—Johnny de Paria from San Fernando, Trinidad—found myself shaking from head to foot with ague at the recollection of my Dorothea cradling that black nigger's—that black African's—head in her lap. My imagination had contracted a strong fever, and I could see the African's head in my beloved's lap as though she were hearing his prayers before bedtime. There she sat—my Dorothea—in blissful reverie, her angelic face rapt as a seraph's, a religieuse at her orisons. I shuddered again in a raging fever, and with such violence indeed that the girl on the bed called out to me in genuine alarm: "O God, man, you cold!" And before I could enter the faint denial that was all I was able to manage, she ordered me to "Come in the bed." She followed this command with a curious non sequitur: "My name is Sita."

Even now I would have resisted her command. Among us Trinidadians, it is the custom to use our hands so as to lend greater expressiveness to our speech. Sita, unthinking, had let drop the coverlet so as to free her hands. There, then, in all their succulence, the size of young green coconuts, cornucopia-full, lactate-rich, were her breasts—twin Fountains of Paradise. I moved toward them, impelled by psychogenetic forces potent as gravity and utterly beyond my comprehension or control.

"Take off your clothes," said Sita. "Yo' keah lay down in yo' jacket an' pants." This was logical enough, but even so I hesitated. I recalled my mother's frequent admonition: "Manners makyth man." Should I not be in breach of good manners by disrobing myself in the presence of a lady and then—occupying the same bed with her? The question deeply preoccupied me.

274

Sita, however, was showing signs of restlessness beneath the coverlet. Yet I remained standing, firmly implanted in the natural diffidence of a well-bred man. A resolve quartered itself in my mind. I would be a gentleman at all costs. Some means must be found of harnessing the turbulence I was experiencing in the vicinity of my loins. The commotion that my "pencil" was engaging in was ungentlemanly. I reproached myself for my Caldeira-like coarseness. It was not the sort of thing a gentleman ever encouraged himself to experience in the company of a lady, and I rebuked myself all the more severely for being guilty of so lamentable a breach of good manners. The same stricture would have to be applied to the lower-class clamminess of my hands. A gentleman was always composed in—

"Come here, boy." Sita's peremptoriness drew my gaze, partly in astonishment but also in part, I must confess, out of an ungentlemanly curiosity, to her. The word that made its way into my unspoken thought was the odious vulgarism I had heard Caldeira employ: "tottots." But I suppressed it at once. Yet I could not bring myself even to contemplate so intimate a usage as "breasts."

Dr. von Buffus was fond of quoting from some poet or other—possibly Goethe, though he told me it was an Englishman who lived on opium and in his narcotic hallucinations sometimes fancied himself the originator of intellectual concepts he had borrowed from German thinkers. Anyway, the lines that the professor liked to quote from one of that Englishman's poems were to the effect that "he"—I never knew who the hell the "he" was—"on honey-dew hath fed/And drunk the milk of Paradise.—" Unfailingly, after his eighth or ninth rum punch, the professor would recite that poem. But a strange thing now was happening to me. Something that the professor afterward explained to me is described by a word I'd never heard before and, to tell you the truth, don't care if I never hear it again. The word, he said, is "atavism." I hope I'm spelling it right. It means, he told me, a species of regression to more primeval habits: a return to the beginnings. Which, he also said, is a notion that has caught the modern imagination of a Swiss obeahman named C. G. Jung and another fella—a Frenchman, Jean Cocteau. It seems that this Frenchman was always talking about an Eternal Return. I thought at first that Cocteau had something to do with cockfighting. The professor said, yes, Cocteau was a kind of cockfighter. He looked very thoughtful when he said this. A different sort of cockfighter, he explained. I was disappointed when I heard that. For I had supposed that all Frenchmen were fanciers, as I was, of those gallant birds who went to their foreordained deaths, like honorable bulls in the ancient Spanish ritual, to the classical measures of a public spectacle. The professor went on to tell me—though I really didn't understand what he was talking about—that "all these terms, cock and so on, are multivalued." He said no more on the subject, and since it was plain to me that he didn't have in mind the fighting cocks I was interested in, I did not pursue the matter any further. But as I was saying, something odd was happening to me right then, as I was standing by the side of the bed in which Sita was lying. The fact that I was weaned at fifteen evidently had the effect, according to Dr. von Buffus, of enduing me with what he described as a "mammary fixation." On the exceedingly rare occasions that I had seen breasts in the nude after I had been weaned, I was seized by an overmastering impulse to nurse at them. This had led to certain difficulties. But inasmuch as in all such instances my aunt Jocasta's female servants were the objects of my irresistible compulsion, nothing much had come of it. They had suckled me, after their initial surprise, without complaint. All they said to me was: "O Gawd, Mr. Johnny! But you funny, yes!" At the same time, I had seen that the effect upon them of their suckling me was dramatic. In every instance they made reciprocal demands upon me, to which I had not yielded because to have done so would have been a betrayal of Aunt Jocasta's confidence and my mother's careful breeding. Even when they had placed their hands on my "person"—an area where no lady's hands ever should stray—I remained adamant, firm as a rock against making the concessions they so passionately desired. I simply would not permit them to take an unladylike advantage of my postadolescent need to be suckled at the breast.

Here now was I, transfixed by the sight of Sita's cinnamon-hued "tottots"—that indecent term forced its way into my mind—the size of young and luscious green breadfruit, leaping away from her chest like spirited cocks eager to fight. The need to be suckled at those twin Fountains of Paradise quite overcame me. Yet I was aware, too, of an explicit warning from my subconscious that if I yielded, as I might be unable to avoid doing, this would be no ordinary suckling. There would be consequences for me beyond any I had ever meditated as the climax of these regressive yearnings. So, although in obedience to Sita's command I began a hesitant but ineluctable pilgrimage to her bed, I did not surrender without a struggle. Clutching my copy of the *Odyssey* as a man eddying in the torrent at the foot of Niagara Falls might grasp a floating spar, a bit of orange peel, a sliver of paper, I paused and opened the book. The effort exhausted me and my hands were wet and trembling with the massive exertion of will opening the book had entailed.

"Put down the damn book." Sita's upper body was completely revealed by the treachery of the absconded coverlet. I could almost hear the lactating murmur of the streaming refreshment of those twin Fountains of Paradise.

I tried to resist. I tried to read. I had opened the book at random and I now began to read: "When Ulysses and Penelope had had their fill of love..."

But Sita, after recovering from her amazement at my recital, sharply scolded me. "Man, w'at de hell de matter wid you? I say, put down de damn book an' come here." Then, as I still hesitated, her tone became wheedling. She commenced to cajole me in the dulcet patois of my native Trinidad. "Come, doux-doux—doux-doux-dahlin'. Come sugarplum. Come to Sita. Don' 'fraid, boy. It go' be sweet. Nice, man. Nice, nice, nice. You go' see. Come, doux-doux—" And she stretched out her arms, like Saint Geneviève over Paris, thereby enabling the Fountains of Paradise to achieve a saliency so sublime that Christ Himself would have succumbed had the Devil appeared before Him on the High Mountain as a Temptress in Sita's guise. But let it be recorded without disrespect to the Christian Lord and Savior that I, Johnny de Paria from San Fernando, Trinidad, stood firm in this hour of supreme trial. Let it be recorded that though a damn fool, I was a gentleman.

Sita accepted defeat like a lady. "What's the matter with you, boy?" Her tone was not unkind, but there was in it a profound wonder, a hint of the need on her part for a radical reconsideration. "You come in the place like a damn ramgoat with a hot pee, you don' even knock on the door—" Then she was silent for a moment or two, plainly in the grip of thoughts too deep for words. Disentangling herself from the web of thought, she said: "Buh lissen, nuh. I warnt to arks you somet'ing—"

As a gentleman should, when a lady addresses him, I came at once to attention.

Her eyes, lustrous as ripe caimite (a delectable tropical fruit) in the moonlight, she put to me the question I breathlessly awaited: "You is a man?"

When I did not reply, since I honestly did not know what to say, being so largely untested, she continued to query me in a tone more puzzled than censorious. "You don' talk, boy? Parrot got yo' tongue?"

At length I said: "I'm sorry. I did not know—"

"How you go' know?" She cut me off, yet not discourteously. "I don' know needer [which was to say, "neither"—how I loved my Trinidadian dialect!]. You not a man—an' I not a woman." She had arrived at a diagnosis. Now for the remedy. "You an' me mus' help one anudder."

She turned over on the axis of her thighs in a slow semi-rotation of her body. She lay now on her side, half-supporting herself on an elbow. I found oddly disturbing the single-minded intensity with which she was regarding me. "You come from Trinidad. Iëre, eh? The Land of the Humming-bird. Dey ain' no place nice so. Nice like Trinidad. O God, man!" She went on speaking more to herself than to me, yet in no sense excluding me. "Why the hell we so foolish, eh? So chupid [stupid], man—leavin' a place like dat to go to dis damn England that only have cold and a lot of white-white people like jumbie [meaning "zombies"]." She pursed her lips and, with the collaboration of her tongue, made a sucking noise of disapproval and regret. "Choops!" Then, "You remember the road-march we sing last carnival: 'Last Train to San Fernando'?"

I shook my head as a sign of my remembrance. I had played mas', jumping up in a band and singing that wonderfully lilting tune.

"You 'member," she said, "the band disguise' as 'question mark'?"

"I played in that band."

"You play question mark, boy?" She sat up on the bed. No longer now could I maintain my feeble pretense of disinterest in the spectacle she presented. I would have to read to her from the *Odyssey* at once. Or as soon as possible, in any case. For my own good—and hers.

"Yes. Me and Tony da Silva. And Roy—you know Roy, the Jew—an' Halsey McSparkle—you know Halsey? He studyin' doctor in England now—and Dinoo Singh—"

"You know Dinoo Singh?"

"Me and Dinoo, we bathe together in the sea every morning, down at Flatrock behind Naparima College—after we play football in Paradise Pasture. Dinoo an' me is best' frien'—"

"But you ever see t'ing so?" She looked at me with pleasure and wonderment at the agreeable workings of chance. "You walk in de damn room an' we find out we from the same place and we know the same people—" She reassessed the present situation. "Lissen, nuh, man. I better put on some clo'es, eh? Yo' tan'-tan' will say I'm a bad girl—"

"No, no, no. My tan'-tan' is not like that." Anxious to change the subject, I continued: "Let me read something for you."

"But I keah leh you see me so, man. After all—"

"It's all the same with me." I had come to feel a deep loathing for clothes and such other civilized impediments.

She gave me a look that, for some strange reason, agitated my "pencil."

"Is all the same? You sure?" She rolled with a smooth, neap-tide motion onto her back, drew up her knees, placed her hands beneath her head, and scanned the ceiling.

I became aware of a profound inner turmoil, an odd sense of having lost my bearings in an alien land, uncharted yet giving promise of vast and novel enchantments. Holding fast to the *Odyssey*, I moved toward her like a drunken acrobat teetering on a slack tightrope.

I was afterward to reflect with a knife thrust of self-censure that in all this time the thought of Dorothea never once entered my mind. It was not that I had forgotten her; nor, despite her oversolicitous mothering of the African, had I abandoned my intention to make her my wife. She had simply been momentarily displaced by the upheaval that had occurred in me when I had blundered into this room and found Sita here. As my mother had so often said: "There's a divinity that shapes our ends/Rough-hew them how we will." Whenever she said this, she would toss her head in a sort of defiance to the despotism of fate and then exclaim,

280

the insane light of excessive erudition gleaming in her eyes: "Shakespeare." This name was so often on her lips that I came in time to feel some slight curiosity about it. Yet no one—not even Dr. von Buffus—seemed inclined to talk about him, whoever he was, so I concluded that, like my father, he was a member of the family. I let the matter rest there. For, what the hell, boy, don' trouble trouble, unless trouble trouble you. Mind yo' own business. Praise yo' God, eat yo' peas-an'-rice, drink yo' rum, and sing yo' calypso. That's me, man. Me, Johnny de Paria. A calypso took shape in my mind:

"Leave Mr. Shakespeare alone,
De man jus' a heap o' bone,
An' 'e eh got nutt'n' to say
Dat better dan tay-lay-lay."

It eh bad, man. I could sing it in a ré-minor. I was seeking the key to set the melody for my composition when Sita's voice recalled me to the present circumstances. I tottered off the tightrope.

"Buh lissen, nuh—" she commenced.

For the moment, however, seeing had taken precedence over hearing insofar as I was concerned. "What lovely knees!" I inwardly remarked, appraising the patellar dimples, at the sight of which, for some odd, ill-bred reason, I developed a strong turbulence in my "person." I was aware of an imperative need to avert my eyes or run the certain risk of forgetting that "Manners makyth man." As even in the most intricate situations I seldom failed to do, I was resolved to place manners first. Aunt Jocasta and my mother would have been proud of me. I opened my copy of the *Odyssey*. It is true that my hands trembled and my fingers fumbled, and that because of my agitation I almost dropped the book, and that I opened it uncertainly and at random. There, however, I stood, holding it before me like Father Maginot clutching his pectoral cross whenever he went to

281

give extreme unction or administer the last rites to some sinner or other in the whorehouse on Mucurapo Street in San Fernando.

"Buh you is hell, oui, boy. You not even ask me my name—" (But was I mistaken in my recollection that she had already told it me?)

As a result, no doubt, of her having maintained her knees in their previous position for an uncomfortably long time, they now wearied, it seemed, and in their fatigue parted ever so slightly. I began to tremble again and to experience seismic tremors at whose epicenter stood my "pencil." My breathing grew difficult. I tended to gasp, a condition I had only once before known with Dorothea and thought that I never would know again with any other lady. I had been mistaken. That was plain. For, if anything, my present symptoms were more turbulent even than they had been in her case. I had a malarial sensation of breaking out into a cold sweat while running a high fever. And I could only return a vapid smile in response to her wry reproach. The gap between her knees was widening—distractingly, I thought. It was high time that I began to read to her.

"I name Sita," she said, perhaps for the second time. "Sita Maraj. You don' know me farder—Balgobin Maraj? He have a dry-goods store on High Street—on the right-hand side, jus' befo' you come to the Black Cat Bar. An' he does give plenty prize for cricket an' runnin' an' t'ing. Balgobin Maraj—people does call 'im Balgo. You don' know 'im?"

Yes. Indeed, I did. But I omitted to say that it was here, at Madame's, that I had made his personal acquaintance.

Her knees came together for a moment, then parted again so that I felt like a manicou in a forest fire. No matter where the hell I ran, the fire was scorching my backside. So I took one last glimpse to make sure that I wasn't missing anything. Then I started to read. " 'For shame, Sir,' answered Ulysses, fiercely, 'you are an insolent fellow—so true is it that the gods do not grace all men alike in speech, per-

282

son, and understanding. One man may be of weak presence, but heaven has adorned this with such a good conversation that he charms every one who sees him; his honeyed moderation carries his hearers with him so that he is leader in all assemblies of his fellows, and wherever he goes he is looked up to. Another may be as handsome as a god, but his good looks are not crowned with discretion. This is your case. No god would make a finer-looking fellow than you are, but you are a fool...'"

As though in confirmation of the judgment of Ulysses, Sita's voice cut in: "W'at the hell wrong wid you, boy? You there readin' book like a damn fool. You don' see—?"

Briefly, I thought that my voice had displeased her. It had sounded to me debilitated, unsure, like a wind instrument with a defective reed. I could scarcely recognize it as my own, so different was it without the vigorous resonance of my habitual timbre. Was this the voice that had launched at so many sunsets countless galleons of full-rigged calypsos on multitudinous seas of ice-cold rum punch? This—this cracked and quavering castrato? In addition, as I had been reading, an instrusive urge, imperious in its intensity, compelled me to check, as a mariner does his course, the current position of Sita's knees. My "pencil" reacted to what I saw like the needle of a compass responding to extreme polar magnetism. I was barely able to retain hold of the book. In the midst of my struggle to do so, Sita's voice cut in again: "Man, you' stannin' up dey like a damn fool. You don' see—?"

I had indeed seen, plainly enough. Though, as I later congratulated myself, I was too well mannered to betray any sign of it. Moreover, I was finding it hard to repress a discourteous urge to exchange my grip on Homer's *Odyssey* for an unrelinquishing hold on Sita's knees. I tried to recall my mother's admonition concerning good manners, but for the first time in my life I was unable to do so.

"You readin' all dat damn foolishness—wey de hell wrong wid you? Come in de bed, nuh. You don' see—?"

Sita apparently set great store by perception. "W'en de mango ripe, eat it! You hear me? Come eat de mango, man! Come! Come, boy!" Her sublime knees were visibly branching apart. "De mango ripe—come, boy!"

The copy of the *Odyssey* slid from my grasp and I moved toward Sita in helpless obedience to the mandate of a tyranny established as primal sovereign in my loins. "W'en de mango ripe, eat it!" Sita's voice, Circean, compelled me. My loins, collaborating, urged me. At the interior angle of her parted knees was a navigational beacon guiding me into port. As I came within range, Sita disrobed me with a nimble skill that disarmed my modesty. But the accumulated instinct of all the unweaned years of my infancy and early youth supervened. I took hold of the Fountains of Paradise and began to suckle myself in a headlong passion of reawakened pubescent craving. I nursed at each in turn—at her magnificent breasts, the color of sun-saturated sapodillas. As I nursed, Sita moaned with rapture, flailing her arms, tossing her legs, clutching me in a murmurous frenzy to her bosom as if I were a prodigal and insatiable infant whom she, bliss-laden, evermore would nurse in ever-mounting transports at her fruit-firm, sapodilla-shaped, sandalwood-colored, well-springing, milk-giving, joy-geysering, Mother-Indian, Trinidadian breasts. I would have been content to spend the rest of my life appeasing my quenchless thirst at Sita's Fountains of Paradise. Sita's purposes, however, were not quite the same as mine. For calling imploringly on God and beseeching me with greater and greater intensity to "eat the mango," she sought to deflect me from my single-minded preoccupation with her breasts into other channels of enjoyment. But I, resolved to remain a gentleman and to hold fast to good manners despite my unassuageable thirst, was impervious to her blandishments. My sole interest lay in her suckling me as in the time of my unweaned infancy and adolescence. Those first fifteen years of my life had irreversibly formed my tastes and determined my needs. I was intolerant of substitutes for the raptures of suckling, even when they were proffered me under such ineffable pressures as Sita evidently was experiencing. She seized me where, until her frantic hand had violated that space, I—and only I, and two or three of Aunt Jocasta's female servants—had had access. It was no easy matter to disengage her grip from what had hitherto known no touch in its nude state save mine. This was rendered all the more difficult by the treachery of that organ itself, which, in a state of violent insurrection, showed every sign of willingness to cooperate with her in her effort to initiate me into premarital pleasures. I stood granitelike in my tacit refusal. Extricating my private possession from her grasp, I retained it in the protective custody of my clenched fist while she supplicated me piteously for its release and surrender to her.

"O God, Johnny—!" she pleaded in whispering abjection.

"No, Sita, no," I replied, with all the decisiveness of a thoughtful parent withholding candy from a child. "Not now. It's not right." Even in that desperate pass, I knew that no gentleman worthy of the name would stoop so low as to take advantage of the temporary weakness of a beautiful girl. What would my mother think? Or my aunt Jocasta? What would they think if I were weakly to succumb to momentary passion and thereby compromise and betray a lady? I meanwhile was suckling with gluttonous beatitude at the second of Sita's Fountains of Paradise so as not to cause it to exhibit further tremors of jealousy of the first. Driven to frenzy—so it seemed—by my rhapsodic suckling, Sita made one last despairing appeal to God, with whose sacred name she coupled my own—a great compliment to me—before being convulsed by a series of seismic upheavals, accompanied by loud, shrill, and wailing outcries to God and to me, that subsided presently into a succession of plaintive murmurs followed by uncontrollable spasms, during which her body rose and fell like the earth itself in a severe temblor, and her arms and legs thrashed about with an abandon that might have been the consequence of either insufferable anguish or inexpressible delight. Amidst these clinical symptoms of overwhelming inner disquiet, one of Sita's lovely feet collided twice in rapid sequence with my testicles (I am certain that these terrible blows were accidental), and in turn I, repulsed by these chance kicks from nursing at her Paradisal breasts, shrieked aloud and, shielding the stricken members in a protective grip, collapsed helpless and agonized upon Sita, who took me into her arms and then, detaching my hand from my sorrowing testicles, began gently to stroke their hurt away. And she would undoubtedly have succeeded in altogether weaning me of my virginity had not the door to the room suddenly been thrown open. Like a convention of voyeurs there now entered her father and mother, the professor, the prefect of police, Father Goncalves, Rabbi Eleazar ben-Josephus, Monsieur Gros-Caucaud, Madame, Dorothea, the pimp—and Caldeira.

As long as I live, I shall never forget Sita's display of self-possession. Like the great lady that she was—and has since in such a diversity of circumstances proved to be—so much, in fact, like my aunt Jocasta—she disencumbered herself of me with quite unflustered dignity, sat up in bed, and with her exquisite knees drawn up and her lovely, tendril-like arms embracing them, she demanded of the intruders: "What the hell all-you warnt?" To this day I can still see the fire in her eyes and the look of proud scorn on her face. "All-you eh got no damn manners. You come in here, macco-in' me an' Johnny. You don' even knock, you don' even say, 'Excuse me,' you jus' come in like manicou runnin' from Mapepire snake." She demanded again: "What the hell all-you warnt?" And since they remained dumbstruck, she continued: "The first time since we born, me an' Johnny findin' out wha' you ole people does do. All-you eh shame to do t'ing like dis? An' all-you so ole—dis eh t'ing fer you. Dis is t'ing fer young people—like me an' Johnny. All-you keah do it, but you does try to prevent the young ones like me an'

Johnny from doin' it, because you know we can do it better than you. So all-you does tell we: 'You too young.' 'Young,' me arse. Is all-you too ole. Too ole," she jeered at them. "An too cole. All-you is ashes and Johnny an' me is de fire. An' we jus' startin' to blaze. So all-you get to hell outa here." She pursed her lips and, smacking her tongue against the roof of her mouth, drew in her breath with a suctionlike effect of high moral indignation. "Choops!" Then she turned to me and, indicating the mute and embarrassed assemblage, she said with a mocking gesture of her magnificent head: "Buh look at dem, nuh. Dey look jus' like a bunch o' wet fowl."

That was a descriptive judgment with which, because of its clear accuracy, I was bound to agree. For it was exactly how they looked. By now, though, her father had made a partial recovery from his initial astonishment. He essayed the role of the outraged and dishonored parent. "But Sita, you eh shame? A li'l girl like you, doin' rudeness [a Trinidadian synonym for sexual intercourse] with dat vagabon'—!"

I took instant exception to the insulting reference to myself. "I would have you know, sir," I informed him with great firmness, though I was by no means discourteous, "I am a de Paria." I secreted my penis and testicles as best I could between my thighs and modestly concealed my pubic area with my hands.

"I don' care who de hell you is," the discourteous fellow retorted. "I ketch you sanga-wanga-in' wid me darter—Ah have witness—" His offended gaze encompassed his fellow intruders. "Ah ketch you fair, boy—fair-fair-fair—so wey de hell you playin'? You is big-man? You go marri'd she? Buh look at me damn trouble—" He addressed the world in general. "Ah goin' on a trip to England—England, yes"—he emphasized by repetition the epic nature of his journey—"an' Ah bringin' she an' she modder wid me. Mos' man woulda leave dem home. But me—Balgo Maraj—I bringin' dem, I so damn foolish. An' w'en de mark bu's', fus' t'ing Ah find me wife sanga-wanga-in' in a ho'house an'—lissen to me,

287

nuh, hear w'at Ah'm sayin'—an' Ah find me darter in de same ho'-house—you hearin' me?—sanga-wanga-in' wid a damn li'l stuck-up kiss-me-arse from San Fernando."

At this further insulting reference to me, I objected more strongly even than before. Although you may be certain—and everyone present would bear me out—I was not at all discourteous. "Mr. Maraj," I remonstrated with him, making the most generous allowance for his distraught state, "You are mistaken—" But I got no further.

"Man, w'at de hell dis boy talkin'?" He tacitly consulted the rest of the group, all of whom maintained their silence, even if their sympathy with him was evident enough. "Ah come in here an' Ah ketch 'im on top o' me darter, ridin' she like jockey on racehorse in de Queens Park Savannah, an' he tellin' me now I make a mistake." He paused, perhaps for dramatic effect, then repeated: "I make a mistake." His sarcastic tone, acrid as it was, emphasized his cynicism. He now addressed me directly. "Wey de arse you talkin', boy? You t'ink, because I's coolie and you is creole, I's a damn fool, eh? Dat w'at you t'ink, nuh? But Ah go show you who is damn fool." Making this threat, he looked at me with obvious displeasure. "You go' marri'd she. You go' marri'd she, you hear? Ah'm tellin' you: you go' marri'd she." He made a cross with his two index fingers and kissed it. "So help me, Gawd, you go' marri'd she—or me name eh Balgobin See-persad Hanoomansingh Maraj."

Mrs. Maraj intervened at this point. "Balgo, man, you don' have to get on so. De on'y man Ah ever sanga-wanga wid is you, an' we jus'—" Delicacy would not permit her to continue.

Maraj himself looked abashed and at the same time pleased that his manhood had been publicly intimated. Yet, as his rejoinder to his wife now made clear, he was concerned about the propriety of his having sanga-wanga'd his wife in a whorehouse. "We coulda do it on de ship—but you wasn' able. An' den we find we'self in dis ho'-house—wid dis ho'-master"—he indicated Caldeira, who acknowledged the compliment with an inclination of his head that was astonishingly gracious in so ill-mannered a fellow—"an dis"—he gestured agreeably toward Madame—"ole ho'."

Madame accepted the reference to herself with a heightening of the color of her classic Lusitanian face and the compression of her lips into a taut line of conscious respectability.

"Look at she," Maraj went on, "de ole soucouyant."

Madame's dignified reserve made it plain that she intended to ignore him. I, myself, thought that I ought to clarify the situation in at least one detail that was of importance to me. So I cleared my throat courteously, announcing in this way—as I had often seen Father Maginot do—my wish to be heard. With flattering celerity the group directed its attention to me. I felt I should not be unworthy of the circumstances. I would show myself a gentleman, a man of honor, a de Paria, with or without clothes on. So I said, speaking directly to Sita's parents, though not singling them out by name: "I must tell you," I began, speaking as often I had heard gentlemen do on visits to Aunt Jocasta, especially when they were the bearers of bad news, "I am already engaged to be married." And I looked across the room at Dorothea, whose waist I now saw for the first time was encircled by the pimp's arm. Indeed, his arm was considerably above the level of Dorothea's waist, and his right hand—unless my eyes were obscenely deceiving me—might well have been thought by a fiancé more jealous and possessive than I to be reposing on her left "tottot." (Ah, that odious word! I mean, of course, breast.) But a gentleman is never suspicious of a lady's conduct, and in any event, as Aunt Jocasta always said, he must stand prepared to give her the benefit of every vestige of doubt. So I was ready to believe that the position of the pimp's hand was purely accidental and only tolerated where it lay by Dorothea's exquisite politeness and disinclination to give offense. Even when I noticed that her left arm also encircled his waist and, in so doing, reposed familiarly in the area between his lower spine and his upper backside, I allowed her the advantage of any insidious doubt that might have slithered into my mind and sullied my credentials as a gentleman, a man of honor, and a de Paria. There was even a moment when his fingers made strumming motions across Dorothea's breast, as if he were playing a short riff on a guitar, and she in response snuggled closer to him and her head declined tenderly upon his shoulder. Even then I conceded her that latitude of innocence which it is the mark of a gentleman, such as I, a de Paria, to extend in all circumstances to a lady. Moreover, this lady—Dorothea—was my fiancée, and this my wedding day. There could, then, be no room for boorish suspicions. Were I to discover them in actual performance of the rites of love, it would be my duty, as a gentleman, to believe her culpable of no more than accepting treatment for a severe cold. The question whether or not her concelebrant was in fact a physician might occur to a quibbling peasant but never to a gentleman. I was obliged to recognize, however, that Dorothea had not returned my reassuring smile of absolute trust and unalterable devotion. But before I could draw any conclusions from this, Mr. Maraj issued a moving appeal to his wife for conjugal unity in the face of the threat I represented to the honor of their family. "We business is weown," he reminded her. "Wey we do is between de two o' we. Not'in' go bodder us. Me an' you is marri'd twenty years. You had eleven years w'en we marri'd, an' I had fo'-teen. We was like child, de two o' we. We grow up togedder."

There was no mistaking the sincerity and depth of his attachment to his wife, or of hers to him when she replied: "Is true wey you say, Balgo. All-you"—she turned accusingly to the rest of the intruding group—"all-you fast to be lissenin' to wey husban' an' wife sayin' to one anudder. All-you eh shame? My husban' can do w'at de hell he like, an' I can do w'at de hell I like, buh we's still husban' an' wife. So all o' you can kiss my arse."

The expression on Madame's face reflected her wish that Mrs. Maraj's alluring invitation had been more exclusive—a point of view that the prefect of police ardently shared. While the professor himself displayed a marked eagerness to respond in the affirmative. But quite unexpectedly, Mrs. Maraj rounded on him, referring to the great scholar, the most learned man in the world, as "dis ole w'ite manicou playin' doctor."

To his everlasting credit as a gentleman, the professor refrained from entering into disputation with Mrs. Maraj on such complicated matters of zoology and the medical sciences. With his universal and unequaled learning, he would have had her at a considerable disadvantage. He merely coughed politely behind the back of his hand, a look of scholarly abstraction on his centuries-old face, as if—as if— he were uncertain whether to cite in his defense a mild objurgation from the Vindiciae Contra Tyrannis. Because of the professorial deliberation with which he addressed himself to all questions, he had not quite made up his mind when Mr. Maraj directed to me the query that he had previously put in the form of an ultimation: "You go' marri'd she?"

Mr. Maraj's eyes journeyed slowly away from me and came to rest on Sita in mingled hope, sorrow, and parental reproach.

Before responding to Mr. Maraj's plaintive and fatherly appeal, I thought it only gentlemanly to consult with Dorothea. She was, after all, betrothed to me. Indeed, this was our wedding day. Yet how strange, how startling, these unforeseen developments! As the old Trinidadian creole saying goes: "Man say do-so; but God say foutez-you." You never can tell, boy, how anything will be. You wake up in the morning and you feeling like a champion race-horse the first time he going to stud a female, and the next thing you know, my friend, you in the hospital because you swallow a big ole safety pin. You just put the thing between you' teeth to hold it for a minute while you brush your hair—and, so help me Gawd, before you could say "foute'," de doctor an' dem cuttin' you wide open. I leave home—lemme see—nine days ago. Ah goin' to marri'd Dorothea. All of a sudden, bam! Dis coolie-man tellin' me I have to marri'd *he* daughter. What the hell it is at-all-at-all?

Musing in this vein, I looked across the room at Dorothea and in that moment suddenly remembered that I was stark naked. Modesty quite overcame me. I made a valorous attempt to conceal my "pencil" behind a screen that I contrived with my hands. Mrs. Maraj, however, observing my embarrassed efforts, remarked sardonically to the others in the room: "Look at 'e, nuh; 'e tryin' to hide it."

I was displeased by Mrs. Maraj's indelicacy, but just then I was in no position to reprimand her. When Sita had disrobed me, she had tossed my clothing to the far side of the bed, and I could not recover it without exposing my "person" and subjecting myself to further vulgarities. I have all my life been careful to maintain my "person" in decent seclusion, and until Sita's violation of my private space, no one had been permitted the slightest familiarity with it—except, of course, two or three of Aunt Jocasta's female servants who had taken unladylike liberties with me as I had been suckling at their breasts. If there was one thing you could say about me, it was that "that boy don' let nobody see 'is t'ing." And it was true. Even when I went to the sea to bathe with my close pals, as Ah Sam and Ah See could tell you, I would hide behind a tree to put on my bathing suit. I didn't want nobody—I didn't care who it was, it could be the governor himself—to say, "I see Johnny"— But now, man, look at my damn cross: everybody peepin' at it. O God, boy! And only nine days—

" 'E eh got much to hide," that untrustworthy fellow, Caldeira, remarked with the coarse, jocular leer that, I regret to say, was typical of him. Then he added, with an affected air of friendly reassurance: "Buh size eh everyt'ing, Mr. Johnny—" And he launched into an obscene tale of "the biggest ho'-master" he had ever known, who possessed a t'ing that was smaller than his little finger—he held up the finger to illustrate his point. "But I eh tellin' you no lie—" He made, as Mr. Maraj had done, a cross with his two index fingers and fervently kissed it. "S'elp me Gawd, I eh tellin' you no lie.

All dem gal used to pay 'im." He returned his specific attention to me. "Is not w'at you got, Mr. Johnny"—his tone was
consolatory—"is how you make yo' parang." He thrust his
hips backward and forward, then rotated them. And as if by
this repellent display he had achieved an Olympian humor,
he burst into a loud bray of self-approving laughter.

To my astonishment, Mrs. Maraj greeted his performance
as though he had just returned from Mount Sinai with a bad
case of smoke inhalation, suffering from hallucinations contracted from carbon monoxide in the burning bush, and carrying rough-hewn Canaanite marble inscribed with an illit-
erate, indecipherable scrawl. "Yo' see w'at Ah'm always
tellin' you, Balgo," she said to her husband. Her tone conveyed her unreserved acceptance of the Gospel according
to the Prophet Joe Caldeira.

As yet, however, Mr. Maraj was recalcitrant to conversion.
Discipleship does not come with equal ease to everyone. So,
deaf of ear and blind of eye, insensitive of soul and hard of
heart, he responded to his wife's evangelism merely by re-
peating his question to me: "You go' marri'd she?"

Not even the most loyal incredulity could conceal from
me the meaning of the communication I now received from
Dorothea. It was as plain as the overhead sun upon the Pitch
Lake at La Brea in southern Trinidad at midday. She was
telling me, in effect, to go jump in the lake. For when I
looked to her seeking, as it were, open confirmation of our
solemn pledge to wed each other, she literally turned her
back on me, and there, in the presence of the assembled
company, threw her arms around the pimp, who, first of all,
directed at me a malevolent look of vengeful triumph and
then, with the protective air of a magnanimous conqueror,
accepted her into his embrace.

Well, you could have knocked me flat on my backside
with half a feather from the fluttering wing of a fledgling
hummingbird. Me, Johnny de Paria. So help me Gawd. But

life funny, yes. Jus' two hours before, I'm getting married to that girl—my eyes averted themselves from Dorothea. And now—I looked with profound yearning at Sita.

Caldeira's voice tore asunder the veil of my inner reflections. "O Gawd, Mr. Johnny! You get horn, boy!"

I knew of course that Caldeira was referring to Dorothea's abandonment of me. Nor, indeed, could I have missed the point. For there was a general noise of jangling, ill-tuned laughter, which, with the composure of a gentleman in the face of a mob, I ignored. The professor could not have been displeased by the fortitude I was exhibiting under the buffetings of a capricious fate. But he chose to be silent, doubtless because of his unequaled wisdom. His face wore the expression of a hungry dog whose sadistic master has thrown him a rubber bone. Standing there and, in a manner of speaking, facing a howling mob, with my hands I shielded my penis from envy, disparagement, admiration, criticism, or desire in a superb demonstration—even if I myself say so—of the inborn dignity of a de Paria. Without revealing the least resentment at Dorothea's withdrawal and transfer of allegiance—and indeed I felt none—I replied to Mr. Maraj in a manner that was at once honorable, just, succinct, and well proportioned.

"Sir—" I felt Sita's eyes upon me. Dorothea, too, had squirmed around in the pimp's embrace so that she now faced me across the hushed, expectant room. I glanced down at my "person" so as to be sure that my modesty was intact and that my hands had not betrayed their trust. Sita noted my concern and said, extending to me her comradely support in these unsettling conditions: "Don' worry 'bout dat, Johnny. You' t'ing is you' own. You don' have to hide it. Who don' like it, s'affaire dem." She cast a disapproving eye at the whole lot of them, one and all. "All-you never see t'ing befo'?" she inquired of them. There was mockery with a mordant, scalpel's edge in her tone.

"Sir," I said, "you cannot have known that I had reason to

entertain tonight somewhat different expectations—" I looked pointedly though not reproachfully in Dorothea's direction. I liked the way my voice sounded. It was strong and manly, and I could see that Dorothea, even though she was still hugging and nuzzling the pimp, was impressed. As for Sita, when I paused at this point to secure the studied effect of my oratory, she interjected the proud endorsement: "O Gawd! But he can really langwidge, boy! All-you pisspot ever hear talk so? Lissen, all-you damn fool! Parlez, boy, parlez!" I was most deeply touched by her loyalty and no longer felt the need for any recourse whatever to Dorothea. What is past is past. Is true, oui: yesterday don' full today belly. And when I looked at Sita, reclining at her ease, dégagée, with all the royal hauteur of an unclothed princess of the blood being waited upon at toilette by her servants, I felt so assurgent a crest of pride in my "pencil" that my hands strove modestly to conceal my jubilant "person" from the prurient gaze of these vulgar intruders. Sita and I had been on the brink of a transfiguring consummation when they broke in, and I did not as yet find it possible to excuse their breach of good manners. However, I continued to speak. Inspired by the spacious dimensions of the moment and the grandeur of the duty that devolves upon a man of character to consort memorable action with lofty occasion, I recalled a saying that was often on my mother's lips: "Circumstances alter cases." And in order, I declared, "To relieve other parties"—I meant, of course, Dorothea, but this time I did not so much as glance at her—"of obligations they are no longer able to discharge, I now have the honor to announce my wish and intention to marry Miss Sita Maraj, with your generous permission, sir and madame"—I bowed to Sita's parents—"and her gracious consent."

May Almighty God on Judgment Day deal with me in a manner condign no less than merciful if I lie when I tell you that on hearing this speech, Balgobin Maraj threw his hands up toward the ceiling of the room as if he was playin' mas' at

297

carnival time and shouted like a British West Indian who had just been told that the King of England was coming to have dinner with him: "Jeeeee-sussss Chris-s-s-s-s'! Dis boy can talk like pidgin does shit!" I winced at the vulgarity of my prospective father-in-law. Yet what is to be will be. He proceeded: "I eh hear nobody talk so—not even Captain Cipriani [a celebrated Trinidadian orator]. You got to study lawyer, boy," he said to me. "You go' marri'd to my darter. You got to 'come lawyer, man. Balgo son-in-law go' be big lawyer in Port-of-Spain. S'elp me Gawd! I pay fer you meself, boy. Anyt'ing you want, Balgo go pay. Ah know you eh go' be like some o' dem boy—nigger an' coolie, too—who win scholarship to go an' study in England. De guv'a'ment does pay fer dem wid de people' money. Lissen to w'at Ah'm sayin', man. All-you lissen. An' dese same coolie an' nigger, dey get so big after dey finish studyin' an' dey feel dey is big-man now, dey cuss Trinidad w'ats matter—Trinidad dis an' Trinidad dat, Trinidad eh no good, de people an' dem eh nobody. All-you lissen to me: I's coolie meself. But if dey didn' drag me gran'farder' arse from India to Trinidad, wey de hell you t'ink woulda happen to me? Ah woulda bin shit in India—coolie shit in Bombay or Calcutta. But Ah get a chance in Trinidad—an' you see me now? Ah is Balgobin Maraj an' Ah can sen' me darter to Oxford, Cambridge— anywey she warnt to go." My father-in-law-to-be gave me a stern, admonitory look. "Don' be ungrateful to Trinidad, boy. Especially when de po' people an' dem pay fer you to go to Oxford or Cambridge or weyever de arse you warnt to go to 'come big-man. Jus' remember: if you is a coolie-man like me, you woulda bin eatin' dog shit in India if dey didn' haul you' gran'farder arse to Trinidad." His gaze returned to me. "Don' worry, boy. Ah know you is creole, an' you eh smart like Indian, but dat eh you' fault. Balgo go' pay fer you. Anyt'ing you warnt. Balgo go' pay."

I thanked him politely, but explained that a de Paria stood in no need of financial assistance from anyone. I went on to say that I had not even decided whether or not I wished to become a lawyer. Whereupon Sita, my wife-to-be, put in: "True, we go' marri'd, man. Buh wey de hell—? You might as well 'come lawyer. You can still play yo' mas an' drink yo' rum. It eh go' prevent you. So w'y you eh study de damn foolish law, man, an' done wid it? Den we go' go home an' you want to wo'k, you wo'k; you don' want to wo'k, you don' wo'k. We eh go' starve. An we drink we rum an' we play we mas', an' if you feel like takin' a case, you take it, an' you don' feel, you don' take it. Buh you is lawyer, and sometimes you put on yo' wig an' gown an' walk down Saint Vincent Street [where the law courts and the lawyers' chambers are situated], because w'en Miss So-an'-So talk 'bout she husban' dis an' she husban' dat, I can say—" And ever so sweetly she pouted her lips into a little *moue* of satirical disdain and, speaking in accents of the most unexpected refinement, declared: "My husband told me that while he was in court today, appearing on behalf of a client, the old, dried-up judge—the foolish sonofabitch—pissed himself on the bench."

Listening to Sita, I found her argument in favor of my qualifying for practice at the bar persuasive. And her mother nourished my incipient resolve by remarking to me with admirable shrewdness: "I know you' tan'-tan' have money. An' me an' Balgo have, too. But always remember, boy: 'Mother have an' Father have, but blessed is the child that have his own.' So w'at de hell, go do yo' business, nuh, man, an' 'come lawyer."

As dawn dawdled on the distant Atlantic horizon before descending upon Madeira in a coat of many colors, a double wedding took place in Madame's parlor. My father-in-law had objected at first to his daughter's wedding taking place in a "ho'-house." But my mother-in-law had overcome his objection with the argument, "You don' see, Balgo, dese two [meaning Sita and me] keah wait to get belly-to-belly. An' if we put them off, dey boun' to see dey Easter befo' Good Friday." (This latter phrase implied that Sita and I would engage in sexual intercourse regardless of marriage and that Sita in consequence would become pregnant.) Maraj yielded to the force of this argument. His ultimate defenses were breached when Mrs. Maraj reminded him: "Dey already start, man. You see dem you'self playin' Mooma an' Poopa. Sita open de door, but"—Mrs. Maraj contemplated me with a mixture of maternal gratitude and feminine puzzlement— " 'e didn' walk in because de two o' we [referring to herself and her husband] wasn' home, an' he is a gentleman, he say." She now addressed herself to me. "Lissen, nuh. Lemme tell you somet'ing. Always remember dis, boy: W'en you have to be a gentleman or a man—one or de odder— don' forget: be a man." The immemorial eyes of Mother India penetrated and interfused with my own, the Caribbean eyes of Arawaks, Caribs, together with Spanish, British, French, Portuguese, and Africans. "Be a man."

My eyes gave promise to hers. In that moment, her daughter, Sita, became my bride and the ceremony of marriage that would shortly take place a trivial formality.

Sita herself, as always indefeasibly my champion, assured her mother: "You don' have to bodder 'bout dat. Johnny is a man. My man."

Naturally, Caldeira could not be content unless he played some part in this intimate, domestic interchange. "I only have one t'ing to say." He considered me with the air of a sage about to initiate a novice into the ritual mystery of the universe. "W'en de mango ripe, eat it."

Father Goncalves joined the respective couples together, and Rabbi Eleazar ben-Josephus pronounced the blessing. Madame was matron of honor to Dorothea, and the prefect of police stood as best man for the pimp. Dr. von Buffus carried out the role of best man for me, and Mr. Maraj gave his daughter away.

Moved by the spirit of the occasion, and their reticence

dissolved in a flood of champagne, Madame and the prefect of police publicly acknowledged their son, the pimp. This heroic gesture added much to the happiness of the circumstances. On being called upon to offer a toast, I took the opportunity, while so doing, to read a concluding passage from the *Odyssey*. This was intended as a compliment to the professor, who immensely relished the subtlety of the tribute. In the course of his own remarks, he referred to himself as having in some sense fulfilled the destiny of Prometheus who (and he gave me a look of the most flattering comprehension and regard) had brought the gift of fire to mortals. Dorothea and her husband declined the invitation to speak, preferring instead to squeeze and nuzzle each other throughout the proceedings. But my Sita rose superbly to the occasion. Speaking with the most limpid refinement and a simple, pellucid loveliness of diction, she said that she was not too young to have noted, as she had done, the fickle waywardness of the meandering stream called life. "My husband and I will do our utmost to be good companions in its flow and flood, ebb and decline. At best, everything human rests on friendship. We have begun as friends, and as friends we shall continue our journey, be it long, short, or eternal."

O God, man! W'en Sita sit down, water is in me eye. I look at she an' I say to m'self: "Dis girl is my wife." In all my life I never feel proud so. Then she turn to me an' she arks me: "How you like me?"

I say, "Girl, Ah'm tellin' you, man, there ehn't nobody can talk like you. True-true-true! You can really parlez, girl."

"Don' make joke, man," she said. "You don' hear yo'self?"

But I really meant it. "No. Is true, man. You mek a hell of a speech, girl." I took her hand in mine. I was aware that in my wife there was a majesty of unfulfilled renown. Until now (and I was not alone alluding to the abilities she had just displayed), I had undervalued her—much as I loved her. "I didn' know you was so good, man."

She gave my hand a gentle, sustained, and loving squeeze.

301

"Wey de hell you t'ink, boy? I got me Higher Cambridge Certificate, yes."

Caldeira took us back to the ship after the wedding breakfast at Madame's. The ox-drawn cart made a brief honeymoon tour of the city before heading for the wharf. As we dismounted from the cart, Caldeira drew me aside for a moment and pressed something into my hand. It was a gold ring. "Put it on 'er finger," he told me.

I took Sita's hand in mine and on the third finger of that hand—the left hand—following Sita's prompting and Caldeira's directions, I placed the ring. It fitted perfectly.

"Gi'e she a kiss," he bade me.

I obeyed, inexpressibly happy.

"Now you marri'd fer true," Caldeira assured us. "All-you don' forget. Me, Joe Caldeira—I marri'd you."

Sita threw her arms around him and kissed him once, twice. I swear, the old rascal blushed, shy as a boy.

Recovering himself, he turned to me. "Tell yo' tan'-tan'," he said, "is all right. Tell she, don' worry. Tell she, Joe Caldeira—her ole frien'—say, is all right."

"W'en you comin' back to Trinidad?" I asked him.

He pondered the question for a moment or two. Then, as if having made up his mind, he answered: "W'en you finish studyin' in England—w'en you do yo' business an' you goin' back home—pass here fer me. Ah'll go wid you—wid de two o' you."

And Sita told him: "We goin' to come fer you."

He walked with us to the ship's gangway. "Any time you have a chance—an' you remember Joe Caldeira—drop me a line an' tell me how t'ings is." He handed me a card. It was inscribed:

> Joaquin Caldeira
> The Cloisters
> 12a Rua Sanctissima
> Funchal
> Madeira

In the bottom left-hand corner he described himself with the most commendable reticence as "Director of Social Relations."

Sita and I were unable to consummate our marriage during the remainder of the trip because of Sita's temporary incapacity. Mrs. Maraj was quietly sympathetic, but my father-in-law derived a boisterous glee from the situation. In the hearing of all and sundry he rallied me: "The jockey ready to ride, but de horse lock-up in de stable." And so it was that I arrived in England still, technically at least, a virgin.

We shared my cabin on shipboard, Sita and I. The very first thing she noticed on entering the room was the brass-bound box protruding slightly from beneath the bed.

As I later discovered, the box had originally been labeled "PLACE IN HOLD." In the course of the rough handling it had received, as it was transported from one place to another, that label had been more or less defaced. All that was left to indicate its ownership was a torn scrap of paper that still clung to the box and that, deciphered as best it could be, appeared to read: "Cabin 207." Following the last digit was the initial portion of what might have been the letter "D" or, possibly, "E"—one could not be certain. I was occupying cabin number 207D and my African fellow passenger the adjacent cabin number 207E. The on-shore porter, stowing away the luggage designated for the respective cabins, was unable to decide which of them would be the correct depository for the box. He was about to place it in 207E when he thought that he had heard something like a sound of movement within the box as he was bending over to lift it to his shoulder. He had listened, heard nothing, and concluded that he had been mistaken. He opened the door of the cabin 207E and saw that some baggage had already been stowed away there. He then opened the door of the adjacent cabin 207D and saw that there was no baggage in that room. On the cabin door was a name printed in black letters on a narrow strip of white pasteboard. "John Sebastian A. C. O. de Paria." The porthole was open, giving passage into the room of a cool, revivifying breeze. Again he bent over the box and again thought that he heard a rustling sound inside it. The breeze coming through the porthole ventilated his brow. "It's cool in here," he thought. He entered, carrying the box, and, having briefly studied the layout of the room, he stowed it away beneath the bed, pushing it neatly out of sight.

When Sita remarked to me on the presence of the box, I said that I was aware of it, but that it did not belong to me. "You think we should open it?" I asked her.

"It don' belong to you?"

I confirmed that this was the case.

"So why you want to open it?"

I pushed it back beneath the bed.

On the morning of our arrival in England, I was arraying myself in my best suit, in order, I hoped, to make the best possible impression on my first contact with English soil, when Sita, who had been studying me attentively for a few minutes, said: "Buh lissen, nuh. Dey have carnival in England?"

To the best of my knowledge, I replied, the English were not quite so civilized as that.

"So wey yo' goin' dress-up as if you playin' clown?"

"You mean you don' like the suit?"

"It make you look like a damn ass. Who do you dat?"

I explained the circumstances and mentioned the name of my East Indian tailor at San Fernando.

"Aha," she said. "I know 'im. He think that all creoles do is play mas'. So every time he sew fer them, he make a carnival costume. Take it off, boy. Put on you' blue serge."

With anybody else in this world, I would have put up a big argument. Even with Aunt Jocasta. But with Sita, I simply did as I was told. The next time I saw that tailor in San Fernando, however, he'd better hide his behind. My foot was itching me.

I had just changed into another suit when there was an agitated pounding on the door of the cabin. I opened it. There stood a ship's porter accompanied by Professor von Buffus and Monsieur Gros-Caucaud. The last-mentioned was in a state of considerable excitement. This perhaps explains the discourtesy with which he pushed past me into the room without so much as the merest hint of an invitation from me to enter. I was astounded. These damned Africans, I thought—no manners. Even after several weeks in Trinidad, where he'd been on some mysterious errand or other, he still had not acquired sufficient politesse to enable him to say, "Excuse me." His manners were exactly those of the ship's porter who had thrust himself into the room in the same untutored fashion. Professor von Buffus apologized on their behalf, as Sita was demanding their instant withdrawal from the room. "Wey de hell you t'ink," she was upbraiding them, "you comin' in here as if you livin' in de place. Haul you' arse—" At the sheer vigor of her attack, the African and the porter stood about uncertainly, peering around the room as if in search of some object. It was the professor who resolved the situation for all concerned by drawing the porter's attention to the brass-bound box beneath the bed, the protruding edge of the box being once again visible.

The sight of the box produced the most remarkable transformation in Monsieur Gros-Caucaud. He whirled like a dervish in solitary exile on the Côte d'Ivoire who has just learned that his banishment has been terminated and that he has been promoted to the position of high priest of his local sect. For minutes on end he spun like a human top grotesquely out of control. Sita and I conferred anxiously with the professor, who seemed not at all perturbed by these strange gyrations. But Sita was on the point of dousing Gros-

Caucaud with a pail of water when he abruptly ceased to spin. By now the porter had drawn the box out into the middle of the cabin. Sweat welling out of him and dripping onto the floor, where it threatened to form a shallow lake, Gros-Caucaud prostrated himself before the box. Mumbling incantations and making the barbaric gestures of a high churchman celebrating an orthodox religious rite of a Christian cult, he now knelt and placed his forehead against the lid of the box, his lips moving in silent prayer and supplication. Then he arose and directed at me a look of unfathomable menace compounded at one and the same time with reluctant and only partial absolution for whatever I had done.

"The box is yours?" Sita demanded of him.

He nodded. Yes.

"So take de damn t'ing out o' de room. How de hell it get in here to begin wid?" But as no one offered her an explanation, she told the African: "From the first time I see you, I know you is a obeah-man. Don' come back anywhere near me or Johnny, or Ah go' put somet'ing on you. My obeah"—she challenged him—"stronger than yours."

Their eyes met. An eternity ensued as they confronted each other. The African dropped his eyes.

"Take de damn box an' go," she commanded him.

Gros-Caucaud took hold of one end of the box, the porter the other, and together they carried the brass-bound box from the room. The professor accompanied them.

"You see dat man," said Sita, pointing at the retreating African. " 'E mix-up wid some bad t'ing—but Ah too much fer him." She moved with the swiftness of a wave outstripping the wind to the door of the cabin. " 'Ey-y-y-y!" she shouted at Gros-Caucaud. He stopped and looked around. "The nex' time you bodder us, Ah go' kill you!" Even at that distance, there was no mistaking the terror on the African's face.

On landing at Plymouth on the west coast of England, whose continental neighbor at that point is Brittany on the

306

French shore, we were required to comply, as is necessary, with customs and immigration formalities. My father-in-law was looking around for an Englishman to shine his shoes and had to be recalled by his wife to the normal obligations of legal entry into England. For myself, I was not displeased to be in England, though I found it odd, and unpromising, that with the sun shining the air was yet so chill. This hinted to me a contradictory dualism about England in marked contrast to the straightforward simplicity of my native Trinidad. Back home there was nothing chill about sunlight. The sun was warm. It didn't pretend to be shining when at the same time your very bones were shivering with cold. That only happened if you were sick. So I began to wonder: in a place like this—this England—was everybody sick? I was aroused from these scientific speculations by the audible murmur of a conversation proceeding at the customs examination of passengers' luggage between Monsieur Gros-Caucaud and an inspector who was rummaging through the contents of the former's traveling bags. I was two turns distant, so I could easily hear everything that was being said. First to one bag and then to another the inspector affixed a cabalistic mark with a stick of white chalk. Last of all, he pointed to the brass-bound box.

"O God!" Mrs. Maraj remarked to Sita, who was immediately behind me. "But it cold, eh!"

"Like dog' nose-'self, man," said Sita. A view I myself shared, but was too engrossed in the colloquy between the African and the inspector to do much more than record the exchange of initial impressions of England between my wife and her mother. Nor was I able to follow with any closeness the efforts of my father-in-law to have his shoes shined.

"Yours?" the inspector was asking the African.

Gros-Caucaud nodded his head in acknowledgment of his ownership of the box. "Yes."

"Open it."

"It is not possible, M'sieu."

"Not possible—?" The inspector's hands, relaxing from their explorations of the passengers' belongings, came to rest on his hips. But even in that negligent pose, he had all at once been subtly transformed into the actual semblance of an official symbol of interrogation. He looked up at the African. "Haven't you a key?"

"*Oui, M'sieu. J'ai le clef. Mais—*"

"Then why—?" The inspector's head described a short arc of official puzzlement. He massaged the back of his neck. And when the African did not reply but only looked at him apprehensively, his suspicions became robust. By this time, too, the queue of passengers had sensed that something unusual was taking place. It did not seem to me that a box that had so thoughtlessly been stowed away by an errant porter beneath my cabin bed should command so much interest. Yet this innocent box, the occasionally obtrusive companion of my voyage to England, was at issue between Monsieur Gros-Caucaud and one of His Majesty's Customs Inspectors. But why wouldn't Gros-Caucaud open it, anyway? He must be trying to hide something. The other passengers in line struck varying attitudes of curiosity and impatience.

The inspector's head half-pivoted to rest on a line which, because of the African's height, inclined upward straight to midpoint between the African's eyes. "I must ask you," he said, speaking in quiet tones but with Britannic firmness and well-trained bureaucratic courtesy, "to open that—" With a gesture of his head he indicated the brass-bound box.

Conditioned by tribal tradition, reinforced by his colonial experience, to be subservient to authority, the African shrugged his shoulders in a mechanical reflex of submission. Lowering his head as a sign of compliance, he placed his hands palms downward on the box. Then he closed his eyes, uplifted his head, and uttered a series of incantatory sounds in an unfamiliar tongue. I heard my father-in-law, who was standing next in line to Dr. von Buffus, exclaim in a penetrating whisper to the latter: "O God, man! But nigger have style, yes!" Then the African slowly, cautiously, raised the lid of the box. Even as he did so, something sinuous and malign swayed upward, its flat, triangular head moving toward the African's hands, which were poised, partly outstretched at shoulder level, over the open box.

"Put that thing back!" said the inspector, retreating with official celerity out of range, as the other passengers—with the exception of Sita—considerably exceeding his somewhat deliberate speed, emulated his example.

I recognized the distinctive markings, the scaly, pineapple-yellow configuration of the Lord Most High, the Emperor Mapepire Zanana, All-Conquering Potentate of the Bush. I found myself quite unable to move. I had a sensation of complete paralysis. I could only stand there, no more than a foot away from the undulating Lord of All, and watch its liquescent, uncoiling ascent, which halted in the space between the African's outstretched hands. The latter meanwhile, his eyes still closed, continued his incantations. Majestically, the serpent revolved its head until its eyes met and held mine in deadly thrall. I felt the graveyard chill of my own death. And then Sita had glided past me and the serpent had abandoned the space between the African's hands and was moving now between Sita's caressing motions, which were circular, slow, fluid, and predominant. I became aware that the African had ceased his incantations and that the whole universe was a vast stillness, a formless void upon the face of a fathomless deep. My paralysis had vanished. I could observe the serpent with something very like inhuman detachment. I was no longer under its spell. I saw Sita's hands direct the serpent's head until its eyes had transfixed the African, to whom my former paralysis had transferred itself. I saw the apprehended knowledge of his own death in the African's eyes—and beyond death itself— the occult awareness of his eternal submission to Sita's will. Then Sita, with the same plastic, undulant movements of her hands, guided the snake's head away from the African.

309

In a continuous, streaming movement the serpent poured itself back into the box. Sita replaced the lid. And now she turned to face the African, who prostrated himself at her feet. He knew that he was in the presence of a high priestess, at whose sovereign will was his life or death.

"Please, let me explain." Dr. von Buffus addressed the customs inspector and pointed to the brass-bound box. "It is the sacred fetish of the ancient Caribbean tribe of the de Parias. It is accompanying the heir-apparent to the tribal throne, who is on a journey to this country in order to render homage to the king-emperor. He is"—with a deferential gesture he indicated me—"the prince of San Fernando, and"—he bowed low in Sita's direction—"the princess. Naturally, they are traveling incognito. I myself am tutor and companion to His Royal Highness." He inclined his head toward Sita's parents and the still prostrate Monsieur Gros-Caucaud. "Members of the royal entourage," he told the inspector. "Herr Kapitän and Frau Gebumst." He glanced toward the obeisant Gros-Caucaud. "Herr Doktor Gross Schwanz." Then, with the viceregal air of a court chamberlain, "May I bespeak on behalf of His Royal Highness the usual diplomatic courtesies?"

In the general commotion following upon such uncommon events, Sita and I, and her parents, were ushered with unostentatious ceremony into a waiting room for railway passengers. Dr. von Buffus and Monsieur Gros-Caucaud remained behind in order to arrange for the disposition of the brass-bound box and its contents.

And so Sita and I, together with her parents, at length reached the Beefeaters Hotel, traveling through the night by train to London.

The first thing I did on arriving at the hotel was to inquire if there was a message for me from Trinidad, for I had telegraphed Aunt Jocasta and my mother from aboard ship informing them of my marriage. Yes, there was. The hall porter delivered a telegram to me. "Your mother and I," it read, "are very happy to learn of your marriage to the maharajah's daughter. Does this make you a prince? We are sending the princess a wedding gift of rubies that we had in any case intended for your wife whenever—some ten years from now—you married. Your mother and I expect to be in England within the next month or two—or as soon as the necessary travel arrangements can be made—in order to meet your bride and her parents, the maharajah and his wife. We are ever so proud of you. Our warmest love and affection to you both, dear Johnny. Signed: Mother and Aunt Jocasta." There was a postscript to the telegram. "Which maharajah is this? Mysore or Patiala? Either of these would be suitable for a de Paria. And how shall we address you now? As Your Royal Highness? (Smile). Our respectful compliments to the princess. Does she eat roti? Dahl? You were always so fond of curry, dear Johnny. Strange, is it not? Your dog, who is so much more sensible than some people we know, howls his remembrances to you. He sounds quite mournful, as if something dreadful had happened. Father Maginot reminds us that dogs have a sixth sense and he will pray for you. So shall we, dear Johnny."

In the first place, I was disquieted by the length of the telegram; and there was, too, something about its tone. . . . But when, later that day, Professor von Buffus joined us at the hotel, he counseled me not to worry. There would be, he told me, a bit of a *Kulturkampf,* but he assured me that in the end there would be an *Aufklärung.* Sita's insight into the matter differs substantially from the professor's. She is of the opinion that my mother and aunt, being intelligent and loving women, will readily overlook and forgive any little mistake—or even a big one—that I may have made. She herself will do her best to ensure their conclusion that, in all the relevant circumstances, the very highest wisdom has prevailed. I shall leave it to Sita. In any case, after tonight—nature having removed its officious impediment to Sita's consummation of her marriage—I shall be a man—no longer a virgin—and prepared to take on the full responsibility for myself and my wife, and any and every consequence of my actions.

I love my wife, my wise, strong, and delectable Sita. Aunt Jocasta and my mother, whom I also love, will simply have to understand.

Tonight I shall be a man. I dress for dinner with extreme care and then escort my wife to join her parents, with whom we shall dine this evening, in the lobby of the hotel. Tonight I shall enter Heaven's Gate and drink deep of the Fountains of Paradise. Tonight. Tonight. O God, man! Tonight I shall be a man. I feel a sudden urge to make water. I ask the hall porter for directions to the nearest urinal. He indicates a pissoir. "The Marquis of Padbury"—he informs me with a benign and British smile, and with precisely the proper degree of deference, self-respectingly distant from servility and decently short of unctuousness—"the Marquis of Padbury has preceded you, sir."

These people have good manners.